IMMORTAL COIL

A DRAGON SPIRIT NOVEL: BOOK 1

C.I. BLACK

Gryphon's Gate Publishing

Gryphon's Gate Publishing

550 King St. N.

PO Box 42088 Conestoga

Waterloo, ON

N2L 6K5

ebook ISBN978-0-9919229-0-1

Print ISBN978-1-988115-30-6

PROLOGUE

F ire consumed him. It burned cold and blue from within, igniting bone and sinew into searing agony. He beat his wings, fighting to remain airborne, to escape the sorcerer's spell, but each muscle contraction spread it closer to his heart. The scales on his chest blackened and cracked, and the soft skin underneath peeled and burst, raining blood on the earth below. He roared, spitting fire from between his teeth and snorting smoke from his nostrils.

An updraft forced him higher into the sky. Minuscule thatched roofs dotted the landscape, like game pieces scattered along a winding dirt road. A patchwork of fields stretched as far as the eye could see and only small forests, not nearly big enough for him to hide within, stood on the edges. His wings trembled. His whole body trembled, the fire blurring his vision. He couldn't remain aloft for long, but every instinct he had screamed not to land so close to the humans.

And yet each movement, even the tiniest ones made in order to stay aloft, sent sharp agony straight to his heart.

More scales blackened, cracked, and peeled away. He strained ahead, stretching his snout forward as if that would make him fly faster. Each stroke burned, more unbearable than before. If he could just get away, maybe, just maybe, he wouldn't be the next of his kin to die. The next to fall to human treachery. But that was just a desperate wish. The spell had been cast. Dark Egyptian magic cast by Greek sorcerers frantic to not let his kind become another weapon for the Roman army and nothing could stop it. No one could hide from it.

Sharp, sudden pain clutched his heart. He gasped, and with that inhalation, the spell entered his veins and consumed him. It burned brighter and hotter than even the core of a lava bath. He couldn't move, couldn't breathe. All he could feel was pain. An all-consuming agony. He hurtled toward the earth, the wind biting the soft flesh exposed by his broken scales.

With the last of his strength, he roared the words his goddess had sacrificed her entire being to give to her children and cast the only counterspell he knew.

A naea climbed over the railing of the Queen Street Bridge and watched the streetlights' flickering reflection on the sluggish water and ice of the Allegheny River. She hadn't stood on this side of the railing since childhood. Then, it had been summer. Her heart had pounded with exhilaration, and her friends, already swimming in the water below, cheered her on.

Now, her heart still pounded, but no one swam below. Now the river's cold embrace called to her, promising to wrap around her and pull her down until she was numb and sleepy.

She sucked in a shaky breath, not believing what she was thinking.

Jumping would end it. End the fight, end the isolation, end the slow wasting loss of self and life.

She hadn't thought this was how she'd die. Pills had seemed more likely. Heck, she had hoped she could win her fight and die of old age in some retirement home, not at thirty-three when her life was just getting started. But her doctor had said it: metastasized.

And now she was here.

She hadn't even thought about it, just fled from his office and aimlessly driven around and around. The sun had set, but no clarity had come with nightfall, nor hours after. All she knew was she didn't want to waste away, fading into death in some hospital bed. She had fought so hard and had still lost. Lost her job, lost her right breast, lost her husband—and good riddance to the cheating bastard—and now she would lose her life. It wasn't fair. And while she knew life was like that, she had hoped so desperately for something better. But now the only thing left under her control was how.

Ice lined the river's edge, but its heart still flowed, even in mid-January. If she jumped, her winter coat would drag her down, the cold would dull her senses, and she would slip into that which she had feared the most.

Her gut churned at the thought. She wanted to scream and rant and cry but knew it would be all for nothing. It wouldn't make her feel better. It wouldn't make her stop trembling.

She closed her eyes, imagining the summer sun warming her face, the laughter of her friends. But the winter's evening wind picked up, biting her cheeks and nose. That little girl was gone, her friends grown up and moved, the courage for summertime swimming frozen by a loveless marriage and consumed by cancer.

In a way, it was a relief. Good or bad, her battle was done. Finally. And if she kept telling herself that, maybe she wouldn't lose her nerve.

Really. There was no more left to do. She supposed she should call Mark, her best friend—ex-best friend—and say goodbye. But her marriage had isolated her, alienated her even from him, and she didn't know if he wanted to talk to her anymore.

"Hey."

Her heart leapt, pounding furiously. This close to midnight the bridge should have been deserted.

The voice was firm and masculine.

Oh, great. A good Samaritan. Just what she needed. Why did this have to be more difficult that it already was? She should jump, avoid the conversation, save herself the trouble, but she couldn't make herself let go of the railing. It wasn't a sense of self-preservation, she was sure of that. It was something else, perhaps the tone of his voice.

"You know, whatever it is, I'm sure it won't seem so bad in the morning."

She snorted. Nope. She'd still be dying.

"Listen, I'm sure you mean well..." She leaned back and glanced at him. He stood a few feet away, one side of him illuminated by his car's headlights, looking every bit like his voice, firm and masculine. He wore a double-breasted coat cut to mid-calf that accentuated a broad chest and narrow hips. His face was square with high cheekbones and dark eyes. A brush-cut of dark hair finished off the look. The overall impression was deliciously handsome, and if it were a different day or she a different person, she might have considered flirting with him.

Maybe she should. She wasn't dead yet. But that was just a fantasy. No one would be attracted to her bald head and sunken eyes and cheeks. Her illness couldn't be hidden.

He stepped toward her, crossing the headlight beam until it completely backlit him, casting his face in shadow.

"Why don't you just climb back over the railing?" His voice held a tenderness she hadn't expected from someone who looked so... well, so masculine. It was just fate being cruel that made them meet under such circumstances, and that, really, was neither here nor there.

"And once I'm safe on the bridge, then what?"

He hesitated.

Ah, he didn't want to waste extra time on her. Typical. He wanted to be the hero then rush away. He'd run even faster, if only he knew...

What the heck was she waiting for anyway? This stranger didn't know her well enough to care, and even if he did, there was nothing he could do for her. No miracle cure for cancer expected in the next three months.

She let go of the railing, spread her arms, and leaned forward. This was it. She didn't want to do it, and yet she didn't want a slow death, either.

From the corner of her eye, she glimpsed a flash of movement, then something jerked her back. Her collar dug painfully into her throat, and she struggled to breathe. Shit. He'd grabbed her coat.

"What the hell are you doing?" he demanded.

She twisted in his grip, but he held tight. "What does it look like?"

"It looks like you're crazy."

"Then let me go."

"No."

God. She couldn't even kill herself in peace. She fumbled with the buttons on her coat, her fingers numb from holding the metal railing.

"I will not justify myself to you." He had no right to tell her what to do. Her fingers weren't working, were too slow. Grabbing the edges of her coat, she yanked, hard, popping the buttons off. She twisted to face him, using his grip on the coat to shrug out of it.

He dropped the coat into the river and seized the front of her sweater. She clawed at him and he pulled her close, wrapping an arm around her back. She twisted, squirmed, but her last bout of chemo had left her weak, and the railing between them made it difficult to fight back.

Sudden, sharp pain bit into her shoulder. She gasped and froze. Samaritan's eyes hardened, his mouth a tight line. Behind him stood a blond woman, whose smile sent a shiver down Anaea's spine. A blade protruded from the man's chest. The weapon had gone right through him and cut into Anaea's arm. The blade had—

Oh God! That woman had stabbed him. Right here on the bridge. Anaea couldn't make her mind work beyond that. She had no idea where this new stranger had come from. She hadn't noticed the woman's approach, but then she hadn't been paying attention to the road, only to her thwarted desire to jump off the bridge.

The woman leaned against the man, pinning him to the railing. "Give me the medallion."

Samaritan shook his head. His eyes were fierce, dark.

"You're so predictable." The woman jerked the blade from his body.

Samaritan coughed a mist of blood into Anaea's face, making her eyes sting. Through her tears, like a slow-motion scene in a horror movie, she watched the woman raise her sword to swing at the man's head. A sword. An actual, honest-to-goodness, medieval weapon. What kind of trouble was this man in?

He tensed and his grip on her sweater tightened. Something flickered in his dark eyes, a decision, but she couldn't fathom what. With a ragged breath, his face contorted in pain and he threw himself over the metal barrier, his weight slamming into her. The railing tore from her grip and they tumbled off the bridge.

For a heartbeat, Anaea was weightless, her mind unable to focus on anything but the woman standing on the bridge. Her expression was stunned, eyes wide, mouth hanging open. The headlights from the man's car glinted off the sword blade and blood ran down its length onto her hand. The man's blood. Anaea's blood. And now they were falling.

Falling!

Her heart pounded hard, and the world leapt back into real time. She drew breath to scream and they hit the water. The air burst from Anaea's lungs. Water whooshed around her, cold and stinging. She couldn't see, couldn't feel, couldn't breathe. Her brain screamed at her to surface, but if she let go, relaxed, everything would be over. Wasn't this what she'd wanted? To end her struggle and finally beat the cancer?

Her Good Samaritan appeared inches from her face, water billowing his coat around him, his eyes peering into hers. Good God, he was still alive.

He clutched at her arm and pressed something hard and round into her palm, his expression pleading, desperate. Then his demeanor changed, hardened. He jerked her toward him and smashed his lips against hers.

What the hell was he doing? She struggled against him, but he grabbed the back of her head and thrust his tongue into her mouth, forcing it open. A ferocious heat raced down her throat, pouring across her chest and deep into her gut.

The heat grew, melting away the bite of the freezing water until fire radiated from every pore. An inferno rushed through her veins, raced into every organ, muscle, and bone. Expanding, burning, until she felt she'd burst or burn up or both.

She threw her head back and screamed. Water flooded her mouth and white light shot out.

2

W ater surged around Anaea and the man. The light vanished, leaving her numb, confused. She had no idea what had just happened. A hallucination from the cold? But it had felt so real.

The man's kiss had certainly been real.

She turned her attention to the stranger. His gaze was unfocused and his face slack. His hands were limp between them. He was dead.

Letting him go, she kicked at the water, pushing herself up toward the surface. His body drifted down, sucked into the murky depths, and disappeared. She hadn't even known his name. It wasn't fair that she, who sought death, should live when a stranger trying to do the right thing had died.

She scissored her legs against the water, again and again, her lungs burning, her limbs numb from the cold, her arm aching from the sword cut.

Breaking the surface, she spat out the water that had filled her mouth when he'd kissed her. She gulped in air, dipped back beneath the surface, and forced herself back up.

The bank lay only a few feet away, snowy ground and trees rushing past as the current swept her farther and farther from the bridge. She struggled to the edge and clambered onto icy rocks, half in the water and half out, stopping to catch her breath. A gust of wind whipped through the naked branches of a tree beside her, but she was too numb to feel its sting.

If she didn't get out of the cold and change into dry clothes, hypothermia would take her. Why hadn't she just stayed in the water and died like she'd planned? The shock of seeing the stranger die must have broken her concentration, causing her survival instinct to kick in. That, along with the strange light and his kiss.

She shivered, not wanting to think about the sizzling lip-lock and the fact that moments afterward he had died.

She dragged her attention to the object in her hand: a brass medallion the size of her palm, with a square hole in the center, similar to some Asian coins. Intricate symbols were carved around it on both sides and a thick, masculine chain looped through the hole, long enough that she didn't need to open the clasp to pull it over her head. She slipped it inside her soaked sweater and hauled herself the rest of the way out of the water.

Her vision blurred and darkened, and she felt as though the world was spinning even though she knew she was on her hands and knees, hunched over in the snow. She blinked her vision clear, determined to get her bearings. Trees and scrubby bushes surrounded her. Thick yellow stalks of dead grass and weeds poked through the snow, and far off to her left the city lights twinkled. Before her lay a rusted chain-link fence and beyond, the shadowy mounds of ruined cars.

The Allegheny had swept her into an industrial area. She doubted she'd find a payphone in the vicinity, and she'd left her cell in her car. Her best bet was to follow the shoreline back to the bridge. Of course, her car keys had been in her coat pocket and now they were at the bottom of the river.

And then there was that woman. She'd stabbed the man right in front of Anaea. It was possible the woman was still on the bridge or searching the bank for the man's body... for Anaea's body.

This wasn't what she wanted at all. A death of her choosing, not someone else's, and definitely not a violent one. That made her stomach churn, and she forced the thoughts from her head. No, she needed to think of something else, anything else.

She had to go to the police and tell them what had happened.

It seemed a silly thought, all things considered, but she clung to the idea, determined to focus only on it. The right thing to do was go to the police, tell them what she'd seen. The thought made her snort, which made her vision blur and darken again. *While I was attempting to commit suicide, officer...*

Maybe she should leave that part out.

She grabbed a low-hanging tree branch and hauled herself to her feet. Her head felt stuffed with wool, and everything about her was heavy and slow. Her waterlogged clothes weighed her down, but the heaviness was more than that. It had to be hypothermia. She couldn't feel the cold, and she knew she should.

Blackness washed over her. She sucked in air and put one foot in front of the other. The police needed to know about the man's murder.

Another wave of darkness crept over her vision and the frozen ground hurtled up to meet her. She put her hands out to stop it, realizing too late that it wasn't the ground moving, but her.

———

TRAPPED IN THE WOMAN'S BODY, HUNTER FOUGHT TO SUPPRESS HER spirit. It had been close to two thousand years since he'd shared a body with its human soul, and the sensation was disorienting. Regardless, he needed control now, before whoever had attacked him came looking for him. If the assailant was a dragon like himself, she—and from the timbre of her voice it had definitely been a woman who'd stabbed him—would have seen the transfer.

Hell, from the power and light that had poured from the woman's mouth, half of the town had seen the transfer.

He struggled to concentrate, but the woman's soul fought against him, not knowing it was him making her numb and drowsy. She thought it was hypothermia. That at least helped. It made her weaker and easier for him to take over. But it didn't solve the root of the problem.

Which was the complete loss of all his common sense.

It was the only explanation for whatever had compelled him to choose saving her instead of fighting his assailant. He couldn't have done both. But when he'd transferred into the woman, he'd been met with so much more than he'd anticipated.

The cut in her shoulder was insignificant to the cancer consuming her. And above it all, her strength of will threatened to subdue him. It took everything he had to divert a small portion of his soul magic from healing this new body to overpowering her consciousness.

Concentrating on the snow stinging his hands, he used the pain to anchor himself within her. He mentally boxed her up until she was contained and asleep, whispering to her that what she'd seen and experienced was all a dream. He could hold that for a few hours. After that, she'd wake to discover herself a prisoner in her own body and what she'd thought were dreams were in fact reality. But he wouldn't allow it to come to that.

He pushed up to his hands and knees... her hands and knees, and studied his surroundings. He stood on an unkempt riverbank on the edge of a fenced-in industrial yard. It was the likeliest place to find a car since he wasn't going to risk returning to the bridge.

Marching through the snow, he slipped through a break in the fence and stepped into a storage yard filled with long rows of rusting cargo crates piled two and three high. Shadows filled the pathways, giving ample coverage for him as well as anyone who wished him ill.

And there was definitely someone out there who wished him ill. It was only a matter of time before his assailant discovered where he'd emerged from the river, and that made haste essential.

He jogged down the closest path to what he hoped was the front of the property, scanning for trouble and a working vehicle. But after a minute, his breath burned in his chest and he had to slow down. He wasn't healing fast enough, and his soaked clothes weren't helping.

His usually rapid ability had diminished to a level that barely sustained him.

The woman had been right when she'd told him she didn't have to justify her suicide to him. Regardless of whether she'd killed herself tonight or not, she would die soon. Unless, of course, he remained inside her.

If he did, his soul magic would cure her cancer within four or five hours... along with the possibility that she'd go crazy and he'd become soul sick. It wasn't likely—usually it took days or months—but to have it happen within hours wasn't impossible.

At the end of the row lay an open, well-lit area. Hesitating in the shadows, he glanced around. The fence was taller here, with a gate wide enough for a transport truck. It was open, and beyond lay a road, void of any traffic. Beside the entrance sat a small security station, no more than a shack with a window. Light flickered within, and noise from a television blared deafeningly through the thin walls. A few feet from the shack was a beat-up white hatchback.

There was no sign of anyone else around. Hunter stepped into the open area, sauntered to the hatchback, and tested the latch on the driver's side door.

Unlocked.

How convenient.

He loved the human fallacy that if it was old no one would steal it.

Sprawled, half in and half out of the car, he hotwired the engine then slipped behind the wheel and drove out of the yard. The closest point of contact for a member of the Royal Coterie was almost four hours away in Newgate. The woman he possessed didn't have that kind of time. Well, she did if he intended to kill her afterward, which would possibly be a blessing to her.

It wouldn't be for him. He might be the prince's assassin, but he'd lost the taste for killing humans centuries ago, particularly innocents who became involved in dragon business because of his mistakes.

Which meant Memorial General for a new, uninhabited body, preferably male, and while there were funeral homes closer to this end of town, he couldn't guarantee they'd have a John Doe lying around. Of course, there was no guarantee the hospital would have a John Doe in its morgue either, but the odds were better.

This was such a disaster. Hunter didn't even know who'd attacked him. Although if he had to guess, it was probably one of Nero's or Zenobia's flunkies. The woman he possessed might have seen whoever it was—

No, he wasn't possessing just some woman. Even if he was only with her for the next twenty minutes, he could in the very least learn her identity. He drew her name from her consciousness. A-nay-ah.

Her essence poured through the connection he'd made, and he scrambled to sever the flow. She hated her name, no one could pronounce it. But her mother had loved that one quarter of herself that was Greek, honored her connection to that ancient society. She'd become a professor of Greek mythology, married a good Greek man, and named her daughter after an Amazon warrior—

He shoved the rest of Anaea's essence back, shaken by the strength of her will even when she was asleep. He wasn't going to do that again, not even to find out who'd attacked him.

Stopping at a red light, he glanced around the empty intersection. No sign of trouble, but the roads before him and to the left curved sharply up around snow-draped hills. If anyone was coming, he'd have little time before they were on top of him.

He squeezed the steering wheel, testing his new vessel's grip while fighting the urge to gun the car and draw unwanted attention to himself. Anaea's body was less than desirable. It astounded him that she could function while so weak, making him all the more aware of what he'd lost. Damn, he was going to miss his old body, miss its strength, even if it was only human.

Mother of All, he needed a new job. Collecting Saber's soul for supposed treason should have been an easy contract, but someone had tipped Saber off and the hunt had lasted months instead of days.

At least the medallion with Saber's soul in it hadn't been lost in the river. Bully for one good thing coming out of this mess. Saber could be reborn and become a pain in Hunter's ass again in another couple hundred years.

The light changed to green. He urged the car up the hill. Not too fast. Don't draw attention. People were looking for him, and with so few cars on the road at this hour, a speeding vehicle would draw interest. It was only ten minutes to the hospital. He'd practiced being unnoticed in the human world for almost two thousand years. He could handle ten more minutes. No matter how much he wanted out of this body.

AT THE HOSPITAL, HE BYPASSED THE EMERGENCY ENTRANCE. WITH HIS appearance, he was sure he'd get swarmed by nurses and rushed through triage, even if he was gaining strength by the minute. It was after one in the morning, and the main entrance was locked, so he continued around to a side door of the four-story structure, avoiding the construction scaffolds covering the massive sagging and stained building.

The snow in front of the door had been packed down, and an ice-filled metal bucket sat precariously on a drift against the wall. Yellow and white cigarette butts dotted the ice in the container.

If bad human habits held true, the door would be unlocked so the smokers could get back in. Unlike many dragons, Hunter hadn't completely embraced human behavior, just enough to hide among them. But a smart drake still knew as much as he could about it, as baffling as it was.

Besides, who was he to argue? He'd smoked, too, for a good hundred years. It had made him feel more like the fire drake he'd been before, puffing small clouds of smoke from his nostrils and hissing it out between clenched teeth. But the thrill had worn off, and he was left with the bitter reminder that the smoke would never be of his own creation ever again. Not since the Great Scourge so many years ago, when the last of the natural human sorcerers had banded together against his kind.

He tried the door. Not locked. It opened into a narrow hall, and at the end lay a wider, brighter corridor. He eased to the intersection and glanced around.

Laughter to his right made him draw back. Two nurses left a room one door down and headed away from him. Smokers would take the exit closest to their staff room, and usually near that was a storage room where he'd find scrubs and physicians' coats.

He slipped around the corner, reading the labels on the doors and finding the storage room. Inside were metal shelves filled with mundane supplies—anything specifically medical was kept in more secure closets. He peeled off his still damp sweater and jeans, quickly noting Anaea's slim figure and plain bra and panties before looking away, since it wasn't polite to stare when a lady wasn't awake to blush.

Everything about the woman he possessed screamed sense and practicality. A warm sweater, jeans that were thick enough to keep out the winter's chill, and winter boots with rubber soles to protect against slipping. Even her choice to kill herself had been practical. Given the option, he'd pick a quick death over a long, slow diminishing one, too.

For a fleeting moment, he wondered if she'd been less practical prior to her illness. From his quick glance, he knew she'd done everything she could to destroy the cancer. It showed in every aspect of her body: noticeable ribs, elbows and wrists just a little too bony, and a red puckering scar peeking from the edge of her bra line. In spite of that, he couldn't deny she was beautiful. Even as a human, she would have caught his eye.

He could have really liked her. Maybe he could still get to know her. She had a few months left, if she didn't kill herself first. After he returned to the Dragon Court with Saber's soul in the medallion, he could come back and visit her. Just because he didn't tend to have trysts with humans didn't mean he couldn't, although there were laws concerning how much could be revealed and how long the relationship could last.

He shoved her clothes to the back of a bottom shelf, put on a set of green scrubs, and threw on a lab coat. Grabbing a larger set of scrubs, he left the linen room and looked in the next door, the room where he'd seen the nurses exit.

Sure enough, it was a staff room. His luck held and it was empty. He chose the combination lock on the nearest locker, twirled the dial, and listened for the clicks that released it. Inside, he found a purse and took enough money for a taxi along with a bobby pin to pick the key lock on his emergency supplies locker at the train station. With that done, he headed to the elevators to find the morgue.

At the basement level, the doors slid open, revealing a long, bright corridor, just like all the others in the hospital. A sign said the morgue was down the hall and to his right, and Hunter headed in the direction indicated, the rubber soles on his boots squeaking on the worn linoleum floor.

He turned the corner. The door at the end of the hall swung open, and a man in a long black coat stepped through. A fedora shadowed his face, and all Hunter could see of him was a pale chin and the hint of thin lips.

Adrenaline burst through Hunter and he sucked in a calming breath. There was nothing to indicate this man was trouble. And yet, there was nothing to suggest otherwise. Merely an instinct honed over hundreds of years.

Hunter didn't need to look for a door. He'd already scanned the hall when he'd first entered and there were none. Which meant no escape but forward or back.

The man gave no sign that he noticed Hunter. He kept walking, his heels clicking on the floor.

Another burst of adrenaline made Hunter twitch and pain shot from the back of his head to his eyes. He stifled a gasp and stared at the man, searching for signs of assault. Those few dragons who had earth magic strong enough for an attack needed a gesture or word to focus it.

But the man's hands hung at his sides, and his mouth was closed. He wasn't casting anything. Which meant the pain in Hunter's head could only have originated from within. Anaea was waking, and much sooner than expected. Hunter needed to get to the morgue and make the transfer, but he was practically defenseless, and he had a bad feeling about the stranger.

Just a few more feet and he'd be within reach.

Anaea's consciousness pressed against his and he could sense her groggy confusion. She wasn't yet aware of her situation, a prisoner in her own body, but she would be soon.

Hunter picked up his pace. The pressure in his head increased, drawing more of his concentration. And while the stranger in black was still a potential threat, he hadn't done anything, yet. Maybe luck was on his side again and there was nothing to worry about.

As they passed each other, the man grabbed for Hunter's wrist. Hunter dropped the extra scrubs and jumped back, but Anaea's body wasn't fast enough to avoid the grasp or strong enough to break it.

The stranger hissed something in ancient Egyptian, and sharp pain lanced up Hunter's arm.

Anaea pounded in his head... her head. Her fear grew, filling his thoughts with cold, burning panic. She knew she was trapped. She screamed and clawed at his will power.

Hunter jerked his arm, but the man's grip was strong, like iron around his thin, feminine wrist. Damn this body. The brute strength he'd become accustomed to was no longer available, and he didn't have time to search his memory for those years when he'd studied martial arts. It had been so long ago, and he'd never thought he'd need them. Not a Crusader like him. But now he needed to know how to fight in her weaker body, and he had no clue how to do that.

But she did. She had to. He delved into her wild thoughts, tapping into her knowledge of combat, what little there was. But before he could do anything, she poured into him, unknowingly taking advantage of their increased connection.

He fought to contain her, but couldn't. Her will was too strong, wild with panic and fury and determination. If her cancer had been a man, it would have been long dead and buried, probably in dozens of little pieces. She had a will unlike any he'd encountered before.

The door at the end of the hall opened and another man in black strode in. He barked words, also in Egyptian, and bullets of ice materialized before his outstretched hand.

Hunter struggled against the first man's grip. A fight against one drake mage while in a body that had yet to connect to whatever magical potential it had was difficult enough, but two was suicide. And if he didn't contain Anaea's consciousness they'd both be dead.

3

Anaea screamed. Her body was numb, and no matter how hard she tried, she couldn't make it obey her commands. A fog pressed against her senses and wrapped about her, freezing her in place. She felt disembodied within herself, like she was floating through a dream, simply watching.

And *herself* was in danger.

Some man held her arm and another threatened her from down the hall. Somehow, she knew she was in a hospital basement, but had no idea how she'd gotten there. She beat at the fog again and again. It swirled, thickening where she pushed. She clawed and kicked, and heard herself curse. No. It wasn't her. There was someone else in the fog with her.

It was a dream. All a dream.

More like a nightmare. She struggled against it, regardless of how hopeless the situation was and whether it was even real or not.

Something nicked her side. Whoever was in the fog with her gasped, and a sliver of light sliced open the miasma. This had to be her chance, and she shoved through.

Her side stung, and the man had a bruising grip on her wrist. He squeezed, sending lightning shooting up her arm and across her chest. With a scream, Anaea realized she was back in control of her body. She rammed her fingers into her assailant's eyes. He let go and she stumbled back.

Down the hall! Look!

She glanced at the second assailant. Tiny white balls—they looked like ice—shot toward her. This was a horrifying dream. It had to be. But even knowing it was one, her heart still raced.

She twisted sideways, but wasn't fast enough getting out of the way. The balls nicked her arm, five sharp slices. Her fingers went numb and slick heat welled around the wounds.

The first man seized her wrist again and jerked her forward. She stumbled and contorted her body to the side, twirling him around as the next barrage of white bullets slammed into his back. He sputtered and sagged, collapsing on the floor, and she ran, knowing he was dead.

But they were in a hospital, weren't they? Maybe her attacker had a chance at being resuscitated.

No, he didn't. It was too late for him. It would be too late for her if she didn't keep running.

More bullets hit the wall by her head as she scrambled around the corner. The elevator sat before her, but she flew past it to the stairs. There wasn't enough time to wait for it and she wasn't dumb enough to try.

She yanked the door open and took the stairs two at a time. Her breath burned in her chest and her limbs ached. She wasn't recovered enough from the chemo for this kind of exercise.

But she had to keep moving. They were going to kill her.

She just couldn't understand why or where that thought had come from. For that matter, she couldn't understand how she'd gotten to the hospital.

All of which didn't matter right now. Someone was after her for some reason, and she had to keep going. The stairwell door below her clicked open and shut and rapid, heavy footsteps thudded up the stairs.

"Come on, Hunter. How far do you think you'll get in that body?" a masculine voice thick with malice asked.

Anaea stumbled and caught her balance, a glimmer of relief forming in her chest. They had the wrong person. Maybe if she just—

But they didn't care. She just knew they didn't.

A bullet whizzed past her head.

"Don't make this difficult."

Pain lanced through her thigh. She careened around the corner, using the railing for leverage, and lunged against the door. It swung open and she rushed into a hall, empty of people and lined with construction equipment. The cinderblock walls were primed but not painted, and the panels in the drop ceiling were missing, exposing the metal frame above. Doors lined either side, and she ran to the first one, grasping the handle.

No. Not there. He'd be able to find her.

She jerked back, leaving a bloody handprint on the door. Her only way of escape was to find people, but she didn't know where she was.

The door to the stairwell opened, and the man stepped through. His trench coat whipped out behind him as if caught by the wind. He tilted his hat back, revealing a dark, emotionless gaze. More white bullets appeared before his outstretched hand.

It wasn't possible, but the ache in her arm and thigh were proof she wasn't hallucinating. And as soon as she found help, she promised she'd think about it.

For a brief moment, she wondered if it was really happening, if she wasn't still lying on the riverbank in the snow, dying. Maybe this was hell, or a near-death delusion. Which meant it didn't matter if she ran or not, she was still dead. She wasn't even sure why she was running in the first place. Hadn't she wanted to die?

No, not like this. Not shot or tortured or beaten. And somehow, she knew this man wouldn't let her die a quiet, peaceful death.

A corridor lay ten feet away. She threw herself at it, but two bullets still pierced her back, sending a spray of blood exploding out of her chest. White-hot pain ignited within her. She gasped, too shocked to scream, stumbled and caught her balance. Blood seeped into the front of her top.

She staggered around the corner to find a dead end. No door, no stairwell, just a fresh cinderblock wall. She pounded on the stone, her mind unable to accept that there was no place to go.

The man eased around the corner and leaned against the wall, his hand raised, more bullets hovering before him. A wicked smile curled his lips, revealing yellowed teeth.

"I'd ask for the medallion, but I'll just take it from your cold, dead hands."

How clichéd. She snorted and coughed blood. It was ridiculous she'd even think that. She was about to die. She should be dead already, but maybe she'd gotten lucky and those bullets hadn't hit anything vital. She had believed cancer would have been the harder death.

A million thoughts flashed through her mind and a new, encroaching fog threatened her consciousness. She struggled against it. She would not succumb, would not lie down and die. This was not her choice, and she'd be damned if she'd let him kill her.

She lunged at him.

He shot at her, and two more bullets lanced her chest. She staggered, grabbing the front of his coat. Heat poured down her arms and blue flame burst from her hands, hissing and snapping. Anaea screamed and batted at the fire. She was burning, bleeding, dying. The fire leapt from her fingers to the man. His trench coat ignited and he, too, screamed and flailed.

She staggered back, and the flames on her arms extinguished, her flesh unharmed. But the man continued to scream and burn, the fire engulfing him until he was consumed.

Bile burned the back of her throat. It was such a horrible way to die. Not much worse than being shot to death, although, now that she thought about it, the absence of extreme pain or burns on her hands astonished her. She hurt, and every time she moved it felt like sharp pokers were lancing through her, but it was almost bearable.

Perhaps she was light-headed from the blood loss, or too numb to feel the pain she knew she should.

Regardless, she needed a doctor.

Not a good idea.

Which didn't make any sense, unless her death wish had finally kicked in. She could just fall asleep as she bled to death, and that would be the end of it. Besides, if she found a doctor they'd keep her in the hospital. Which was the last place she ever wanted to be again. That, and someone would find the bodies and questions would be asked. She couldn't afford to still be here when that happened.

Yes, that made sense. She didn't want to spend what little time she had left talking to the police and wrapped up in some court case.

No. No, that was ridiculous. She had holes in her body. Admittedly, they were small ones, but they went all the way through. It was a miracle she was still standing and not feeling much pain. But maybe that was just shock.

The fog pressed at the edge of her senses.

It was a dream. All a dream.

She stumbled, caught her balance with a hand against the wall, and left a bloody smear on the white primer. It didn't matter how she felt about hospitals or the police, she needed help.

HUNTER SHOVED ANAEA'S CONSCIOUSNESS BACK INTO THE PSYCHIC BOX he'd constructed for her. The whole situation was racing out of control. The fact that his two assailants hadn't healed meant they were human mages, not dragons. The only way for a human to have magic was if someone had intentionally broken dragon law by body-sharing until the human's body had connected to the earth's magic. And when he had time, he'd consider all the ramifications of that. None of them were good.

To make matters worse, Anaea shouldn't have woken, and if her body hadn't been so damaged by the cancer, she wouldn't have. His soul magic was divided among too many things. If only he could make it not heal her, but that happened on a subconscious level. It would be easier to tell himself to stop breathing.

Fiery pain washed over him as he regained control. He gasped and sucked in a slow breath. It would pass. Not soon, but it would pass. As much as Anaea wanted to find a doctor, he didn't. He'd tried to convince her otherwise, but he couldn't get through to her with subtle suggestions, and revealing himself to her was the very last option. Thank goodness she'd so quickly established a connection to the earth's magic or they'd certainly be dead.

Although that created a whole other problem, since now Anaea was evidence that Hunter had broken dragon law as well. If he was lucky, really lucky, he might still be able to convince her subconscious that calling fire had been a hallucination or a dream and he wouldn't have to uphold dragon law and kill her.

He coughed blood and shuffled to the stairwell door. If he could get to the morgue, he could get a new body, but Anaea was too damaged to survive. She lived only because his magic was focused on her body's injuries. It would take time to heal. Sure, the bleeding had stopped, but internal organs took longer to repair and his magic was the only thing keeping them alive at the moment. It wouldn't be safe for him to transfer out of her for at least a few hours.

He had hoped to be long gone by that time. Of course, the woman was dying of cancer. Wouldn't it be a kindness to transfer to another vessel and let her slip into death while still unconscious?

The stairwell door swung open before he could reach it, and a woman in a long black coat strode toward him. Her blond ponytail swished over her shoulders, accentuating her long neck. She flipped her coat open, revealing a long sword strapped to her hip.

Shit. At least they were recognizable by their dress code. Hunter felt for his body's magical thread, the single thing connecting him to the earth's magic. It wasn't there. He concentrated, searching faster, but couldn't find it. It had to be somewhere. There was no other way Anaea could have called fire.

4

"All I want is the medallion, Hunter," the woman said. The fact that she knew his name suggested she was in league with a dragon, or was a dragon herself. And until he had a stable connection to the earth's magic, he wouldn't be able to sense if she was or not— and maybe not at all, depending on how this body connected to it. He didn't recognize her, but that didn't mean anything. Accidents requiring a transfer into a new vessel, while infrequent, did happen. The irony of this situation was not lost on him.

She drew her sword. The ponytail made her face look pinched and stern. "The medallion."

He scrambled back, and pain washed over him. This damned body wasn't healing fast enough. Gulping air, he kept moving, past the dead-end corridor where the seared corpse of his new assailant's associate lay, and continued to the next one. This wasn't a dead-end and he turned down it. With the clean edge of his lab coat, he twisted the handle of the second room he found and leapt in. He searched for a lock but there wasn't one. So much for that idea.

Pressing his back to the door, he took a cursory note that it was an unoccupied private room with nothing in it that looked as though it could bar the entrance or be used as a weapon.

The handle rattled and the door shoved forward. Hunter stumbled, and it flew open. The woman jabbed her sword at him, and he twisted out of the way, shoving an empty trolley between them.

She kicked it aside and lunged again.

Hunter rolled over the bed, grinding his teeth against the pain. If he were in his old body... but he wasn't, and he needed to stop thinking like that. He needed to get creative. He yanked open the drawer of the bedside table in search of a possible weapon. Inside was a leather-bound Bible and nothing else. The woman slashed at him over the bed. He ducked and grabbed the book.

The woman shoved the bed toward him. He slid under it and slammed the Bible into the side of her knee. She dropped to her other knee and brought the sword around at his head. He deflected her swing with the Bible against the flat of the blade, thankful she didn't have enough room for full range of motion. With a growl, he smashed the book into her face, up and back.

He didn't wait for her to react. He needed to stay close, making it impossible for her to use her sword. He launched forward and rammed the Bible's spine into her temple. Her eyes rolled back into her head and she crumpled to the floor.

Hunter tossed the book on the bed and staggered out of the room. He'd bought just enough time to escape without drawing more attention by running. If the woman was a dragon, she'd wake soon and be back on the hunt. As much as he wanted to search her for clues to identify the traitor she worked for, there just wasn't the time. He needed to put as much distance between them as possible.

He went back down to the first dead mage in the basement, wiped his hands on a clean corner of the dead man's shirt, and shrugged into his trench coat. It wouldn't be good if someone stopped him to ask about the blood on his clothes—or the rest of him—and while this man's coat was stained, it looked more like water on the black fabric than blood. He continued down the hall, past the morgue, and up a back stairwell.

The first exit he came to opened onto an alley lined with dumpsters. Still aware that his misappropriated body was healing, he eased down the stairs and headed to the busy main street where he could hail a taxi or find a phone and call one.

What a mess. But with dragonkind growing frustrated over Prince Regis's laws restricting dragon liberties—particularly concerning the duration spent among humans—it didn't surprise Hunter that some drakes would attempt subversion. And now Hunter was the one being hunted.

He amended that. It wasn't really him they were after, but the medallion. Not a comforting thought since he was still in their way. Without a doubt, there was a dragon pulling strings and intentionally breaking dragon law.

Only a dragon would know the power the medallion had over dragonkind, or want it. With the use of ancient Egyptian, the likeliest suspect was Zenobia, but he hadn't thought she'd be so foolish. But then again, for all he knew, Regis had grown tired of Hunter's service and was trying to eliminate him—since murder was how Royal Assassins were fired.

A taxi a few feet away flicked on his 'in service' light, pulled a u-turn, and drove away. The next closest one was three blocks down in front of a billboard touting the town's urban revitalization plans tagged with black and red graffiti.

"Hey, baby," a masculine voice said.

Hunter glanced at the man leaning against a pizza shop window. His clothes were stained and ripped, and his hair was greasy and unkempt. Ah, the human race at its best. He pitied the poor woman who'd attracted this man's attention.

"Sweetie, don't give the cold shoulder."

Hunter kept walking. He wished he could do something for the woman being accosted, but he wasn't in any kind of shape for more confrontation. Besides, he was trying to keep a low profile.

The drunk ran up to Hunter's side and draped a heavy arm across his shoulders.

"Baby," Drunk said in a low voice.

Shit.

He'd forgotten he was a woman.

How did a woman brush off a man? They always made it look so easy. Not that he'd been on the receiving end very often, but it was bound to happen at least a few times in two thousand years. He needed to keep walking.

Hunter shrugged off Drunk's arm and sped up. The taxi was only one more block away.

Drunk scurried to Hunter's side and put his arm back across his shoulders. "Is that the way to treat a fine man like me?"

Hunter rolled his eyes. He'd seen finer. Heck, he'd *been* finer.

He should say he was married.

He didn't know where the idea had come from, but he couldn't say that, he had no proof. His gaze jumped to his hands. He hadn't even thought to check if Anaea was married. Her fingers were splashed with blood, Anaea's and the mage's, but she didn't wear a ring.

Relief flooded him. He wasn't sure why. In truth, it was sad this woman was so completely alone. Kind of like him. Except his empty life was by choice.

Of course, he didn't really know anything about her at all. There probably was someone who loved her and waited for her to return home. Which meant he had two days to take care of business before a missing persons report was filed and the police started looking for him... her.

The Dragon Court Clean Team was going to love him. Blood and an abandoned car on the Queen Street Bridge and two, maybe three, bodies in the hospital. He was going to have to buy Capri a half dozen more rare orchids for her hoard just to stay on her mostly pleasant side.

"Listen," Hunter said, "my boyfriend is waiting for me."

Drunk squeezed Hunter close. "I'm sure he'll share."

"After ten years in the state pen for manslaughter... I doubt it."

Drunk leapt back as if he'd been stung.

Hunter bit his lip, forcing his expression to remain blank. He wasn't sure where that line had come from, but it worked wonders.

He'd have to keep it in mind the next time he was stuck in a female body—which was going to be never if he had any say in it.

"You're joking, right?"

Hunter shook his head. "I suppose we could ask him."

Drunk didn't respond. He spun on his heel, found a new target across the street, and rushed away. Hunter didn't wait for anyone else to take his spot. He marched to the closest taxi and got in then instructed the driver to take him to the train station.

As the taxi pulled up to the station, Hunter scanned the area for anyone dressed in a dark trench coat. There was no one around. It was late, at least an hour past midnight, and passenger trains didn't run at this hour in Elmsville. Good, since it would be easier to spot danger, and yet bad since he'd stand out like a sore thumb on the security cameras.

He paid the driver and got out. He'd need another taxi to get to his hotel, but he'd call one from a different company to cover his tracks.

The snow had been shoveled from the walk, and his boots crunched on the salt. He checked out the waiting area through the large windows as he approached.

Still empty.

The glass door was heavier than he recalled, reminding him that the last time he was at the station he'd been healthy and male. Little things seemed off to him, ever-so-slightly bigger or taller, and he wondered how long it would take for him to get used to it.

He shook his head. He wasn't going to get used to it. He'd contact Grey, have him arrange for an appropriate body, then hand over the medallion with Saber's soul inside ready for rebirth and make his own discreet transfer. Grey would know what kind of body to look for. They both had an appreciation for warriors after taking their Crusaders.

The lockers sat to the right of the building in a narrow hall just past the public washrooms. He'd lost his key when he'd lost his body, but a dragon didn't go more than a few centuries without picking up some useful skills.

He eased over to his locker, at the far end, almost out of sight of the security camera, and blocked the view with his body. He could only get away with blocking the camera for a moment before drawing attention to himself, but the lock on the door was simple and would only take a few seconds to pick.

He bent the bobby pin at a right angle, scraped the plastic tip off one end, slid it into the lock, and froze. His fingers held it, he could feel it, but he couldn't move his hands. He tried to glance over his shoulder but couldn't turn his head, either.

Where am I? What am I doing? Anaea's sudden thoughts washed over him.

He gasped.

No, he didn't gasp. She did. He dove into his mind to find the breach in his psychic box. But it was gone. There was no indication it had ever existed. He hadn't even noticed its disappearance and he couldn't figure out what had happened.

Neither can I. Anaea looked at her hands, making his head move against his will.

He struggled to regain control, but couldn't break her will this time. He had to do something or a security guard would figure out that something wasn't right.

5

H unter grasped at the first thing that came to mind. *You're having a bad dream.* The situation was past any graceful salvage. He'd take whatever worked.

How can I be having a bad dream when you just thought about needing to do something about me?

Who do you think you're having a conversation with?

Her thoughts flashed through him as she considered the possibilities.

Someone shot me, she said without the panic he'd expect.

A dream, remember.

Oh.

You should go back to sleep.

She giggled at the ridiculousness of that, but thankfully their body stayed silent. *How can I go back to sleep when I'm already asleep?*

Why don't you try to find out?

She yawned and it felt as if she rolled over in his head and drifted off. He wove another quick box around her consciousness but didn't believe it would hold her. His first box hadn't disappeared because of his lack of skill, but because the strength of her will was something he'd never encountered before.

He finished picking the lock and fished out a small backpack containing cash, a prepaid cell phone, and a key ring with spare hotel and car keys. As he walked back to the front door, he called a cab on the phone. It had been a long night about to go into a long day. He needed to get to his hotel room, pick up a few things, call the Clean Team to take care of this mess, and make arrangements for a new body. His current one was too crowded.

ANAEA FLOATED IN A VISCOUS WARMTH. IT ENVELOPED HER, CLOUDING her vision and soothing her senses. She felt at ease for the first time in a long time. It had been months since she'd felt so truly and completely relaxed. Her fight against the cancer had seemed never ending, and yet there had been an end. She'd chosen it and jumped... no, she'd...

Memories of the bridge and the man swept over her, and she sat up with a start.

She was in her mother's hammock, swinging from side to side. A gentle wind sighed through the twin maples above her and caressed her face, bare neck, and arms. She wore the breezy white sundress she'd purchased for her honeymoon with John three years ago. And while she still loved the dress, she had serious second thoughts about her husband.

Dappled sunlight danced over her but she couldn't bring herself to ease back into the hammock. As wonderful as it all seemed, it wasn't right. She'd never sat in this spot while wearing that dress. She'd torn the hammock down the night her mother had died— joining the father Anaea had only known through photos and stories.

And then she realized she was whole. Impossibly perfect and complete. The curve of her right breast was fleshy and real, matching her left, not a falsie like it had been before. Her throat and chest tightened at everything she'd lost.

The weight in the hammock shifted, and a masculine hand slid up her arm to her shoulder.

"Lie back, Anaea."

Strong, muscled thighs braced her on either side. They were draped in thin cotton, and she ran her hands over them, feeling their chiseled contour.

They reminded her of Mark's legs, of his lean-muscled body, and of the relationship that would never be between them because she'd married John instead. She'd often dreamt of Mark, her college sweetheart, but never like this. Those dreams were soft and aching, filled with what-ifs, where he stood at a distance and reached out for her. But when she realized she could run to him, that she was free of her husband's charm, he turned his back on her.

Whoever was behind her eased her back against his chest and she glanced up. It wasn't Mark, but the man from the bridge. A thin scar sliced through his left eyebrow, and his nose was offset as if it had been broken a long time ago. His eyes were deep brown and filled with such warmth.

That warmth seeped through her, heating her from within, radiating safety and comfort.

"What are you doing here?" she asked, even though she felt he belonged there.

"You're dreaming."

He had said that before. She'd believed him then, but she wasn't so sure about that now, although it certainly felt like a dream with the hammock and the dress and him.

"Just relax," he said. "Enjoy this moment, this serenity."

"But who are you?" She couldn't get the sensation out of her mind that something wasn't right.

"I'm only a dream." He wrapped his arms around her, offering the comfort she'd longed for since her husband had left.

If she relaxed, she might be able to believe this was a dream. A soothing, comforting dream. Better than the heartbreaking dreams about Mark. She certainly wanted to let this man hold her and ease everything that ached within her. But the faint buzzing at the edge of her senses wouldn't let her melt into his embrace.

He whispered her name. "Anaea."

She closed her eyes, savoring the gentle tone. It had been too long since anyone had said her name with affection.

A chill swept over her. Something wasn't right. She could feel it niggling the back of her mind. Something about this man and people shooting at her.

She pushed away from him, making the hammock rock. Cold panic swept through her. She'd been shot. She was in trouble, hurt, and had to wake up.

"Relax," he said, reaching to pull her back into his embrace.

She scrambled out of the hammock.

"No. I'm hurt. I need help." She shook her head. "I have to wake up."

"But isn't this better than reality?"

"Yes…" She stared at him. His face was full of acceptance and understanding. "No… Someone has to tell the police what happened to you."

"Anaea."

She squeezed her eyes shut, forcing all thoughts of him from her mind. Just wake up. It's just a dream. An amazing, wonderful, dream—

No. Wake up!

She could feel consciousness just out of reach. Just a little farther.

6

A naea woke with a start. She lay on the floor on a thick carpet. From her vantage in the shadowy room, she could see a pair of table legs and beige-on-beige striped wallpaper lit by a stream of weak sunlight.

Taking a slow breath, she waited and listened. She couldn't hear anyone nearby so she sat up to get a better look. She was between a simple desk with padded chair and a king-size bed. The heavy drapes across the window were closed tight, and pale light slipped between the cracks around the edges. To her right was a door with a floor plan and fire escape routes plaque-mounted above a peephole. To her left, a door leading, presumably, to the bathroom.

Her body ached, but not as much as she'd expected from getting shot.

Shot!

She'd been shot. She reached for her coat and froze. She wore a black trench coat.

Where the hell had that come from?

She couldn't remember putting it on. Ripping open the coat revealed a lab coat and green hospital scrubs. She ran a hand over the front of her top. It was sticky with blood and there were holes in it big enough to fit her finger through.

It wasn't a dream. She scrambled to her feet and raced into the bathroom. Shedding the coat and lab coat and dropping them to the floor, she yanked the top over her head. Crusted blood pulled away from her chest with a sharp sting.

She flicked on the light and stared at herself in the large mirror. Her chest, plain white bra, and the strange medallion were covered with a black crust. Oh God, someone really had shot her. Admittedly, she couldn't see any holes in her body, but there were holes in her shirt. And all that blood.

How was she still alive? She snorted at the thought. A few hours ago—well, maybe more since she had no idea what time it was—she'd stood on the Queen Street Bridge contemplating killing herself. And now she was upset that someone had shot her.

But someone had shot her! Her mind kept repeating the thought. She couldn't focus on anything else. There was no logical explanation for her survival. None.

Her heart skipped a beat. She was in someone's hotel room, and she had no idea how she'd gotten there. She stared at her reflection, gazing into her blue eyes. If she looked hard enough, maybe she'd be able to see what was wrong, why she still lived.

Red flashed, haloing her entire body for just a moment. She jumped, her heart pounding and blood rushing in her ears.

She'd had a close call, that was all. It was making her see things, but she still turned back to her reflection to see if it would happen again.

It didn't. She raked a bloody hand over the half-inch-long stubble on her head and the panic subdued to an ache in her gut.

And then she realized she was topless in a stranger's hotel room. She snatched the robe off the hook beside the door and wrapped herself in it. She needed to get to the hospital, do something about the holes that were... had been in her chest, but there was no telling when whoever had kidnapped her would return. Against all logical thought, it didn't appear as if she needed immediate medical attention, so getting someplace safe was her first priority. She needed a top that wasn't covered in blood and then she was out of here. And if she couldn't find something in the next few seconds, she'd put the disgusting hospital shirt back on.

There was no evidence in the bathroom that the room was occupied. No toothbrush, cosmetics, shaving cream, nothing. Not even a toiletry bag tucked away on the corner of the vanity. She didn't even know if she'd been abducted by a man or woman.

She returned to the main room, spying a leather bag on the desk. She rushed to it, yanking the zipper open. Inside was a plain black T-shirt and a pair of blue jeans. Both were too big for her and were cut in a masculine style. Underneath the clothes was a laptop, a cell phone, a knife the length of her forearm, and a thick wad of cash.

What kind of person had her? Everything since standing on the bridge was fuzzy, save for a few shocking moments of clarity where she'd run for her life and been shot.

She dragged the T-shirt over her head. Then she pulled the knife from its sheath and flipped it into a reverse grip so the blade lay flat against her forearm. This was crazy. She should hold the knife out, ready. But somehow she knew she needed to keep the blade hidden until the last moment. Was it a fleeting remembrance from her childhood, something from a book or a TV show?

Besides, if she did manage to make it out of the hotel without running into whoever had abducted her, she didn't want to draw attention by holding a knife. Then again, maybe a quick call to 911 would be the smartest option. They could trace the call and find her even if she had no idea where she was.

She needed help, but there wasn't anyone she could turn to. Her ex was in Tahiti with his healthy, perfect girlfriend, and she'd rather eat dirt than ask him for anything. The only other person was Mark, and he hadn't returned her calls in two years and lived three hours away in Newgate.

The lock clicked open. Anaea froze and stared at the door. A rapid succession of thoughts raced through her mind: hide in the bathroom—the shower was obvious and she'd be found—go out the window—didn't know what floor she was on—stay and fight—

Shit.

She squeezed the grip on the knife as the door swung open. The woman from the bridge, dressed all in black, stood in the hall with a sword as long as her leg peeking out from the folds of her coat. A strange yellow light danced around her, crackling and hissing.

It was powerful magic.

Anaea had no clue how she knew that. The thought just popped into her head. Maybe she'd seen one too many sci-fi movies, but without a doubt, it was powerful, and in her weakened condition, it was deadly.

Strange thoughts kept jumping into her mind, thoughts that couldn't possibly be her own. She should be panicked, desperate, but she wasn't. Instead, she was itching for a fight, even without magic.

See, there it was again. Magic was crazy, impossible. It wasn't real. Nonetheless, she eased into a wider stance and held her hands up, ready for battle. She shoved all resisting thoughts about what she was doing to the back of her mind. There was no other place to go but past that woman, and it looked like that would involve a fight.

"Should I even suggest handing over the medallion?" the woman asked, cocking her head to one side and staring at Anaea with feral intensity.

Anaea clutched the medallion through the T-shirt. If that was all the woman wanted…

No, once she gave up the medallion there was nothing to stop the woman from killing her.

The woman sneered at Anaea's silence. "Glad to see you're willing to entertain me." She drew her blade and lunged in one quick motion, bringing the tip of her sword up and pointing it at Anaea's heart.

Anaea stumbled back, her expected panic still absent. She should have used the knife. Well, yes, but using a knife against a sword wouldn't give her very good odds.

The woman pressed her attack, dancing into the room with whirling sword and precise footwork. Anaea scrambled away. The backs of her thighs hit the edge of the bed as the woman lunged forward. The blade bit into her side, sending pain shooting through her.

Anaea gasped and swung her knife. The woman leaned in, grabbed Anaea's wrist, and bent it back, sending hot spikes of pain up her arm. Anaea's fingers went numb, and the knife fell to the floor. The woman kicked it aside and rested her sword against Anaea's neck.

"The medallion, if you please."

So much for fighting back. Anaea slipped the medallion outside of the T-shirt. It was sticky with her blood and warm from being against her body.

A small voice in her head told her to resist, fight, anything but give over the medallion.

But there was nothing she could do. She didn't know how to fight, and she had a sword against her neck. Maybe if she handed it over she'd live. She doubted it, but maybe.

The magic aura around the woman flared and crackled like electricity. It bit Anaea's skin with tiny painful jolts. The pressure from the sword against her neck increased, and the woman's lips curled back in a dark, satisfied smile.

"Now."

Don't give it to her. The voice was louder this time, filled with urgency.

Anaea squeezed the medallion, feeling its heat against her fingers and the edges, crusted in blood, digging into her palm.

Don't.

She tried to break the chain, but couldn't move. The muscles in her arm twitched and heat burned from her hand up toward her shoulder. She ground her teeth and shot the entire force of her will to her arm. With a jerk, the chain broke.

The voice in her head howled and she trembled as if someone else fought her for control of her body. The heat from the medallion poured over her, tinting her vision red.

7

The woman grabbed the chain, but Anaea couldn't make her fingers release the medallion, and her other hand clamped on top of the woman's, pressing the medallion to her palm. The heat intensified, burning through her veins. She was on fire. If she opened her mouth and released the scream boiling at the back of her throat, she was certain flames would roar out of her.

The woman's eyes opened wide. She dropped her sword and used her free hand to pry at Anaea's fingers. Against her will, Anaea held on tight, every muscle burning, smoke muddling her thoughts. Then words popped into her head. Three short words in a language she didn't recognize.

She forced them out, and the heat rushed through her hand, into the medallion, and enveloped the woman.

"It's too soon," the woman gasped and her face went slack.

Anaea's heart pounded once, twice. With a sudden whoosh, the heat poured back into the medallion.

The woman dropped to the floor. Anaea kicked the sword across the room and nudged the woman's shoulder with her toe.

She's dead.

It was the voice in her head, the one that hadn't wanted her to give up the medallion. Without the panic of a fight, she had the time to concentrate on it. It was within her, but not a part of her, and with a pitch closer to tenor, it was definitely male.

She shivered and hugged herself, but the shakes continued.

Take her coat.

Anaea's gaze went to the woman of its own volition. No, not its own control, the voice's. She squeezed her eyes shut, shaking so hard her teeth chattered.

You're in shock.

"Yeah, I'm hearing voices." She pressed her palms to her ears but knew that wouldn't keep him out, since he was inside to begin with.

Anaea, you're still in danger. Get her coat and put it on.

Her arms reached out and she yanked them back. "Stop that."

Then you do it.

"Get out first."

The voice—he—hesitated. She sensed he was deciding what to tell her, but she couldn't determine what options he was considering. It was a strange sensation, similar to the frustration of knowing you know something but being unable to bring it to mind.

I'm here to help you.

She snorted. "I don't even know you. For all I know, you're just some hallucination and I can add paranoid schizophrenia to my list of problems."

I would beg to differ. You know for certain someone's trying to kill you so you can rule out paranoia.

"Gee, thanks." She squatted beside the woman on the floor and nudged her. "Do we know who she is?"

You don't. I do. And trust me when I say you don't want to be here when her friends come looking for her.

"Well, I'm not going anywhere until you 'fess up."

Don't be stupid.

She sat back on her heels and crossed her arms. Her muscles twitched, and she willed herself to stay where she was. She could feel his frustration and beneath that a hint of fear, although she doubted he'd admit to it.

Pressure built in her head, a heavy darkness pushed against her vision and threatened to wrap her consciousness in sleep. Every muscle trembled until she lost her balance and toppled onto her rear. She ground her teeth and shoved back with her thoughts. He could try to take over, but she'd be damned if she'd make it easy on him.

Spots danced across her vision, bright specks and black voids, and her blood pounded in her temples. Then, without warning, the pressure disappeared. She gasped at the sudden release.

Please. Need and desperation filled that one word. Then he clamped down on the emotions. *I'll explain on our way.*

"On our way where?"

I'll explain that, too.

She could feel his indecision. Images of a monstrous creature wreathed in shadow flashed through her mind. She gasped, and he clamped down on whatever that was, too, before she could get a good enough look.

"Why should I trust you?"

Because I've already kept you alive. The strange words she'd spoken earlier while fighting over the medallion entered her thoughts.

"Easily said. If I die, you die."

A hint of frustration flittered over her, before he forced his presence back to calm authority. It felt like he was keeping himself from her, hiding away who and what he really was. From his reaction, she knew he wasn't some projection with an essence outside of her. He was stuck in her head. That meant there was no way he was human. He might have been human at one point, but he certainly wasn't that now.

Which was ridiculous. Impossible. Crazy. That was it, she had to be crazy.

Her throat tightened, and her eyes burned with tears she refused to shed. She didn't want to be crazy. She was already dying. Couldn't God or fate or whatever was out there be satisfied with that?

You're not crazy. His voice was soft, filled with warmth, but there was an undertone, a concern, on the edge that she couldn't put into words. *It's just that the situation is complicated.*

"I'll say." She reached for the dead woman, uncertain if the impetus to move came from her or the man in her head. Pearl, her name was Pearl. Certainly, Pearl's name had come from him. It didn't matter. Her options were limited. She could try to carry on and hope no one else came for her because of the man. She could go to the police, but she didn't think they'd believe her. Or, she supposed, she could re-attempt her suicide, but her heart wasn't in that idea anymore, although she couldn't figure out why.

It's great that you're thinking about this, but we don't have a lot of time. If Pearl found us— He cut himself off.

She sensed he wasn't sure who else would be after him, but was certain that there was someone else. Pearl wasn't powerful enough to attack him alone.

"Pearl is merely a henchman... henchperson?" she asked in an attempt to confirm if the thoughts flitting through her head really were his.

Which is why I suggest we get moving.

"Fine." She wasn't thrilled with the idea. In fact she wasn't thrilled about anything, but she didn't see she had much choice. How could she? She had no clue what was going on.

———

IF HUNTER HAD TEETH, OR AT LEAST TEETH WITHIN HIS CONTROL, HE'D grind them. As it was, Anaea's will was so powerful he was now the one trapped in his... her... their body. And damn, if he could get her to listen to him. Any suggestion he'd tried to put in her mind during the fight had been ignored. It had taken all of his will just to keep holding onto the medallion. It was a miracle he'd managed to put the words to activate it into her head.

Of course, now he had two souls to deliver to Regis and one heck of a mess to clean up. He could just imagine the look on Capri's face when she heard she'd have to clean up the corpse in the hotel room. A dozen orchids and a lot of sweet talking would be in order.

All he had wanted was to grab his stuff from the hotel room and move on, since anyone at Court could find out where he was staying.

And now he'd lost control of his body and couldn't even physically vent his frustration.

Anaea worked at removing Pearl's coat while Hunter worked at containing his thoughts. Now it was him stuffed into the tiny box of his making, hoping as little of him as possible seeped into her consciousness.

He had no clue how much he should reveal to Anaea about her situation. Of course, dragon law stated he couldn't reveal anything, but he didn't think that was practical given the situation. Besides, with a will as powerful as hers and a thread to the earth's magic already established, Regis would proclaim her a sorcerer. It didn't matter how much she learned about him and dragons. Her execution was a certainty.

He clamped down on that thought, fast. That was definitely something he couldn't share.

Even if she were only a mage, which was more than likely the case, and not a true sorcerer, Regis would still want her dead since the idiot was unable to see the distinction between the two. Which meant if Hunter didn't want to kill Anaea, he'd have to break even more laws and keep her hidden. It was her only good option, although Hunter had a sinking suspicion she wouldn't just accept it.

"So what now?" she asked, the coat in her hands.

He considered flashing into her mind what to do to save time. But that would break the thin wall he'd managed to erect between them and just as he would be able to read her thoughts and memories, she'd most likely be able to read his. *Put the coat on. Does she have car keys?*

She put the coat on and reached into the pockets. A set of keys was in the right pocket, along with a wallet. In the left was a cell phone.

Dump the phone, grab the duffel bag, ensure the 'do not disturb' sign is on the door, and let's go. He concentrated on sounding commanding, while letting a trickle of urgency slip through. The short list of dragons who wanted him dead popped into mind, but he put it aside.

There was no point in making her panic, as much as they really did need to leave—and five minutes ago, at that.

Anaea dropped the phone on the floor, took the bag, and opened the door. The 'do not disturb' sign hung on the handle. She glanced up and down the hall, looking for trouble.

Strong willed and smart. He could really get to like this woman.

"Which way to the exit?" she whispered, as she stepped into the hall.

Stairs to your left. Don't take the elevator.

She rolled her eyes. "I wouldn't dream of it. You've made it quite clear we don't want to wait around any longer than we have to. I'd hate to meet your short list."

He jerked away from her consciousness and threw up another layer of soul magic around his box. She shouldn't know about the short list. He was slipping.

She strode to the end of the hall, eased open the stairwell door, and checked for trouble. All was quiet and she continued down the stairs.

"So I'm doing what you want…"

She was also persistent. He should have known she wouldn't give up on the idea of knowing what was going on. And yet, there was no way she'd believe him.

Let's put a little more distance between us and the body. And try to think what you want to say. Hopefully by then he'd have a chance to figure out what to tell her.

"Oh, no, you don't." She plopped down on the second-story landing and crossed her arms.

Fantastic. If he had eyes to roll—

Do you think we have time for this? There have been at least two attacks on your life already.

"Death—" She snorted. *Death doesn't scare me.*

Of course it wouldn't, what with her having terminal cancer and all. Just his luck he couldn't use loss of life as a motivator. Unless he used the loss of his life. No, that wouldn't work either. There was no way he could make anything, even the truth, make sense… not without a very long talk. Something he didn't have time for.

Trust me when I say it's just better you don't know.

"I doubt that."

All right. Then it's easier for both of us if you don't know. It's a little difficult to explain. More than a little difficult, and then he'd have to kill her. Although as it stood right now, he still probably had to kill her.

"Try me."

I could just make you miserable for the rest of your life.

She snorted again.

Right. She thought her life wasn't going to be that long and she'd already been miserable for the last year of it. *If we just go to a friend of mine, everything will be resolved and we can part ways.*

"I don't even know what will be resolved."

Damn, woman. Would you please… just… An internal roar escaped, just a tiny one, but even that hint of his dragon self made her jerk up.

Shit, shit, shit.

Anaea sped to the bottom of the stairwell without question. She trembled, inside and out, as her thoughts grappled with what he'd let slip.

He wished he could take it back, soothe her, lie to her. But she didn't seem to want lies. That made him like her even more and it stung to think that no matter what happened, the situation would end badly for her.

She paused at the steel side door. There was no way for either of them to know if Pearl had a partner waiting by her car, let alone what simply lay beyond the door.

They would just have to take a risk.

She eased the door open and glanced out. There were half a dozen cars in the parking lot and thankfully no people around. Anaea pulled the keys from her pocket and used the fob to flash the headlights of a Buick at the back of the lot.

She slid into the driver's seat, put the key in the ignition, and started the car, but didn't put it into drive.

Where to now?

Newgate.

"Newgate? That's three hours from here."

It's not my fault your town is pretty much nowhere.

"And that's where your friend is?"

He could feel her suspicion overriding her fear of him and her nagging thoughts that maybe she had lost her mind and he was merely a figment of her imagination. She didn't like the situation. Well, he didn't like it either. If she would just give him control of their body she could go to sleep and everything would be solved when she woke up.

If, of course, he could keep her hidden from Regis. There was still time for a transference before she suffered soul sickness, although things were now complicated by her becoming aware of him. If he wanted to make her forget, he'd have to involve Capri, the only dragon he knew who could manipulate a human's mind. And a part of him didn't want Anaea to forget.

"Fine," she said.

He'd waited too long to answer her, and now she didn't even believe that going to Newgate would solve her problem.

"At least tell me where we are so I can get us to the highway."

Turn left on Maple. The highway is a few blocks up.

She put the car into gear and pulled out of the parking lot.

Once they were on Route 62 and headed in the correct direction, he gathered his mental shield around him, thickening it to allow only a sliver of consciousness out. He needed to figure out what the hell was going on, and the less Anaea knew, the better.

The medallion was at the center of the problem, and he was getting tired of every dragon's political maneuverings surrounding that piece of jewelry. Twelve hundred years ago, things would have been different. Then, there had been seven medallions that could absorb a dragon's soul in preparation for rebirth. Each one had been created by the Handmaiden and they ensured a balance of power among the dragon coteries. Over the centuries, however, the medallions had changed hands, were stolen, or lost until only two remained, the one in the arena and the one controlled by the Royal Coterie. But there were also any number of other dragons, not just Zenobia or Nero, who could be responsible for this mess. Anyone could be vying for greater power. And he'd be damned if he was going to be collateral damage.

First order of business was to get the medallion to the Handmaiden for the rebirth ceremony. He'd collected Saber's soul more than twelve hours ago and needed to get it into the stabilizing magic of Court so it didn't lose cohesion. But that meant he had to put off getting a replacement body and would have to show up as a woman.

He was never going to hear the end of it.

Unlike some drakes, he'd never been a woman and never felt inclined to learn how the other half lived. Some dragons had changed bodies yearly, like fashion. That was before they'd discovered how dangerous frequent body hopping could be. Dragon law now banned body hopping, so even more questions would be asked if he arrived in Court as a woman and then returned a few days later as a man.

Shit. He was going to have to be discreet. Avoid everyone save the Handmaiden. And if he could avoid her, too, even better.

He made a crack in his mental defenses and checked on Anaea. They were moving steadily along the highway, and she was concentrating on driving. Snow dusted the windshield, melted, and was swept away by the wipers.

He had no idea how he was going to explain that Newgate wasn't their final destination, but he'd deal with that when they got there. They were actually going to an anchored, magical gate in the city leading to an inter-dimensional sphere. Centuries ago, the Handmaiden had discovered the sphere, inaccessible from anywhere on earth save through magic. She'd used her massive power to shape the caves and passages within it into an underground city, the Dragon Court. It was supposed to have been a sanctuary. A place to protect dragonkind from humans. But as the pain of the Great Scourge faded, Court felt like a prison to more and more dragons. Particularly as laws grew more and more restrictive in an attempt to protect dragonkind.

Which led back to his current predicament: caught in the middle of political maneuverings.

Hunter couldn't really blame them. He didn't like Court or Regis's rules either. Sure, he kept a suite at Court, but it wasn't home. Some dragons, like earth drakes, enjoyed being surrounded by all that stone, but Hunter ached for sky.

He ached to fly.

Which would never happen again and, like every other dragon, he'd just have to live with it.

At least there was one small blessing in this situation. Anaea's body had connected to the earth's magic and in record time, since it usually took days or even years for the connection to awaken. Thank the Mother of All. He didn't understand how earth magic worked, something about the innately magical spirit of a dragon awakening a dormant connection to the earth's magic within a human vessel—so dormant that a human hadn't connected with the magic without dragon assistance for two thousand years. But he wasn't going to look this gift horse in the mouth.

Even better, her magic seemed strong enough to activate his private gate. Which meant he wouldn't have to face the humiliation of having to ask the gatekeeper for help. Particularly for Newgate's gate, since Jade, an ex-lover, minded it.

Anaea's magic actually was surprisingly strong. She hadn't needed power words or gestures like most dragons, and she could call fire. In most cases, a dragon's magical ability was small, like seeing auras. But about twenty percent of dragons developed something significant as well, like lightning, or wind. Hunter's old body had had null magic. But he was gone, and earth magic changed with each new vessel.

It stung that Anaea could call one of the rarest magics, fire.

He dipped into Anaea's mind, searching once again for her thread to the earth's magic.

It was nowhere to be found.

Hot panic raced through him as it had before. The thread had to be there. She had called fire and activated the medallion. That could only be done by earth magic.

He searched harder, looking for a weak or inconsistent thread, and found a fluttery connection. Which didn't make any sense. It should either be there or not. Not there one minute and gone the next. The only time he'd heard of a connection feeling fluttery was if the human body was somehow actually dying. But Anaea was very much alive. The wounds, ice-shot and otherwise, were healed, as was the hypothermia from her swim in the river, and now all of his soul magic was focused on eradicating the cancer from her body. She'd be cured by the time they reached Newgate. Which was information he buried as deep as he could within his consciousness. It would be cruel for her to learn the accident that cured her would result in her execution.

And the risk of that had just increased. If he couldn't open a gate by himself, he couldn't sneak into Court. He was going to need help getting in, and that meant going to the gatekeeper.

Jade was going to revel in ridiculing him about his new female body, likely announce his arrival to Regis, and cause an entourage to meet him in the receiving hall. The gossip would spread like wildfire.

To top it off, he'd have to be overly cautious, since Jade was one of two dragons who could see multiple souls in a single body. But if he asked another drake, even a friend, to open a gate, more questions would be asked and that friend could be put in danger—and he wasn't going to do that to a friend. Which meant Jade was his only option and he'd just have to pray he was too useful to Regis to be reborn when he body hopped to a new male vessel later.

Now he really needed Anaea to hand over control.

8

Anaea parked the car on the top of a six-story garage on Third Avenue and turned off the engine. She still couldn't believe what was happening. But her acceptance, or not, of the situation didn't stop anything. Of course, how she could explain the man in her head and the attempt on her life was beyond her.

Grab the bag and head to the stairwell.

She did as instructed. There wasn't anything else she could do. Well, she supposed she could go running to the closest psychiatrist. She wasn't sure why she hadn't. Perhaps she could beg Mark for help since she was now in Newgate. But the voice in her head hadn't tried to take control of her body since the hotel room, three hours ago. She didn't even know his name.

It's Hunter.

She jumped and sucked in a slow breath, trying to still her racing heart. God, how intrusive. Listening to her thoughts. Of course, he was in her head and might not be able to help himself. But still no excuse to act on what he overheard. She was going to have to be careful what she thought about.

That made her snort. Sure, she could control what she consciously thought about, but not any of the unconscious thoughts.

Hunter, huh? she asked, dragging herself back on topic. *Is that a name or a title?*

She felt what she could only describe as a shrug in her mind.

Both.

I see. She concentrated on him, trying to find more meaning in that single word. If he could hear her thoughts, maybe she could hear his. But his answer was ambiguous and so was any sensation that came with it.

Dropping the keys in the garbage bin by the door to the stairwell, she took the concrete stairs down to the street. It wasn't fair that he could keep his thoughts from her and yet hers were an open book.

More like a megaphone announcement.

"Would you stop that?"

Don't speak out loud.

She bit her lip. *So now what?*

Now we visit a friend of mine. Turn left here.

She stepped into the flow of pedestrian traffic shadowed by the towering skyscrapers. Here in the heart of the city, the vehicular traffic was thick and plumes of exhaust clouded the street. The snow had stopped falling but the sidewalks were edged with filthy brown mounds and cars splashed slush on those too close to the edge.

This friend will solve this little problem of mine... ours?

She could feel him trying to figure out what to tell her. Hints of emotions and thoughts flitted too fast and too ephemeral for her to catch and examine.

Not exactly.

At least he hadn't outright lied. She didn't know if that made her feel better or not. She pulled Pearl's coat tighter around her. With only an oversized T-shirt and no hat, she was starting to really feel the cold. It had been fine in the car with the heater blasting, but now, out on the street where the wind whipped down the road and the tall buildings created a wind tunnel, it went right through her thin clothing and chilled her to the bone.

Should I even bother asking what 'not exactly' means? she asked, recognizing the ridiculousness of the question.

No answer. And more hints of thoughts.

Great. It was probably something she needed to know and he wasn't going to tell her.

Stop here at the bus stop and get out some change from the side pocket of the bag.

She unzipped the small pouch and pulled out a handful of coins. *You're going to have to explain it sooner or later.*

No, I'm not.

You really think keeping me in the dark is an option?

A mix of emotions swirled through her, then he spat out a string of curses in a variety of languages, most of them dead.

Wow, you can curse like a sailor in Latin and Old English. That's impressive. Maybe if she tried humor, he'd open up a bit.

How—?

She bit back a chuckle. All things considered, it felt good to catch him off guard. *Didn't bother to find out anything about me, huh?*

I was respecting your privacy. He practically growled the words.

I'm a— Her throat tightened. She wasn't anything anymore. *I was a linguist.*

He didn't respond, but she could sense a thoughtfulness to his silence.

The 81B pulled up to the stop and she got on, taking a seat close to the back.

Now that you know something about me, why don't you tell me something about you? Like what the heck is going on?

You're not going to believe me.

She snorted and a woman with a toddler a few seats down gave her a concerned look.

I'm talking to a voice in my head. I think I've already made the leap to unbelievable.

Oh, it could get weirder than she imagined.

The thought was so clear he might as well have said it.

Would you just spit it out? His reluctance to share was driving her crazy.

It's better if you don't know all the details. We'll talk to... a friend and then talk to... another friend and...

And then our problem will be fixed with vague unknowns who don't even have names.

That's not fair.

"Life isn't fair."

The woman gave Anaea another furtive glance and hugged her child close.

It's better this way. And it would be easier if—

No.

But you don't even know what I'm going to say.

Oh, yes I do, and this is my body. You're the interloper.

The bus turned a tight corner and she clung to the pole beside her to keep from sliding from her seat.

It's dangerous if they don't think it's me.

I'm sure it's more dangerous if I don't have a clue about what's going on. Dangerous so far had involved getting shot in the chest and almost run through with a sword. But damn it. It was her body and the more she knew, the better she could cope.

Hunter growled another string of curses. *Fine.*

Fine.

All right. He squirmed, twisting around within her and making her stomach churn. He really didn't want to tell her anything, but it couldn't possibly be worse than her current situation.

Oh for goodness sake, spit it out already.

I'm a spirit—

I kind of got that.

—of a race of spirits.

"A race of what?"

In your head.

The woman with the kid stood and shuffled to the front of the bus.

How can there be a race of spirits? And why can't you just be spirits someplace else?

Bitterness washed over her, but he sucked it back before she could identify any specific details about it. *Without a human vessel, I'll lose cohesion and die, and there are consequences to changing vessels too often. As for the rest, you're on a need-to-know basis, and that you don't need to know.*

She bit back a nasty retort. Making demands just seemed to make him clam up. So he didn't want to talk about his spirit state. Fine. She could relate, she didn't particularly want to talk about her cancer. *Okay, so you're stuck in me.*

Until I can make arrangements for an appropriate, unoccupied vessel.

And that will be when?

As soon as business is taken care of.

And that's what we're doing now? Taking care of business?

Uh huh.

And you said it was dangerous if they don't think it's you.

My people have laws to protect us, to keep us a secret. Sharing a body with a person breaks one of our oldest laws. If they realize we're both in here, they'll kill us. Hunter's presence softened and regret seeped through her. *I didn't mean for you to get caught up in this. I had thought—*

The image of her standing on the bridge on the wrong side of the railing flashed through her mind's eyes. He had thought he was doing the right thing by saving her. And now he was stuck in her, and she was stuck with him... at least until business was taken care of.

From the turn of his mood, she didn't think she'd get more information. But there was time to learn more later, hopefully before she needed it. *You still don't get to use my body, but I promise I'll do what you say.*

And you'll say what I say?

She nodded without thinking then ran her hands over her head to hide the action. Everyone on the bus must have thought she was crazy. Talking to herself and nodding. She probably was.

She could feel his thoughts churning, but couldn't get a sense of what he was thinking.

Deal. Get off at the next stop.

She pulled the cord and shuffled to the door.

Remember, you need to do what I say, even if things get...

Weird? she said, filling in the blank for him. She wasn't sure what could get more weird than what had already happened, but she supposed she'd find out soon enough.

I suppose so, he said.

Stop that. The bus shuddered to a halt, and she got off.

Antique shop, red house on the left.

The house couldn't be missed. It sat in silent defiance to the modernization of the neighborhood. A stately Victorian with single gable, turret, and yawning front porch, it was crowded on one side by a three-story, concrete and glass office building. On its other side lay a parking lot with two scraggly trees marking the entrance.

A neon red-and-blue "open" sign shone in the house's large front window, the colored light reflecting on the icicles hanging from the porch's awning. The snow had been cleared off the path leading to the porch steps, and Anaea's boots crunched on ice, sand, and salt. She reached for the brass doorknob, noting a small sign in beautiful black calligraphy: "Please push. This door sticks."

She could feel Hunter's hesitation, as if he held his breath. No, it was more thoughtful than fearful. He was coming to a decision.

It'll be easier to communicate if you're... if we're not so closed off.

The idea of opening up to him held mixed appeal. On the one hand, she was dying to know more about Hunter and his race of spirits. On the other, the idea that a race of spirits existed made her question everything she knew about the world, and she feared knowing the truth would drive her crazy.

She entered the shop—the door indeed required a shove—and stepped into a dark, dusty, crowded house. She'd never hidden from the truth before. With three months before her death, it was probably pointless to start now. *Okay.*

A sudden wave of masculine presence filled her. She clutched the empty coat rack just inside the door to keep her balance. Flashes of thoughts, feelings, memories that she couldn't quite bring into focus, raced through her. Then he pulled back and the sense of him lessened, as if he'd hit a dimmer switch.

Sorry. I've never done this before.

She could sense his sincerity, and was reminded he was stuck in this predicament, too. *Let's just get this over with. Who are we here to see? Try the back.*

On any other day, she might have paused to look at all the treasures. And there were a lot of treasures. They weren't arranged in any sort of artful display, but instead were crowded this way and that on shelves and clustered on the floor in what were once a stately living room and dining room. She continued to the back of the house and found a curvy blond in a green pantsuit, lounging in a chair that might or might not have been merchandise. Anaea couldn't tell. The room had once been a kitchen and was packed with strange metal, wooden, and ceramic gadgets and furniture that she could only assume were related to a kitchen.

The woman's brown eyes narrowed while Hunter squirmed in Anaea's head. She had the sense that she— No, *he* knew this woman in a very, very friendly way. It was difficult to tell her memories from his, even with Hunter at this 'dimmer' setting. He knew the woman from a long time ago. Preferred her hair long, not the bob it was in now. And her eyes were the wrong color. Whatever that meant.

The image of her with some complicated hairdo piled on top of her head and a corset that barely maintained her modesty popped into Anaea's mind.

Heat raced up her neck and she turned away to hide her blush.

Don't break eye contact.

What?

Just don't.

His fierce tone shot her gaze straight into the woman's.

The woman's lips curled with a hint of a sneer.

Hunter was right. If she were him, she wouldn't have looked away at the thought of some woman's breasts. She wouldn't have blushed either, but she had less control over that.

"I see a familiar aura but not a familiar body." The woman burst into laughter. "Oh, this is rich. The mighty Hunter reduced to a woman."

Anaea bristled.

"Just open the gate," she heard herself say.

"Heavens, no. I want to laugh at you a little more. There's no way you'd have willingly given up your Crusader. You were more in love with him than me."

"Jade—"

Do you mind? Anaea said. *You're not allowed to have a conversation without me.* She wasn't sure what most of the conversation was about, but couldn't stand that somehow he had appropriated her body again.

Sorry, it just happened.

She couldn't tell if he felt contrite or not.

"You know I have to announce your entrance into Court."

He had expected no less, but Anaea heard herself protest anyway. "Only if you choose to. You could just let me slip in."

Would you stop that. Nope, definitely not contrite about taking over.

Jade stood, sauntered to Anaea, and leaned close, brushing her lips against Anaea's. Hunter shivered with disgust as Anaea did, and they both pulled back.

"I suppose I could let you... slip in." Jade curled her top lip back revealing her teeth and Anaea got the impression it was supposed to be a come-on. "As best as you can, all things considered."

Jade slid a heated gaze down Anaea's body and her face burned. This time she did nothing to hide it.

"I'll grow my hair out for you." Jade's hair lengthened, like stop-motion photography on fast forward. It spilled over her shoulders in long golden locks.

Holy shit!

"If I recall, you preferred a curl." Her hair bounced into gentle ringlets. "And green eyes." Green light flashed over her eyes. When the light dimmed, they were a breathtaking emerald.

What was that?

Jade playing games.

In the back of her mind, Anaea felt Hunter's disgust that Jade would use what little sorcerer ability she had to change her appearance. It was such a waste of energy. She was about to ask what that meant when she realized he was considering Jade's sexual invitation. Not in terms of attraction but in terms of what best suited his needs.

Absolutely not! She shoved Hunter to the back of her mind. "Announce me or don't. Open the gate," she said while Hunter fought against her.

Jade pouted, her full bottom lip drawing memories of lingering kisses from a long time ago. Anaea ground her teeth. There was no way she was going to have sex with some strange woman who thought Hunter inhabited her body just to have some stupid door opened.

God, Anaea. Couldn't you have played along? We could have made a date for after this situation is fixed.

She hadn't thought of that, and a small part of her still didn't like the idea of Hunter sleeping with that woman even in a different vessel.

"Be that way." Jade's pout dropped away and she walked to a slatted-wood door marked "Employees Only." It opened into a narrow pantry crammed with china and knick-knacks. At the back, a rickety set of stairs led into a cavernous basement—not the low-ceilinged dugout Anaea had expected.

It was the most space she'd seen in the house. The walls and ceiling were plain concrete. Half a dozen doors led to other rooms to Anaea's left, right, and behind her, but the wall in front of her was unbroken.

With one last heated glance, Jade sauntered to the wall before them, her hips swaying with exaggerated movements. She placed her palm on it and closed her eyes.

So, about the hair thing?

It's comp—

Don't you dare say it's complicated. I've already figured that out.

The air around Jade quivered, like heat radiating from asphalt in summer. Anaea's skin tingled.

Hunter sighed. *And it's about to get more complicated.*

Jade chanted, her voice hushed. She wasn't speaking English. Perhaps it was that strange language Anaea had spoken earlier when Pearl died.

Jade never learned Sumerian. She spent most of her time in China, Hunter said, as if Jade not learning Sumerian lessened her somehow.

Mandarin or Cantonese, maybe. Anaea's Mandarin and Cantonese weren't great, and Jade was using strange phrasing, but now that Anaea knew what to listen for, she could make out a bit of what she was saying.

How did—?

Linguist, remember.

Light flashed across the wall and the air around them shook.

What is she doing?

Making a gate to our inter-dimensional sphere.

A speck of black pierced the center of the concrete.

You know you sound like a bad Star Trek *episode.*

Hunter snorted. *Think more like* Lord of the Rings. *Jade has the ability to channel the energy of the universe to create a gate between your dimension and ours.*

Dimensions? Energy of the universe?

In the old days, it was called magic.

What do you call it now?

Magic.

Spirits, magic, other dimensions. Yep, she was losing her mind, but all of her senses told her the black void growing with every second was real. The darkness devoured the light and the wall until it reached the corners. Anaea couldn't see anything beyond. It was a big, gaping nothing.

Any more magic you need to tell me about?

Not at the moment. Now, remember to do what I tell you.

She felt the urge to step toward the black nothingness and Hunter's intention that they walk through it.

You want me to go in there?

Where else would we go?

She bit back her rising panic. There was no way she was going to walk into that thing.

It's the only way to get me out of your head.

Crap. In for a penny, in for a pound, right? Besides, what did she have to lose? Her life? Hunter, more like it. And irrationally, she wasn't sure she wanted to lose him. But then he'd die with her when the cancer had run its course, and he didn't deserve that. She hadn't managed to save him, or rather his body, in the river, but she could save him now.

She gulped in air and stepped into the black nothing.

9

The world twisted and spun. Anaea was weightless. The void pressed against her senses, plugging her ears and pouring down her throat. She gasped, struggling for air.

Then her foot hit something solid. Her leg buckled and she fell. Hard, cold stone met her knees and hands.

Hunter shivered in her mind. *God, I hate that.*

Gee, I can't imagine why. She glanced up. They were in a large empty chamber, with open archways on either side. Rough-hewn granite walls, floor, and ceiling surrounded them. There were no windows and no obvious light sources even though the room was as bright as where they'd just left. There also wasn't a door or a black hole or anything else behind her.

Welcome to Court.

What?

Our inter-dimensional sphere.

Footsteps rushed down the hall to her right and she scrambled to her feet.

Brace yourself, Hunter said, as a large man hurtled toward them. His name popped into her head: Grey. His name was Grey, and Hunter didn't recall him being so large before. He looked like a

Viking, all towering muscle with long, wild, blond hair. It struck her as odd that he was dressed in a modern suit.

He looked furious and ready to bowl her over. She searched for a place to run or hide, but there wasn't one.

No, brace yourself and meet his gaze.

But Grey stumbled to a halt. "Mother of All, Hunter. What the hell happened?"

Grab him.

You want me to what?

Hunter seized control of her body, closed the distance between her and Grey and yanked the front of his dress shirt. He brought her cheek to Grey's and hissed. And for a moment, she didn't feel entirely human. No, it was Hunter, not her. There was something feral, something primal about him. Part of the same whatever it was that she'd glimpsed when he'd lost his temper in the hotel. He filled her thoughts, as if his soul was too big for her tiny body.

With another hiss, Grey grabbed the front of her coat and pulled her in until their chests. Then he shoved her back and widened his stance. "Where have you been?"

She shrugged. Against her will.

Damn it. She wanted her body back.

Hey. Hunter. He didn't answer and she could sense him determined not to let anyone know anything was wrong. But, damn it, it was her body and he'd promised not to take over. Well, if nice wasn't going to work, maybe force would. She'd done it before, if only she could remember how. She pressed against his consciousness, but couldn't break his hold on her.

"I've been on assignment."

"Yeah, well, Regis has been trying to call you."

"Things got complicated."

"I can see that. You never struck me as a gender hopper." Grey glanced over his shoulder at the archway. "Have you had the new digs long enough to connect to the earth's magic?"

Hunter's emotions surged, and it felt like it had something to do with magic, but Anaea couldn't place it.

"If I'd been in this body long enough do you think I would have gone to Jade to enter Court?"

"Shit."

"What's going on?"

"There's been—"

"Hunter," a new voice called from down the same hall where Grey had come from. Hunter recognized the voice as his prince's, but his emotions about the man were mixed.

Anaea thought about the primal, feral aspect to Hunter. Perhaps man wasn't the right word. He'd said he was from a race of spirits. He hadn't said what kind of spirits, although if he hadn't been human, she had no idea what else he could be.

A swarthy, heavyset man, Prince Regis stepped into the chamber dressed like Henry VIII. Or maybe it was his girth that made him seem like those pictures of the English king. Half a dozen men and women in a strange array of historical garb, all matched to Regis's orange, beige, and gold, clustered behind him.

Both Hunter and Grey dropped to one knee and bowed their heads.

Anaea struggled to twitch a finger, blink her eyes, something, anything, that would get her back in control.

"I see your hunting was complicated." The prince motioned for them to rise.

Anaea put all her will into not standing, but Hunter remained in control.

"To put it mildly," Hunter said. "You'll need a second body for the rebirth ceremony. Tell Pearl's doyen the Major Green Coterie can have her hoard."

The image of a tall woman, a hooded cloak shadowing her face, flashed into Anaea's mind.

Regis narrowed his eyes, the only indication Hunter might have said something he didn't like. "I see. But you got Saber?"

"Yes. Would my prince like a report?"

Regis faked a yawn. Hunter had seen that too many times to count. "Not personally. You've been called to *wasu tahazu*."

A small, hunched man in an orange and black harlequin costume shoved through the crowd, clapping hooked, arthritic hands. "Goodie, goodie. A fight."

"I've what?" Indignation washed over Anaea and what little flashes she'd received of Hunter's memories were cut off.

"That's what I was going to tell you," Grey mumbled.

The small man cackled.

"Who?" Hunter's fury boiled around her, and he clenched his hands, fighting to control it.

Anaea unclenched her right hand. Strange, she'd have thought his emotions would have made his grip on her body stronger. She seized her chance and shoved him to the back of her mind.

Not now! he growled.

This is my body and you promised.

I did, but—

Are you kidding me? No!

Grey shrugged as if the situation didn't bother him like it did Hunter, but she could tell from the look in his eyes he was just as troubled.

"Welkin," Grey said.

"Welkin. Welkin," the harlequin giggled.

Regis glared at him and he fell silent, shying away. "It's his right to call for *wasu tahazu.*"

Ask him when the wasu tahazu *is. Maybe we'll get lucky.*

"When's the… *wasu tahazu.*" The words felt strange on her lips even to her, and she spoke nine languages.

"He called for it last night, on the second day of the *pahar,* as is also his right."

Shit.

Hunter's thoughts whipped through her. No one had challenged him for his position in Court in six hundred years. It didn't make any sense to start now, unless Zenobia—or whoever was after him—was using the *wasu tahazu* as a backup plan. He wouldn't put it past her.

So what does all this mean? she asked, her head swimming at the thought that Hunter had been alive, more or less, for six hundred years. Of course Jade had referred to him as a Crusader. Perhaps she hadn't just meant his outlook on life.

It means we have to fight a duel to the death. Now.

But you're already a spirit.

Trust me, death comes in many forms. And for me to die, you have to die.

Death is kind of a moot point, Anaea said.

It's not to me.

She couldn't see how that worked since he was already dead.

Give me control of your body.

She bit her lip, about to refuse. A duel to the death wasn't something she knew how to deal with. In the back of her mind she had the nagging feeling she knew how to fight, but that could only be because of Hunter. She was a linguist. Nothing more. For the last year, she'd been her disease—and that kind of fight, while still involving death, had nothing to do with fists.

Or magic, Hunter said.

Stop eavesdropping.

He sighed. *Darling, I wish I could. But first, I have a* wasu tahazu *to win.*

You mean we *have a* wasu tahazu *to win. It's still my body.*

"I trust you'll be around to report to Tobias when this is done." Regis chuckled. It held a strange joy, as if the thrill that Hunter might not be around to report excited him. The group around him matched the laugh with nervous titters. "You're permitted to go to your room and change. Don't tarry." His voice darkened, a warning. Stalling would show weakness, and the prince's assassin could not be weak.

Nod and take the hall to your left, Hunter said.

Anaea obeyed. The hall was the same as the cold receiving chamber. The walls, floor, and ceiling were rough-hewn granite. There were no windows, and she couldn't tell where the light emanated from. Grey fell into step beside her.

So I'm thinking now is the time to tell me a little more about my... our situation.

"Welkin is young." Grey ran a hand over his hair, doing nothing to tame it. "If you were in your old body the fight wouldn't be much of a match."

But he wasn't in his old body.

And as soon as I find a new one, you won't have to worry about me.

"The point is kind of moot," Anaea said, hoping Grey wouldn't continue the conversation. *I think if we're going to fight to the death, a girl should know what kind of trouble she's gotten into.*

"Moot?" Grey asked.

Damn, Anaea, I wouldn't have said moot.

"Do you have any earth magic?"

Anaea shrugged. It seemed like a Hunter kind of thing to do. "Don't know. Remember, had to use the gatekeeper to get here."

They walked in silence until they reached another large empty chamber that could just as easily be the same one they'd left.

Take the hall to your right, down the stairs at the end, sixth door on the left, Hunter said. *And please. I know I promised, but give me control of your body.*

Fine. She tried to relax, while still walking and not revealing anything to Grey. If only she could stop for a moment, sit, take a few long breaths. That might make it easier to let go. He slid around her thoughts, but that sense that she was trapped in her head never came. It was her walking, breathing, seeing.

Just relax. I'll give it back.

She didn't think that was the problem. Well, maybe it was. It was her body, after all.

Perhaps if I sit.

Fine. We'll try again when we get to my suite.

How fancy. The man had a suite.

The stairs at the end of the hall were wide and wound both up and down, disappearing into dark shadows. She followed it down one level then counted doors and stopped at the sixth one.

"I'll wait outside." Grey gave her an appraising look. "Better yet, I'll find you clean clothes that fit. Maybe that will buy you enough time to find your new magic. If you have any… which I'm sure you do… because you've never not."

She considered saying thanks, but didn't think Hunter was a thank you kind of guy. Instead, she nodded and gripped the door handle. A shiver of electricity raced up her arm and touched something in her mind. No, not something. Hunter. The door recognized Hunter. The lock clicked opened, and she entered.

The room wasn't what she expected. She wasn't sure what she expected, or that she'd been expecting anything. Perhaps she'd been thinking his suite would be distinctly male. Sleek, modern, nothing overly sentimental. But the moment she stepped inside, she was surrounded by sky: summer sky, stormy sky, sky with puffy clouds, sunset, sunrise, vast expanses of it on canvas, tapestry, and photographic paper. Even the ceiling was a sky mural. The art was crowded on the walls, covering every available square inch. More pieces sat on display on easels while others were piled in the corners and against the walls and furniture.

On the left wall, framed by more art, sat a large bookshelf, half-filled with books and half with mini skies. To her right was a conversation area with a worn leather couch and matching chair, and a carved wooden trunk between them. Above the couch on the wall hung an enormous sword, the edge nicked and the leather grip worn down to the wood. A shield, almost as big as her, leaned against the couch. It looked like it had been used, with chunks hacked from its edges. The paint was faded, a green and yellow background with a black dragon dead center.

Strangely, Hunter had been quiet. Not interrupting her thoughts or inserting some quip. He seemed... melancholy. Looking at all that sky made her ache. But it was an old pain. Whatever kept him silent was new, fresh, as if he missed the man he'd once been and was content with her making her own opinions.

She supposed it didn't matter anymore since he was now at the bottom of the Allegheny River. That man was no more. And he'd been that man for a very long time. If she ignored all rational thought, then perhaps the sword and shield had been his.

Of course, could she even consider any logical thought? She had the spirit of a man, or something, stuck in her head. The sense that

Hunter wasn't quite man, but something else, something feral, made her shiver.

Anaea turned her attention to the bookshelf. She didn't want to think about what Hunter was or was not. There was an out-of-place collection of Louis L'Amour westerns on the top shelf, the paper covers creased and torn. The rest of the books were leather-bound hardcovers. She ran her fingers across the spines and stopped at a random book. She tipped it out of the shelf and opened the cover. The paper was dry and yellow with age.

You should be careful with that.

Her gaze fell to the inside cover. *A Gutenberg Bible?* She gingerly eased the book back into place. *How did you manage to get your hands on that?*

She felt him hesitate. *It's kind of a long story.*

"Like the matching sword and shield over there?"

Use your thoughts. Someone could be listening.

She glanced about. The room was empty. The back wall had a dark hall and window-sized cut-out opening into an eat-in kitchen.

"Who—" *Who could be listening?* She sighed. *I think we're at that point where I need a little more information. Duel to the death? Magic? Antiquated monarchy?*

We're old. My... people have been in this spirit state for a long time, and it's difficult to change the old ways.

So when you say old, you don't just mean your race, you mean you?

Yes. With that one word he suddenly sounded tired, as if the loss of who he'd once been weighed heavily on him. *You've already figured out that I took my last vessel during the Crusades. The Fifth one to be precise.*

How old are you? She knew it shouldn't surprise her, he was a talking spirit after all, but it was a lot to take in.

I lost count.

She had a feeling he hadn't, that he knew exactly how old he was.

A knock on the door made her jump.

That's probably Grey.

She opened the door. Grey pushed past her into the room, a

bulging laundry bag slung over his shoulder. He dropped the bag at her feet and plopped down on the couch.

"You're not very big. It was difficult to find armor. And no. I'm not going to ask Capri."

Anaea swallowed and resisted asking the obvious. She was about to fight a duel to the death. Why wouldn't she have expected armor. Images of an ancient Roman gladiatorial brawl danced through her mind's eye.

You're not that far off.

This is so not civilized. Whatever happened to submitting a resume and making a better offer to get someone's job?

Trust me, this is civilized, Hunter said.

Compared to what?

Get the clothes.

Compared to what? she repeated more insistently.

But he didn't answer. She grabbed the bag and headed down the hall in search of the bathroom.

It lay on the other side of the kitchen, and was enormous with a separate glassed-in shower and a four-person Jacuzzi bathtub. The entire ceiling glowed with a gentle white light. The illumination around the mirror over the vanity was twice as bright and it showed her sallow face.

She shrugged out of Pearl's coat and let it drop to the floor, then kicked off her shoes. The marble floor was heated. She considered standing there until her toes warmed up, or perhaps lying down and letting the warmth seep into her body.

After the fight, perhaps a shower, Hunter said.

Perhaps? There are no ands, ifs, or buts about it. I'm filthy.

She opened the laundry bag and pulled out what Grey had brought. It really did remind her of gladiator armor. There were leather bands that strapped around her arms and shins and something with metal studs that attached around her chest and neck, protecting half her torso and right shoulder. At the bottom of the bag were a pair of black jeans and a small black T-shirt.

Whatever happened to Kevlar? It's not the dark ages.

Kevlar stops bullets. It won't necessarily stop swords and it certainly won't stop magic.

There's that word again.

Yep.

She stripped out of his oversized T-shirt and the tattered hospital pants and put on the jeans. They were tight and low slung. *So much for protection.*

I'm good enough I won't need it. The other stuff is also just a formality. Now hurry up so I can— So you can give me control.

The clean T-shirt didn't cover as much as she liked, either. It stopped just below her ribs and exposed an alarming amount of flesh at her midriff. At least her ribs were covered. Last time she'd looked, she could count them. A sign, just like her hair, of her illness.

She sat on the edge of the tub. *All right. How do we do this?*

Just relax.

His presence pressed against her mind as it had before. She sucked in a slow breath, feeling him ease over her, like oil on water. The pressure increased. She thought about the place in her mind where he'd kept her when he was in control. Really, that would be a better place to be while he fought this duel. Just for a moment. Not long. He would give control of her body back to her.

Really?

Really.

And she knew that was the truth. He didn't want her body. He wanted someone else's. Actually, he wanted his old body back.

Just relax.

I am relaxing.

Well, think about going to sleep.

She thought about going to sleep. Spikes of pain shot through her temples. She gasped. The pressure stopped.

She gasped again at the sudden release.

This isn't working, he said.

"No, really?"

In your head.

Sorry.

You need to relax.

I am relaxing. She felt his disbelief. *Well, I'm trying.*

Try some soothing breaths. His voice was calm, but she could sense his rising panic. They were running out of time to make the switch. Any time now, someone would come to call them to the arena.

"Hey, Hunter," Grey said through the closed door.

Anaea jumped.

"I know you got yourself a sweet little body now. But Regis's page has arrived with the summons. You can play with yourself later."

She felt Hunter grimace, but whether it was at Grey's comments or the fact that they were out of time, she didn't know.

Pick up the armor and tell Grey to help.

After that comment, I don't know if I want him touching me.

Maybe not, but you're not going to get into it on your own, or at least by the time required.

Fine. She opened the door and held up one of the forearm protector pieces.

It's called a grieve.

She resisted the urge to say something nasty and instead decided to focus on the problem at hand. *So, how is this fight going to go?*

Hunter didn't answer and she could tell he was thinking. How to win a fight while stuck in a body with a person who didn't know how to fight.

Grey strapped on the first grieve then the second. He helped her shrug into the weird shoulder and neck piece thing and tightened the straps around her chest.

So?

Well, we don't have magic...

I noticed that.

That decreases our odds, Hunter said.

I kind of figured that out on my own.

Grey brushed his hands down the front of his thighs and stepped back. "Man. I never thought of you as a gender hopper. This is just too weird."

Anaea shrugged. "Yeah, well. It's weird for me, too."

Don't improvise, Hunter said.

Sure. I'll just become the unsociable silent Hunter.

He harrumphed and she got the sense she wasn't far off the mark on his actual behavior. It was a little sad. She at least had a good excuse for cutting herself off from the few friends and family she had. He just chose a solitary life.

My job doesn't allow attachments.

She didn't really know what his job was so she couldn't comment. In fact, she knew very little about this man... spirit... creature... whatever. And without a doubt, he was holding things back. She could feel it. If she just had a few more pieces to the puzzle, everything would make sense.

I doubt that, Hunter said.

"Well, come on." Grey motioned to the door. "Can't keep royalty waiting."

Hunter snickered. Royalty didn't mean much to him, but she couldn't determine why. Loyalty, however, did. And he was loyal to Grey. She got the sense that Hunter had been friends with Grey for a long time.

A very long time.

The image of Grey pulling a heavy medieval helmet off his head and grinning back at her flashed through her mind's eye. He wore classic, knight-in-shining-armor armor except it was covered in filth and blood and dents.

Hunter had said his people were old. It was still just so difficult to wrap her mind around it, though.

Grey grabbed a sword from a rack by the door and led her back down the hall to the circular stairwell. Instead of going up, they went down four flights to the very bottom. The illumination here was dim. Before her rose two towering arches, filled with blinding light, and beyond she could hear the rumble of many voices. She wasn't as exhausted as she'd expected with all the physical activity she'd done over the last however many hours, and adrenaline pounded through her with every rapid beat of her heart. She didn't feel like a gladiator anymore, but a Christian being led to the lions.

Grey thumped her on the back. "Happy hunting."

She stumbled but caught her balance before falling.

"Sorry, forgot. Half your usual size." He handed her a heavy sword, turned, and headed back up the stairs. She could only guess that 'audience' seating was accessed on an upper level.

So. She hefted the weapon. What was it with these people and swords?

So. Hunter almost sounded apologetic. Then images and emotions and thoughts flooded her mind. She was drowning. They rushed over her, filled her, pressed against the essence that was her and permeated through her. They moved so fast she couldn't grasp onto any one thought and examine it. All she could tell was that they were violent, desperate, primal. Years upon years of struggle and death, edged with a strange satisfaction.

This was who Hunter really was. He was a hunter in the most basic of terms. No, that was what hundreds of years had made him. Deep down, at the very beginning, she sensed the spirit of a proud, majestic creature. A leader in his own right, not one subservient to a prince.

Sadness crept through her, and as abruptly as the experience began, it ended. He was not going to allow her to see his true soul, only the warrior he'd made himself into.

She fought a hysterical giggle, but it escaped. The whole situation was crazy. She knew—not in any specific kind of detail, but still— violence. Hundreds of years of combat experience.

That wasn't supposed to be amusing, Hunter said, his voice dry.

I think I know Kung Fu. She couldn't resist.

He groaned. Obviously, he'd watched that movie as well. Too bad this wasn't some Matrix-like dream.

You only know it mentally. Your muscles don't know it at all.

What does that mean?

Fighting is more reflex, more muscle memory, than anything else. You train until you don't have to think about it, Hunter said.

So why fill my mind with— You know?

Because some knowledge is better than nothing. The overtones of what she was about to face swept through her, and she couldn't ignore the inevitable anymore.

Great. She stepped to the edge of the closest arch and peered out. It was too bright. She'd have to step into the light, blind, and hope there was honor among Hunter's people.

10

Transferring his memories had been the only thing Hunter could think of to save Anaea. Sure, she was glib about death. She thought she was already dead, but that wouldn't help him. Besides, she wasn't dying anymore.

Boy, that was going to be a shock.

If they survived the next ten minutes, he'd consider telling her. Of course, that was only if he could finish the rebirth ceremony and sneak away from Court to find a new body without anyone noticing her soul was still present. The Mother of All only knew how they'd managed to escape so far.

He was in so much trouble. He'd already told her too much. If anyone found out she knew anything about dragons, regardless that he'd managed to keep that particular detail from her, she was dead. Dragon law demanded she be hunted down and eliminated to keep dragonkind safe.

He pushed those thoughts aside and focused on the matter at hand. First, survive the duel. Then they could deal with her illicit knowledge of dragons.

His martial experience was extensive. His last body he'd picked up during the Fifth Crusade and with it, he'd survived hundreds of battles. He'd studied style after style to ensure his place close to the throne, because a drake without a coterie was a victim waiting to happen. But passing his knowledge to Anaea might not be enough.

She stepped into the light and squinted, refusing to close her eyes against the brightness. Good girl. Welkin would be disqualified if he attacked before Regis made the proclamation, but if he got in a killing strike the point would no longer be debatable. Hunter would be dead. His soul would be absorbed into the heart medallion at the center of the arena and he'd be one of the three dragons being reborn at dawn instead of Welkin.

Anaea's vision cleared, and she studied the man before her. He was small, thank the Mother of All, but Hunter didn't know what kind of magic Welkin possessed, if any.

The crowd went silent, and Anaea glanced up.

Regis stood in the royal box, his arms raised. "By the power bestowed upon me by the Mother of All, I proclaim the *wasu tahazu* begun."

The crowd burst into a deafening roar and Regis sat.

Nod, and get your eyes on your opponent.

She nodded and turned her attention back to Welkin.

In a way, he was Hunter's doing. Three hundred years ago, Welkin—who'd been Eton at the time—had pissed off Regis, and Hunter had been sent to reclaim his soul. Welkin was a product of rebirth. He had no memory of his previous life, only what was permanently imprinted on his soul, that he was a blue drake, the lowest member of his coterie, and a baby by drake standards.

Hunter had never bothered to ask what Eton had done. That wasn't his job. And these days he asked even fewer questions. Go out. Get the soul. But perhaps avoiding questions and politics had gotten him into this predicament. If Welkin had been told about Hunter's current weakened condition, it might explain why he'd called—or been goaded into calling—the fight. Nothing else would possess anyone to make the challenge. Hunter had had one of the most powerful earth magics at Court: null magic. Which made it difficult, although not impossible, to use magic against him. With magic mostly out of the equation, a *wasu tahazu* became a matter of martial prowess, and Hunter was efficiently deadly. And as soon as this was over and he had a new body, he was going to turn that prowess onto whoever was responsible for this mess.

If only Anaea could call her fire. Even just a few small balls of flame flying through the air might be enough for Welkin to reconsider the challenge. Fire was as rare as null magic and almost as powerful.

You can do this. The probability that he has magic is slim, which means my skill will be more than enough to take care of him.

I can do this. But she didn't sound confident.

Yes, you can.

Welkin flashed his teeth, a demonstration of aggression or sexual attraction—in this case Hunter doubted the fight had anything to do with sex. The young drake swished his sword, a two-handed blade close to four feet long, and started to circle to the left, but didn't come any closer. Anaea matched him step for step, but also didn't close the distance.

Interesting he'd pick Hunter's preferred weapon. Then he saw the faint crackle of electricity along the blade. Anaea saw it, too, and her heart pounded her fear through her... their... body.

Stay calm.

But you said he probably didn't have magic.

I was wrong. Most of us don't have anything dangerous.

She gulped air. *Swords are bad enough.*

It's just lightning.

She bit her lip, stifling a manic laugh.

He couldn't bring himself to tell her lightning was significant. It was surprising Welkin had managed to spend the last three hundred years with that earth magic and not have drawn Hunter's attention. Again, it made him wonder if something more was going on than just a simple *wasu tahazu.*

He searched for Anaea's connection to the earth's magic, but it remained elusive. Oh, for just a little fire.

My kingdom for a flame, she said.

What?

Nothing.

He's got the advantage with distance, his arms are longer.

Which means we need to eliminate that, she said. He could hear the resignation in her voice. She had his memories and knew, as well as he did, that for someone with her lack of experience close combat was the last thing she wanted.

You've no choice. You need to end this fight before it can begin.

She ground her teeth and gave a barely perceptible nod. If anyone was paying exacting attention they'd know something wasn't right. While he was a thoughtful combatant, he never spent an excessive amount of time considering his options. They had stood in place for too long.

All he could do was hope everyone would chalk it up to him not being familiar with his new body. It was a big difference from what he'd come from. His over-six-foot-tall, well-muscled Crusader had been perfect for the job of prince's assassin. Tiny Anaea, at five and a half feet and just over a hundred pounds, wasn't your standard warrior type.

Close the distance.

She inched closer, still matching Welkin's wary circling.

Lightning danced along Welkin's blade. He needed a physical focus to maintain his magic. He wasn't as strong as Hunter had first thought, which meant the lightning was new. Some dragons didn't develop earth magic until an extended period in their human body... and while this was all interesting, it could still kill them.

You've got to move in faster.

I am.

But he could feel her hesitation. It took a lot of courage to ignore one's natural desire for self-preservation and throw one's self into the path of danger.

No, rush him. Don't give him time—

Lightning arced down the sword.

Anaea threw herself to the side, curling herself into a ball at the last minute. She rolled to her feet, sword up, and rushed at Welkin without missing a step.

Perhaps his transfusion of memories was more effective than he'd thought.

She brought her sword down in a fierce overhead swing. It was obvious. Too obvious.

Welkin blocked and rammed his hilt into Anaea's blade, knocking it aside. Anaea clung to her sword and twisted, dodging Welkin's thrust.

She stumbled away and renewed her guard, but had missed an opportunity to gut her opponent. Not that it would finish the fight. The only surefire way to kill Welkin was to take his head.

I've got to what? When were you going to tell me this?

If I had told you before you started the fight, would you have stepped into the arena?

Probably not. But don't you think there was a more appropriate time?

We can argue about it later. This is a duel to the death. It's his or ours. And I'll be damned if it's ours.

Welkin jabbed at her. She parried, and lightning danced from his sword to hers, zapping her hands.

She gasped, but held onto the weapon. Welkin swung again. She parried again, and he countered, more lightning crackling over her. It charred her T-shirt and seared her skin, leaving painful black welts that Hunter could feel, even disconnected from her body.

Welkin forced her back toward the arena wall. Her breath was already labored, and her mostly-healed body wouldn't last much longer with the stress and physical exertion. Hunter had to figure out how to end this, and fast.

He's going to jab when you back into the wall. Your next two steps.

I know.

Take the thrust.

Do what?

He could sense her panic and tried to keep his voice calm. He hated taking an unnecessary injury in a fight, but in this case the end justified the means.

He's going to play with us. He'll jab for the gut or chest before he takes our head. Take the thrust, it won't kill us. I heal too fast for that. And while you've got his blade trapped in your body, take his head.

Welkin swung again. She stumbled back. Hunter saw the gleam in the other man's eyes.

Here it comes.

Welkin lunged. Lightning danced up his blade as it slid between her ribs. She gasped. Pain exploded through her.

Now. Do it now. He felt her struggle, the pain threatening her consciousness. Control of the body flickered between them, but she kept hold. Her force of will squeezed him back until he watched everything from the end of a long tunnel.

The fire of earth magic washed over him and ignited in Anaea's mind. She lifted her sword and swung. It imbedded in Welkin's neck. She didn't have the strength to sever his spine.

Welkin howled and pulled his sword from her body. She sliced her blade down and across, severing both arteries.

Blood spewed from his neck, bathing Anaea, and he dropped to his knees. As serious as the wound was, he'd still heal. An arterial strike would only incapacitate him for a minute, maybe a little more. She had to finish him now. Take his head. It was the only way.

Strike again, he yelled, but she couldn't hear him. He was too far away.

Her magic crackled just under her skin, pulsing with her heart. Her breath gurgled and the metallic tang of blood filled her mouth. She dropped her sword and grabbed Welkin's face in both hands. Blue fire, called by instinct and desperation without gesture or incantation, burst from her fingers. It raced over his body and he wailed as the flames devoured his too-human flesh. Black smoke billowed around them and the acrid reek of burning skin washed over her.

The powerful magic of the arena medallion flared to life, blinding Hunter, even from his distant vantage point, trapped deep in Anaea's mind.

And then it was over.

The crowd burst into a thunderous cheer as Anaea sagged to

the arena floor beside Welkin's charred and soulless corpse. The front of her T-shirt was stained with both her blood and Welkin's, but her wound was already healing, the tissues knitting back together.

She coughed. Her mouth filled with blood and she spat it onto the arena floor. *Let's not do that again.*

He could have laughed. Mother of All, he was so proud of her. An unblooded warrior taking on a drake with lightning.

The thought was sobering. She should never have been put in this situation in the first place. He should have minded his own business and let her jump off that bridge.

Of course, then he wouldn't have gotten to know what a strong woman she was. She was a warrior, and he had to find a way to get her body back to her. She deserved at least that much.

You'll never have to do that again. I promise.

She shuffled back to the double arches where she'd entered. *Now I really deserve that shower. A few stitches.* A panicked giggle escaped and she bit her lip. *How in God's name am I still alive?*

That's long and complicated.

Of course. And let me guess, it involves magic. Eventually, all this will bite you in the ass. She sighed and leaned against the arch at the edge of the darkness. *I guess that would be my ass. Since my ass is currently your ass.*

And for a moment, he wished her ass was his. He shut that thought down fast. It was completely inappropriate given the circumstances, and he couldn't afford to think of her that way.

Since we're on the topic of magic, I thought you said Welkin wouldn't have any.

I thought we were talking about your ass?

Don't avoid the question.

Fine. If she wanted to know, he'd tell her. *One of the side effects of my people's... condition is magic. The magic, or rather energy, is every-where, and it's particularly in our spirits.*

You mean your people's spirits are magic?

Yours is, too, but not to the same extent. We call it spirit magic. But what you have that we don't is a connection to an external magic, earth magic.

Earth magic?

The ability to do things like create gates, or make lightning or fire. It's dormant in you, and only about twenty percent of you have the connection, but our spirit magic can waken it.

So I could do anything I wanted?

At the moment, he really wished she could. They wouldn't be in this predicament if he could cast spells like a true sorcerer. *No. We can't cast spells, only true sorcerers can. Usually we can only do one or two things, and often that second thing is being able to open a gate between dimensions.* He checked the connection within her but it remained thready, as if she could only access her earth magic when desperate. *Your connection is still developing, and I wouldn't consider it reliable.*

So no making a magical gate and getting the hell out of here.

No.

Lovely.

As soon as I take care of business here, we'll leave.

Promises, promises. She pushed away from the arch and stepped into the darkness of the corridor. A hand seized her and shoved her against the wall. Her head hit the stone and lights danced across her vision.

Grey pressed his massive weight against her, his muscled arm on her chest, his face close to hers. "Who the hell are you?" His voice was low, a hiss that wouldn't carry.

She struggled to breathe. "Excuse me?"

"You're not Hunter."

Hunter felt Anaea freeze, a deer caught in headlights. He couldn't let her reveal herself. That would endanger both her and Grey, and he needed to keep them safe.

Don't let him know you're not me. But as soon as he told her that, he knew Grey would have figured everything out during the fight. They'd fought side by side for hundreds of years. Hunter should have finished off Welkin without a scratch. The fact that he had to impale himself on Welkin's sword was a sure giveaway. Hunter could only hope no one else, particularly Regis, had noticed.

"What are you talking about?" Anaea asked.

Good. Now shove him aside.

How am I supposed to manage that? He's twice my size.

Before he could answer, she rammed her heel onto Grey's foot and shoved him back. Grey stumbled but regained his balance. He grabbed her wrist and yanked her to his chest.

"I know you're not Hunter. That was the most pathetic fight I've ever seen." Grey grasped her chin with his free hand and forced her to look at him. "Is he in there?"

Anaea's heart pounded and Hunter could feel her struggling with her answer.

Don't say it. Please don't say it.

Suddenly she deflated and nodded.

Shit.

Grey released her and crossed his arms. He glanced at the arches to the arena and over at the stairwell. "Let me talk to him."

"If I could do that, do you think I would have dueled some guy to the death?"

What the hell are you doing?

You know he wouldn't believe me, so I'm just cutting to the chase.

You don't know how dangerous this is. It was bad enough he had put Anaea at risk, but now Grey could be accused of being an accomplice.

"This is one big mess," Grey said.

She snorted. "You're telling me."

"But Hunter is in there? It's the only way you're managing to pull off his aura."

"Yeah."

It bothered Hunter that she didn't sound happy at the thought. Of course, would he be happy if he had to share his body with some strange man?

Tell him it's temporary.

"Hunter says it's temporary," Anaea said.

"I see. Why don't you just let him out for a minute and we'll fix things."

She put her hands on her hips and pursed her lips. Hunter was sure she looked the warrior that he thought she was: proud, strong, and covered in blood.

Grey ran a hand over his head. "Right. Yeah. What's the exact problem with that?"

"I don't know. We tried to switch earlier and couldn't."

Grey hissed a curse. Yep, he'd figured it out. Anaea had a stronger will than Hunter, which was almost unheard of in the dragon world. It meant it wasn't just Anaea who would fall to the soul sickness, but Hunter as well, and, according to all he'd heard, her strength of will was terrifyingly similar to the Greek sorcerers who'd used Egyptian magic to cast the Great Scourge. The only thing he could do was hope that when her soul and earth magics fully awakened they would be at the usual human level. Regardless, any dragon who remembered that terrible day and discovered her would see her as a threat that had to be eliminated.

"This is not a problem," Grey said, although Hunter could tell from the subtle undertones in his voice that he thought it was a disaster.

"Tell me another lie. Hunter knows you know something, I just haven't figured out what that is."

"Excuse me?"

There's nothing wrong, Hunter said.

Bullshit. You were just thinking this was a disaster.

Aside from the fact that it is.

"All right. We have to get you out of Court." Grey grabbed her wrist.

Not until after the rebirthing ceremony.

She jerked free from his grip. "Not until after some ceremony."

"Damn. I'd forgotten about that. Okay, well, you just stay in Hunter's room until the ceremony and I'll—"

He might as well say it, Hunter said.

"Say what?"

"A new body. I need to arrange for a new body for Hunter."

"And how do you go about doing that?" she asked.

If it was a legitimate request, Tobias, the Court's chamberlain, would call up the drakes positioned in the half-dozen Medical Examiner offices and hospitals scattered over the world, to see if someone had something appropriate—appropriate being the correct gender, with a fully matured body, that no human had claimed. This, however, wasn't legitimate and would likely be a raid on a body bank for a learning hospital or a body farm. The farm was definitely less desirable since the state of the bodies usually required a lot more healing. Either way, Hunter could only pray Grey wouldn't go into the gory details.

"Well—"

The jester's insane giggling echoed down the stairwell. Hunter was never so happy for the annoying human's interruption. But the tread of half a dozen pairs of feet shattered his joy. Regis, and his entourage, were coming. Grey froze, his eyes wide.

Regis can't know, Hunter said, hoping he'd infused his thoughts with enough urgency.

Anaea nodded. "He can't know."

"No. He can't." Grey's eyes remained wide.

"Then stop looking terrified."

Mother of All, she was fabulous. Why couldn't he have met her sooner? And yet, if he had, in his other body, she would still be dying.

"What a fabulous *wasu tahazu*. You finally played one up to entertain me," Regis said as he appeared around the curve of the stairwell. He stopped on the steps, towering above them, with his followers gathered behind him. How typical. Hunter had displayed his strength, yet again, and Regis was using petty tricks to remind him of his power. As if Hunter needed someone to stand at the top of a stairs and talk down to him to reinforce who was in control.

"We will feast in an hour. You better hurry up and report to Tobias."

"Now?" Grey asked.

Regis pursed his lips and raised an eyebrow.

"He's covered in blood."

"Are you still sworn into the Handmaiden's service, silver drake?"

Drake? Anaea asked. *I thought his name was Grey?* She froze, then started to tremble. Realization dawned on her. It billowed into a panic that threatened to envelope Hunter's consciousness. He had to stop it, now.

It's a term of endearment. Shit, of all the stupid things to say. But he had to say something. Perhaps she wouldn't completely figure it out, but she was too smart for that and he'd let too much slip—like that dragon roar back in the hotel room.

Grey squared his shoulders. "I serve the Handmaiden until she releases me from duty."

Baby, bunny, snuggle-umpkins. Those are terms of endearment. But drake—!

Not. Now. A growl escaped and Anaea's heart pounded faster. Hunter forced calm into himself and his voice. *Regis can't know about you. Please.*

Anaea shoved her fear back with a force of will that made Hunter shudder. If she could do that with her emotions, no wonder he couldn't regain control of their body.

"Pity. When she tires of you it'll be fun to see how long you last… in the arena, of course." But Regis's tone gave away his disappointment that Grey had to be reborn instead of permanently eliminated. "Fine. Dress for dinner then report."

Anaea drew breath to speak. Even terrified of what Hunter had let slip he could feel her intention to stand up for Grey. Which would get them all reborn.

Don't say a word. Just bow.

She hesitated for a heartbeat, thankfully not long enough for Regis to notice from his perch on the stairwell, then she dropped to one knee and bowed her head.

The jester giggled again. If Hunter had a body he'd shiver. That laugh was like nails on a chalkboard.

"I'll send appropriate clothing to your suite," Regis said over his shoulder as he left.

He can't just make threats like that. The bastard thinks he's in charge.

He is. Unfortunately. The Mother of All only knew why the Handmaiden continued to support his claim to the throne. But given that she was the most powerful dragon among them, no one was going to publicly oppose him. Privately, games Hunter didn't want to know about or participate in were being played. Some to win Regis's favor, others to undermine his tenuous control over dragonkind.

But—

He could sense his distaste for Regis coloring Anaea's opinion of the prince. Not that Regis hadn't been his usual malevolent self. Anyone who had a mind of his own quickly learned that Regis got off on games, particularly the painful kind. *It's complicated.*

Nothing is ever that complicated.

But it was. And, regardless of politics, dragons still needed to protect themselves. Perhaps draconian-styled laws and leadership were necessary, although Hunter was loathe to agree with that. He sighed. *He's my prince. I must obey.*

She bit back a huff. *You should really think about a democracy.*

We tried a democracy. It didn't work. Our culture is old. The strong lead and the weak follow. If you don't like something, become strong enough to lead.

Why doesn't that surprise me?

ANAEA ROSE FROM THE BOW. HER GUT ACHED, AND SHE REALLY JUST wanted a hot shower and a long sleep. Why did she have to give a report and then go to some stupid dinner?

"We can manage this." Grey brushed nonexistent dirt from his knees. "Hunter doesn't say much. Tell Tobias you'll write something up, then just sit and eat."

Is that true?

She felt Hunter shrug. *I'm usually not around Court enough. Not quite my place.*

Gee, I wonder why. His welcome home hadn't been overly welcoming, to say the least.

"I'll go and make arrangements for... you know... after the rebirthing ceremony."

"Which will be when?" She didn't want to think about how Grey would go about finding a new body for Hunter. The image of bulging body bags being tossed into the back of a black van flashed into her head and she shoved it back. Nope, she really didn't want to know.

"Dawn."

She nodded and he scrambled up the stairs and out of sight. If her situation wasn't so bizarre she'd have found it amusing. Instead, she just climbed after him, her pace slow and steady as she tried not to jar the hole in her. It should have felt worse. She should probably be bleeding to death. But she accepted she wasn't as part of the insanity that had the presence of a strange man... spirit—or rather drake?—trapped in her head.

God, she didn't want to think about that. She didn't want to think about any of it. Just a flicker of thought on that topic made her heart race and her skin clammy with fear. Instead, she embraced the numbness seeping over her, making her limbs weak and filling her head with a strange buzzing.

She made her way to Hunter's suite, thankfully without meeting anyone. Hunter didn't say a word as she'd shuffled along the strange halls. Perhaps he felt it. She didn't know why he wouldn't. How was she going to go to some public event and calmly eat? She had just killed a man... a drake...

No. Stop. She couldn't think that... couldn't... She'd killed another per— thing. Burned him to a crisp after being doused in his blood. All that blood. Her hands had taken a life.

It didn't matter that the man had tried to take hers and Hunter's lives. It didn't matter that the situation was beyond bizarre... No, she couldn't start thinking about that again, either. She couldn't stop thinking about anything no matter how hard she tried, couldn't stop coming back to... oh, God.

She stumbled into Hunter's suite, closed the door, and pressed her back against it, as if that would keep everyone and everything out. Her eyes burned with tears and her throat tightened. This was all just a bad dream. That was it. Just a bad dream. It had to be. Please, let it be a dream.

She began to shake, her knees buckled, and she fell to an all-too-real floor. A sob escaped before she could stop it. She was stronger than this. She had to be. But she couldn't make herself stop. Her body was wracked with tears and she fought to muffle them against her arm for fear someone was listening to her.

All she wanted was to scream and yell and cry. How had her life rocketed out of control? Of course, she didn't really have a life. In a few months, none of this would matter. She just never thought she'd die with someone else's blood on her hands. But she hadn't, no. This was a fantasy, a psychological meltdown, a hallucination, a... a...

She squeezed her eyes shut as if by blocking out her vision she could block out her thoughts as well.

Hunter remained silent. His presence hummed at the back of her head but he didn't say anything, as if he knew the reminder of him would be too much for her to take.

GREY STRODE DOWN THE HALL TO HIS SUITE. THIS WAS A DISASTER. A complete and utter disaster. Hunter was body-sharing with some human, and it looked like she had a stronger will than him. Human consciousnesses were supposed to be weak, easily contained, and always susceptible to soul sickness. Even after a dragon's presence awakened whatever soul and earth magics the human possessed, that stress induced insanity.

It was even worse that the human had already established a connection to her body's earth magic. Such a fast awakening of both magics had the possibility of creating a true human sorcerer.

This was really, really bad. Hunter had killed more than enough mages and even a few sorcerers in the early days to know better than to body-share. He certainly knew what he was doing was punishable by rebirth. Everyone did.

Now he had to attend dinner. And not just any dinner, one of the feasts of the *pahar*. Every doyen from every coterie and their seconds, possibly their thirds as well, would be in attendance. Sure, no one really knew Hunter as well as Grey did, but someone was going to notice he was acting weird and ask questions.

If only Hunter had control of the body and not the human. Although Grey had to admit, she'd handled herself well in the *wasu tahazu* as well as when she'd faced Regis. It was sort of a pity they'd have to kill her. They certainly couldn't allow her to live. Even if Hunter hadn't told her anything about dragonkind, it was too great a risk. He wondered if Hunter had known that, or if he'd lied when he'd said he didn't have magic. Regardless, it was a serious crime to body-share and create a human with earth magic, even if in the end she only fit Regis's definition of sorcerer and not the real kind that endangered them all.

Mother of All, what was going to happen when Hunter went to the Handmaiden? She was certain to see the double souls crammed into that emaciated body. He needed a replacement before dawn. It was the only answer.

But if Hunter showed up at the rebirthing ceremony in a different body, he'd be charged with body hopping and that was a sentence of rebirth, too.

Shit.

Grey dragged his hands through his hair and glanced up. He'd walked right past the door to his suite.

Double shit.

Now he was acting the fool that human woman had warned him against. How could she keep her head when both hers and Hunter's lives were on the line? He needed to keep it together. Besides, the human was probably in shock from killing Welkin. Humans were fragile like that. But once the shock wore off, she'd be a mess he'd have to deal with.

The hall darkened, and pain raced across his neck. Crap, a flash-back. The metallic tang of blood filled his mouth and every little detail of that terrible night from sixty-four years ago flooded his senses.

He fought to breathe. This wasn't real, just his Mother-cursed memory making him relive it. But logic couldn't combat the emotion.

"Hey, Grey."

The darkness wavered.

The voice was female and without menace. It was so familiar, her name hung on the tip of his tongue.

"You okay?" This voice was male, young, a reedy tenor.

He knew that voice, too.

He blinked. The hall materialized out of the darkness. Capri stood a few feet away, petite, defiant, and beautiful. Her strawberry blond hair was tied back as usual, accentuating the fine lines of her cheeks and straight nose, and did little to age her youthful appearance. Although her perpetual shadow, Gig, looked even more like a teenager with his shaggy mop of black hair, even though his human body was at least twenty-five.

"Visiting the Handmaiden before dinner?" she asked, meeting his gaze and staying there. Her tone was neutral, but her blue eyes had narrowed. She knew something was wrong.

"Well, he's not going to his suite," Gig said.

Grey glanced back at his door. "Yeah."

Capri's perfect, pale eyebrows drew together ever so slightly.

Damn. He should have said something witty. But he couldn't flirt with Capri like he did with everyone else. She mattered. The others were just a way of coping. Hope still sprung eternal, although after a couple hundred years he was pretty sure she didn't feel the same way.

"Seeing if the Handmaiden needs anything." Now he just looked like a loser. "Can I get you anything?"

Please say yes.

Maybe after so much time her feelings had changed. It happened all the time in the movies.

A smile pulled at her lips. It was only a hint of its full self, but his memory could fill the rest of it in. Every detail. Her dimple. How her eyes shone. The way sunlight would kiss her skin. Her impossibly long lashes.

"Did you see Hunter fight?" Gig said suddenly, looking every bit the part of the little cartoon dog bouncing excitedly around the big dog. "Amazing. And in an unfamiliar body, too."

"I'm pretty sure he saw Hunter fight." Capri's smile deepened just a little bit more. Not with sexual overtones, but that didn't matter. It still made Grey want to rush out and get her things. She hoarded the most amazing flowers, so definitely some of those. And definitely things that sparkled in the sunlight.

He struggled to remind himself that she wasn't interested. Who would be? He'd sworn himself into the service of the Handmaiden and she didn't even want him.

"Will I see you at dinner?" he asked, grinding his teeth against his self-pity.

"I doubt it, and you can blame Hunter for that. He hasn't left such a mess since the 40s. I suspect when I check in with Tobias, Hunter will have left more than just the abandoned car and the bodies in that small-town hospital."

No, Hunter hadn't left a mess, not since he'd hunted down those drakes who'd attacked Grey. He'd ripped off their limbs and claimed their souls for rebirth. That had been messy and Hunter hadn't cared. And Grey could never repay the debt.

Grey's throat ached. "I don't know what went wrong, but it had to be big. He's not a messy guy."

"Yeah, give the dude a break. He's now a dudette," Gig said.

Grey barked a quick laugh before swallowing it. Capri slid her gaze to Gig, her lips twitching. What Grey wouldn't give to hear her laugh. Even if it was Gig's joke and not his.

Now Grey's chest hurt as well.

"Well, catch you later," he said, fighting to keep his voice even.

Capri nodded and sauntered past with Gig close behind. The hall darkened around him, and he blinked it back. Not yet. If he concentrated, he could keep his memories at bay for a while yet, at least until he got Hunter through this disaster.

Mother of All, just let them get through dinner.

12

A fter a forever that didn't last nearly long enough, Anaea sat up from her fetal ball against Hunter's door. She wiped the tears from her face with the back of her hand and took in a shaky breath. She still had a report, a dinner, and some ceremony to get through before she could be free.

And yet, a part of her didn't want to be free of Hunter.

Even when he was silent, hiding in the back of her mind, making himself as small as possible, she was comfortable with him. Certainly, more comfortable with him than she'd ever been with her husband or even her college sweetheart, Mark, as if she could be herself without fear of rejection.

If only she'd met him while he had a body. One that wasn't hers. Even if it was a single last fling with a sexy, mysterious stranger—and she was not going to think the D-word, referring to a mythological serpent. She'd focus on the man, or rather his vessel, the one from the bridge and her dreams. She'd only seen him briefly, but she imagined he was as handsome as his voice and presence seemed. The thought sent shivers over her that she was sure he noticed.

Her face burned. There was no reason to feel embarrassed about being attracted to someone. Maybe, if they had a spare moment, she could get him to read the phone book.

She stood and went to the bathroom. What a horrible, terrible mess, and as much as she knew a shower wouldn't solve her problems, she was at least looking forward to something.

She turned on the taps to let the water heat up and struggled out of her armor, leaving the pieces on the floor where they fell, then grabbed the bottom of her T-shirt. Blood crusted the material to her skin. She eased it up over her head, letting the shirt drop to the floor, too. She didn't want to think about the hole in her gut, or rather the hole that should have been there but wasn't anymore. There was nothing ordinary about her situation so she shouldn't expect the usual effects of getting run through.

When she'd woken in the hotel room with foggy dreams of being shot, she hadn't had holes in her then, either. And now she was sure she had been shot. Okay, so the blood on the hospital shirt and the matching holes had been a giveaway, but she'd been whole, healthy, more or less, and alive. It made her wonder what had happened to her cancer. With Hunter in her head, she could heal gunshot wounds.

A part of her wanted to ask if, when he left her body—which he was certain to do—would the cancer finally kill her, but another part of her hesitated. Perhaps she didn't really want to know. Not yet, anyway. Besides, it felt good to be alone for the first time since all this insanity had started. She could always ask him those questions later.

The mirror was foggy, which meant her shower had been ready a while ago and she'd spent too much time thinking. She unhooked her bra and slid out of her underwear, keeping her gaze away from her impossibly healing wounds. Then she stepped under the spray and let the water sluice over her. It ran red down the drain until all of the blood was sloughed from her skin. The heat seeped into her aching muscles, and she savored the luxury of hot water on clean flesh. She picked up the bar of soap on the ledge in the corner and scrubbed at her skin, rubbing a thick lather around and around on her belly.

I hate to interrupt, but we can't keep Regis waiting.

Anaea jumped and dropped the soap.

He was back.

And she was reminded of the reality of her situation. No, she was not going to think about it. Not yet. She couldn't, not without losing her mind. But she'd already learned denial didn't make something go away and promised herself when the shower was done, she'd face it. Whatever it was.

She glanced down to find the soap, and hot desire washed over her. His hot desire. With a gasp, she realized her naked body was within her field of vision, and therefore within *his* field of vision. Oh, God!

She jerked her gaze to the ceiling, her cheeks burning.

You know you shouldn't sneak up on a girl while she's in the shower. She suppressed her thrill of pleasure at the thought that he found her attractive. So there actually was something good about the situation. Of course, he'd missed the worst of it. She hadn't had to amputate a leg.

Isn't that the best time to sneak up on a girl?

She could feel the innuendo in his words. It heated her veins with more than just embarrassment. Of course, which were his emotions and which were hers was a different story. Perhaps she'd just imagined it all. Having a sexy masculine voice stuck in her head did make a girl fantasize.

Well, you're not getting a peep show. She closed her eyes and knelt, feeling around on the floor for the soap. Her hand knocked it into the corner and she chased it, eyes squeezed shut.

This is going to take forever. Warning deepened his voice. *We don't have forever.*

You don't get to see me naked. She captured the soap and at a record pace scrubbed herself down, including the stubble on her scalp. At least she was a low maintenance kind of girl. Only mere minutes required to style her hair.

Hunter's impatience grew along with another emotion that she couldn't quite place until she realized he could feel what she was feeling. Like her soapy hands running all over her body.

God. You're impossible.

She rushed out of the shower and dried herself off as fast as she could, then wrapped the towel tight around her and opened her eyes.

There should be clothes in the bedroom, Hunter said.

Of course. None that would fit, but she didn't say that to him. She headed farther into the suite to the bedroom, somehow knowing, probably from Hunter's infusion of memories, where to go. It felt kinky going into his bedroom wrapped only in a towel. Her, with a strange man. She'd never had a fling before. Of course, that strange man was in her head. Did that count? How could a relationship between them work? The thought of self-pleasuring jumped into her head, making her blush.

Stop that, she said.

His bedroom was a masculine room done in dark woods. Midnight blue walls speckled with stars, low light, and matching blue silk sheets finished off the look. In the corner sat a massive wardrobe and beside it a large leather chair.

A sleek red dress was draped over the bed. She wanted to ask how the dress had arrived in the room with the front door locked, but wasn't ready yet to know. Sure, her shower was done, but she'd feel braver, ready to handle anything, if dressed.

Really.

She picked up the gown. The front would cover her all the way up to her neck, but the back plunged dangerously low. She wouldn't be able to wear a bra, and would be forced to reveal her deformity. So much for the idea that clothing would make her feel safer.

Anything else? she asked.

I think you'll look great in it.

Still, she said. *I'd like something more modest.*

Hunter chuckled. *Modesty isn't something worn at Court dinners.*

She swallowed. *I see.*

I don't see what the problem is.

Of course he wouldn't. He obviously hadn't seen all of her. If he had, she was sure he'd have said something. Every other man had. It was shocking he hadn't pulled it from her thoughts, even though she was determined to keep that locked away. Surely, he would find her repulsive when he realized the lengths she'd gone to in order to stop her cancer.

But it didn't matter. She hadn't had a choice then. Just like it seemed she didn't have a choice now. Perhaps it was a good thing she wasn't well endowed to begin with. Barely endowed was more like it. The fact that she was lopsided might not be obvious. She supposed it helped that the dress didn't reveal any cleavage. It could have been low cut in the front as well as the back.

She closed her eyes and let the towel slip to the floor.

Hunter snorted.

She suspected if he had control of her eyes he'd roll them. Well, actually, he'd probably steal a peek. Men.

Stepping into the dress, she slid the smooth material over her hips and chest and fastened the clasp at the back of her neck. Then she opened her eyes and looked around for underwear.

Whoever was thoughtful enough to provide the dress hadn't thought of underwear. Great.

You don't need it.

Spoken like a true man. She went back to the bathroom and put on her dirty undies. The dress revealed the panty line. Better they look at her panty line than her misshapen chest. Besides, she didn't want to face a room full of strangers who'd happily watched her battle someone to the death without underwear. A girl needed all the protection she could get.

And now she couldn't put it off any longer.

She paced into the living room and sucked in a slow breath.

You look great.

She could feel Hunter's rising concern and paced back down the hall to the bedroom door.

She had to ask. Had to face it. Knowing was better than not knowing. Right?

She sucked in another breath.

Right.

We will get through this dinner, he said.

That's not what I'm worried about... I mean it is, but— Tell me about the drake thing. The words spilled out in a rush.

Hunter grew still within her. *Like I said, term of endearment.*

Yeah, right, she thought at him, the muscles in her jaw trembling with the effort to remain calm. *You said you were a spirit.* She paced back into the living room. She couldn't seem to stop moving.

I've already told you too much.

I don't think you've told me enough.

I know. His thoughts swirled through her, as if he was deciding what to tell her and what to keep secret.

This was ridiculous. Even if she didn't need to know everything, she certainly needed to know more. She pushed against Hunter's consciousness. The wall between them was thick, impenetrable, and she couldn't tell what he was thinking. She pushed harder, skittering across his defenses, digging a deep rent in its dark mental surface as if with mental claws.

Memory flooded her. Majestic creatures with scales gleaming in the sunlight, dipped around and through clouds.

The memory snapped shut. *Stay out of my mind, woman.*

That's a little difficult since you're in mine.

Another memory blossomed around her. Hunter trying to stand on shaky legs, but he couldn't find his balance. Having only two legs and no tail sucked.

I said, stay out, he growled but the memory continued. He felt so small, so fragile.

Please. That one word was filled with pain and vulnerability.

Appalled, Anaea shoved the memory away and imagined her own wall between them. She shouldn't have gone prying. That was wrong, akin to a form of rape, even if she hadn't realized what she was doing. His thoughts and memories were private, as were hers. The thought made her sick. She hadn't meant—

What was she turning into? All she wanted was to understand what was going on.

She stopped pacing and hugged herself, willing her twitchy muscles into stillness. But they wouldn't obey. She was so sorry.

I know.

Did you hear that thought?

No, just sensed your emotion. You've closed yourself off from me. His presence stilled within her. *I'll tell you what I can, but it's dangerous.*

You've said that before. Don't you think at least mentioning you were different than say a human spirit was important?

Is it?

Yes— Maybe— She ground her teeth. *I don't know. Can you at least explain the drake thing?*

It's slang for dragon.

And that's what you are? As in scales, tail, wings, breathing fire?

Only a few of us could breathe fire.

Of course. Nothing in her world made sense anymore. He was a spirit talking in her head and she'd set someone on fire just with her thoughts. Impossible or not, she was going to have to accept these new rules to the universe or die in some horrible, probably painful way. *Okay, so you're a dragon?*

The remains of one.

Sadness enveloped her, a deep throbbing ache that felt ancient yet still raw. And somehow, she knew his people were trapped in human bodies, unable to survive without the vessels, as trapped in their lives as much as she was in her death. They were so few, so very few. Only half had survived to take the parasitic spirit state they lived in now, and their numbers dwindled every year. They were down to less than fifteen hundred worldwide.

Now come on. His lack of comment on what she'd learned made her wonder if he knew the thought had leaked through their walls. *We've spent too long getting ready. Certain people will be becoming impatient.*

A pair of four inch pumps, conveniently her size and matching her dress, sat by the front door. She put them on, hung the medallion around her neck, and opened the door to find Grey leaning against the wall.

One of those aforementioned impatient people? she asked.

But not one we have to worry about.

"Wow." Grey stepped up to meet her.

She smiled in spite of herself and dipped her head to hide her reaction.

He leaned close, his lips brushing her ear. "I'm flattered, but none of that. Hunter's not shy."

She bit the inside of her cheek and schooled her features into a wary calm. It was what Hunter was really feeling. She could only hope she could keep it up all night.

Yes, you can. I'll help you.

But she knew coaching would only get her so far. She was surrounded by dragons in disguise and didn't think their human condition lessened their bite.

An insane giggle echoed down the hall and Hunter felt Anaea shiver.

"Jeez. I was hoping we'd get through dinner without Giacomo," Grey said.

Giacomo? Anaea asked.

Grey's nickname for the Court jester. He could sense Anaea's confusion. *It comes from a movie. Jester of kings. King of jesters.* Thankfully, she didn't ask for more details. But, as Grey would put it, she was paying attention to the man behind the curtain and Hunter couldn't hit rewind to undo it. In fact, as much as he hated the idea, the more she knew, the better their odds of surviving this mess.

The jester cartwheeled into sight, stopping upside down and walking on his hands the rest of the way.

"Come on," Grey said, his voice low. He shoved past the crazy human, knocking him over.

The jester hissed and growled.

Hunter cringed. He'd always wondered why King Constantine and Regis kept the human around. He didn't have any earth magic to be useful, but perhaps he was a physical reminder of what would happen if a drake body hopped or body-shared. Hunter would have thought Constantine's soul sickness and Regis banning body hopping after the dangers were discovered was proof enough, but Hunter couldn't deny the effectiveness of the jester.

Anaea shoved past him, but he grabbed her wrist in his fleshy, ruined hands.

Glare at him.

She did. The jester let go and shrank back.

"The king must see you," he said in a tiny voice.

Not what Hunter wanted to hear.

Grey grunted. The jester mimicked him, then giggled.

"Come, come. The king calls."

What do I do? Aren't you supposed to report or something?

Hunter sighed. They really didn't have a choice. *When the king calls, every drake answers, regardless of anyone else's schedule. Go with him and remember, stoic.*

You mean sullen and silent.

If that's what it takes. Maybe they could get in and out. If Constantine was having a bad day he'd be incoherent. That tended to make audiences confusing... and blessedly short.

The jester bounced from foot to foot. "Come. Come."

"Coming," Anaea said.

She started down the hall. Grey fell into step beside her and the jester leveled a hard stare at him. "Not you."

Grey slid his gaze to her.

Shit. Grey should know better. *Don't react. Just go.*

Anaea ground her teeth. He could feel her fighting the urge to let Grey know everything was going to be fine. Then she jerked to face the jester and marched down the indicated hall.

So remember, we need to play this cool, Hunter said.

I kind of got that impression.

Constantine is... unstable.

They turned a corner into the hall leading to the royal chambers. This was one of the only two adorned parts of Court—the other being the rebirth chamber. Here the walls were carved with forest scenes and painted in bright colors. It was a dazzling difference from the rest of the corridors and public chambers. Hunter suspected Prince Regis liked it that way. Everything was a manipulation, a reminder of whose coterie was the most powerful.

What do you mean by unstable?

Remember when I said it was bad to change vessels too often? Constantine is an example of that. Part of our spirit can get warped if we body hop too much and we go... well, crazy.

So why did Constantine do it?

We didn't know until it was too late. Hunter bit back a sigh. *There was so much we didn't know when we first ended up in this spirit state. Some drakes loved the idea of changing their vessels regularly, kind of like clothes.*

That's disgusting, Anaea said.

I always thought so. But others felt differently and by the time we realized it was dangerous it was too late.

The jester snorted and started zigzagging from one side of the hall to the other.

Is that what happened to Giacomo?

He's a different problem. And one Hunter didn't know how to explain to Anaea.

And what problem would that be?

Nothing you need to worry about.

They reached Constantine's chambers, the double doors inlaid with gold leaf.

I'm starting to get the impression that "nothing you need to worry about" is code for something I definitely need to worry about.

Can we talk about this later?

I'd rather not.

And I'd rather get through this meeting.

The jester shoved the doors open, straightened as best he could with his twisted body, and strode into the king's suite as if he owned it.

Anaea stopped at the threshold and crossed her arms. *How about the abridged version?*

Anaea.

She didn't move. *Hunter.*

If he had eyes to roll... Mother of All, she was going to be the death of both of them. He didn't want her to panic, not in front of Constantine, and he was certain that she would once she knew the jester was crazy because his human spirit hadn't been strong enough to share a body with a dragon.

Oh my God, it's bad!

Not that bad.

Yes it is. I can feel you thinking about it.

"Enter," the jester said with a manic giggle.

He's me. It just flashed in my head. He was a human who had a dragon in him and now he's a raving lunatic. Her heart raced and even without control of their body, Hunter could feel a clammy sweat chilling her hands and neck.

He jerked his consciousness back and threw up another mental shield between them. His concern was making him slip, and she was hearing his private thoughts. He hadn't believed he was leaking so many of his unconscious thoughts to her. And he couldn't risk letting it continue. It would only accelerate their spiral into soul sickness.

But she felt his sudden withdrawal, and her heart raced even faster. Shit.

I won't let you become soul sick.

The jester cleared his throat and waved his hands around his head. "I said, enter."

But—

Hunter could feel a ragged sob threatening to escape. *You won't go crazy. I'll get out before that happens. Now please. We have to get through this.*

Anaea sucked in a quick breath.

He could feel her fighting the urge to nod. *You can do this. Just be stoic.*

Yeah. Stoic, she thought at him.

And don't make eye contact.

What?

Think of dragons like big cats. Eye contact is a sign of aggression, a contest for dominance. Constantine might be crazy, but he's still king.

She sucked in another breath. *Anything else you want to add?*

Nope, I think we're good.

You have a strange definition for good.

Given the situation, I'll take what I can.

You have a point. She crossed the empty receiving room and entered the king's private chamber. It shimmered with mounds of coins—gold, silver, and bronze—and all types of jewels. There wasn't any furniture. Constantine sat on a pile of coins, his already small stature dwarfed by his dazzling hoard.

Anaea dropped her gaze and without prompting, knelt.

Good girl. If she kept this up and luck was on their side, they might make it through this evening alive after all. When this was over, he'd disappear for a while, leave the Royal Coterie, and let someone else be prince's assassin. He might even be able to survive without a coterie. During his long life, he'd developed financial resources that should be enough to sustain him. Maybe now was the time to use them.

But that was a fool's dream. Others had tried it and failed. What made him think he could do it? Leaving made a doyen and the coterie look weak, and every doyen, not just Regis, would chase down the deserter to maintain power. And while neither death nor rebirth were options, since desertion was a private matter, there were other disciplinary alternatives that were painful and maiming.

Constantine sighed, sounding very much like his sane self. Not good.

"Rise," Constantine said. "I would congratulate you on maintaining your position in my coterie."

Anaea trembled but didn't stand.

Anaea.

The trembling increased. It thrummed through her, her muscles twitching.

Get up.

"False humility doesn't become you, Hunter."

Anaea, stand up.

"I said, rise." Constantine's voice was dark, promising danger. And with the king more than halfway to crazy, Hunter didn't even want to guess where that would take him. More than one dragon had been reborn merely on the fact that Constantine didn't like the color of his eyes—and that was his own eyes, not the reborn dragon's.

What do you think I'm trying to do?

Something snapped within her. It zinged through her head into his thoughts.

This was going to be a disaster. He should have told Regis he was staying in his chamber until the rebirth ceremony. Meditating or something. Not that he'd ever meditated in his life, but there was always a first time for everything.

He ground his teeth.

Wait a minute.

He could feel that.

He bit the inside of his cheek, or rather, Anaea's cheek.

Praise the Mother of All, he had control of their body.

He stood. "Is Your Majesty attending the feast?"

"Falsely humble and falsely polite. One would think you had a personality change as well as a physical one. How am I supposed to show my appreciation now?" Constantine's voice turned petulant and he slapped the pile beside him, sending coins skidding across the floor.

The jester cartwheeled to Hunter, grabbed his chin, and peered into his left then right eye.

Hunter jerked back, and in his head he felt Anaea shrink away. Smart girl. Getting caught wasn't a good idea. Not that anyone could tell two souls were inside just by staring in his eyes. Only someone with sorcerer ability could tell and there were only two who were strong enough. Jade, who remained by her gate, and the Handmaiden —a true sorcerer—who stayed in her chambers. With luck, the Handmaiden would be too busy tomorrow with the ceremony to notice.

What is he doing? Anaea asked, her mental voice a whisper.

Giacomo clicked his tongue three times, hopping on one foot and humming 'Twinkle, Twinkle, Little Star.'

Being annoying.

"Your Majesty, no appreciation is necessary," Hunter said, unable and unwilling to keep the growl from his voice. It sounded strange with Anaea's higher pitch, but he was sure it got his point across. Mother of All, just let him leave.

"I don't know why my son is so fond of you," Constantine said.

Regis wasn't fond of him. Not really. But Hunter wasn't going to remind the king of that.

"You're trouble."

The jester giggled. "Gimmie a T."

If the fool didn't shut up Hunter was going to strangle him. Both him and Constantine. Boy, that would feel good.

I'm inclined to help, but I think that's your emotion.

And right now, you're not helping.

Hunter dragged his attention back to Constantine. "You should be glad then, that I'm trouble for your enemies."

"You are my enemies." Constantine gasped and clutched an armful of his hoard to his chest. "Who are you? What do you want? Guards! Guards!"

Anaea trembled within Hunter, but he could sense she was still watching, studying, collecting even more questions he was sure he'd have to answer at the most inopportune time. But she was also facing her fears like a dragon should—but unlike many of dragonkind these days.

The jester took up the call for guards, laughing and dancing, kicking coins and gems this way and that. Two drakes rushed from an inner chamber, swords drawn, but stopped when they saw Hunter.

He fought the urge to roll his eyes. There were reasons Regis didn't listen to Constantine anymore, and had likely stopped centuries ago. Trapped, half-sane, in his current form, Constantine needed to be reborn, but Regis refused to do it. Of course, with only two gold drakes left, Regis and Constantine, that meant there was no one directly behind Regis to contend for the throne. A convenience that likely helped with the stability of Court but left a bad taste in Hunter's mouth.

"Your Majesty." Hunter nodded to the king and then the guards. They'd been in this situation too many times before, and Hunter knew the sooner he left the easier it would be for them to get Constantine calmed down. Rebirth would be a kindness to his king. And execution one to the jester. But neither was going to happen while Regis was in control. Court was simmering with discontent but not one coterie seemed confident enough in its strength to make a play for the throne. Not against the Handmaiden's chosen coterie. Although perhaps that wasn't true. Someone had broken the law. They'd shared bodies with humans, created human mages, and tried to take the medallion. Very likely Zenobia, doyen of the Major Green Coterie. Something was stirring, Hunter just didn't know what.

13

Hunter left Constantine moaning and clutching his hoard and headed to the Chamberlain's Office to finally get in his report before dinner. The office sat at the end of the Greater Promenade, one of two major corridors that crossed, making the heart of the Primary Level at Court. The office's enormous, plain double doors lay open—they only closed during a security lockdown, and that hadn't happened for a good four hundred years—and beyond lay a 20th century, modern-office maze: partitions, desks, water coolers, photocopy machines, and rows and rows of shelves and cabinets filling the area.

I feel like I've stepped from one nightmare into another.

He felt her shiver again and knew it had nothing to do with the office. *I'm told the environment is good for productivity.*

Anaea snorted. *I doubt that.*

He could sense her fighting to keep her tone light. He didn't want to draw her attention to the emotions he could sense her struggling with, but didn't know how to distract her. *This, my dear, is the heart of Dragon Operations.*

Every Clean Team, every head of Coterie Security, those drakes placed in key human positions, and the head of Identification Replacement, all went through the Chamberlain's Office. Not to mention the covert teams few drakes knew about: Internal Inspection—assigned to monitor dragon activities—and the mysterious Asar Nergal—assigned to eliminate any human-mage threat accidentally or intentionally created by dragons. And given that Hunter had killed two mages in the Elmsville hospital, the Asar Nergal obviously weren't doing their job.

Hunter wove around cubicles to a small office, complete with large glass window and closed vertical blind, at the back of the maze.

All the day-to-day minutiae of running a small kingdom also went through the office, although the chamberlain's second-in-command oversaw that. Tobias, the chamberlain, was most concerned with following the Handmaiden's directive to keep dragonkind a secret from humanity and in doing so, safe from themselves.

Hunter crossed the threshold into the office and Tobias looked up from his computer monitor. He narrowed his muddy brown eyes and pursed his thin lips. "So it is true."

Anaea's presence trembled then abruptly stilled. Mother of All, just let her make it through this and dinner.

"Too busy to watch me fight?" Hunter forced his tone into a casual drawl.

Tobias leaned his massive, six-foot-five, all-muscle frame back into his deluxe office chair away from the delicate antique writing desk. Hunter always thought it strange that the brown drake would upgrade to a chair with lumbar support but keep the rickety desk with its spindly legs. But he supposed it was only as strange as a former pirate, who still kept the dark, wild pirate hair and attire, becoming the most efficient security manager dragonkind had seen in a thousand years.

"Tell me there weren't more complications than this." He gave Hunter a pointed stare. "And the mess you left was only on the bridge and in the hospital."

Anaea shrank back from the look.

"The job's done." Maybe if he was brisk the interview would be short. He hated reporting in the first place, and he had less patience for it now. Not with Anaea on the verge of a breakdown. He needed to get through this dinner, switch bodies, and ensure payback for the situation.

"And?"

"Capri will also need to make a trip to the Rest Well Hotel in Elmsville." Come on, come on. Assign the homework and be done with it.

Tobias typed something into his computer. "You know I'll want a report."

Of course, and Hunter would do it as soon as Anaea was safe and his hunt for the drake responsible for this was over. "Absolutely. But I'm late for dinner already, so I'll do it later."

"Like all your other reports?" Tobias raised a dark eyebrow. It was a fight they'd been having for centuries. Tobias hoarded his paperwork, and Hunter gave him a hard time about it.

Hunter sighed. "I'll get Grey to do it."

What, is this high school? Anaea asked. He could feel her forcing the quip but at least she was still trying.

Something like that. Please just let her hold it together. The knowledge of dragons and magic were just too much for a human. It had been proven time and again. He'd thought with her strength of will she'd resist the soul sickness long enough for him to find a new body and transfer out. But now he wasn't so sure. Her emotions sat on a razor's edge. The slightest thing could push her into a spiral that he wouldn't be able to save her from—or save himself, either.

"Grey wasn't there," Tobias said, jerking Hunter's attention back to him.

"Do you really think that matters?" Hunter's reports were sparse at best. Grey's secondhand account would be as wordy as if Hunter had written it, probably more.

Tobias's gaze lifted, focusing on something—most likely someone —behind Hunter.

"Oh, man, I never thought I'd see the day. Hunter a woman," a husky feminine voice said.

He clenched his jaw and turned to face Capri, a red-haired beauty whose petite figure disguised how lethal she was even in human form. "Hello to you, too."

She chuckled, not bothering to hide her amusement at his predicament.

Tobias cleared his throat. "Hunter left you another cleanup."

"Are you kidding me?"

Guess the hospital hadn't been a simple clean and go. Of course, he hadn't expected it to be simple, but a drake could hope. He'd need lots and lots of orchids, just as soon as he took care of his situation.

"Am I going to find the local P.D. swarming that place, too?"

Oh, probably. But he wasn't going to point it out. For a water drake, Capri had a whole lot of fire. He could see why Grey was so interested in her. Too bad it was as plain as day she wasn't interested in him.

"Not a problem," lanky Gig said from halfway behind the door-frame, his perpetual state of disarray still obvious even dressed in a Victorian-styled suit. Maybe it was the mussed hair, since the suit would probably look clean and tailored on anyone else.

Capri glared at him. "That's because there won't be anything for you to do at the hotel."

Gig ignored her, his gaze locked on Hunter in wide-eyed admiration. Damn, even hopping into a woman hadn't discouraged the hero worship. And if Hunter wasn't careful, the kid would get himself killed over it.

Which, at the moment, wasn't on the top of his list of problems. He shrugged. "Grey's report of my misadventure will be on your desk eventually."

Capri barked another laugh and Tobias glowered. At least that was business as usual.

Now, onto 'business unusual.' He headed to the feast hall with two hurdles down. Only the feast and the rebirth ceremony to go. Thank goodness he'd regained possession of their body. Everything could go smoothly now until Grey found him a replacement.

You okay? he asked Anaea. He didn't know if checking in would push her over the edge, but her growing silence was unnerving. And with her building strong soul magic shields around her thoughts, he couldn't tell what she was thinking, only feeling.

Yep. Just trying to keep my eyes closed for the rest of the rollercoaster ride.

Funny how just a few hours ago she couldn't even keep her thoughts private. She certainly was a fast learner. But that didn't surprise him. Her situation was beyond bizarre and she'd adapted to it all. He damned well was going to make sure she didn't go crazy and lose that which attracted him the most: her spirit.

It burned to know she was under such stress and there was little he could do about it. Meeting Tobias and Grey and learning the truth about dragons was difficult enough, but Constantine and his jester was worse, particularly now that Anaea realized the jester had lost his mind by body-sharing, just as she and Hunter were doing.

He rounded a corner and found Grey leaning in the doorway of an antechamber.

"So?" Grey asked, straightening and stepping into the dim room.

Hunter followed him in and the ensorcelled light brightened. Every time that happened he was reminded of how much dragons owed to the Handmaiden: discovering and shaping Court, and enspelling lights, air currents, room-to-room delivery systems, and other magical features. Even if all she did was rebirth dragons, there was no way dragonkind could survive without her.

"Is it you?" Grey kept his voice low and his gaze on the doorway. "Or... her?"

"Her name is Anaea."

"Jeez, Hunter. You know her name?"

"Kind of hard not to when I'm in her head."

I heard that, Anaea mumbled.

"Yeah, but you're using it."

"Tell me you found a suitable replacement," Hunter said.

"I've got Cole on it."

Swell. How many more drakes could he get involved in this disaster? "You couldn't have gone out and taken care of this yourself?"

"Cole is discreet, he doesn't know any details, and he can slip almost anything past Tobias. For all he knows, I've taken up pathology."

"Fine." Hunter supposed it would have to do. He ran a hand over his head. The stubble, usually his preferred haircut, felt out of place on Anaea's scalp. "Let's get this over with."

He strode out of the antechamber too fast and wobbled on the heels, unfamiliar with balancing on that kind of shoe. Grey grabbed Hunter's arm and snickered.

"Now I know it's you and not the woman."

Hunter jerked out of Grey's grasp. "She has a name," he growled.

"Yes, and better balance." Grey wasn't even trying to hide his amusement. Why did everyone have to find this so funny?

"When I get an appropriate body back I'm kicking your ass all over Court."

"Merely incentive for me to find the smallest, wimpiest man I can."

Hunter swallowed another growl. He really just wanted to slug Grey, but with Anaea's strength, the silver drake would likely mistake it for a love tap. Instead, he focused on making it the rest of the way to the feast hall without falling over.

This night couldn't end soon enough.

He'd eat his meat then leave. In and out. No problem. Really.

He stepped through the enormous arch into the mostly empty feast hall. The room could hold close to two thousand but was only set for the hundred and fifty drakes attending the *pahar* dinner. Their tables huddled at the far end near the dais, making the room look desolate instead of grand. Less than a thousand years ago, the hall had been full. It was a testament to their declining ranks and the growing disinterest toward Court activities among the younger dragons.

He squared his shoulders. Walking the length of the room to his seat beside Regis's at the royal table unsettled him more than any other duty as prince's assassin. But it was necessary if he wanted to keep his position in the Royal Coterie. His heels clicked on the polished marble floor, and the room fell silent before he'd even reached the first tables.

Everyone looked at him. Every doyen of every coterie—major and minor—their seconds and thirds, their mates, their advisors, and every coterie's security detail. Any one of them could be responsible for the human mages, although he had a short list of suspects.

He ground his teeth. Fine. They could look all they wanted. He'd still won the *wasu tahazu*. He was still Regis's Assassin. And if he told himself that enough times perhaps he wouldn't feel like an insect on display.

Striding the length of the hall to the dais, he passed the tables of the minor coteries who, for the most part, had made alliances with the more powerful ones. Closer to the dais sat the doyens of the Counseling Coteries and their seconds. Depending on where the coterie's doyen stood in Regis's favor at the time would determine how close he or she was placed to the throne.

Nero, doyen of the Major Black Coterie and always Regis's favorite, sat the closest. Barna, doyen of the Major Brown, was next. Zenobia, as expected, sat with her Second and Third and their mates as far away from Regis as possible without actually proclaiming that she'd been ousted from the Counsel. Her coterie wasn't magically powerful, but it was large and Regis would be a fool to completely alienate her.

"Look who lived to fight another day." Zenobia leaned back in her chair and traced the lip of her wine glass with her index finger. "Didn't think you had it in you."

Hunter bit back a growl but still showed a little teeth. "I always have it in me."

"Not from what I hear, Prince's Assassin." She brushed a dark lock from her eyes toward the pile of black curls and braids cascading from her head down her back. Her enormous, almond-shaped eyes narrowed, drawing focus to how dark her irises were. "Even the best get tired every now and then."

The nerve. She was barely veiling her threats now. "I wouldn't hold my breath on that."

Who's the bitch? Anaea asked. She sounded far away, as if she was peeking out of a crack in her mental box.

Top suspect for our current situation. "I'm not so easily killed."

Zenobia swirled her finger in her wine then slid it into her mouth and sucked on it. "That's what makes it so fun to watch."

Someone's soul needed collecting and writ or no writ, he was going to come calling soon. Trying to kill him or making a play for the throne was one thing. But breaking dragon law to create human mages went too far. Screw the Asar Nergal taking care of it. This was personal.

He marched the remaining feet to the dais and eased into his seat beside Regis's empty throne. The prince wouldn't arrive until just before the ceremonial meat. Which meant Hunter had a much-needed moment to compose himself. He reached for his glass of wine. Boy, did he need a drink. Something stronger would be nice, but he'd just have to be satisfied with rotten grapes.

His hand didn't move.

He concentrated on raising his arm, flexing his fingers, moving, twitching, anything.

Nothing.

Shit.

Shit, shit, shit, shit.

Like the last time, he hadn't noticed the switch. There was no box, no sense he was cut off from the physical form he inhabited. He really hadn't wanted Anaea to have to act her way through this dinner. He didn't know if she could.

Grab that glass of wine, will you? We need a drink.

Are you kidding me? She didn't sound happy at all.

I wish I was.

His hand jerked forward, or rather, her hand did. She took the glass and sucked back a large swig. *How soon can we get out of this?*

Look sullen, eat the meat, and then we can leave.

She finished the glass. He could feel her struggling not to shake. She didn't want to be here, didn't want to think about what had happened in the *wasu tahazu* or about Constantine and the crazy jester. She didn't want to think about what was going to happen now.

It will be okay. I promise.

Rivers of blood, pouring over her, flashed through her mind.

And to top it all off, she was still in shock from the fight. It made him ache to know he was the cause of her turmoil.

You did what you needed to do.

She blinked and he felt her throat constrict.

I don't know if I can do this.

Yes, you can. She couldn't cry. He needed to distract her with something, anything.

Raise a finger. Let's get our glass topped up.

She obeyed, and a young woman in a gossamer gown refilled the glass. Regis's imagination reflected a time period long dead, along with its misogynistic beliefs, but Court still mirrored that in hopes of winning his favor.

Anaea didn't comment on the dress or lack thereof. He would have thought she'd make a biting remark of some kind.

This wasn't good.

Maybe a familiar face would help. *Grey is on your left, halfway to the dais.*

She didn't look up. *Everyone's looking at me.*

That's because you look hot in this dress.

You mean it's because they all think you *look hot in this dress.*

That was better. *I suppose so.* If a little laugh at his expense helped her to calm down, so be it. What he really needed was to get her emotionally detached, make her see the situation from a distance... appeal to her intellect. She was already curious, but too afraid to ask anything. *Now, look at Grey. Over there. He's with his coterie.*

His coterie? Anaea's gaze darted to the left, hit Grey, then returned to the wineglass.

Excellent. He'd hoped the interesting word would catch her attention. If he could keep her intellectually focused, perhaps she'd be able to ignore her emotions enough to get through this. *We're organized in groups or clans called coteries.*

That's why a democracy didn't work. Everyone was loyal to their coterie.

Yeah. Some habits die hard. We lived this way before we lost our physical forms, and nothing else seems to keep order. There used to be a lot of coteries, family and extended family groupings. But with Constantine being unstable, there's safety in numbers, and the smaller groups have joined more powerful ones.

Anaea swallowed. *You have a complicated society.*

You have no idea. It's been around for thousands of years. Currently there are thirteen coteries and everyone sits by color association. Even if they were at the dinner for other reasons, like Grey who sat with the Silver Coterie but represented the Handmaiden who never attended events.

That's why Regis called Grey a silver drake?

Exactly. For the most part, they're based on our original dragon form colors. He really shouldn't be telling her any of this, but thank the Mother of All it was working. Her panic had eased a bit even if she was still staring at her glass.

Dragon form colors?

Our original colors reflect a drake's primary element: fire, water, earth, or air, and therefore his weakness, but with the discovery of magic that's no longer important. Although after a couple thousand years without bodies, seeing a dragon for his color seemed pointless, like the humans' prejudice to skin color.

But you said only a few of you have magic.

It's enough to distinguish leaders from followers. We live in a precarious state between order and chaos. If the leaders of the coteries are roughly equal in strength, no one will try to upset the balance.

But if nothing changes, Regis will stay in control until he dies.

And if he stays safe, he never will.

Her shock billowed over him. *You don't die?*

We're spirits. The magic in our spirit stops our vessels from aging. We can still be killed, but we don't die from natural causes.

Her thoughts stilled, and a chill went through him. He couldn't tell what she was thinking, but he could guess. If she had survived the wounds she had, and he stopped his vessel from aging, was her cancer gone? He didn't know what he'd say if she asked.

So if you can't die and no one challenges Regis, he stays put.

Hunter swallowed his relief. He should probably tell her the truth about her cancer, but if it was discovered that they were body-sharing there wasn't anything he could do to save her. It would be better if she thought she was still dying. To give her hope and then take it away would be cruel. Once he knew she was safe, he'd tell her the truth.

You don't like Regis, she said.

No. Regis held onto his power through cruelty and fear. He supposed that was one way for a leader to keep power, but he didn't agree with it.

You don't think he should be in charge.

He's not in charge. Constantine is.

Anaea snorted, but still didn't look up from her glass. *Even I can tell Constantine isn't in charge.*

But that was all part of the tentative balance as well and likely the reason for the attack on him. As soon as they were through this and Anaea was safely away from Court, he would prove he wasn't a blind follower. Until then, he needed to keep his goal in mind, getting through dinner without anyone noticing that he wasn't himself. And to do that, he needed to get Anaea to look up. *Enough about Constantine. Let's see who's here.*

Okay. She gathered her courage and scanned the area.

Good. All the usual suspects are here. He hadn't missed anyone on his way in.

The usual suspects?

All the coterie doyens, the leaders, are here. There isn't anyone I wasn't expecting. Attending the pahar *and its feasts is all about maintaining or gaining political power.*

Just by showing up? she asked.

It's more complicated than that.

I figured as much. But why don't you continue trying to distract me.

And yet again, she demonstrated the depth of her acuity. He

supposed he wasn't being particularly subtle about his intentions, but he hadn't been trying to be obvious either. *I shouldn't be telling you this.*

I know.

You shouldn't be reading my thoughts, either.

I'm not. They're like... well, they were *like a megaphone announcement.*

Now that wasn't fair. How had she managed to turn the tables on him and use his own words from earlier that day in the parking garage against him? Fine. How had she put it? In for a penny, in for a pound.

He double-checked his mental shields to ensure she couldn't hear anything he didn't want her to. *All right. Fine. A coterie's influence can be determined on many levels, such as the number of its members, like Zenobia's major green.*

You mean the bitch?

Yes. The bitch. The Royal Coterie has the most members with the strongest magic.

Which makes them dangerous to annoy.

That was an understatement and definitely something he wasn't going to go into details about. The knot between her shoulders was just starting to ease, he didn't want to scare her about Regis's predilections. *A coterie's power can also be determined by a significant city or geographical region controlled in the humans' realm. The Major Brown controls Newgate, where the main gate to Court is.*

But the most important indicator of power was whether a coterie was in or out of favor with Prince Regis.

As if he could read Hunter's thoughts, Nero, doyen of the Major Black and Regis's favorite, met Anaea's gaze and raised a glass in salute. Light shimmered from the streaks of silver at his temples in his immaculately short-cropped dark hair. He raised a black eyebrow, drawing emphasis to his dark, hard eyes.

Anaea maintained eye contact without prompting until Nero dropped the eyebrow, sneered, and downed his drink.

Do the same, Hunter said.

I was planning on it. She took a sip, letting the wine spread across her tongue.

Nero and his coterie were a prime example of power through royal favor. Before dragons discovered Newgate's dimensional instability, Bath in England had been the primary gate into Court's inter-dimensional space. There were other unstable pockets, Cadiz in Spain, Xi'an in China, but none as unstable as Newgate. As a result, dragons who couldn't open anchored gates before now could, giving almost half of the population freedom to move between Court and the human realm without assistance. Bath lost significance and the black coterie that had controlled it was politically weakened, opening the way for Nero to sweet-talk Regis into turning his minor black coterie into the Major Black.

You don't want to have a conversation with that drake.

Nero leaned over to a young woman in a black strapless gown, her hair artfully piled atop her head. Hunter couldn't tell if she was his new Third, or just eye-candy.

I don't think I want a conversation with anyone.

Probably not. But Nero is the worst person here for us. He's a Traditionalist.

Anaea took another sip of wine. *And that means?*

He'll kill you if he discovers what you are.

Could you get any more medieval?

That's probably an accurate analogy. Think of the doyens as lords or dukes. They've sworn their allegiance to the crown, the coterie members have sworn their allegiance to their doyen. A doyen will do anything to protect their members, or a good one will. Some drakes, like Nero, believe the only way to keep us safe is to keep us hidden. Any human who knows about us is a liability and must be eliminated.

On top of that, Anaea had earth magic, which would make the Traditionalists fear her even more. But he wasn't going to point that out. Her earth magic connection was still uncertain, and maybe when he left her it would go dormant again. Regardless, even though she could only call fire and couldn't cast spells, which technically made her a mage and not a sorcerer, Nero and Regis, and many others for that matter, would demand her death. Which meant once Hunter transferred out of Anaea's body he wouldn't be able to see her again. He couldn't risk someone like Nero finding out about her.

It stung just thinking about it. Irrationally, he wanted to spend more time with her, real time to get to know her better. Which was ridiculous. How much better could he know her? He was already in her body, sharing her thoughts. But there was something about Anaea's spirit that compelled him and teased his primal dragon nature to hoard and protect.

Gig stood from a table at the back and sauntered up to the dais with exaggerated confidence, drawing Hunter's attention. What the heck was the kid up to? He looked... ridiculous. There wasn't any other way to put it. His clothes and hair seemed more unkempt than when he was in Tobias's office and he'd pushed out his chest, likely in an attempt to make himself look bigger, but it only drew more attention to his lanky build.

"Hi, Hunter." Gig leaned against the table, placing his hands on the top. "That was a great fight." When he leaned back, a tiny *ensi* coin remained, half-hidden by the flower arrangement.

Of all the stupid times to show a coin—

The damned things were dangerous.

Anaea reached for it. *What is this?*

An ensi *coin. It represents support for political maneuvering.* Usually for overthrowing a doyen and taking control of a coterie. *And before you ask, no I'm not interested in gaining more power.* The coins had once been used in early *pahars* where each doyen and their seconds presented the coins to King Constantine. Funny how the *ensi* tradition had stopped after Regis had proclaimed his father crazy and took the throne in 1521.

Slide it back, but be subtle about it. If anyone sees it both of us... all of us will be arrested. They'd likely be tortured then reborn for treason, but he wasn't going to mention that to Anaea.

Anaea placed her finger on the coin and inched it back to Gig.

Disappointment flashed across his face. But before she could say anything, Tobias stepped up to the head table and Gig's expression jumped to panic. Tobias would certainly turn them over in a heartbeat.

Take the coin. Hide it. Hide it now!

Anaea scrambled to palm the coin, knocked over the flower arrangement, and spilled water across the tablecloth. Gig's eyes widened even more.

Tobias righted the vase and flowers. "I don't think I've ever seen a drake have so much trouble adjusting to a new body." He patted Gig's shoulder. The young dragon squeaked and fled back to the safety of his seat.

Ask him what he's doing here. Tobias hadn't been to a *pahar* dinner in centuries. These days he hardly left his office.

"Decided to join us for supper?" Anaea asked.

Tobias shrugged, the movement languid and completely danger-ous. "Strangely enough, I do get hungry. Besides, I have a feeling tonight's dinner will be interesting."

Anaea snorted. Interesting was overrated, she'd had more than enough of it lately, and didn't want any more. All the work Hunter had done with the lesson in dragon politics was evaporating.

"Enjoy your meat." Tobias flashed a hint of teeth and took his seat at the far end of the head table.

God, he terrifies me and I don't even know why.

Yes, she did, but Hunter wasn't going to point it out to her. Tobias frightened her because he was a big bad dragon hiding in a human suit. When she was safe, Hunter was going to tear the limbs from whoever was responsible for this mess. The thought was starting to become a mantra. If he thought about the situation, it reeked more and more of Zenobia's handiwork. Stabbing a dragon in the back was just her style. But first things first. *Please tell me you have the coin.*

Yes.

Pocket it.

I barely have a dress, let alone pockets.

Okay, this was going to be a problem. He couldn't be caught with the coin.

Can you slip it into your shoe? he asked.

Anaea eased the coin into her shoe, her gaze darting over the room.

No one appeared to notice, although Hunter wouldn't be sure if anyone had until someone tried to manipulate or arrest him.

The room went quiet and all eyes turned to the entrance. Regis posed under the arch, resplendent in golden robes. He flicked a finger and a woman, naked save for the flowers in her hair, danced down the aisle, scattering white rose petals. He followed, strutting more like a peacock than the drake he was.

A drake without a coterie was a dead drake. Really.

Regis settled on his throne and leaned toward Hunter. "I think you're overdressed."

Anaea raised an eyebrow and let her gaze travel over the voluminous robes. The man was covered from neck to ankle.

"It was what I was provided," she said before Hunter could feed her an answer.

Hunter held his mental breath. There was no right way to answer Regis. Anaea's response was as good as any.

Regis sighed. "I'll have to look into that." He raised a hand and the meat was brought in. The cow was a good size. It would feed the Royal Coterie and the doyens of the coteries: counseling, major, and minor. The animal rolled its large brown eyes. They always did, as if the creatures could sense it wasn't surrounded by humans but by predators.

One of Regis's guards presented the ceremonial sword to him. He nodded his blessing and selected Nero, as always, to swing the killing blow. Nero raised the blade and Anaea tensed.

Shit.

Her stomach roiled.

He should have warned her, he'd just gotten distracted and—

Drink your wine. Fast.

So I have something to throw up?

So no one sees I'm upset.

She pressed the glass to her lips and stared into the liquid.

The room erupted into cheers and roars.

It's dead, isn't it?

Please tell me you're not a vegetarian. That would make the evening complicated on so many levels.

No. But I don't butcher cows in the middle of dinner parties.

A servant placed a plate of raw cow in front of her. Hunter could feel the bile burning the back of her throat.

And I cook it first. She finished her wine and called for a refill. *Please tell me we can leave before I have to eat this.*

It would be rude not to partake. But given the situation, he doubted Anaea would be able to stomach it. *Tell Regis you need to prepare for the ceremony and leave.*

She shoved back her chair.

"You're not leaving?" Regis asked.

"I need to get ready for the ceremony."

Regis narrowed his eyes.

Maintain eye contact.

She leveled her gaze on him.

He might be prince, but you're the better man... woman... whatever.

Regis looked away first. "You've just done the ceremony so many times before."

"Doesn't mean I still shouldn't prepare."

Good. Now go before he can think of anything else.

Anaea stood and smoothed the sides of her dress. She caught Grey's gaze, who gave an ever-so-slight nod.

Good girl.

Someone at the back of the room among the minor coteries yelled, and a young drake leapt up. "I challenge you."

The room erupted into chaotic babble.

You've got to be kidding me. Zenobia must have goaded the fool into action because he'd neglected all the fancy phrasing to call a *wasu tahazu.*

Anaea's heart skipped a beat, then pounded. *What do we do?*

Well, he wasn't going to put her through another *wasu tahazu.* Damn it. He didn't want to put her through anything else, but something had to be done.

Grab the steak knife and confront him. These challenges were going to end now, and he didn't care if he broke tradition or the rules or whatever.

Anaea clenched the knife, hidden along her forearm. Anger flooded her. Good. He was angry, too. She needed to get angry. It would make everything more believable.

She strode around the table and leapt off the dais.

Get him to come to you. You'll need to do this fast.

She gave a slight nod. "You want to challenge me?"

The man smirked and sauntered up to her. He towered, head and shoulders, over her, but she didn't shrink back. Something had snapped. Whatever had made her tremble earlier now shook her with rage.

He stepped so close that if Anaea took a deep breath, they'd brush chests. "Yeah, little girl, I challenge you."

Now cut his throat.

Fine. Grim resignation washed over him. He hated what he asked of her, but there was no way in hell he was going to take her into the arena again.

She grabbed the man's shirt and slashed his throat open without warning and without flinching. It stung to think she was numb to the violence. But as he thought that, he felt her shudder and sensed her iron grip on her stomach keeping her from throwing up.

She shoved the drake back. He fell on his ass, his mouth working like a dying fish. Blood poured from the wound. She'd cut deep, hitting both arteries. Good.

The drake's gaze grew glassy, but that wouldn't last for long. He stared at the red stain seeping down his shirt, then back up to Anaea.

"I'm done with challenges." She held up the bloody knife and leveled a hard stare at those in the great hall.

Mother of All, she was fabulous. An Amazon like her namesake. And in that moment, he realized he could fall in love with this woman, regardless of the fact that she was a human.

Regis stood, his chair squealing against the floor, loud in the stunned silence. "There are ways things are done."

A distant heat rippled through Hunter. Magic. Hot, fiery magic. It poured into Anaea's hand, covering it in undulating blue flame. He could feel her intent to end this and kill the challenger.

You can't kill him.

Then I'll use the medallion. The words growled through her as if she were a true drake.

You can't.

Why not?

There are some rules even I'm not willing to break. Mother of All, help him. If he broke the Handmaiden's personal mandate to him now, to never take a soul indiscriminately, he might not be allowed to leave Court for years, and they would fall for certain to the soul sickness.

Fine. What do I do?

Make him rescind. Scare him into it.

The flame on her hand billowed and the drake on the ground whimpered.

"There are rules, Hunter," Regis said.

Even Grey looked as if he was going to have a fit.

She leveled her gaze on her challenger.

He inched back, smearing his blood on the floor.

"Rescind."

The drake whimpered. His gaze flew about the room.

Why couldn't the fool just call uncle? Even if he was almost healed enough to fight, with Anaea's fire already called, he didn't stand a chance.

"Rescind," she said again, her voice low. Just like Hunter's would have been if he had control of the situation.

It made his stomach churn. How much of himself had imprinted on her? She hadn't been like this before the *wasu tahazu*.

The drake stared at the tables where the Major Black Coterie sat. Nero's expression was flat, unreadable. Interesting. Perhaps Hunter's initial assumption about Zenobia had been wrong. Nero wasn't who he'd expected, but he wasn't entirely a surprise, either.

"The *wasu tahazu* must be done properly," Regis said.

Anaea shoved her hand against the drake's face. He screamed and she eased back, leaving a charred handprint that oozed fluid. "I said, rescind."

The drake moaned. "I take it back."

"I can't hear you."

"I take it back."

The flame on her hand vanished. "Anyone else want to challenge me?"

Silence filled the room.

14

Anaea stormed out of the feast hall and back to Hunter's suite, slamming the door behind her. Hot, ferocious rage consumed her. She wanted that man dead, had wanted to burn the life out of him. She wanted to wreak vengeance for all the hurt laid upon her, and she'd finally cracked. Her soul was bare before her and she no longer liked what she was. Blood, blood, and more blood. She was bathed in it. She drank it, reveled in it. She was a beast.

No.

The word was soft, gentle. Hunter had merely thought it, not spoken it… or projected it, or however they communicated.

She'd done what she'd had to do.

Grief and shame washed over her, but it wasn't hers.

She pressed her forehead to the door. God, what was happening to her? Please let this be a dream, a bad, bad dream.

Her breath hitched in her throat.

But it wasn't a dream. It was all too real.

Trembling shook her. She hugged herself but couldn't stop the tremors.

He whispered her name. *Anaea.*

"I—" Her teeth chattered. "I—" *I can't—* She couldn't think, couldn't move, couldn't stop shaking. She'd thought she was strong, but she wasn't. She couldn't even recognize herself anymore. There was something horrible within her.

That's me, Hunter said, his mental voice thick with regret.

No. It came from within.

From the memories I gave you.

But she couldn't completely believe that. She'd already gone to terrible lengths to save her life. Lord help anyone who threatened her or those she cared about. She would rain fury upon them. She knew it deep within her. These awful events merely galvanized that part of her.

We don't blame the mother bear for protecting her young. Or the lioness. Or the soldier.

I'm not a bear or a lion. She sniffed. *I'm not a soldier.*

But you are a warrior. You've faced every creature's greatest fear.

She sniffed again. *Yep. And I'm on the verge of tears.*

A true warrior is allowed to cry.

Oh, and you've cried.

Sure.

She could tell he was keeping something back. *Really?*

Well, Grey has.

She snorted. *At least I'm in good company.*

Warmth and fraternal affection washed through her.

Grey is very good company. Now, if I promise not to look will you take that bath you wanted earlier?

She didn't want to think about what she was or wasn't, or what she had done. But for now, Hunter had blunted the edge of her panic. He seeped understanding and compassion and a little confidence into her. For a moment, she felt as if she had some of his deep affection that he carried for his friend.

Even if she knew, without a doubt, that he'd try to sneak a peek. He was, after all, still a man.

GREY STAGGERED AWAY FROM THE FEAST HALL, HIS NECK BURNING, HIS breath hitching in his throat just like when he'd been attacked back in 1946. The room roared with wild conversation from the shocked drakes at the dinner. Hunter had been amazing. Even stuck in that woman's emaciated body he'd taken on that young drake and won. But the sight of that slit throat and all the blood released the cascade of painful memories Grey had been struggling to keep at bay.

Mother of All, he couldn't bear it any longer, and he couldn't wait for the mess with Hunter to be resolved. He needed the Handmaiden's soothing magic now before he drowned in remembrances.

With the hall seeping in and out of darkness, Grey gated to the door to the Handmaiden's chambers, not trusting he'd last the ten-minute walk to the other side of Court. This time she had to do it. She had to rebirth him. It was worse than any time before, although this was the longest he'd held out before seeking her help. The attack in the alley had only been sixty-nine years ago, but it felt an eternity to him. The agony of that knife slicing his throat. The heat of his blood pumping down his chest, mixing with the icy rain.

The memories of everything, all he'd done and survived as a human, were just too much. Every wound, physical and emotional, was ready for crystal-clear recall.

"How fast can you heal?" they had hissed at him, knowing he wasn't a fast healer, not like other dragons, not like Hunter. Certainly not fast enough to recover before they decapitated him. The pain had even made it impossible to create a gate, the one thing he was really good at.

He pounded on the Handmaiden's door.

In truth, he hadn't healed at all. Not on the inside.

She had to do it. This was a practical, necessary use of the spell, although he knew she'd argue it wasn't. Everyone else saw rebirth as a punishment because a drake lost everything: status, hoard, wealth, and memories. But Mother of All, Grey would give everything for the fresh start.

The door cracked open. He took that as permission to enter and rushed in. "Please."

He didn't need to say more. They'd had this conversation count-less times, and every one he could recall in perfect detail if he put his mind to it, which he didn't. Mother of All, just turn his memory off.

"Please." He couldn't bear to remember in excruciating detail every bad thing he'd experienced. "Please just rebirth me and make it stop."

"And what about Hunter?" The Handmaiden sat in the chamber's only chair. Her grimoire lay on the table beside her—the only other furniture in the room.

"Hunter can take care of himself. He's a big boy."

"That's not what I hear anymore." The corners of her eyes soft-ened. The room's magical illumination shimmered in her salt-and-pepper hair, and the hint of lines around her eyes, denoting her false age, made her appear as profoundly wise as she really was.

"Do it tomorrow after the others." He jerked his gaze to the walls. He couldn't look at her when she wore that expression. It was too close to pity. The walls were bare, smooth, perfect, breathed into existence with a thought. No tool marks, nothing. "Tobias won't care if I bring in another body."

"No." She said it so matter-of-factly.

His frustration exploded with the verbal blow, white and hot in his chest. He rushed at her, raising a fist. Her silver gaze met his and held it.

Then she blinked, her lids closing and opening as if in slow motion, and blue power flickered over her eyes. But she didn't cast anything. She didn't move, didn't subvocalize, not that she needed to. A true sorcerer who wasn't magically depleted could gather energy and will her spell into existence.

In that moment, she seemed more than just a dragon. She was otherworldly, divine. Perhaps it was because she was a true sorcerer, more powerful than any other dragon. Perhaps it was how she kept herself apart from dragonkind, isolated in her magically shielded suites, not part of any coterie. And perhaps it was because Grey didn't know what color she was. Sure, she gave the impression of being a silver drake, and most times so did her aura. But while other dragons accepted that, Grey couldn't because he couldn't remember her from before the Great Scourge. And yet, when he wasn't desperate, he adored everything about her, even her mystery.

More energy crackled over her eyes.

Grey's knees buckled and he collapsed at her feet. Surely attacking the Handmaiden was evidence he'd lived too long. His eyes burned.

The Handmaiden ran a hand over his hair. A gentle stroke. Then another. Energy tickled his skin, seeping her soothing magic into his flesh. It eased the knot in his chest and his memories grew distant and murky, as they always did when her spell slipped into him.

"I barely have any magic." How could he call himself a dragon, a warrior, when he felt such relief over forgetting?

She shushed his weak argument. "We've already discussed this."

"My memory isn't magic. I don't have to cast, it's always on." But the ache that had propelled him to her chamber no longer filled him.

"Just because it's 'on,' as you put it, doesn't mean it's not magic." She hooked a finger under his chin and raised his head. "Now, I have a job for you."

"Mother of All, you have a request?" Since he'd sworn himself to her just after the Ninth Crusade, she'd refused all but the most basic services—although many at Court assumed he was being used in one very particular way.

"Don't get tart with me." She swatted playfully at his head, stood, and headed toward her inner chamber. Probably where she kept her hoard, but since no one, not even Grey, had ever seen inside, or managed to get past the wards on the entrance, no one knew for certain.

"What can I do for my lady?"

She turned, swishing her robes. The toe of a soft brown shoe flashed beneath the fabric and then was covered. "And now you flatter."

Grey frowned. The Handmaiden never wore shoes. Unless she was leaving Court. And she hadn't done that since 1521 when Regis had taken the throne.

"You will need to deliver my book."

"Your book?" He glanced at the grimoire. He doubted she used it often, not since she'd created Court and had needed to conserve her earth magic by using power words instead of exhausting herself by willing spells into existence. But the incantations within the book, honed over the years, harnessed magic with extraordinary force and in the wrong hands could be used to subjugate dragonkind completely. However, if she planned to leave Court and feared she wouldn't return, someone needed to take over the rebirthing ceremonies. But no other dragon had that kind of power. Only a true sorcerer could cast that spell.

"What about the ceremonies? If the souls are left for more than a couple of days without a vessel, even in the medallion while at Court, they'll lose cohesion and can't be reborn."

She raised an eyebrow and more energy flickered over her eyes. "Don't worry about the ceremonies. They will be taken care of."

"Yes, Handmaiden." Of course she knew the souls could be lost. She'd been the one to discover that, and he doubted she'd forget something so important. "To whom should I deliver the grimoire and how soon?"

A wicked smile pulled at her lips and she touched a finger to his forehead. "You'll figure it out."

"I— What?"

Energy tingled over his nose and cheeks as she set her spell.

"I see. When the time is right, your spell will activate and tell me who to give it to."

"You *have* been reading my journals."

"It's the only thing you've asked of me." If only she'd require more of him. Perhaps more purpose to his life could distract him. Flirting was fine, but it didn't fill the void. Unfortunately, his aura sight couldn't distinguish between dragons and mages so the Asar Nergal wouldn't take him. And while he suspected Tobias had a team that reported on the happenings in Court, Grey wasn't interested in spying on his friends.

"And I ask it of you again," the Handmaiden said, drawing Grey's attention back to her. She held out her hands, palms up, and a journal from her secret library materialized on them. It was thick, bound in black leather with a gold '1477' inscribed on the spine.

"I've read that one." He'd read them all, and because of his so-called magic, could remember the contents of every single one. Although so soon after her soothing spell, he'd need to concentrate to recall the details of the book, but the risk of losing himself to his memories was slim.

She held out the book. "I know. It will be important soon."

"How soon?"

A sly smile pulled at her lips. "Read it again."

Right. In her own good, mysterious time, just like delivering the grimoire.

"It's the record of dragon involvement leading up to the Spanish Inquisition." One of her more exciting reads, but having lived through that time and read the book five times already, not something he wanted to revisit anytime soon. "My lady, if you require, I can tell you the twentieth letter of the twelfth line on every page."

She pressed the book into his hands. "Three hundred and nine."

The image of the page flashed into his mind unbidden. "N."

Her smile curled open in full, revealing her teeth in a sexual challenge.

"Would my lady like any of my other services?" She wouldn't accept. It was just the game they played. But it was still fun to flirt, even if he wished it was Capri. Besides, the Handmaiden was still a female. Just because she represented everything that was sacred to dragonkind didn't mean she was without mundane desires.

"For now reread the journal and deliver my grimoire when the time comes." She blew him a kiss and withdrew into her chamber.

He sighed. Right. Reread one of the many bad times of his life and wait for whatever spell the Handmaiden had put in his head to activate. Until then, he had a body-sharing Hunter to deal with, and the odds were bad the Handmaiden wouldn't notice. Here was hoping she'd show the same compassion to Hunter she'd shown Grey.

15

Zenobia strode up the last step of the sweeping staircase to the balcony overlooking the grove and squeezed the railing beneath her palm. This forgotten cavern on the edge of Court, magically able to sustain vegetation, was the perfect place to build and hide her strike force. Containing a large clearing encircled by shaggy pines and majestic oaks, she'd cut off the only entrance, making it accessible only by an unanchored gate so no one could accidentally stumble upon them. Most days she loved watching the twenty-seven trusted members of her inner circle train the fifty human mages they'd created, but not today. It was proving more difficult than anticipated to acquire the medallion, and now she'd lost Pearl and Welkin. Why wouldn't Hunter just die?

The stone under her fingers cracked. Dust drifted down to the moss-covered floor below. She had to have the medallion. The coup was only days away, and without that symbol of power more drakes would oppose her, threatening her success. And she'd seen what Regis did to drakes when their plots against him failed.

Her heart ached, and she shoved the thought aside. Now was not the time to wallow. Her lover's plan had been good. Abduct transients from around the world, particularly those from third world countries who wouldn't be missed, and find a drake who could enspell them to obey commands. Done and done. Then came the risky bit, body-sharing with the humans until they connected with the earth's magic, because well, she could scrounge the earth looking for a natural human mage, but one hadn't been seen in two thousand years and body-sharing was faster. Her lover, however, had made the fatal error of body hopping himself and getting caught before he could finalize his attack. She wouldn't be so foolish. There was too much riding on this, and as much as the Handmaiden wanted all souls saved, a select few, like Hunter's, were going to be sacrificed. It was just the cost of doing business.

Kijani, her Second, and Howel gated onto the balcony a few feet from her, framed by the stone arch to the hall behind them. They were a study in opposites, Kijani's dark skin, short hair, and tall muscular stature, beside Howel's diminutive build, messy brown hair and slightly tanned skin. And while Howel stood straight-backed, he was missing the age and power that Kijani radiated. That, and the still oozing handprint Hunter had seared onto Howel's flesh, eliminated any sense of the young drake's competence. The fool couldn't even follow her simple command to call a challenge, and then he had backed down. At least he'd stuck to the plan and looked at Nero instead of her, redirecting any suspicions Hunter might have. Obviously, the youngling couldn't be trusted with anything more complicated than creating human mages for her strike force.

She would never again welcome another unknown drake to her inner circle. Certainly not someone she hadn't approached herself. She'd only invited two dozen young drakes, those who were the most discontented with Regis's rule, but Kijani had vouched for Howel, and she'd trusted her Second.

"It was rash to challenge Hunter in the feast hall."

Howel shifted from one foot to the other. "Yes, Doyen, but I—"

She jerked her chin and Kijani nudged Howel into the passage behind them. A lesson needed to be taught before he could screw up again.

"Howel, do you know where we are?"

The young drake shook his head.

She hissed her power word and with her earth magic drew a pebble from the ceiling. With a flick of her mind, she sent it skittering down the hall into darkness, drawing a moan from within the walls.

Howel's Adam's apple bobbed, and his eyes grew wide.

Kijani had dubbed this passage the Hall of Lament, a place where she imprisoned those she could no longer trust in the granite walls. Since she didn't have the medallion, she couldn't have them reborn and while souls would be lost during the coup, they didn't have to be lost now. Besides, this was so much more effective as an object lesson.

They stopped at an alcove, sarcophagus sized.

"I told you to challenge Hunter."

"I did."

"But not in the feast hall." She hissed her power word again and whipped a tendril of granite around his legs. He squeaked. It echoed down the hall, drawing more moans and cries from those encased in the walls. "And then you rescinded."

She surged the granite to his waist and shoved him into the alcove, the granite's movement fluid under her control.

"Doyen, please. I—" He clawed at the rock encasing his lower body. "Please."

The cries of those imprisoned turned to wails.

She pressed her palm to Howel's sternum, forcing him to lean back. "If I leave you just a crack for air, I'm told you'll survive for centuries."

"No, Doyen." He drew desperate gasps and his chest heaved under her palm. He clawed at her hand, digging rents in her flesh, but as fast as the pain flared, her soul magic healed her.

"Your human body will waste away but your dragon spirit will keep you alive, on the edge of death, in constant agony." She inched the rock higher.

"No, please! I'm sorry!" Tears streamed down his cheeks.

Mother of All, he was disgusting. No true drake begged. And they certainly didn't whimper and cry like Howel. She yanked the rock away and he collapsed at her feet. "Perhaps you'll be more use to me making mages… if it doesn't make you soul sick."

Howel babbled hysterically, but she didn't wait for a response. Kijani would see it done if he didn't want to take Howel's place in the alcove. She strode back to her balcony, the wails grating on her nerves.

Kijani followed.

Good puppy. She needed his abilities, even if he was a lousy judge of character. But for all of this to work, there was one thing she really needed. "Get me that medallion."

"With Hunter in Court that will be more difficult," he said.

She hissed her power word and with a flick of her thoughts jerked the rock under his feet, throwing him back into the Hall of Lament. "I don't need you to state the obvious. I need you to get the medallion."

"Yes, Doyen."

"Make sure you use those drakes who've recently changed their allegiance so it's not blatant we're making a move."

Kijani scrambled to his feet and gave a curt nod.

She was so close. Soon she would have the throne and dragonkind would once again take its rightful place at the top of the food chain.

16

Wind caressed Anaea's face and the ground slid by far below her. She was flying, her body held aloft by large, leathery wings that caught and adjusted to the air currents. And while she was flesh and bone, weighted and solid, she felt buoyed, supple, magical.

In that moment, she realized she was dreaming. The current she'd been riding dissipated and she faltered, dipped, then glided into the next updraft and rose higher and higher until she skimmed the bottom of the clouds.

So what if it was just a dream. It was the most pleasant thing that had happened to her in days, perhaps even months. There was no appeal to waking up, either. Hunter's people… dragons… whatever, were crazy. Every single one of them. No matter how hard Hunter had tried to intellectualize the situation for her, she couldn't deny the terrifying truth about them. After that dinner, she couldn't get through the rebirth ceremony fast enough. Sure they looked human, but there was nothing human about them. They were predators. All Hunter's friend, while nice enough, still gave off the predator vibe.

Even Hunter had darkness about him. And Anaea had the feeling he was the most dangerous of them all.

There she went, making assumptions again. She didn't know

anything about Hunter, not really. As much as he'd been forth-coming about what he really was, she still felt he was giving her the watered-down reality of their situation. But perhaps that was a good thing.

Yet even with his memories swirling through her head like a montage of the world's history of violence, she felt there was some-thing more to him than just a predator. She felt it in her gut and at the back of her mind. It was like a glimmer seen from the corner of her eye that disappeared when she tried to get a better look. If only she could put her finger on what that was.

Of course, maybe that was just her mind trying to justify how Hunter's presence made her feel. She couldn't possibly be attracted to a cold-blooded killer dragon. She wasn't that kind of girl. She couldn't be. There had to be something more to him. If only he'd let her in long enough to figure out what that was.

But after the last couple of hours, she didn't know what she was anymore. There was blood on her hands now. Lots of it. And if confronted again she knew she would defend herself.

She stretched her wings, reveling in the weightlessness of flight. She could almost imagine her soul was weightless, too.

Miniature houses dotted the landscape, surrounded by a patch-work of yellow and green fields. A narrow road wound through the fields into the villages and disappeared into the horizon. Crisp, fresh air flooded her nostrils. It was beautiful, wondrous. She had never experienced anything like this before, so it had to be one of Hunter's memories. A good, non-violent one, at that.

Sudden, sharp pain pierced her chest. She gasped and a burning sensation rippled over her skin. It subsided for a moment, no more than a heartbeat, then flared, hotter and more intense. It zinged through her, igniting sinew and bone.

The acrid scent of smoldering flesh stung her nostrils. She tried to shake the sensation from her body, twisting and turning in the sky with strong beats of her wings. But the fire increased, filling her with hot agony. She was burning from the inside out and there was nothing she could do about it.

Something on her chest cracked and scales fell to the ground. The soft skin underneath peeled and burst.

She screamed, hearing a roar instead. Fire exploded from her mouth, and smoke poured from her nostrils and yet, in only the way of dreams, she knew the fire and smoke were hers, not whatever consumed her.

An updraft forced her away from the ground. Her wings trembled, and the consuming blaze blurred her vision. But she couldn't land, not so close to the humans. And yet, each movement, even the minuscule ones to keep aloft, sent sharp agony straight to her heart.

More scales blackened, cracked, and peeled away. She strained forward, desperate to get away and find safety. She refused to be the next to die.

She beat at the air, each stroke more unbearable than the one before. Her breath caught in her throat, the ground below swam in and out of focus, growing darker and darker. Just a little farther. She could do it.

The fire pierced her heart and she couldn't move, couldn't breathe. All she could feel was pain. An all-consuming pain.

And then she plummeted toward the earth. The ground hurtled toward her faster and faster. She squeezed her eyes shut, unwilling to witness that last moment of her life.

But she didn't hit the ground. There was no excruciating moment as every bone in her body shattered or as her skin and muscles burst from the impact.

She cracked one eye open. The leafy canopy of the twin maples in her mother's backyard stretched above her. The hammock lay at the base of the one on the left. She'd torn it down when her mother had died, making Anaea an orphan at twenty-five. The word 'orphan' had weighed on her. It weighed on her now with a profound emptiness. She was alone, estranged from her mother's family, and unacquainted with her father's. Perhaps that was why she'd been so eager to love John, her husband. But that hadn't turned out right, either. Not her marriage, or her life, or her—

Strong hands slid up her arms, drawing shivers, and the heat of a body pressed against her back.

Hunter.

Guilt twisted, fast and fleeting, through her that she'd assume, even want, Hunter to be the man of her dreams rather than her college sweetheart, Mark. But something about Hunter inspired a desire within her that Mark never had, regardless that he wasn't, spiritly speaking, human. Besides, Mark didn't deserve to bear witness to her too-soon death. Maybe Hunter could just be a fabulous fling. Besides, it wasn't even real. It was just a dream.

"Anaea." His lips brushed her neck.

Surely, she could allow herself a small fantasy.

He kissed a trail along her jaw, his breath caressing her cheek. Desire burned low within her.

It had been too long since she'd been with a man, and even longer since a man had touched her with passion. All she yearned for was to feel normal and loved again. Just for a moment.

His mouth was tantalizingly close to hers. He flicked his tongue against the edge of her bottom lip. She shivered, straining to turn into his embrace. Just a little more. She hadn't realized how much she'd wanted this until it was offered.

Reaching up, she ran her fingers through his short hair to the back of his head and drew him closer, tentatively touching his lips with hers. They were soft, welcoming, waiting.

She released the breath she hadn't realized she'd been holding. This was a dream, her dream. No fantasy lover would refuse her. Here she was whole and well. Here she was anything she wanted to be. And what she was right now, was hot for this man.

She pressed her lips against his, needing, burning. He matched her desperate passion, licking and sucking, as she tried to kiss away all her heartache and pain at her husband's betrayal, her cancer, the deaths by her hands, and her lonely existence. It was all devoured, swirled in a fiery frenzy of breath and lip and tongue.

17

C apri rubbed her temples. Police tape had been strung across the room door at the Rest Well Hotel, which meant the Elmsville P.D. had beaten her to the scene, and she had to go to the police station to finish this cleanup. Hunter was definitely going to pay for leaving such a mess.

Admittedly, she didn't have anything better to do than work, since she wasn't interested in the *pahar* or dragon politics. But it had been difficult enough dealing with the detective at the hospital. He hadn't believed she and her team were FBI—most didn't given that their unit was pretty obscure within the organization. Flashing her badge usually did the trick but this detective had remained skeptical and she'd had to use her earth magic to influence him into releasing control of the investigation and handing over his notes.

Swipe mumbled his power words and made a discreet gesture, casting his magic and removing every trace that a dragon had even been in the hotel room. Less than a hundred years ago not even Swipe had known exactly what he did, but with the advent of forensic sciences, they now knew he cleaned up everything: footprints, blood, fingerprints, hairs, and DNA. Anything that could lead to questions and reveal dragonkind.

After a few minutes, Swipe blew out a long breath. "Done."

"Good." She wanted to get this over with. Facing Mr. Annoying Detective a second time would require even more magic than usual, since meeting him twice in such a short period made things more complicated. It would make her headache worse and the painkiller she'd taken half an hour ago still hadn't kicked in. Damn that her soul magic didn't seem to heal earth-magic-induced headaches.

They left the hotel and drove to the Elmsville police station. Swipe parked the company's black SUV at the curb, and Capri got out. She checked her badge and sidearm.

"Shooting won't make this simpler," Swipe said in his new southern drawl. The green drake was trying on a Texan identity this time, but his turns of phrase kept revealing his Old World background.

"No, but it would make me feel better."

He barked a laugh and flashed her some teeth. "Don't take too long."

She showed a hint of teeth back at him. "Look who's talking." His job could take much longer than hers, depending on how much evidence had been collected.

Swipe shrugged and headed into the building to get as close as he could to the evidence locker to work his magic. At least he looked the part of an FBI special agent: mid-thirties, blond, well-built, and always wearing a suit. If anyone stopped him he could talk his way out of the situation. Gig, the other member of their team, was another issue altogether. He always looked like he'd just woken up in his jeans and T-shirt for the third day in a row. And as much as she begged him to cut his mane of black hair, she found the shag charming—which she wasn't going to admit to anyone.

Thank goodness she hadn't needed his earth magic ability to communicate with technology on the assignment and had left him at Court. Hopefully that would mean one less thing that could go wrong.

After a moment to ensure her temper was in check, she climbed the concrete steps to the front door, entered, and strode across the small foyer to the officer at the reception desk. He was middle-aged, probably near retirement, and the type most likely in Capri's experience to question her presence. And there were always questions. How could the FBI know of anything so fast? What was her jurisdiction and the nature of her team, and why had no one ever really heard of her? It got worse if the investigation dragged on, which, with the mess Hunter had left, was growing more likely by the minute.

"Yes?" The cop sounded bored.

Bored was good. She could work with bored.

She flashed her identification. "I'd like to talk to the detective in charge of the investigation at the Rest Well Hotel."

He stared at her. She got that a lot. She knew she looked professional in her suit, particularly if she offset the color with her strawberry blond hair and blue eyes. But the fact that she was stuck in a body not quite five feet tall made everyone think she was a child—usually Swipe's if they arrived together. Maybe she should add some gray to her hair.

And maybe everyone else should just live with it.

"The detective, please." She subvocalized her power word and slid a thread of magic into his mind. *The lady will stop bothering you if you page the detective in charge. It's easy. A simple phone call. Besides, no one wanted to be on the bad side of the FBI.*

She fortified her magic by forcing a smile, and the man picked up the phone.

"You can wait on the bench." He nodded at an uncomfortable steel beam intended to be a bench running across the back of the lobby.

"Thanks."

He had a ten-second conversation with someone on the phone before hanging up and staring at his computer, an obvious show of ignoring her.

Fine, as long as whoever controlled her case showed up. Boy, did she ever want to blame Hunter. But Gig was right. Having to take that woman's body must have been an act of desperation, since, speaking from personal experience, a human female's strength was not an advantage in a sword fight. And Hunter's human didn't look healthy. Not that the dead ever did look healthy, but his seemed particularly worse for wear. His soul magic was probably working overtime healing whatever was wrong with him, and that likely didn't help his situation either.

The door to the station's inner sanctum opened and her heart leapt in her chest. It wasn't Mr. Annoying Detective. It was Eric.

She swallowed at the constriction in her throat. Logic dictated it couldn't be him. Their affair had been two human lifetimes ago. She'd snuck into Eric's funeral when old age had taken him. But the man's face, his square jaw, his eyes…

"I'm Detective Miller. What can I do for you, Special Agent?"

Those eyes still haunted her. The way he'd looked at her when she'd had to follow Regis's laws and leave within the appointed time frame. Above all else, dragonkind had to be kept a secret. It still hurt so much. And yet she still considered herself a part of the younger generation who insisted on living in the humans' realm. For centuries now, humans had blithely lived next door to dragons. Their favorite teacher, trusted accountant, and even lover could be a drake, and since there were too many of them, Regis couldn't stop them.

But she'd never take a human lover again. Not after Eric.

"Special Agent?" Miller's eyes narrowed.

"Jones," she croaked out, then mentally jerked herself back together and thrust a thread of magic into his mind. "I'll be taking over the investigation of the Rest Well Hotel." Life will be easier. No messy murder investigation.

"Dan mentioned something about you. What did you say your unit was?"

She pushed harder into his mind, cursing Dan. The obnoxious detective from earlier was still making her job difficult. Her unit's name didn't matter. They were legitimate—it helped to have a drake involved in the creation of the FBI—but their unit was so small most hadn't heard of them, so naming names usually didn't help.

"I'll need your notes," she said, trying to steer him back on topic.

"Sure." But he didn't sound certain.

She concentrated on her magic, but flashes of passionate nights with Eric flitted through her mind. The two men sounded so much alike. If she closed her eyes, she could imagine herself wrapped in Eric's embrace again.

"Let me buy you a coffee," he said.

Yes. Anything.

"What?" She dragged herself back to the conversation.

"Coffee, so I can talk you through my shorthand."

She glanced at the ratty old coffeemaker behind the reception desk. The usual station brew often ranged from bad to worse. She suspected Elmsville's wasn't any different.

"But not here," he said as if reading her mind.

Mother of All, she wanted to say yes. But the more time she spent with the man, the more difficult it would be to adjust his memory.

And yet, not impossible. Just a little time.

Surely she deserved a little something for herself. She'd never taken anything in the hundreds of years she'd worked for the North American Clean Team.

Besides, it was just coffee.

"Come on, it'll be faster if I take you through it." He flashed her a smile heartbreakingly similar to Eric's.

She never could say no to that smile. "Sure."

"Great." He rushed back into the secured area and returned with a file folder. "It's just across the street." He opened the front door and motioned her out.

The winter wind bit her cheeks and slipped down her collar but she didn't care. It had been too long since she'd pulled these memories out and wrapped herself within them.

Cars drove past, churning the morning's snowfall into brown slush. Headlights reflected white and red blobs on what little wet pavement was visible. They rushed across the street between a break in the traffic, dodging puddles to a twenty-four hour coffee shop across from the station. It had been buggies and early motor vehicles when she'd run across the street with Eric. She had felt light, free then. In love.

A chime on the door announced their entrance, and a pimple-faced teen glanced up. "The usual, detective?"

But she wasn't free. And she wasn't with Eric. He was dead.

Miller nodded. "And for the lady?"

"Coffee, black."

The teen filled their order, Miller paid, and they took a seat by the front window. The place was empty, but that wouldn't last long, not with such a prime location on Beaumont Street across from the police station.

Miller blew steam from his paper cup and took a slow sip.

Even his mannerisms were like Eric's. But perhaps that was just what she wanted to see, a means to flame the fantasy. That knowledge didn't stop her heart from beating just a little faster or her skin from tingling at the thought of his touch. She felt like a youngling, fresh hatched from the egg, and a part of her didn't care.

He glanced at her over the rim of his coffee. "So what does the FBI want with this case?"

"Straight to the point." And as much as she had momentarily fantasized that this was her old romance, it wasn't. Confusing romance, even just a remembered one, with business could get a drake in trouble.

"I like to finish what I start, not pass it along to someone."

"I'm not just someone." But she could tell that didn't matter, particularly in the way she wanted him to think of her.

"Yes, you're FBI." He didn't sound pleased.

This was going to take a lot more magic.

With a sigh, she subvocalized her power word. Her magic flared and so did her headache, but she didn't push into his mind right away. If this was going to stick, particularly with skeptical Dan back at the station for Miller to talk to, she needed the right moment to make the manipulation undetectable.

She took a sip of coffee. "The event at the Rest Well Hotel is connected to the incidents at the Queen Street Bridge and Memorial General."

"And you know this how?"

"This is one small part of a larger investigation we've been building for a while." She pushed a thread of power into his mind. It was a long-term investigation. Handing over the information would be helpful. He wanted to be helpful. He wasn't giving up, he was aiding the FBI.

"I'm not sure I see the connection."

She pushed harder. Pain radiated behind her eyes. "And I can't fill you in. It's a matter of national security."

"I'm not just some small-town cop." His tone darkened.

It sent shivers of anticipation through her. No, he wasn't just a cop. He was her Eric look-alike. If only he'd show a little teeth, she'd be completely turned on.

But she needed him compliant, not randy.

Mother of All, her head hurt. When was that painkiller going to kick in? Why was he being so difficult to manipulate? She took another sip of coffee to cover her discomfort. "I'm not the enemy."

He rubbed his face with his broad hands. "You're right. Elmsville just isn't the right speed for me."

"And what is your kind of speed?" She shouldn't have asked, but she couldn't help herself. She didn't feel good about shoving thoughts into his head. She wanted to feel sexy for him—even if he was just the image of her dead lover—and not like the manipulator she really was.

His eyes lit up and he raked a heated gaze over her. Guess he'd caught the innuendo in her question and had similar feelings. Her heart beat a quick tattoo at the thought.

No. This was not good. She shouldn't be flirting with him.

"If I hand over my notes, does that mean you'll have to leave right away?"

"Not necessarily." Her body tingled at the idea. She wanted to stay, but she couldn't and had to keep reminding herself of that.

Her magic billowed within his head and she gained control of his thoughts.

He jerked forward. "I haven't filed my report yet." His eyes glazed over and he shoved the file folder across the table to her. "Here's everything I've got."

Ice ate away her heated attraction. She was an awful, awful dragon. But the job had to be done.

Out of the corner of her eye she saw Swipe leave the station and head to the SUV. Thank God. She needed to get out of here before she did anything really stupid.

"Thank you." She made a final push into his head. He'd make a new case file and note that the FBI had taken over and that would be the end of it.

"It was a pleasure meeting you, Special Agent Jones." He stood and held out his hand.

She stared at it, afraid if she made contact she'd forget herself and let her longing consume her.

"The same." She took his hand, feeling slimy and horny all at the same time. Life just wasn't fair. It was obvious she was overdue for a lover, but at the moment, the only one interested in her was Grey. But that idea seemed too much like sleeping with her brother. Which was a shame because he was hot and a nice guy.

She rushed out of the coffee shop, leaving Miller inside, and headed to the SUV. Who she really wanted was Eric. She'd always wanted Eric. And her attraction to Miller was just the long-held dream, nothing more. She'd be fooling herself if she pursued anything. Besides, the more he saw her, the harder it would be to keep his questions about the investigation at bay. It would have been nice if he'd just been some Joe on the street. As it was, she'd just have to return home and try not to think sexy thoughts.

A naea woke tangled in a towel and Hunter's silk sheets, with the medallion by her cheek and the chain loose about her neck. One of her hands rested on her good breast and the other clutched her inner thigh. The clock by the bed said 6:53 a.m. It was getting close to dawn. Hunter's consciousness felt fuzzy, and when she gave him a mental nudge he mumbled something in a language she didn't recognize and seemed to roll over.

Still asleep, it seemed. Good, because she couldn't help thinking about that dream. And God, what a dream. She was liquid heat, caressed and loved by Hunter, no less. Perfect and whole. She'd never felt loved like that by anyone before, not even Mark.

Just thinking about it made her trembling and hot all over again. She wanted to go back. It wasn't fair that she was once again in her cold reality. But life wasn't fair. She knew that as well as anybody. Perhaps even more so. Besides, the Hunter of her dreams was who she wanted him to be, not who he was. She didn't belong in his world, and she was damaged goods about to hit her expiration date. She just wanted…

Her eyes burned. She blinked back the tears. She'd be damned if she'd cry any more.

She wanted what she couldn't have.

So get on with it already.

Hey, Hunter said, his voice thick with sleep. *You okay?*

She shoved all thoughts of the dream aside. Best if he didn't know. *You keep asking me that.*

Heat simmered through her. But she hadn't thought—

Oh, God. Her hands were on—

She yanked the sheets around her, heat of her own making flooding her face.

So we're going to play this game again, are we? His tone was steeped with the sexual invitation he'd had in her dream.

Boy, if only.

He chuckled, sending shivers of anticipation over her. Good God! She couldn't believe she was even considering it. Even for a heartbeat. Besides, once he realized she was scarred it'd be over, and she didn't think she could stand the rejection. Not with him stuck in her head.

Don't we— She sucked in an uneven breath. *Don't we have that ceremony or something?*

He sighed. *Yeah.* He almost sounded disappointed.

Or maybe she just wanted him to be. Jeez. *So the ceremony?*

Something flittered across her senses, but she couldn't tell what it was, and he clamped down on it, leaving a gut-churning emptiness. She wasn't sure if she wanted to know what he was feeling, but surely it would be better than him closing her off.

Ah... yeah. The ceremony.

Images of a vast chamber flooded her mind. Giant pillars with carved dragons curling around them, clinging from their tops, or sleeping at their bases, supported a domed ceiling. A stone altar sat in the center engraved with more dragons and at its foot stood a woman wearing a shimmering, silver dragon cloak.

The vision snapped to black. *You should get dressed.* His tone remained strange as if, in this quiet moment, he wanted to but couldn't deny what he was, wanted to deny his magical ferociousness. He thought all he'd done was fill her head with horrific, violent memories, but there were wondrous ones as well, she could sense them on the edge of her consciousness and yearned to look at them. But she wouldn't. Not without permission. She wouldn't abuse their connection like that.

It didn't matter that he was a dragon and she a human. She couldn't deny it. She was inexorably drawn to him. His spirit.

Which wasn't fair. Not now, not when her time was so short. She supposed it was fitting, though. She'd drawn the short stick in her marriage and in life. Why stop now?

Anaea, I—

His voice was soft, heartbreakingly tender, like it had been last night.

Any more kindness and she'd shatter. *Let's get going.*

But—

Please. She sniffed and wiped her eyes. They were dry. Good. *It wouldn't do for you to show up at this ceremony weepy and red-eyed.*

Okay. He didn't sound as if he agreed. But he didn't push either. *Put on the robe hanging in the wardrobe.*

She clutched the sheet around her, padded across his plush carpet, and opened the cabinet. There wasn't a lot inside, a black suit, a knee-length black leather coat, and a red robe that looked more like armor than clothing.

It's scale mail. Pieces of metal, shaped like scales and sewn to create a cloak.

She slipped it off the hanger. The thing weighed a ton, but was gorgeous. It reminded her of her dragon hide from the dream. Red with a hint of gold, darker on the back and arms, and paler on the front.

It represents what I— He grew quiet, as if steadying himself. *What I once was.*

It's beautiful.

Thanks. The heat of embarrassment rippled through her. *Now put it on.*

I need some clothes first.

He chuckled. It seeped into her. *Dragons aren't shy, remember? The ceremony requires the cloak and only the cloak.*

You mean— She shivered at the thought of putting it on. *This is going to be freezing.*

It warms up.

Swell.

He chuckled again, and warmth eased over her bare skin. *The cloak resembles what we were. And we were also naked and fragile under our scales.*

Before you became spirits?

Yes.

She shifted, uncertain what to say next. She was dying to know what had happened. What could possibly turn all the dragons in the world into spirits? But just the thought seemed to fill Hunter with such pain. *It must have been terrible.*

It happened a long time ago. But the weight of his emotion told her it still hurt.

And everything your people do is somehow connected to it.

That kind of attack isn't something easily forgotten. But now I'm not sure if I can blame those humans. They were afraid.

Fear makes people do stupid things.

It certainly makes dragons do stupid things. A few Greek sorcerers just before the first century were terrified the Romans would enslave dragonkind and use us to conquer them. Because of them, we lost everything. Our bodies, our families, our sense of safety. Even our goddess. She gave up everything she was and had, and diminished into another dimension so our spirits could survive. I remember her flying among us, a great shimmering dragon, and now she's gone. We hide in this inter-dimensional sphere and make laws that restrict what we can do and how we can live, because we're afraid that you'll discover our meager existence and try to finish what your ancestors started.

The ache of that betrayal brought tears to her eyes. She could only imagine how devastated she'd feel if everyone and everything she knew was destroyed. Dragonkind wasn't living, they were barely surviving.

Hunter growled and the pain radiating from him was muted. *Come on, we've got a ceremony to complete.*

That they did. She dropped the sheet and pulled on the cloak. Cold red silk lined the inside. It slid against her skin, setting her nerves on high alert.

A low rumble filled her, vibrating through her head. Was that another growl? No. Not a growl. There was nothing angry about it. It was a purr, a heated, sensual purr. As soon as she realized it, Hunter stopped.

What was that?

Nothing.

She could sense his lie, but had no idea why he'd said it, or what it meant.

Pull up the hood.

She shoved the too-long sleeves back to free her hands and snagged the hood, pulling it forward. It hung low, obscuring her vision save for a few feet before her. *I feel like I'm a little kid in my father's shirt.*

It is a little big.

Hope looking ridiculous will work for this ceremony.

Hunter snorted. *You couldn't look ridiculous in anything. Besides, we're just there to present the medallion and take it back when everything is done.*

That I think I can handle.

And then we'll gate out of here and meet up with Grey.

Yeah. A sparkly new body for you. And then all of this would be over and she could go back to the business of dying. She didn't know how she felt about that. In a way, it would be a relief to have Hunter out of her head, to not have to kill anyone else. On the other hand—

At least she'd have her dream. The one she really wasn't going to think about right now.

———

THE MEMORY OF THEIR SHARED DREAM FLASHED THROUGH ANAEA'S mind. Hunter fought the urge to start purring again, but had to admit it was a better feeling than remembering the pain of the Great

Scourge. If he wasn't already a spirit, he'd swear she was going to be the death of him. Death by sensual thought. Not necessarily a bad way to go.

Thankfully, she clamped down on the memories and focused on closing the many clasps down the front of the cloak. He was in deep trouble if that simple dream, the one he'd guided within her mind to keep her soul from becoming sick, was affecting him as well. Although the feel of the silk lining sliding over her skin wasn't a dream and so much more enticing.

It was a good thing they'd have separate bodies within a couple of hours.

And then he'd be free to explore her for real, all of her, not just her lips. He had no idea how he was going to make it work, but there *would be* something between them. If he hadn't been certain of that before, he was now. The panic that had threatened her sanity earlier when she'd discovered what he was had eased, and she hadn't lost her mind. In fact, she seemed more comfortable with him now than she had before. Of course, that didn't mean the next little thing couldn't send her spiraling into insanity while he remained within her. But once he was out, surely there was a way to keep her safe from Regis.

Mother of All, who was he kidding? Once a mage was discovered, Regis and the Asar Nergal were relentless in pursuing them. Or at least so he'd thought. Those mages who had attacked him in the hospital were the first he'd seen in three hundred years. Still, he had to sever all ties with her. And yet he couldn't deny his attraction to her.

For goodness' sake, he'd purred. Dragons only purred with their inamoratas. Which meant no matter how ridiculous it seemed, his spirit had made a decision. One that in no way was fair for Anaea. Dragons didn't mate often, making them rare even before the Great Scourge, but like swans and wolves, once inamorated, they mated for life. And as much as they'd taken on some human traits with their human bodies, like promiscuity, the compulsion to take a permanent mate still compelled some dragons.

He just never anticipated an inamorata would ever be in his future, let alone a human one. Humans' lives were so fleeting, even those few who had soul magic. Which made his spirit's choice all the more complicated. Humans thought the secret to healthy old age was green tea, but in truth, those centenarians had a hint of soul magic slowing nature's course. Hunter could only hope that Anaea was the very rare human with strong soul magic and would live an unnaturally long life, like Methuselah. But that went hand in hand with sorcery, which hadn't been seen since the Great Scourge and, again, he was back to it being complicated.

Regardless, Hunter faced a shattered heart. Either his human inamorata lived a normal human life, forcing him to face the rest of an eternity of emptiness after her passing, or she was that which dragonkind feared the most, and dragon law demanded be destroyed: a sorcerer.

And none of that mattered. He was compelled to put her needs before his, protect her, even if that meant protecting her from himself. Regis would never accept her as a Court sorcerer, and she didn't belong in his world. Heck. He didn't even belong in his world. The only way for him to be with her would be to leave his job, and the only way to do that was through rebirth, which would mean losing his memories of Anaea. The only honorable solution to this mess was to let her go.

It burned to think the best thing for her was to cut her free, but he could do it. Really. He had to. They hadn't known each other for that long. Perhaps it wouldn't hurt that much.

But inamoratas didn't work that way.

19

The rebirth chamber lay deep within the Dragon Court, accessible only through a maze of passages and unused chambers. Hunter had no idea why, when the magic sphere had been discovered, that a chamber so removed from the rest of Court had been selected. But it had. The Handmaiden's prerogative, he supposed.

She was the only true dragon sorcerer and all that power probably made her feel separate from dragonkind. It certainly gave her an air of mystery. Not that she'd particularly made an effort to fit in. With the rebirth chamber distanced from Court, she could enspell the area so no one could gate in or out without permission and scrying inside was impossible, ensuring the privacy she craved.

For as long as Hunter had known her, her only dragon contact had been brief audiences with Regis, time with Tobias dealing with replacement bodies, Hunter, those she rebirthed, and, of course, Grey—who for reasons Hunter didn't understand had sworn himself into her service even though he still belonged to the Silver Coterie. He'd never seen her at any royal functions or at the *pahars*. She was the sole means of survival for their dying race and yet completely apart from it.

So she's powerful, Anaea said.

To say the least. She's a true sorcerer.

And that is?

Dangerous, in a word. But he didn't think Anaea would be satisfied with such a simple answer. *A true sorcerer can cast spells. They don't just have one or two abilities, they can do anything, and most don't even need words or gestures. The sorcerers who tried to destroy us weren't all that powerful, but when they joined their magic together they had enough collective strength to cast a devastating spell. A true sorcerer is terrifying. They just think about whatever they want to cast, draw on their connection to the earth's magic, and it happens.*

When we were with Jade, you thought about her sorcerer ability.

I was hoping you wouldn't remember that.

Hunter felt a blush creep over Anaea's cheeks. *With the memories you have of her, it's kind of hard to forget. That and the crazy hair thing.*

Yeah, well. She has a hint of sorcerer ability, just enough to change her appearance with a thought, but she's nothing like the Handmaiden. I don't think anyone knows how powerful she is. The Handmaiden made Court, she found this inter-dimensional space, willed all the rooms and halls and galleries into existence with her thoughts. She used her magic to create the air, the light, everything.

So why isn't she in charge?

I don't know. She's an enigma. She keeps herself apart from our society. She doesn't belong to a coterie, doesn't need to, and doesn't seem to want to.

Anaea stopped at the threshold to the chamber, a narrow arch with dragons carved in the stone to create a doorframe. She traced the wings of one with a fingertip. *I got the impression last night that everyone was in a coterie.*

Dragons without a coterie don't last long. Or at least they didn't in the early days. Unless, of course, you're the Handmaiden. My coterie didn't survive the transition from physical to spirit and I had to choose. I chose the most powerful coterie I could, Regis's. But now most of that power is because the Handmaiden supports Constantine and Regis. It's probably the only reason they still rule.

Even though it seems everyone hates their rules.

Many believe that those rules have kept our people, what little we have left, alive.

And you?

He didn't know. In the beginning he'd believed it, believed the only way to stay safe was to remain hidden. But they weren't really dragons anymore, they were something else, and clinging to the old ways no longer seemed to work. *I think at one time the rules were important and change is hard.*

Which is why you're still in feudal clan groupings.

For all their negatives, the coteries are the closest we can get to families now. We're a race of spirits. There are no more of us.

You can't have children?

We lost that ability when we lost our physical forms. The coteries are all we have now.

A hint of melancholy slid through her. She was without a coterie as well. Someone in her life had isolated her from friends and family and now she believed she faced a death sentence. It astounded him how brave she was, not wanting to renew her old connections so they wouldn't have to watch her die.

Anaea— How he wished she hadn't become so good at hiding her thoughts from him.

I don't blame you for throwing your lot in with Regis, or for...

Images of the *wasu tahazu* flashed through her mind and bile burned the back of her throat.

He was such a fool. Just because she hadn't lost her mind the moment she'd learned what he was didn't mean she'd accept him. Besides, it wasn't his original form that he needed her to accept, but the killer he'd made himself into to protect himself. Yes, he was a predator, but he'd encouraged that, embraced it, to become the prince's assassin. And he'd forced her into his world and stained her hands. Mother of All, he really was a beast.

Let's just finish this, he growled.

She jumped and he yanked back his frustration. She didn't deserve anything he'd brought her. Even the new life he'd given her had been at a hefty price to her psyche.

Sorry, I—

It's okay. She stepped into the dim hall that ran left and right. *It's been a stressful couple of days for me, too.*

The hall ringed the chamber, archways opening into it at regular intervals. Anaea entered by the closest arch and strode to the altar in the center of the room. He could sense her desire to gawk at the massive statues and the carved ceiling, but she kept focused on the three naked corpses on the altar, maintaining the guise that she was him. He definitely didn't deserve her.

"I see a new cloak will need to be commissioned," the Handmaiden said, emerging from the shadows at the far entrance. She was a tall, middle-aged woman who had looked middle-aged for as long as Hunter had known her, having never been forced to abandon her original body and for some reason not bothered to change her appearance with magic. Under her jeweled and etched-silver hood were wisps of black and silver hair.

"Ah... yes." Anaea inched the hood back to expand her field of vision.

The Handmaiden's eyes narrowed. Hunter could only imagine what she was thinking. If anyone could see through the charade that only Hunter inhabited Anaea's body it would be the Handmaiden. He prayed she wouldn't notice, but it was probably better to pray that she just wouldn't say anything. Hunter had always respected her and the rules. He could only hope for leniency for his first offense.

"I never thought of you as a gender hopper."

Not this again.

Anaea rolled her eyes. She was getting tired of this as well.

Hand over the medallion, and let's get this over with.

Agreed. She pushed the hood off and slid the chain over her head.

"Business as usual, I see." The Handmaiden took the offered medallion. "Just like your body, things are changing."

What did that mean?

"And that means...?" Anaea asked.

The Handmaiden shrugged and turned to the first body, a

medium-built, thirty-something male. "I don't know, but I can sense it."

If Hunter had brows, he'd furrow them. He'd grind his teeth, too. This was the most conversation he'd had with the Handmaiden in centuries.

"When the time comes, you must look after your own."

His own? He was a dragon without a coterie, or at least one he had any affection for. He didn't have anyone else.

As if she could hear his thoughts, she leveled her silver gaze on Anaea, making her shiver.

"Yes. Definitely a new robe. Narrower in the shoulders, but just as long." Blue flashed around her and she offered a weak smile.

What was that? Anaea asked.

I have no idea.

I think this might be a first. Us not knowing the same thing.

Ha, he said, filling her thoughts with as much sarcasm as he could muster. *It still isn't safe for you to know what you do about me.*

And yet, I feel so much better knowing why I'm supposed to be terrified.

You're hardly terrified. It was one of the things he'd forever be grateful for: her strength and courage to hold on in what had to be a bizarre situation.

I tried terror with... with something else. It didn't get me very far.

The Handmaiden awakened the medallion with a glance and Hunter knew she was concentrating on bringing the spell to life. Heat rippled through Anaea.

Funny, now that the Handmaiden had the medallion, Anaea shouldn't sense the magic within it.

What's she doing?

Casting the rebirth spell.

Oh, that's informative.

Hunter bit back an internal grin. *The rebirth spell is the only way we can get a fresh start. It wipes everything from our soul except what's permanently imprinted on it, color and gender. You have no memories, all of your stuff is given to your doyen, and you're essentially a baby, the youngest member of your coterie.*

That sucks. Anaea shivered. *Have you ever been reborn?*

No, but more than half of our population has at some point. And some found the rebirth a blessing. Two thousand years' worth of memories wasn't necessarily a kindness.

How does it work?

Remember those words I put in your head when Pearl jumped us in the hotel room in Elmsville?

He felt Anaea struggle to hide a nod.

Those words activated the medallion. The Handmaiden made the medallion to capture souls in the event that punishments were needed or a soul could be saved if a vessel was damaged beyond healing. The medallion keeps the soul cohesive for a short period in your dimension, and a little longer in the Court dimension.

The Handmaiden pressed the medallion against the chest of the first corpse and whispered two words in Sumerian.

Anyone with enough earth magic can say the power words and activate the medallion to absorb a soul into it, but only a true sorcerer can cast the rebirth spell. It takes a great deal of concentration to cast the spell and then draw out a specific spirit and encourage it to take host in a body.

And the Handmaiden is the dragons' only true sorcerer?

Yes.

That seems dangerous. What if something happened to her?

I don't think anyone would be stupid enough to try something. If she left, we'd have no way to recover souls. We were rare before we became spirits—

And being unable to have children, your numbers can only diminish.

And that was the sad truth about dragonkind. They were a species facing extinction. It might be a slow extinction because of their indefinite life spans, but there was still nothing they could do about it. It was inevitable.

Energy surged from the Handmaiden's hands, encompassing the medallion in blue flame. The same hues as Anaea's fire, although that was merely coincidence. The Handmaiden's magic always manifested as blue flame surrounding the medallion.

The heat within Anaea grew.

The Handmaiden whispered more words, coaxing the first spirit,

Saber, out. Energy poured from her, blue and silver, in a light show Hunter had never seen before. It had to be a result of Anaea's connection to the earth magic. He just had no idea what it meant. And it had mesmerized Anaea. Hunter could feel her holding her breath, all her thoughts focused on the energy sizzling around the Handmaiden, as if there was nothing else in the room or even Hunter within her.

A shadow moved out of the corner of Anaea's eye. Cold panic shot through Hunter. Something was wrong.

Look left.

Anaea didn't respond, her attention consumed by the Handmaiden's magic.

Anaea. Mother of All. If she could just move her head a fraction in any direction he could see beyond the medallion.

The Handmaiden jerked from the body, the medallion clenched in her hands, fire rippling over the surface. A metal wire appeared, wrapping around her throat.

Anaea gasped, her trance shattered. A cloaked and hooded drake yanked the garrote tighter. It looked like Homok. Which didn't make any sense because he belonged to Barna's Major Brown Coterie and not Zenobia's or Nero's coteries.

Get the medallion.

But—

She'll survive, but she's a slow healer. He could only hope they were just after the medallion and not out to kill the dragons' only sorcerer.

Another drake, Curdus from the Minor Green, rushed at Anaea, slashing with his sword. She twisted out of the way, his blade skittering against the scale mail.

Get the medallion and run.

Hunter had no idea why the Handmaiden wasn't casting something, anything. She just needed to think it. How the hell had the drakes gotten into the chamber?

The Handmaiden sagged to her knees, her face crimson. More drakes, wrapped in black cloaks with the hoods pulled low, stormed in. Hunter recognized less than half and their coterie allegiances were mixed. At least they were the last time he'd checked.

Anaea lunged for the medallion. She wrapped her fingers around it, meeting the Handmaiden's gaze. The sorcerer nodded and drew her hand back. Magic still raced across the surface of the medallion, crackling over Anaea's flesh. But more was building around the Handmaiden. She was casting a spell. A big spell.

Run, Hunter growled.

Anaea scrambled to her feet. Curdus dove at her. She stumbled out of his reach and ran for the archway, her heart thudding in her chest. Hunter could barely hear himself think over the rushing in her ears. They had to move, get away.

A wall of energy slammed into her back, throwing her across the chamber. The magic engulfing the medallion shot through her. She rolled on her shoulder and staggered to her feet. Energy nipped her skin, poured through her veins, and ignited Hunter's spirit. Flame surrounded him, burning through his soul. He retreated to his mental box but it followed. The magic was too strong. Agony burned through his remembered bone and sinew. He was falling, falling, plummeting to the ground, and no spell, known or otherwise, could save him now.

20

Anaea ran from the chamber, the assailants racing after her. Sparks danced over the medallion, around her hand, and dripped to the floor.

Someone yelled behind her. They were close and getting closer, she could sense it. She had to get out of there, but she had no idea where. Surely if she wasn't safe in that sacred chamber, she wasn't safe anywhere else at Court.

She scrambled around a corner, then another, zigzagging as soon as a new corridor presented itself. The heavy metal cloak slapped against her body. She hiked it higher around her knees, desperate not to trip.

Hunter?

He didn't answer.

Damn it, Hunter. What do I do?

Still nothing.

More voices echoed through the passages, but she couldn't tell from which direction. It seemed they were all around her now. She needed Hunter. Why wasn't he answering her?

She pressed against her thoughts. He was there, she could feel him, but something wasn't right. He'd never seemed so removed from her before. For lack of a better term, he seemed unconscious.

She leapt into the next passage. A small, empty chamber. No other exit. Shit.

"There she is."

Double shit.

She spun to face her assailants. There were five of them, all cloaked. How the hell could they see with their hoods pulled so low? She gave her head a quick shake. That didn't matter. Should she give up or fight? Well, she knew what Hunter would do. It didn't matter what they wanted. Hunter's last instructions had been to run, and until he woke up, or came back from wherever he was, she was going to stick to that.

The first man rushed at her. She side-stepped his attack and let him career into the back wall. He punched at her head. She ducked.

The energy still rippling over her flared, but did nothing. She reached for it. The man in front of her swung again. She staggered back, unable to call fire or anything else. If she could just get some-place safe.

A meaty hand clamped around her arm. She twisted in his grip, spinning away, and stumbled against the side wall.

Fire flared over her hands, scorching the rock. A burst of light blinded her, pulling energy from within her that she didn't know she had. It latched onto the thought of escaping and sucked her in, just like Jade's gate had when she'd traveled into the Dragon Court.

She was falling… falling… suspended in a brilliant, white nothing that was warm and embracing, unlike the black void from the gate before. Her skin tingled and the hair on her arms stood up. The nothing plugged her ears and poured down her throat. She was drowning, fully submerged in this viscous light.

She hit the ground, scraping hands and knees, and scrambled to her feet. The men weren't behind her, and she no longer stood in the chamber but on a snow-covered country road. Before her lay the grove she and Mark used to visit while in college. They used to pack a picnic lunch and travel here, to the outskirts of Newgate. A small stream meandered through what Mark described as interesting foliage. She'd bring her books, and he'd take his sketch pad, and they'd while away the hours together. But that was then and this was now. And now things were much different. She shivered in the crisp air and hugged the quickly cooling metal robe closer. *Hunter?*

Nothing.

Come on, Hunter. Please. She hadn't expected his lack of response to unnerve her this much. *Wake up.* She needed him to explain what had happened.

But he didn't answer.

She needed to do something. That's what Hunter would say. She couldn't just stand here and wait for those men to find her. When he woke, they could deal with the situation. Until then, she was on her own.

At least one thing good had come out of this. She was in Newgate. With no money, no winter clothes, and nothing but the stupid medallion that everyone wanted, her options were thin. But there was one person in town who she could turn to. Mark.

She slipped the medallion over her neck and hung it inside the cloak, hoping against hope he'd help her after one year of her not returning his phone calls and two years of him not returning hers.

GREY GATED AS CLOSE TO THE REBIRTHING CHAMBER AS THE Handmaiden's wards would allow and bolted down the hall. Something was horribly wrong. Moments ago, Court had trembled as if struck by an earthquake, which was impossible since it was separate from the physical world. Nothing had ever shaken Court like that before, and the only dragon powerful enough to have caused it was the Handmaiden. And Hunter was with her this very moment.

Grey careened through the arch and skidded to a halt. Crumpled, smoldering forms littered the chamber. The altar and floor in front of it were scorched and the corpses about to receive reborn dragon souls were charred skeletons.

His gaze raced over every detail, searching for any sign of Hunter or the Handmaiden, but everything was black, covered in debris.

One of the smoking piles near the altar shifted and moaned. Someone was still alive. Whoever it was moved again, sending up a cloud of ash. A hint of silver scales caught the light and Grey's heart leapt into his throat. It was the Handmaiden.

He rushed to her side as she pushed back her hood. Soot smeared across her forehead and chin and a thick red line marred the pale skin on her throat. Grey's throat ached in sympathy.

"What happened?" He helped her sit up.

"Politics." Her tone made that one word sound like a curse.

"But you're the Handmaiden." Grey couldn't wrap his mind around that. If anything happened to her all dragons were lost.

"They weren't after me."

"Is Hunter—?" He glanced at the closest corpse. Please don't let it be him.

"I gave him time to escape." She clutched Grey's shoulder and used it to stand. "I do have a soft spot for him. But he'll need help soon."

"Have you seen something?" With the implication that she was leaving for an extended time and this latest comment, it seemed certain she'd looked into the future. He itched to do something. Something for Hunter or the Handmaiden. Right now. An assault on the Handmaiden in the rebirthing chamber required an aggressive response. Something so strong that no one would think of attempting an attack again.

The Handmaiden flicked a finger and the soot slid off her cloak. "I haven't seen anything."

"But—"

"Grey." She cupped his face in suddenly pristine hands. "Things are changing. Like Hunter, you will need to adapt. And this time I can't help you with it."

"You what?" He hadn't heard that right. He couldn't have heard that right.

Magic billowed around her, and she straightened. Behind her, without support of a wall or archway, stood a gate. It shimmered white, the signature of only her gates. All other dragons created black ones.

"You are stronger than you think. Don't forget that."

He snorted. Forgetting wasn't one of his problems.

She offered a gentle smile and stepped into the white nothing. With a whoosh, the gate disappeared, taking the Handmaiden wherever it was she was going. Now he had no idea what to do.

Anaea glanced over her shoulder down the apartment building's empty beige hall.

Please, oh please, let Mark be home. She rapped on the door again. Still no answer. It was late afternoon. He had to be inside. God help her if he'd actually changed his routine since they'd last talked. He had to be home and she was too exhausted for any other option.

She'd spent all day trudging the cold, snowy back roads to get into town where she managed to flag down a woman willing to drive her to this side of Newgate even though Anaea was sure she looked crazy. All the while, she searched in her mind for any indication that Hunter was conscious. She was hungry and tired, still very much alone, and mostly freezing, although to her surprise she didn't seem to have frostbite on her bare feet.

But then she did have the spirit of a dragon in her—a spirit who was going to wake up any minute now. Please. She was shocked to discover just how alone she felt, after all this time with him inside her head. It felt so... wrong. She hadn't thought her life could get more confusing, and yet, she hadn't felt more alive in years. The last time she'd really felt like herself had been here in this hall. That was before the cancer. She had been recently married and had come to see Mark to commission a painting with her newly wedded wealth as a way of an apology for how things had turned out between them. But he'd refused, and they had fought.

Less than a year later, ten months into her marriage, she'd realized she was a trophy wife. And as soon as she'd become sick she was no longer a prize. She had called Mark, realizing how foolish she'd been picking John over him. But he never returned her calls. It was unlikely Mark had forgiven her for marrying John. But he was all she had at the moment, and she was tired enough to accept pity if it got her a change of clothes—although not as tired as she'd have expected with the cancer.

The door to the stairwell at the far end of the hall opened. Her stomach clenched. She looked for a place to hide, but there wasn't anywhere to go.

Metal jingled against metal and she whirled around, ready to make a stand.

Mark dropped his keys.

Her heart skipped a beat. Thank God.

"Anaea?" He didn't move, didn't smile, just stared at her.

Not the reaction she was hoping for. She hugged herself, the metal scales hissing with the movement. "Hi."

His eyes narrowed. After a moment, he broke eye contact and picked up his keys. "Still married to that prick?"

"Unfortunately." Since her lawyers seemed to work at a snail's pace. Please just let her in. All she needed was a moment to catch her breath and figure out what was wrong with Hunter.

"So what are you doing here?" He pushed past her and shoved his key into his lock.

"Well, I..." She didn't know what to say. That she'd been possessed by a dragon spirit and someone was trying to kill her? Perhaps something more believable. She was dying and her husband didn't care—he was already working on his next trophy wife. "I just need..." Shit. What could she say? Screw it. "Don't be a dick."

A slight smile pulled at his lips. "Get in here. You look like crap. And what the hell are you wearing?" He opened the door and ushered her in.

His apartment was as she remembered. A battered orange sofa faced an old computer monitor hooked up to a VCR, and the rest of the room was filled with canvases of various sizes in various stages of completion. A rickety bookshelf sat beside the monitor, the bottom filled with cop movies, the top littered with painting supplies.

"Pardon the mess," he said.

"What mess?"

He flashed her a full smile and pushed a pile of *National Geographic* from the sofa.

"So I love the new haircut."

She ran a hand over her stubble. She hadn't told him about the cancer. Hadn't been given a chance.

"I've been changing it up since college."

"Bet John never saw your pink phase." Mark crossed his arms.

"John doesn't have a say on how I cut my hair."

"Really?"

"Really." She met his gaze, daring him to keep up the line of conversation. She might need his help, but there wasn't any point arguing over old discussions.

He shifted from one foot to the other. "So why are you here?"

"I wanted to see you."

"Uh huh. And you decided to wear a Halloween costume to do it?"

"Fine." She sighed and dropped onto the sofa. "I needed a place to hang out for a while."

"Better answer."

"Gee, thank you."

A FEW HOURS LATER, ANAEA WAS WARM AND CLOTHED AND FED AND alone in Mark's bed. And still uncomfortable. She'd thought going to Mark would be the right thing to do but she wasn't so sure anymore, despite the fact that he'd been her only option. Hunter still hadn't made an appearance, and the thought made her pizza dinner churn in her gut.

The meal with Mark had been rife with uncomfortable silences, and talking about their college days only made her feel more out of place. The freedom and confidence to love from those days were definitely past her. Were past them. She'd made her choice, albeit a bad one. But she'd made it.

And with her situation now, with cancer and being hunted by dragons, she was even further from those days and those possibilities. But Mark knew nothing about that. There wasn't any way she could explain it—at least the dragon bit. As for the cancer... well, it wouldn't be fair to have him suffering along with her for her remaining few months. It was best just to leave it with the only thing he really knew, which was that she'd picked John over him. Anything else would just complicate an already complicated situation.

She hugged the sheets to her chest. They smelled like Mark, fresh and soapy, mixed with a hint of turpentine and oil paint. It was obvious from the way he looked at her—the way he still looked at her—and the things he hadn't said that he still loved her. While she wasn't sure if she had ever truly loved him.

Maybe she had. She thought she had. He was clever and talented. Definitely attractive with gorgeous curly black hair, fine features, and long-fingered artist's hands. But John had swept her off her feet, whirling her thoughts and emotions in a rosy frenzy until Mark was a distant memory. If she could forget him so easily it meant she didn't really love him. Didn't it?

Mark rapped on the doorframe and crossed his arms. "So..."

She clenched the blanket tighter, a weak defense against her unwanted examination of her emotions.

"I'll be on the couch." He pursed his lips, obviously wanting to say more. She could feel his questions like a heavy fog pressing around her. His anger and hurt and continued love hung between them.

She didn't want to reach out, didn't want to acknowledge any of it, particularly the love. Loving him wasn't right.

Images of the sexy dream with Hunter flashed through her mind, and sudden arousal burned through her.

God! Loving Hunter wasn't right either.

He shifted from one foot to the other, the anger dissolving into hurt. "You, uh..."

"I'm good." Boy, she had no right reentering his life, dredging up old emotions. It wasn't good for either of them. But she needed time to figure out what was wrong with Hunter.

"Okay." He clenched his jaw, but made no move to leave.

Her heart contracted. Please don't let him confess his love. Let him rage, shout, make demands. But that was never his style.

"I—"

"I can sleep on the couch instead," she said.

He blinked. "What?"

"You don't have to give up your bed. I can just as easily sleep on the couch."

He opened his mouth then closed it.

She had no idea what he was thinking now but she could tell he was struggling with something.

"Anaea."

Her gut churned even more.

He sighed and gave a slight nod. "You're welcome." Then he closed the door, leaving her alone in the dark.

Her eyes burned and she sniffed. Thank God, Hunter hadn't been awake to witness that. And yet, if he had, it wouldn't have happened. Or, more likely, he'd have something acerbic to say that would make her realize exactly how she felt.

Tears blurred her vision. She wished Hunter were here. Then she wouldn't feel so alone. But it was more than that. Dream or no dream, Hunter's presence made her feel worthy. She couldn't explain it, other than no matter what he said, she knew he respected her, took pride in her, maybe even more.

But that 'even more' had to be fantasy. The desires of a lonely, broken heart.

She sniffed and wiped her eyes. She'd take a page from Mark's book and handle her situation with grace. She didn't have to like it, but she could at least make it easier on herself and Hunter.

21

Hunter floated in a white nimbus without form or sensation or thought. A great, encompassing, timeless nothing. There was no pain, no struggle, no politics, no settling, and no Anaea.

Blue lightning zinged through him.

There had to be Anaea. She needed him.

No, she didn't. Not really. Whether she admitted it or not there was nothing she couldn't face. Even those desperately hard life-and-death decisions.

In truth, it was Hunter who needed her. She gave him purpose. And not just the 'save her life' purpose.

Raw and exposed, surrounded by nothing, he couldn't avoid the truth. She was his inamorata. Humans would call it true love. Grey would say twitterpated. Every primal instinct Hunter had screamed that he belonged to her. She could renounce him and he would never pick another. All the sky in the world paled in comparison to his desire for her. To hold her, feel her nuzzle against him, be enveloped in her scent.

More lightning shot through him.

He needed a body. One separate from her.

His heart pounded.

No. It didn't. It couldn't. He was a spirit.

The lightning crackled, flashing this way and that, revealing a latticework of energy.

Anaea?

The lattice billowed then shrunk.

Anaea?

No answer.

He concentrated on her. She was there. She had to be. He was stuck within her.

A narrow black tunnel formed on the other side of his cage, like the one she'd squeezed him down into during the *wasu tahazu.*

Memory flooded him. They'd been in the Handmaiden's chamber and had been attacked. They were after Anaea.

The lightning snapped, showering him in sparks.

He couldn't see anything at the end of the tunnel.

Anaea. Please answer. She had to be okay. His spirit would heal her. It had to.

He grabbed the lattice. Fire lanced through him. White agony swept over him and the tunnel was consumed by the nimbus.

ANAEA WOKE TO A LIGHT AND PERSISTENT KNOCKING. FOR A MOMENT, she didn't know where she was, only that she was warm and comfortable.

"Hey, Anaea."

She jerked up. That was Mark's voice. She was in Mark's sweats and his bed and…

The events of the past day rushed into her head. Hunter. Hunter was—

The door cracked open, and Mark poked his head into the room. "I've got to go out."

"Uh… yeah."

"I need clean clothes." He pointed to the dresser.

"Sure."

He padded across the room. "You're welcome to stay for as long as you need, you know."

"I know." She searched in her head for Hunter's presence. He was still there and still distant. Her heart skipped a beat but she managed to suck back her panic.

"I'm just at the gallery on 6th Ave." He fished out shirt, jeans, and socks. "The number's on the fridge door."

"Okay."

"I'll be back before lunch."

She nodded.

"And, Anaea—"

She met his dark gaze.

"That asshole can't touch you anymore. We'll get through this." He left before she could respond, which was good since she didn't know what to say. Mark thought John was abusing her, that she'd finally left him and turned to Mark for help. A year ago, he would have been closer to the truth, but now... now it was an entirely new problem that he couldn't help her with. She needed Hunter.

She nudged Hunter's presence. It felt weak, insubstantial.

Hunter?

She nudged again. Harder.

Still no response.

Her gut churned. He felt far away, encased in something, but she couldn't get a handle on what it was or how to fix it.

Come on, Hunter. She needed him. God, what if she'd killed him? Was that even possible?

Please.

She shoved at him, but his essence wavered, becoming less substantial than before. She was making it worse. She had no idea what to do. Hunter was completely disconnected from her. She hadn't even had any dreams of him last night.

She needed someone who had a clue. Another dragon. But the only one she could think of trusting was Grey and she had no idea how to contact him...

But maybe Hunter did. Maybe it was somewhere in those memories he'd shared with her. With them constantly slipping into her consciousness against Hunter's will, she was sure to have access to them even if she couldn't reach Hunter.

She sucked in a quick breath. Please let there be something.

Closing her eyes, she concentrated on Hunter, who and what he was. He was feral. A dragon. She could feel the hint of his essence sliding along the edges of her thought. Dark, primal, and powerful. A deep yearning to be as powerful as him washed through her. She'd been powerless for the last year, longer if she wanted to include the years of her marriage.

She dragged herself back to her purpose. Contacting Grey. She searched her thoughts for him. He'd grabbed her after the *wasu tahazu*, looked at her with a mixture of uncertainty at the dinner, and a bit of lust before that.

No. She needed to go back, further, into Hunter's memories. Not hers. They'd been Crusaders together. Images of Grey, in armor covered with mud and gore, flashed into her mind's eye.

Good. Disgusting, but good. She needed more.

"Come out with me, man."

She shook her head.

No, Hunter had. He wanted to be alone. Empty and alone.

"But they've added sound. It's incredible."

"You've seen that movie five times already."

Grey offered a lopsided grin. "Yeah. And it's still amazing."

The image in her head jumped. Darkness, screams, roars. A face wavered into sight: broken, bloody, swollen.

Hot rage burned through her.

It was Grey. He clung to his neck, blood bubbling over his fingers, and he gasped each breath.

"I swear, Grey—" They were going to pay for what they'd done. Hunter would make them pay. All of them.

The ruined face gave a weak laugh. "Not any worse than the Seventh Crusade."

A growl seethed within her. She jerked back from the memory, panting with fury and fear. Hunter's loyalty was terrifying and exhilarating. There wasn't anything he wouldn't do to protect his own.

Her chest burned with regret and envy. What she wouldn't give to have someone care about her so deeply. But she was broken. Even before the cancer it had been made clear she wasn't worthy, wasn't a woman any man would want. Hunter was only being polite and not mentioning it because he was trapped in her body.

Damn it. Pity parties weren't going to help Hunter. She had to suck it up like she always did. Now concentrate. Did Grey have a phone? Did dragons even need phones?

Yes and yes.

The answers popped into her head. Of course, they needed to communicate and neither Hunter nor Grey had anything like telepathy.

She snorted at the thought. Never in a million years would she have thought about telepathy, and yet she'd spent the last day and a half talking with the spirit of a dragon in her head.

Well, if she just knew he had a phone, maybe she also just knew his number.

She scrambled from the bed, grabbed the phone, and before she could second-guess herself, typed in a number.

It rang once... twice...

Please oh please let it be Grey and let him know how to help.

"Hello?" Grey's voice was rough on the other end.

"Grey?"

"Who is this?"

"Anaea."

"Mother of All. Where's Hunter? Are you two all right?"

She released the breath she hadn't realized she'd been holding. "I'm okay, but something's wrong with Hunter."

"What do you mean, wrong?" Grey asked, his voice darkening.

"I can sense him, but he's unconscious, or far away, or something." Her throat constricted and she sniffed.

"Hey. It's all right. We'll just—" He groaned. "Mother be damned,

Hunter, you are so going to owe me," he said, suddenly sounding pained. "Okay. Remember Jade's shop, where you gated into Court?"

"The antique store?"

"Yeah. Can you get there?"

"It'll take me half an hour."

"Okay, good. Don't go inside. That's too dangerous. And hang tight."

GREY SNAPPED HIS PHONE SHUT. HE HAD NO IDEA WHAT HE WAS GOING to do. If something was really wrong with Hunter he'd need the Handmaiden's help. But she was gone now, and Hunter might be, too. That human, Anaea, had sounded so concerned. It was almost a shame dragon law demanded her death. The only way to find out what was wrong with Hunter was to meet her as promised.

Shit.

Maybe he could send Cole. But that would bring another drake into this mess, and while Cole was discreet he wasn't above using the information for his own gain.

Which meant Grey had to enter the human world.

He stood and paced his private theatre, his heart suddenly pounding. Ten paces to the large screen, ten to the plush recliner. Ten back to the screen.

Sweat beaded on his palms and down his back.

Hunter needed him.

This was crazy. Irrational. All he had to do was open a gate and walk through. Besides, the Handmaiden had eased his memories yesterday. They shouldn't incapacitate or even bother him for weeks, months if he was careful. But going into the humans' realm wasn't being careful.

No, it was just stress, that was all. The stress of keeping the Handmaiden's grimoire safe. It certainly didn't feel safe, hidden in a secret compartment in his wardrobe.

His breath wheezed between teeth he hadn't realized he'd clenched.

Having the grimoire was too much responsibility. There were too many power-hungry drakes who could use the magic within it to control all dragons. Regis was bad enough.

Yes, that was it. That and trying to figure out why she'd asked him to reread that particular journal. And her leaving. And Capri not caring for him. And having no purpose to his life. And—

And that was all a lie.

He shot his gaze about the room, desperate for something to keep the world from spinning. But there were only the chairs and the screen, no other furnishings. Nothing else to impede the joy of immersing himself in the stories captured on film.

He sucked in more air, but his heart only pounded faster. He'd never returned after that night. At first, he'd needed to heal and had holed up in his lair. But that first day had passed and Hunter was already tracking down the remaining drakes who'd attacked him. Then a second and a third day had passed and it seemed easier to remain at Court. Then the nightmares had started.

The room whirled around him. His throat ached, his whole body throbbed. Damn it. The Handmaiden was supposed to have taken care of this.

He squeezed his eyes against the memory. It was a memory. Just a memory. He could do this. He had to do this. Hunter didn't have anyone else. Well, Gig would probably be glad to help, but Grey didn't trust him to keep the body-sharing thing a secret. In the very least Capri would find out and there was no telling what she'd do with the information.

He ground his teeth.

The drakes who'd attacked him all those years ago had been punished and reborn. They were no longer a threat. He didn't even know why the thought of gating over made his heart race. It didn't make sense. Newgate was perfectly safe. Even more so in the daylight. Be the Swoosh. Be like Nike. Just. Do. It.

Before he could doubt himself, he shoved his hand against the screen and yelled the word to power a gate. Earth magic erupted from his palm. Its black energy devoured the white rectangle.

His knees buckled and before he could fall, he staggered into the vortex. The magic of the gate pressed against his senses, filling his mouth and nose and ears for a terrifying moment. Then his hands and knees hit uneven ice-covered asphalt.

Hot and cold billowed through him, one radiating after the other over and over again. He tried to control his breathing but couldn't stop panting. His pulse raced and black specks danced across his vision. He squeezed his eyes shut. It wasn't that bad. Really. He could do this. He was already here.

He clutched at the memory of the Handmaiden's touch on his head and the tingle of her magic easing the sharp edges in his mind.

His racing heart slowed and the rushing in his ears melted away. A mix of low humming noises vibrated the air around him, like a faint bass from his stereo system. It reminded him of movies. The strangely soothing sounds of cars and machinery. Sounds he'd heard millions of times before on film. See, not bad at all.

He glanced up. The world spun and wavered.

He squeezed his eyes shut.

Hunter needed him to do this.

He cracked open one eye. When the world didn't whirl, he opened the other. He wasn't outside of Jade's shop as he'd intended. But given the stress of the situation, it didn't surprise him. Gating to locations without anchors required a lot of concentration, even for those few drakes who could do it. The fact that his gate had latched onto the anchor he thought the safest, Hunter's private gate, didn't surprise him. The alley was more or less as he remembered from the last time he and Hunter had gated there, back in the early 30s... back before that terrible night. Secure behind a warehouse that Hunter had given to Grey.

His throat started to ache and he drew in more slow breaths, shoving the memories back.

Dead stalks of grass and weeds broke through snow drifted against the building's foundation, but the windows were new, even here at the back. Good, his human business manager was keeping up with maintenance as he'd instructed. And if he focused on that, perhaps he wouldn't lose his mind.

He forced himself to stand.

See, everything was fine. He could do it now. He was doing it. Hunter needed help and was depending on him.

Holding that thought close, he left the alley and raced to Jade's shop.

22

A naea peered around the edge of the shop and glanced down the sidewalk. Grey still wasn't in sight. Maybe he wouldn't think to look for her in the narrow alley between the house and the office building, but it was the best place to hide. And he had told her not to go inside.

She had fished coins from a dish by the front door of Mark's apartment and taken the bus across town to the antique shop. The old coat she'd found in his closet had done little to keep out the winter chill and she couldn't help but fear that feeling the cold somehow meant Hunter's situation was getting worse.

No. She was just oversensitive to the situation. Jumping at every little thing. Hunter was going to be fine. He was still within her. He couldn't lose cohesion like he would if he didn't have a vessel. Grey would know what was wrong. And everything was going to be all right.

"Wow, Hunter. I only bite if you ask," a throaty feminine voice said behind her.

Anaea spun around. Jade stood, framed between the red brick house and the gray concrete office building at the far end of the alley.

"Or do you like skulking in alleys in the cold?"

Damn it. Where was Grey?

"The cold doesn't bother me." It seemed like a typical Hunter thing to say.

Jade raised a sculpted eyebrow. "Tell me another one, fire drake."

Anaea pressed her lips tight, fighting the urge to argue. Please just make the woman go away.

"You know," Jade said, lifting her long green coat, stepping over the low snowdrift, and sauntering to Anaea, "all of Court is looking for you."

"So I hear." Anaea's stomach churned. She had no idea if Jade was the type to turn in an ex-lover. What was she thinking? Of course Jade was. She'd already tried sexual blackmail with their trip into the Dragon Court. Why not now?

Jade ran a delicate finger along Anaea's arm. "Must feel good to have fire again."

Even through Mark's coat and sweatshirt, the touch made Anaea's skin crawl. God. She had to get rid of Jade.

Heat bubbled within her, radiating from her chest, down her arms to her hands. She clutched the woman's wrists. "I'm not in the mood for games."

Jade's eyes widened. Blue fire licked her skin and Anaea pulled it back. She didn't want to kill the woman, just make her run away.

Translucent green light flashed around Jade, like an aura. It wavered then took hold, surging until she was completely enveloped.

Anaea jerked back and Jade narrowed her eyes.

"You're not Hunter."

A chill swept over Anaea. "Of course I am."

Jade leaned close, peering at Anaea as if she could see her soul. "No. He's in there. I can see his aura, but— Who the hell are you?"

"Hunter," Anaea growled.

"There he is," someone yelled behind her. Two men rushed from the far end of the alley toward her. More light, muddy brown for both men and not nearly as bright as Jade's, engulfed them. Jade grabbed Anaea's arm. "What did you do with Hunter?"

"Nothing." She shoved the woman but Jade held tight. Fire rippled through Anaea. "Let go."

She didn't want to kill anyone else. All she wanted was to fix whatever was wrong with Hunter and get him into his own body.

"Get the medallion," one of the men yelled.

A heavy hand seized Anaea's shoulder. She wrenched away, shoving Jade into the third man. They staggered back as flames shot from Anaea's fingertips.

She yanked her hands to the side, aiming the inferno at the wall beside her. Energy poured out of her, the flames twisting into thick white threads. The air shimmered and with a flash, a white hole stretched before her.

The urge to leap into it made her limbs twitch. Her stomach roiled. She had no idea what the white nothing was. But the part that had been Hunter knew exactly what it was. A gate. And a well-crafted one at that, even if it wasn't the usual black and even if she hadn't used a power word to make it.

Bully for whatever instinct Hunter had instilled in her. She still didn't know where it went.

The men yelled, the light surrounding them wavering. Jade's aura intensified and gathered around her hands. She was doing something and Anaea was certain she didn't want to hang around to find out what.

Anaea leapt for the gate. Out of the corner of her eye, she saw Grey storm into the alley, but it was too late. The vortex wrapped around her, twisting her essence and pouring into her.

THE LIGHTNING CAGE SQUEEZED HUNTER TIGHT. HE SENSED ANAEA'S heart pounding, felt a surge of panic, and then the suffocating press of a gate.

Images flashed to him. Jade recognizing two souls in Anaea's body. Three drakes he didn't know grabbing for Anaea. Shit.

He fought the urge to squirm in his prison. He couldn't afford to pass out again.

Anaea's pulse slowed a little. Good. Calm was good. A black speck materialized before him, and the tunnel vision came back. He was still a long ways from her, but if he squinted he could see what she saw.

She stood in a parking lot surrounded by a circle of charred asphalt, indicating an astoundingly powerful gate—especially for one created on instinct. Once she knew the proper spell, she could probably go anywhere in the world like Grey could. Which was good, since they'd need a place to hide as soon as he'd gotten his own body and killed Zenobia, or Nero, or whoever was after him.

Anaea's gaze searched the area, stopping on a rusty station wagon. She knew that car, knew the owner.

Relief flooded her. He was home.

Jealousy twinged through Hunter, but he tamped it down. He wanted to be the one to help her, but given their current predicament, he'd be happy if she found a safe place for a moment. Maybe if she calmed down he could work free of this cage.

She rushed into the apartment building, up the stairs and down the hall, but slowed halfway.

Hunter squinted. He couldn't quite see.

A chill rippled over her. She inched forward.

The door at the end hung ajar, ripped free from its top hinge.

Damn. *Turn around.*

But she didn't hear him.

Lightning pulsed over the cage, biting into him.

Calm down and run away. Couldn't she see what was before her?

But of course she could. Whoever he was, he could still be inside. She couldn't turn around any more than Hunter could have.

ANAEA'S HEART POUNDED, AND EVERYTHING WITHIN HER SCREAMED FOR her to run. But Mark's car was in the parking lot below. Which meant he'd returned.

Maybe he wasn't home. Maybe he'd seen whoever had burst open his door and had run away.

Her mouth went dry, and she peered through the crack between the splintered door and warped metal frame. The apartment was trashed. The sofa lay on its back and the monitor was smashed. Pieces of torn and broken canvases lay among the knocked-over books, movies, magazines, and art supplies. Blood was streaked across the far wall by the balcony door.

A faint groan sent her heart racing. Oh, God. She scrambled across the room. There, behind the couch. A hand with twitching fingers.

Mark lay in a pool of blood, clutching his gut and failing to hold an enormous gash together. Both legs were broken, one lying at an unnatural angle while the other's bone protruded through his pants. Blood covered his bruised and swollen face.

His uneven gaze focused on her through slitted lids. "Anaea."

"Just lie still. Help is on the way." She spun around. Where the hell was the phone?

"No, Anaea."

She needed a phone. But in all the destruction she didn't even know where to begin looking. Maybe the bedroom. Surely they hadn't trashed the entire apartment.

"Anaea." He brushed his free hand against her leg. Her heart leapt into her throat. She had to do something.

"I—" His lids fluttered.

She dropped to her knees. "Just hold on. I'll get help—"

He reached for her face, drawing a sticky line across her cheek. She grabbed his hand. Tears burned her eyes.

"Please, Mark." She swallowed hard. Surely someone had heard something and called 911. The attack and all this destruction couldn't have been quiet. Surely Mark had screamed when they... when they had... Oh God.

She had to get help. Now.

Mark gasped.

"Mark?"

His eyes rolled up and his hand went limp.

"Mark, please." She squeezed his hand but he didn't respond. "No.

Please." She shook his shoulder. His other hand fell from his gut, revealing protruding intestines.

Bile burned the back of her throat. Her vision blurred. She'd killed her friend. She shouldn't have turned to him for help. She should have tried to figure everything out on her own.

She brushed a lock of hair from his face. All she'd wanted was to die in peace, and now she was responsible for the deaths of three people. Black specks danced across her vision, blurred then popped into sharp focus. Maybe she should let them take her. Kill her, end it. But then what would happen to Hunter.

The specks swelled. *Hunter?*

No answer.

She was still very much alone.

Her vision blurred again but the tears wouldn't come. Trembling, she fought the dry, silent sobs wracking her body. She couldn't even let go long enough to mourn Mark. It was disgusting. She'd spent too long closing people off under the guise of strength. Surely, she could take a moment and cry. She hadn't even cried for herself, not even when her doctor had said that awful word. She still didn't know if she was worth tears, but Mark... gentle, artistic Mark certainly deserved them. For just a moment. Just to prove she wasn't completely broken.

She sucked in a ragged breath and sobbed it out. The tears quivered in her eyes, and her throat burned. Then one broke free, tracing a hot line down her cheek, and another and another.

A fire ignited in her heart. Gasping, she tried to clutch her chest, but instead reached for Mark, unable to resist the compulsion. She pressed her hands to his temples and smashed her lips against his. Energy flared, burning through her veins, in white-hot agony that bubbled out of her and spilled into Mark's body. She struggled to regain control. Her muscles shuddered, and more energy poured out, burning until she couldn't breathe. The force controlling her snapped, and she wrenched back. Blinding light shot from Mark's mouth and he inhaled a deep, gasping breath.

Anaea's heart skipped a beat. "Mark?"

Mark's gaze darted about the room, his expression shocked for one timeless heartbeat, then he moaned and his face twisted in agony.

"Mark?"

He pressed his hands to his gut and turned his head the fraction necessary to see her. Red flashed around him.

Oh, God. "Hunter?"

"Just… give me… a minute," he gasped.

Anaea's thoughts whirled, a vortex of half-formed questions that she couldn't bring into focus. "Is Mark still there?"

Hunter pursed his lips.

He mustn't want to say.

Which meant Mark was dead.

Her throat tightened.

"Don't fall apart on me," he said. With Mark's voice. "We still have to get out of here."

23

Hunter ground his teeth against the pain. His teeth. Not Anaea's. She stared at him, her eyes wide. He couldn't imagine what was going through her mind. He could barely think past the agony screaming through his new and broken body. Anaea's friend had not died peacefully and whoever had done this could come back for Anaea, if they weren't already hiding in wait for her. What the hell had gone on while he was trapped in her head?

He struggled to sit up. His muscles trembled and partially mended flesh strained against the movement. He just needed to heal enough so his guts didn't spill out and his broken legs held together. Thank the Mother of All for dragon-fast healing and not a drop of water in sight to weaken his fiery nature.

Other bones were broken: the fingers in his right hand, his nose and left cheek, and a couple vertebrae in his back. He didn't want to count the lacerations and bruises. It wasn't the best body to have jumped into, but then he hadn't had much choice. He hadn't initiated the transfer. Anaea unconsciously had, a natural involuntary reaction when two souls shared a body and an empty vessel was presented.

"Come on, help me up."

"But your—" She bit her lip and nodded.

Atta girl. She'd come to the same conclusion he had: they were still in danger.

She stood, braced herself, and offered her hand. He reached for it, but changed his mind. Easier to roll over and stand from hands and knees than using his useless abs to hoist himself upright.

Fire shot through him as he struggled over. His legs, barely mended, trembled with the added weight. Please just let one of them hold. Black specks flashed across his vision and he sucked in a breath. It rasped in his chest. With the exhale, foam bubbled into his mouth and he spat it out. He hadn't been this hurt since the Fifth Crusade.

Anaea placed a tentative hand on his shoulder and heat tingled down his arm and up his neck. "If we're leaving perhaps you shouldn't look like you've killed someone," she said.

"What?"

Her hand withdrew, leaving him cold. "You're covered in blood."

He glanced at the pool beneath him.

"Can you get out of those clothes?"

He wasn't thinking straight. He should have thought of that. He looked like a mass murderer fresh from the kill.

He nodded, spending spikes of pain through his face, and she hurried away.

With sticky fingers, he peeled off his shirt. Agonizing tremors shook him. His damaged gut and chest had knitted shut, but the organs beneath were still damaged, and his soul magic was doing everything in its power to keep him together. He was fumbling with the button and fly of his pants when Anaea returned with a duffle bag, a change of clothes, a ball cap, and a towel. Without hesitation, she pushed his hands away and undid his jeans.

Heat swept over him, pooling low, and it had nothing to do with his damaged body or healing soul magic.

"Lean back."

He worked his pants over his hips and perched on the edge of the toppled sofa. Kneeling, she grabbed the hem and eased the fabric from his body, keeping her gaze locked on his feet. A faint flush of red crept up her neck.

Hunter's heart pounded, and his breath wheezed. Agony battled for a moment with arousal until a fresh wave of pain washed over him. He was damned well going to heal fully, get them out of this mess, and make good on the unspoken promise hanging between them.

"I... ah..." She held out the towel, her gaze not straying from the floor. Her blush swept over her cheeks and forehead.

"Good thinking." He wrapped his unfamiliar hand around hers, their fingers brushing. More heat slipped up his hand, easing some of his pain.

Her gaze jumped to his. He could see her heartache and confusion. All manner of painful emotions flitted across her expression, but behind it was a fierce determination staring back, as strong as any dragon's.

He nodded and she matched the movement, relinquishing the towel. On unsteady legs, he stepped away from the blood. With Anaea's help, he staggered to the kitchenette and washed his face and hands as best and as fast as he could. If the assailants weren't still around, the police would be soon.

Mostly clean, he changed into the fresh clothes—Mark's clothes —and pulled the ball cap low to shadow his face. Leaning on Anaea, he staggered out of the apartment and down the hall to the stairs. Somehow, a miracle beyond miracles, all was quiet. The neighbors were probably hiding in their apartments waiting for help to arrive. He couldn't fathom how their luck had managed to hold, but it did. Maybe the assailants assumed Hunter wouldn't return, which he wouldn't have.

He eased down the stairs, careful of his mending bones. Pain jolted through him with every step. Anaea was silent. He didn't know if he should be grateful or worried.

Reaching the bottom, Hunter glanced into the parking lot through the glass door.

Almost empty and no one looked like a drake.

Good.

They shambled to Mark's car. Hunter hotwired it, and Anaea slipped into the passenger's seat. Still silent. There was a long conversation coming, one he didn't particularly want to have because he had no idea what to say.

Hurt as he was, he still didn't want someone as shocked as Anaea driving. They left the lot as a fire truck turned onto the street with a police car close behind.

Once this mess with people trying to kill him was over, he'd definitely have to leave Newgate for a while. There'd be too many questions concerning Mark's disappearance, and Hunter was loath to find another body. He'd hopped twice in an incredibly short time, making him a perfect candidate for soul sickness induced by body hopping.

They abandoned the car a good distance from the trashed apartment in an elementary school parking lot across the street from a public library. He'd have liked to have parked the car farther away from the library, but he wasn't in much condition to go marching around.

"The library?" Anaea asked, her first words since the apartment. "What the hell are we doing at the library?"

He opened the glass door and ushered her in. "Confirming a place to stay."

"We're what?"

He hobbled through the narrow foyer, up the stairs, and into the hushed main floor. "There must be a thousand questions racing through your mind, and that's the one you ask?"

"I'm warming up."

A clerk behind the checkout desk eyed them as they passed. Hunter could just imagine how they looked and didn't want to think about it. He inched the cap lower to better shadow his ruined face and made a beeline for the computers in the center of the room. Only half were occupied. Thank goodness for small blessings, since he didn't want to stand around and wait his turn.

Going to the closest machine, he entered his library card number from memory. Other dragons had scoffed at the invention of the public library. What good was a hoard if it wasn't your own? But since Hunter wasn't inclined toward books, he found the concept intriguing. Humans hoarding something and yet sharing it. And, quite frankly, with memorized library card numbers for the cities he frequented the most, he always had internet access.

His body throbbing, he leaned against the desk and brought up his email program. He sent a quick note to the CEO of his company to inform the Royal Park Hotel to book two guests into the reserved executive suite and purchase clothes to fit both of them, as well as send over the sealed envelope in Hunter's safe. They could both use a change of clothes and the envelope contained emergency money and new credit cards.

The humans had an organization whose motto was 'always be prepared' and that philosophy had helped Hunter more times than he'd care to count. The hotel was just one of his many secret holdings. He might have aligned himself with the diminished Royal Coterie shortly after the Great Scourge but he'd prepared for the termination of that arrangement. Particularly when it became obvious that Constantine suffered from soul sickness with his mercurial moods.

It was actually surprising that Hunter had managed to go centuries without having to tap into his carefully developed resources. Only Grey knew of Hunter's wealth and business holdings, and anyone else could guess that he had something since most drakes who hadn't been reborn in the last hundred years had created financial safety nets. But even Grey was only aware of a fraction of the details, and the Royal Park was one such secret.

It was a luxury accommodation, unlike any place Hunter usually stayed while hunting. He kept a modest-sized executive suite but had never used it, and doubted anyone would consider looking for him there, including Regis. Besides, he wanted Anaea to feel pampered. She deserved it and needed it. And he needed to give her that. It burned in his newly inamorated soul that he hadn't treated her like he should have, even if the situation hadn't allowed it. That, and he needed to hole up for at least a few days. He could only pray this body had a connection to the earth's magic and he could tap it in record time. Until then, they were going to have to stay put. They might as well be comfortable.

GREY MATERIALIZED IN THE RECEIVING HALL AT COURT'S PUBLIC anchored gate, not in his suite as he'd intended. In his hurry to retrieve a weapon that he should have brought in the first place, along with the stress of keeping his memories at bay, his concentration had slipped—again. He sagged against the wall, black specks dancing across his vision. His throat ached, and every muscle in his body throbbed from being on high alert while in the human world.

Remembered rain rattled against the windowpane, and the reek of rotten food wafted over him.

He didn't have time for this. He wasn't sure what he'd seen in the alley beside Jade's shop, but it hadn't been good. At least Hunter had escaped, although Grey had no idea who'd made the white gate. Maybe Hunter was back in control of the body, or—and this was more likely the case with the white gate—maybe the Handmaiden had helped him.

Wouldn't that be lovely. But Grey wouldn't know until he found Hunter or Hunter phoned. Or the Handmaiden returned to Court and revealed what she'd done. And the more Grey thought about it, the more it had to be true. Only the Handmaiden's gates were white. If Hunter had somehow gotten back in control of his body, his gate would have been black. Which still didn't solve the problem that Hunter was in trouble.

Grey drew power to gate to his suite but stopped. Even if those drakes were still there—which he doubted—Hunter wasn't. And the purpose of the exercise was to find where Hunter was and what was wrong with him.

Damn.

What he really needed was a way to find Hunter. Although

running one or two traitorous drakes through with a dull blade had a certain amount of appeal as well.

He fished his cell out of his pocket. The only person he could think of calling was Capri. Her specialty was cleanup, but she knew more about today's human world than Grey did, and if he could trust another drake with Hunter's current situation it would be her.

He flipped the phone open.

But could he trust her? If he guessed wrong, things would get much worse.

Footsteps down the hall drew his attention. Zenobia sauntered in his direction, followed by her Second. Her eyes lit up when she saw Grey and she sped up her pace.

"Hello, Grey." She showed a hint of teeth. It wasn't a sexual invitation.

Even if it was, Grey wasn't stupid enough to take the bait. Zenobia didn't like him, and she did nothing to hide her distaste. He couldn't tell if she hated him because of his association with Hunter or not, but Hunter was closer to family than his own, and anyone who was against Hunter was against him.

"Zenobia." He flashed a little more teeth than she did.

Her Second, a green drake in a thirty-something male with richly dark skin, stiffened.

"How's Hunter? Still alive?"

A growl thrummed in Grey's chest. "He's fine."

She smirked and raised an eyebrow. "Are you sure? I'd keep an eye on him in his weakened condition. You never know when a drake might take advantage of the situation."

"Are you confessing something?" Maybe he didn't have to go back to the human world for a fight. He could just impale her. She'd heal fast enough, and it would make him feel better.

She opened her eyes wide in a mockery of innocent surprise. "Not me. But just about every dragon has their eye on his position. Who wouldn't want control of the medallion? I can think of a few who'd make excellent assassins."

"I'm sure you could." This conversation was getting old. Fast.

"For one, that little girl leading the North American Clean Team. What is her name?"

Zenobia knew very well what Capri's name was. "She doesn't want the job."

"You so sure? No one talked about taking the job when Hunter was so strong. But now he's a weak little woman."

Zenobia's Second chuckled.

"He has fire," Grey said.

"But will that be enough?" She shook her head as if answering her question and sauntered away with her Second.

"Bitch," Grey growled at her back.

Her Second glanced at him.

"Try me." Grey could take him. He was dying to take him. But Zenobia snapped her fingers and the man fell into step beside her. She hadn't outright admitted to the attacks on Hunter, but she hadn't denied it either.

Grey opened his cell and dialed the first three digits of Capri's number.

Every dragon had their eye on Hunter's position at Court. Surely Capri was happy with the job she had. Yet there was no way to know for sure.

He ground his teeth. Zenobia was playing with him, and he was foolish enough to take the bait.

"Bitch."

He finished dialing Capri's number. But she didn't pick up, and he wasn't going to leave a message.

24

Anaea couldn't make her mind work. She would have thought, given everything that had happened in the last couple of days, she'd just accept Hunter taking over Mark's body. But she couldn't. Couldn't see past her college crush to the predator within. Perhaps this was the last straw. She'd seen more than she could take and was going to lose her mind like the crazy jester in the Dragon Court.

Hunter hotwired the lock to a suite on the second floor of a fancy, towering hotel.

"Isn't someone going to notice?" she asked.

He swung the door open and stepped aside, indicating she should enter first.

"No. I own it."

The suite's sitting room was spacious, with a conversation area comprised of antique furniture near a marble fireplace and an out-of-place large-screen television.

"You own what?"

By the door, to her right, sat an office area, complete with laptop and printer. An enormous oil painting of a clear summer sky hung above the desk.

"I own the hotel. Or rather, one of my holding companies owns it.

You tend to build significant resources when you've been around as long as I have."

She hugged herself against shivers threatening to consume her. It was just another detail. Nothing more. And yet, it was a detail that reminded her of how insane her life had become. Of course Hunter was rich. He'd had a thousand years or so to amass his wealth. Hell, he owned a Gutenberg Bible and had probably bought it new from Gutenberg himself.

"I found in my line of business it helps to have a few contingency plans."

"And we're safe here?" She had no idea how Mark had been found. Magic, probably. Which meant, how could they be safe here or anywhere?

Hunter shuffled to the closest chair, a stiff wingback in dark red damask. "No one knows I own this place, and a dragon would have to do a lot of digging to discover that I do. And by then our problem should be solved."

She nodded, his words washing over her.

"Why don't you go get cleaned up. In a couple of hours I can officially check us in." He offered a rueful smile, looking ever so much like Mark. Her heart skipped a beat and her teeth chattered.

She clenched her jaw.

"It wouldn't do for us to show up mere minutes after the email notification was sent."

"I suppose not."

"There are robes in the bathroom, and I made arrangements for fresh clothing once we check in."

She nodded but didn't move. She couldn't, not without trembling. God, she was going to shake herself to pieces if she didn't do something soon. And without Hunter's soul in her body to heal her, she wouldn't be able to recover if she fell apart.

"Anaea." His voice was soft, heartbreakingly like Mark's the night they'd said goodbye. Her eyes burned and her vision blurred. She turned to the only other door in the suite. It had to lead to a bedroom and the bathroom.

"Anaea."

Not looking at him was worse. Now all she could think of was Mark and what had never been between them. She wanted to rant and scream and pound her frustration into something... someone.

"I'm okay." It hurt to say it, but there wasn't anything else she could say. Nothing that would be productive or make her feel better.

"Are you sure?"

Her throat tightened. Why did he have to push? Mark wouldn't have. That had been their problem. But it wasn't Mark sitting behind her. It was Hunter. Magical, feral Hunter. Who wasn't human. And who had thrown her into this nightmare. But that wasn't a fair thought, either, and she couldn't maintain her anger at him.

She sniffed. "I just need..." She didn't know what she needed. Well, she did. She just couldn't bring herself to ask. She needed to be held and told everything was going to be all right. But it wouldn't be, and it wouldn't be Mark murmuring those words. "I just need a hot shower and something to eat."

"Anaea." He sucked in a noisy breath and shuffled close, but she refused to look at him.

"Something with chocolate would be preferable."

He brushed her shoulder with a tentative hand, but didn't maintain the contact. "Chocolate I can do."

"Thank you."

———

HUNTER DIRECTED THE BELLBOY TO PUT THE BAGS OF CLOTHES ON THE desk. He thanked the young man with a tip large enough to inspire loyalty but not gossip and closed the door behind him, clicking the bolt into place and hooking on the chain. Unwelcome guests would at least be slowed down by the door even if it wouldn't stop them.

He couldn't hear the shower anymore, but Anaea wasn't in the living room. He shuffled to the bedroom door and eased it open. She lay on the bed, eyes closed, wrapped in the blankets, and curled into the fetal position.

His heart contracted. He hated to see her so vulnerable, and sleep revealed the insecurities she kept locked deep within her. He wanted to show her all the strength she possessed and failed to recognize. This woman was a warrior, and more of a dragon in spirit than many dragons he knew.

He inched closer. Pain rippled through him. Not the sharp agony he'd first experienced when he'd been thrown into this body, more a dull ache of healing. It felt strange to be in an empty vessel after the warmth of Anaea's occupied one, even for the short time he'd spent with her. He was alone.

Again.

A creature of magic chained to the earth. A dragon without a real coterie and with very few friends. He had thought the fury brought on by the great betrayal of those human sorcerers was enough to sustain him, but it was empty. As empty as the anger that had motivated the humans in the first place, so very long ago.

But those men were dead, nothing but dust. He doubted any of them had been true sorcerers and were immortal like dragons, seeing as no one had heard or seen any activity from them since. The Handmaiden's fears that the sorcerers lived and would finish off the dragons were unfounded. The Mother of All had destroyed them and saved dragonkind, albeit in spirit form. Humans rose and fell, some by his hand, and he obeyed his king and prince. That was his life.

But there was no comfort there, no love.

Anaea had left the medallion on the nightstand, and he gingerly picked it up, not wanting to wake her, and hung the chain around his neck.

She sighed. Her breathing changed, and her lids fluttered open. A moment of panic, of not knowing where she was, flashed across her face, and then her gaze locked on Hunter. A hint of a smile pulled at her lips, then she pursed them and the expression vanished.

Had she been happy to see him or the man whose body he possessed?

He shoved that thought away. He couldn't do anything about that, as much as he really wanted to. Regardless, she drew him to her, a moth to a flame, his spirit unable to resist hers. He knelt beside her.

She snaked a hand out of the covers and brushed her finger along his jaw, drawing heat with her touch. He wanted to say something, but he had no words. How could he express joy and sorrow all at the same time?

If he were in his true form, he'd leap into the air, roar and spit fire. If he were still in her body he'd sense her feelings and know what to do.

He inched closer. Her breath caressed his cheek, warm and feathery. Just like in her dream.

What they'd started in her dreams, they could finish in reality. But not now. She was his inamorata and in need of comfort. He just had no idea if she felt the same about him. Dreams were just dreams. Nothing more. In fact, she probably had no idea how he felt about her. She thought she was broken and unworthy and ugly. But there was nothing damaged about her and it was he who didn't deserve an inamorata as beautiful in body and spirit as Anaea.

Humans expressed this with touches and kisses. Like when she'd touched his jaw.

He drew a gentle line along her chin. Her wide eyes stared into his. The promise of their dream quivered in the breath between their lips.

Mother of All, he needed to show her how he felt, needed her to know she was more than worthy. He brushed his lips against hers. Heat zinged through him.

She froze. Her eyes widened farther.

It hadn't been enough. That tentative contact hadn't shown her anything. He dipped close again, but she jerked back, pulling the blanket up until all he could see of her were her pale eyes.

His gut churned and all warmth seeped from him. Now he had even fewer words.

Anaea couldn't stop trembling. Hunter had kissed her, tentatively, and all she could think of was him in Mark's body. She shouldn't have pulled away. The pain in his eyes made her heart break. Then he'd rushed from the room without a word. She should call him back and tell him—

Tell him what? That she wanted what she'd fantasized? Boy, did she ever want what they'd had in her dream, and more. But he didn't know about that. And there was Mark. Or rather, there wasn't Mark but his body. She wanted Hunter. Not Mark. The two weren't one and the same, and yet…

She squeezed her eyes shut.

This was complicated. So very, very complicated. Too much had happened, too soon. She needed time to think and adjust. She could deal with this. Honestly.

If she were in her right mind, she'd get up and run as far away from the mess as possible. But she couldn't abandon Hunter.

She snorted at that thought. Hunter was more than capable of taking care of himself, particularly in this situation.

Fine. She'd admit it. She liked Hunter and missed having him in her head. Yeah, she'd wanted him out, but now that he was gone, she felt empty and abandoned again.

Which was completely ridiculous. He was still with her. He'd even tried to kiss her. Of course, all she'd seen was Mark, and she'd pushed him away.

And she was back again to everything being complicated.

Swell.

25

Hunter splashed water on his face but it did little to ease the confusion of emotions within him. And they all had to do with Anaea. Every fiber of his being now knew she was his inamorata and he had no idea how she felt about him. Which still didn't mean anything if they were dead.

He stared at his new face in the mirror, the glaring light from the hotel bathroom accentuating the sharp features. A stranger stared back at him. Dark hair, tousled from sleep, curled around his ears and the nape of his neck, too long for his liking. His dark eyes stood out against slightly tanned skin. If he squinted he could imagine they were still the eyes of his previous body. At least he was back to being tall.

He dragged his T-shirt off.

And strong again. He was lean-muscled, reminding him of the wiry black belts in Japan who'd kicked his Crusader's ass centuries ago. He could work with this. Attack and bash was no longer his best style. But he had others and suspected this body was faster on its feet than his last one.

Did Anaea like it or was that why she'd refused to kiss him? From their shared dreams, she'd appreciated the Crusader. But there had been something between her and this man. He wasn't sure what and didn't know if he wanted to ask. Sometimes the hope, before receiving the answer, was better than the knowing.

Which was ridiculous. He'd always wanted to know, always wanted to plan with all information available. Anaea was something different.

She was confusing, that's what she was. She was human and, because of him, a mage. But she was so much more than that. A warrior, a linguist, a woman.

His inamorata.

Mother of All, he was losing his mind. The instinctual need to prove himself worthy of her was overwhelming, but he wouldn't be able to do that until the attacks on his life had been stopped—he'd worry about Regis demanding her life when the immediate threat was over.

Which meant he had to get off the defensive even if his body hadn't connected to the earth's magic yet. Every time he turned around another drake was after him, and as a result, Anaea as well. He couldn't let anything happen to her. Whether he liked it or not, it was his turn to do some hunting.

He had no proof Zenobia was responsible and in this case, his gut didn't count since the challenger from dinner last night had looked to Nero for help. What he did know was that everyone who had attacked him, who hadn't been a human mage, had been young. So he'd start by talking to the younglings. He'd have to change his appearance a little, so he wasn't recognizable as the human they'd just tortured and killed, but there weren't many young drakes who'd recognize his aura. They'd only know he was a dragon. With luck, he'd confirm Zenobia's involvement, make short work of her flunkies, and collect her soul.

He snorted at the thought. Not likely. Not with the way things had been going lately. He'd probably have to call in a little help. Grey was always up for knocking a few heads together, even if the drake didn't want to go into the human realm anymore. But Hunter needed to expose the root of the problem so he could defend his actions when Regis and the other doyens of the Counseling Coteries found out. Taking Zenobia's soul without a writ would be too much like proclaiming himself independent. The doyens would demand Hunter's rebirth for killing one of their own, even if they didn't like her, and Regis would have a fit at losing his assassin. Taking her soul with proof would still end in a fight, but it was the best he could come up with.

He really wished he had the time to wait for this body to connect to the earth's magic. But that would cool any possible leads and continue to endanger Anaea. He wondered what magic he'd develop this time. More fire would be nice. He could practically feel it rolling over his tongue like it had in the old days.

Which was neither here nor there. The odds of him getting fire were slim. The odds of finding two bodies in a row that could were practically impossible. There was no guarantee this form could even connect to the earth's magic. Many dragons couldn't.

There was nothing he could do about that. All he could do was focus on making Anaea safe. First things first. A change of appearance. There wasn't a whole lot he could do in a short time save shave his head. He'd prefer a buzz cut, but beggars couldn't be choosers. And hopefully a haircut would make him feel more like himself.

After shaving his head, he dragged on a clean T-shirt and strode through the bedroom into the sitting room. Anaea sat on the couch watching the local news. She stared at him, her mouth drawn into a tight line, her disapproval palpable even from across the room.

His heart flip-flopped. Damn it. It was his body now. He could cut his hair any way he liked.

"I'm not into the solidarity thing. Now we won't be able to stand beside each other in public for a good couple of weeks," she said.

"What?" Not the response he'd expected.

"We'll look like the Bobbsey Twins." She ran a hand over her stubble. It seemed longer than before.

Nah, he was imagining things. He was seeing her as he'd envisioned in her dream because that was what she wanted him to see.

"Yours'll grow back in no time."

She opened her mouth but closed it without speaking and turned back to the television. "There's nothing in the news about…" She glanced back at him, her gaze sweeping over his body, sending heat washing through him. "Mark."

"There was a lot of blood. The police might be holding details from the press."

She swallowed. "He has— had a family."

"Everyone does." This wasn't a conversation he wanted to have. He didn't know what to say and couldn't begin to imagine how she felt to look at her friend and know he was dead. Hunter had never regretted taking a deceased human's body before. But then, the last time he had, he'd known nothing about the man. "I need to go out for a bit."

She jerked up. "What for?"

"To find out what's going on. I'm tired of running."

"Well, so am I."

So brave, he could hug her. But dragons were dangerous, and he didn't know what he'd do if anything happened to her. Man, he really was in trouble. He'd fallen down the rabbit hole of inamoratas and didn't want out. "This isn't your fight."

"I beg to differ."

Okay. Fine. She had him there. If no one realized he'd switched bodies then they were still looking for her. And now she didn't have rapid healing.

"I'm just going to talk to a few drakes. Find out some information. That's all." But from her pursed lips, he could tell she saw right through the lie.

"I'm not going to sit here while you go out and fix everything."

"Of course you are." Every cell in his stolen body screamed for him to do this for her, get his hands bloody so she wouldn't have to. He wanted to give her everything, including every piece of sky he cherished.

"No. I'm not." She stood and strode to the door.

"They'll know you're human." He seized her arm and jerked her close. Her hands pressed against his chest, drawing an inferno within him. The odds were slim that any drakes would be able to tell the difference between a dragon and a mage. Only a lucky few could see the difference in their auras. But Hunter wasn't going to tell Anaea that and wasn't willing to take that risk. "I'll not permit you to go."

Damn, he shouldn't have said that, but now that he had, he didn't want to take it back.

"You'll not permit?" She shoved him back. "Not permit? Been there, done that. No man tells me what to do anymore."

"I'm not just any man." A growl rumbled with him.

"You're acting like one."

The rumble grew, and the room was washed in red. Mother of All. She really was a drake in spirit. "We can argue about this later. Besides, I'm not going to fix anything right now, just speak with a few younger drakes at Baltu. I want—" He sucked in a ragged breath. "I need you to stay here, safe, so I can focus on the hunt."

He grabbed his coat and stormed out the door. It was either that or take her there on the floor. When this was done he'd court her properly with shinies and meat and—

Shit. Human women might like shiny things, but did they appreciate whole cows? He couldn't just kill something, present it to her, and expect her to fall in love.

He ground his teeth. He hadn't integrated well into the human realm at all.

ANAEA HUGGED HERSELF, UNABLE TO TEAR HER GAZE FROM THE DOOR. It was her life, too. How dare he proclaim he would fix everything and she should just sit around and wait. She'd never sat around and waited for anyone. The fact that her life had somehow spiraled out of her control just made her want to do something even more.

And now, every time she looked at him she saw Mark. She supposed she saw more of Hunter now that he'd shaved his head. Mark's head. She'd loved those curls. Every woman she knew was jealous of them. Now they were gone. Probably a mess on the floor for housekeeping to sweep up.

Her eyes burned. That wasn't fair. She knew Hunter better than that. He wouldn't intentionally leave a mess for someone else to clean up. Their whole fight had been about that. The mess was his, and he had to deal with it alone. The problem was that she knew everyone after him was also after her, since they'd have no way of knowing Hunter had changed bodies. Which meant, damn it, it was her problem, too, and she was going to do something about it. She could gather information just as well as Hunter could.

Besides, she felt better, felt alive. It was a misconception, she knew that. Nothing could heal cancer. But she'd spent so long being weak and insignificant. She had to do something now. If Hunter had shown her anything in the last couple of days, it was that she, too, could face her death fighting.

And damn it, bad idea or not—and she was sure going after Hunter to get information from other dragons was a bad idea—she wanted... no, needed to do this.

Hunter had said he was going to talk to the younger drakes at Baltu. She had no idea what that meant, but Hunter did, and she could still feel the memories he'd infused into her brain hiding at the back of her consciousness.

She concentrated on those memories. Images of a medieval battlefield filled her mind.

Not what she wanted.

She clamped down on the vision, drawing her sight back to black. She needed his modern memories. Something about Baltu. Perhaps concentrating on how their connection had felt when he'd been in her head would help her tap into something more recent.

The sensual dream flashed to the forefront, and her body heated. At least the memory was of this century. She reveled in it for just a moment then clamped down on it. But the glow of Hunter's presence wrapped around her and remained. It almost felt as if he was in her head again, a strong, sexy presence.

Boy, she missed him. But that was just her fantasy imposed on the situation. Not anything true. Although maybe the memory of his presence would help her better connect with the thoughts he'd left behind.

She focused on the desire he inspired, how he'd made her feel and how she wanted to continue feeling. What was Baltu? And why would he talk to dragons there? Who would he go to for information on their current situation?

The image of a steel and glass high rise flashed across her mind's eye and information flooded her. Baltu. A private spa. A place where drakes likely wouldn't recognize him and would gossip. He'd mentioned younger drakes, which made sense. Most wouldn't have been at the *pahar* so they wouldn't know Hunter had been in her.

The address popped into her head along with the sense that it was hidden inside the building.

What were the odds that Hunter would be pissed when she showed up? Too good to take that bet. But she needed to reclaim her life, stop being scared and reacting. She was tired of being a passenger. It was time, ready or not, for her to do something.

26

Hunter's taxi pulled up to the sleek glass high rise at the corner of 5th and 6th Avenues. Barna, the doyen of the Major Brown Coterie, owned it along with large chunks of the city. It would have been nice if the easiest portal to Court had been someplace with more temperate weather. California would have been great. Australia, Bermuda. Any place that wasn't freezing close to six months of the year. Even the climate in Bath, although less than fabulous, was still better.

But Newgate was the most unstable place between dimensions, making it the easiest location to open a gate into Court, so this was where the majority of young and weaker drakes resided. And Barna, ever the entrepreneur, had established all manner of entertainment for his fellow dragons to squander their amassed fortunes—or, if they had been reborn, their coterie's fortune, since a reborn drake's hoard, if it was of any value, went to the coterie's doyen.

Baltu, for dragons only, was a preferred hangout for the younger dragons, regardless of coterie affiliation. To the average human observer the building was a regular office tower, but in the back and basement was a private spa.

Hunter entered the lobby, while searching within himself for his body's connection to the earth's magic. In reality, it was still too early, but it was worth a look. It would have been nice to arrive in the spa's gateroom and not have to slink in like a weak, lesser drake. If they thought him too weak, they might not talk to him. Of course, if they thought he was too strong they wouldn't talk to him either. It was always a balancing act with the young dragons, many of whom were young because of him. The other risk was the chance that whoever had killed Mark would recognize him, shaved head and all. But he'd already decided the risk was worth taking. If he found evidence that Zenobia was trying to kill him to get the medallion and making human mages to do it, he could focus on Anaea.

The memory of his hands... her hands... on her naked body in the shower back in his suite at Court rushed through him, drawing heat. What a complete mess. He would fix this. It didn't matter how impossible the odds, he owed it to her. Mother of All. He would fix this.

He strode through the expansive lobby to the back and pressed his palm against the keyhole for the cargo elevator. A tingle swept up his arm as the magic guarding the spa recognized his dragon soul. The bell dinged, and the doors slid open. He entered and waited. There was no need to press a button. He'd already indicated where he wanted to go by activating the magical lock.

The doors closed and the one behind him opened. Beyond lay a modern reception area, all chrome and glass and white paneling, with soft lighting. Large plants clustered in a corner beside a small glass reception desk. Save for monitor, keyboard, and telephone, the desk was empty. A young female drake emerged from a doorway behind the desk, dressed all in black, her blond hair pulled back in a tight chignon. Minimalistic like the spa.

"Afternoon." She spared him a quick look then dropped her gaze before it could be interpreted as a challenge.

"I'm here for lunch." He presented his new credit card.

She swiped it along the top of the keyboard and handed it back, still keeping her gaze lowered. "The lounge is to your right." She indicated a pair of smoky-glass doors then retreated back through the doorway behind the desk.

Here went a whole lot of nothing. He usually had stronger leads when chasing down a warrant. And he'd always known who he was after.

He pulled open the door, squaring his unfamiliar shoulders. The lounge had a tent-like feel, in drastic contrast to the reception area and the building behind him. Miniature trees, large ferns, and planter boxes bursting with exotic yellow, red, and orange flowers made the room feel like a tropical summer garden, while gossamer silks were draped from the ceiling, creating the suggestion of privacy. It made it difficult to see everyone in the room, but it also made it difficult for everyone to see him.

Please no one recognize his new body.

White panels on the walls and ceiling, lit with a soft glow, created a sense of natural sunlight. Matching palm trees framed the entrance to the gateroom. A possible exit, if he somehow connected to the earth's magic while here, but more likely a place for an attack. Most tables were booths with benches, ranging from two-seaters up to ten or more. There were about a hundred drakes in the room.

A man in a nearby booth leaned forward, catching Hunter's eye. Nero. Hunter inched back. The black drake would surely recognize him by his aura, but it was interesting that he was in Baltu. While not against a Traditionalist's beliefs, it was still uncommon to see one here. Unless, of course, Hunter had been wrong about Zenobia. Why else would Nero be in the spa surrounded by young dragons?

The person across from Nero, a man by the tenor of his voice, said something in Italian.

Hunter swallowed a curse. It was no good eavesdropping on someone if he couldn't understand the language. He should have brought Anaea with him. He bet she spoke Italian.

No. Really bad idea. If Nero saw them together he'd know Hunter had body-shared and then it would be impossible to keep her hidden from Regis. It was almost impossible now, without anyone else knowing.

Better to stay focused, pick up whatever gossip he could, and return to Anaea. They could come up with a plan together.

Hunter turned his back to Nero, looking for someone to chat up. No one looked familiar. Good. That meant they didn't hang out at Court and wouldn't recognize his aura. Laughter at the back drew his attention, a mixture of male and female voices all nervously excited. Hunter rounded a topiary shaped like a dragon to find half a dozen drakes, two men, four women, in an enormous booth.

"And I heard the great and mighty Hunter has been reduced to a woman," the larger of the two men said. He was built like a line-backer with a swarthy complexion and dark hair. Not a threat. Or he wouldn't have been if Hunter had been in his old body. Probably still not in this new one.

The group tittered with laughter. Even the other man seemed to titter.

Hunter snorted, and the swarthy drake's gaze jumped to Hunter, challenging for dominance. The man's size made him an obvious choice as leader of the group. Hunter held his gaze long enough to make the drake ever-so-slightly uncertain of his position in the unspoken dragon hierarchy, but not enough for an outright challenge.

"I heard he's practically a skeleton," a full-figured blond woman said.

"And bald." Hunter forced a smirk. It stung to make fun of Anaea's ailment, but he had no choice. Her hair would grow back, she'd regain a healthy weight, and her beautiful soul would be matched by her magnificent body.

The swarthy drake barked another laugh, sending the rest of the group into more giggles. Hunter laughed with them. It didn't matter what they thought about the prince's assassin, only that they trusted him enough to gossip. Besides, he didn't have that much of an ego. Okay, who was he fooling? Ego was the only thing keeping him going these days.

Except now he had Anaea and a new purpose.

"I'm not sure I'd laugh so hard," another muscular drake said as he approached. "Even as a woman Hunter still killed Welkin. And I heard he played with the idiot first and then lit him on fire. Not a pleasant way to die."

Hunter didn't recognize this guy, either. Jeez, he'd really fallen out of touch with the younger generation.

The swarthy drake frowned, but the others nodded, their expressions suddenly solemn.

Great. How was he going to get them to talk now?

***

ANAEA STOOD AT THE BACK OF THE SHINY OFFICE TOWER BY THE elevators with no idea how Hunter managed to get the damned thing to open. Somewhere, in the flashes of the murky memories he'd shoved into her head, she knew it would recognize her and let her in, yet no matter how many times she pressed her palm across the button nothing happened. If she didn't do something soon, someone would notice. And getting noticed wasn't on her list of things to accomplish.

Just a few more moments and she was sure she'd figure it out. But if the building had security those moments could create trouble and anyone from Court would still recognize her as Hunter. She should have put on a disguise in the very least. But in her haste to take control of the remains of her life, she hadn't thought of that. Twenty-twenty hindsight at its finest.

She pressed the call button for the regular elevators.

Then she remembered Grey. Last time she'd seen him was just before she'd gated away from Jade and the thugs. He probably thought Hunter was still in trouble.

Damn, she should at least call him and tell him everything was all right… more or less.

The door slid open and she pressed the first button she saw. Fifth floor. It was as good a choice as any.

First problem first: getting into the spa. She'd give it another shot, and if she couldn't figure out how to get in then she might as well leave. Then she could call Grey once she got back to the hotel.

She thought back on the door to Hunter's suite in the Dragon Court. Something magical had tingled up her arm and recognized Hunter, permitting her to enter. The door to the spa was probably something similar. Perhaps not attuned to a specific spirit, maybe just to dragons. And since she no longer had Hunter's spirit in her, the door didn't recognize her.

Just great. She didn't want Hunter to have his way with this. Sitting around helplessly, waiting for someone or something to kill her, had never been acceptable before and it wouldn't be now. This was a problem she *needed* to solve.

The elevator door slid open, revealing a wide hall as shiny and clean as the lobby. A few frosted glass doors broke the white and chrome paneling on the walls. Silver plaques mounted beside the doors indicated which businesses occupied the offices inside.

There had to be another way to get into the spa. She drew on Hunter's memories within her, but her frustration grew instead of easing. How was she going to get them to talk now?

She ground her teeth and strode down the hall. What was that all about? Where did that bizarre thought come from? She was alone up here. Who exactly was she supposed to talk to?

Despite the logical questions, the strange feeling remained. It was supposed to be a simple, quick information grab. That was all.

Yes. Exactly. She needed to get in and learn whatever information she could. It felt as if Hunter was back in her head, as if they had renewed their mental connection.

She reached a tall window at the end of the hall and stared at the street below. If she didn't get a grip, she was going to break something. She should have shown greater strength than arriving by mundane means.

Her heart skipped a beat.

No, *she* shouldn't have. *Hunter* should have.

Surely, this was just a memory, not a side effect of having had Hunter within her. But it couldn't be a memory. It was too unnerving, too close to her current situation.

Anaea held the thought, not shying away from it the way her

instincts insisted she should. There were answers in her head...
somehow. If Hunter should have arrived differently, how would that
have been?

A gate would have been nice. It would have demonstrated a
strength in earth magic that less than half of drakes possessed and
might have been enough to convince these fools to go back to
gossiping.

Of course. A gate. She could do that. She'd made one to escape
from Jade and suspected she'd created one to flee the Dragon Court.
Although she hadn't used any magic since Hunter had taken Mark's
body. Could she even still use it? Was it still a part of her?

She turned back to the elevator. If the door wouldn't recognize
her, gating in was her only other option.

A tiny, rational part of her brain berated her for acting like an
idiot. This was insane! She couldn't do magic. She was a normal
human being.

Then why did it feel so possible?

Heat seeped into her, ignited by that thought, and sent tingles
racing across her skin. The hair on her arms stood on end and she
shivered, but not from cold. The tingles raced over her again,
building up speed and energy, swirling around and around.

She called the elevator and rushed into it. Tendrils of white light
spun from her hands, caressing the back of the car. With a spike of
fire, the light latched onto something she couldn't see and the
tendrils jerked taut. The energy roared through her, pouring into the
elevator, drawing out sparks of herself along with it.

A dazzling speck formed in the center of the back wall, growing
with every beat of her heart until it was as large as her whole body.

The elevator dinged, indicating the main floor. She stepped
through the gate, the vortex encompassing her for a heartbeat before
she arrived in a bright alcove, the walls and ceiling glowing with soft
light. To her left and right were hallways marked with silver direc-
tional plaques. To the gym and pools. To other spa services.

Before her, a gossamer curtain covered a doorway. She inched
forward and drew the curtain aside. A tented wonderland of orange,

yellow, and red diaphanous fabric, cushioned booths, and greenery lay on the other side. Men and women socialized in knots of various sizes, standing, sitting, eating, drinking. A tall man with brown, stylishly mussed hair, sitting at a nearby booth, glanced at her. A hint of yellow light radiated around him. "A new arrival."

The other man and woman in his party turned her way. The light around them was both weak and yellow as well. And when she had a moment to figure out what that meant—not to mention wrap her mind around the fact she was seeing auras—she'd deal with it. As it was she froze, uncertain what to do. How did she think she could fit in with Hunter's people well enough to pass as one of them without his coaching?

"Very new, from the looks of it," the other man said, a blond. A smile spread across his classically handsome features.

The woman crossed her arms and frowned, but the man ignored her. He eased over to Anaea and held out his hand. "First time?" His voice slid over her, oil on water.

"Looks like Dune has this one handled," the first man said.

The woman rolled her eyes. "Just great."

"Catch you later," the first man said, and he escorted the woman away.

"Got a name, sweetie?" the blond, Dune, asked, holding out his hand.

Anaea bit the inside of her cheek. Why couldn't the others have stayed?

"Or should I just call you Sweetie?"

"Sweetie—" She swallowed back her harsh remark. She needed information. Not a fight. With luck, she could get what she wanted from Buddy here and extract herself before he got the wrong idea. Although from the looks of it, he already had the wrong idea. "Sweetie will do just fine. Care to give me the tour?"

"But it's lunchtime." He flashed a perfect, gleaming smile, and she suddenly felt like a mouse cornered by a cat.

"What has that got to do with anything?" Perhaps going against her initial instinct to blow Buddy off was a mistake.

"You can't go wandering around on an empty stomach."

She fought the urge to punch him, not sure if the desire was hers or a residual emotion of Hunter's. "Right."

He flexed his hand, drawing her attention back to it. It was still held out, an offer for her to accept his invitation.

Fine. Besides, she knew Kung Fu, not to mention a dozen ways to incapacitate a man. Thank you, Hunter. She brushed her palm against his and he snapped his hand shut before she could change her mind.

"Excellent." He flashed his smile again and led her into the room.

She felt like a new plaything on display. People watched her, all with various strengths and colors of auras, most with knowing or evaluating expressions.

More like an edible plaything.

Now she knew how that poor cow must have felt at the feast. It wasn't anything in particular that she could put her finger on. Nothing overt. Only that she knew, without a doubt, that she walked into the lion's den. Or rather, the dragon's den.

They rounded a pillar of silk. The main entrance lay only a few feet away. She could change her mind and get out. Go back to the safety of the hotel. Hunter really was much more capable of solving this mess. They were, after all, his people.

But that thought stung. It was her life, too. For once, she wanted to be in control of it. That, and she wanted Hunter to respect her, see her as an equal. She was tired of men looking at her as if she was a prize, or helpless, or just a thing.

A man two booths up ahead leaned back on his bench, the movement catching her attention.

Her heart skipped a beat. It was Nero.

She couldn't let him see her. He was sure to recognize her from the *wasu tahazu* and the feast, and then she and Hunter would be in trouble.

Nero's gaze lifted and she slipped into the small, dimly lit booth in front of his before he could see her.

"Why don't we sit here?" Anaea forced a flirty smile.

Dune grinned back. He glanced at the two-person seat, the curtains, and tropical plants. All of it suggested intimacy. "Absolutely, Sweetie."

He waved a waitress over, ordered a bottle of wine, then slid onto the bench opposite her.

"So are you new to town or just plain new?"

"New?" She had no idea what that meant. The memory of the rebirth ceremony flashed into her mind. "Oh, ah... new to town."

"Then you've certainly come to the right place." He sneered. She didn't think it was supposed to be a sneer, more like a seductive smile, but that wasn't how it looked. It sent shivers up her spine, and they weren't the good kind.

The waitress arrived with the wine, poured the first two glasses, and left. Anaea grabbed her glass, realized her hand trembled, and added her other hand to the stem to keep from spilling her drink.

"And you've definitely met the right drake."

She doubted that.

Nero said something in Italian, catching her attention. There were only a few reasons people conversed in foreign languages and one was to keep the conversation a secret.

"Well, you don't have to worry about Hunter anymore," the other man with him said, also in Italian.

Definitely a secret conversation.

Dune leaned into the table. "I'm available to show you... the town."

She nodded, only half listening to Dune and straining to hear Nero's voice.

"Hunter's resourceful and Howel's challenge only drew more attention to us," Nero said.

"You shouldn't have left him hanging."

"He got what he deserved." Nero's voice darkened. "And he'll get worse if I find he's changed allegiance. If another drake calls a challenge without my consent, he won't just have a handprint burned into his cheek. Are we clear?"

The other man didn't respond.

"Howel put us on Hunter's radar and I doubt Regis will call for his rebirth even for fleeing Court with the medallion without permission. Particularly with the Handmaiden missing. Which means we need to turn Hunter's attention away from us."

Anaea's heart skipped a beat. Dune said something, his lips moving, but she was no longer listening to him. Her thoughts whirled. She had no idea what Nero's conversation meant, but he obviously was hiding something.

Dune wrapped his hands around hers. "Why don't we skip lunch?"

"What?"

A heated look burned in his eyes. He eased the glass from her hands and placed it on the table, keeping her fingers captured with his free hand.

"I can help you fit in." His tone claimed the only way to do that was to sleep with him.

She caught movement from the corner of her eye as Nero stood, and she leaned forward, praying he wouldn't see her. "I'm sure you can," she said to Dune.

Nero strode past.

"But I don't have the time this afternoon—" she slid her fingers from Dune's grasp "—for a man so... versed in fitting in."

"Blow off the rest of your day."

She glanced away, hoping she looked coy and not desperate to leave. "I can't."

"Sure you can."

A polite 'no' was getting her nowhere. "I'm sorry. Not today." She stood. Maybe if she made a date he'd give up. "I'm free tomorrow."

He rose from the bench, the feral dragon within him radiating anger. It practically billowed off him in waves like heat from hot asphalt.

"A smart drake would listen to me." He grabbed her wrist and jerked her close.

"I'm sure." She fought to control her disgust and not make eye contact. Heat rippled over her skin, pooling in her hands.

"I don't think I've made myself clear." He seized the back of her head with his free hand and mashed his lips against hers.

Her heart leapt into a rapid tattoo. She twisted in his grip, but he held tight. She wondered if she should feel flattered that even bald and emaciated, someone found her attractive. But the man had no tact and crazy wasn't her type.

She shoved at him and he bit her lip.

Energy roared down her arms to her palms.

How could she have been such an idiot to assume she could handle this? She dragged Hunter's battle memories to the forefront, but there were too many, and they were too disorienting. Really, a quick knee to the groin was the easiest way to solve the problem. So much for being subtle.

She rammed her knee into him. He grunted and shoved her. She stumbled backward into the bench and toppled over.

"You won't get far in your coterie if you're not willing to play the game."

"Can you get any more clichéd?"

A man the next table over chuckled, while men and women at nearby tables stared. Some stood, many pointed.

Dune growled, fully releasing the feralness radiating from within. But he was nothing compared to Hunter. An infant in a world of adults. The energy within her surged. It poured from her heart across her chest and down her arms to her hands.

Dune scrambled back. "What the—?"

Something bright flickered at the edge of her vision, and she glanced down. Flames licked the cushioned seat, dancing along her fingers and clinging to the fabric. She leapt up, batting her hands against her legs. The fire on her hands went out. But with a whoosh, tendrils raced over the back of the bench and caught a curtain.

Someone yelled as the fire swept from one curtain to the next. Smoke billowed around her, stinging her eyes and making her cough. Dune was gone, and the flames encircled her.

27

Screams jerked Hunter's attention from the drakes at his table. Smoke swelled on the other side of the lounge, and people ran for the exit from a growing inferno. The fire alarm wailed to life. A heartbeat later, water spewed from the sprinklers but it did little to diminish the blaze. The flames were persistent, which meant magic, and there were only a few drakes who could call fire.

Dragons scrambled from their booths, rushing from the room. Those who could open gates without an anchor popped away in the chaos of bodies and smoke and water.

Something on the far side of the room caught his attention. The flames were thickest there, and smoke swelled and fluttered as water pelted through it. A figure stood in the center of the cloud. It looked liked Anaea, but there was something different about her.

The inferno surged, whipping in an unfelt wind, framing her in a perfect, horrific frieze. His stomach churned. She wasn't supposed to be here, and he had no idea how she'd found him. The place didn't even have a phone listing. How the heck had she even gotten in? Didn't she know being here was dangerous?

Her gaze lifted and met his. His heart skipped a beat. If the fire was of her creation, it shouldn't harm her much. The fire licked at her legs and her eyes widened then hardened.

Mother of All, he was in love with that woman. Surrounded by flames and drakes, and she still wasn't going to give in to fear.

He started to run toward her but a man leapt through the flames and grabbed her arm. She twisted in his grasp, her gaze still on Hunter, but the man was too strong and dragged her to the far exit.

Hunter ground his teeth. It should have been him saving her. He glanced around the room, checking for anyone else in trouble, but it appeared all of the drakes had managed to get out safely. Hurrying through the back door, Hunter ran down a narrow hall and out into a crowded alley.

Drakes and humans milled around on the shallow pink steps of the high rise across the street, bubbling with excited talk. He shoved through them. He had to find her. Now. Blood rushed in his ears, roaring away the sounds of the people, the traffic, and the emergency vehicles. Capri was going to have a fit when she heard about this.

There, on the edge of the crowd, in conversation with the drake who'd pulled her out of the flames. Thank the Mother of All she was safe.

He took her arm, leading her away from the commotion and shooting a glare at the drake who'd saved her, daring him to argue. "What the hell are you doing?"

"I'm fine, thank you." She yanked her arm out of his grip and hugged herself.

His heart clenched at the look on her face, but he pushed the feeling away. Damn it, he was mad at her. She could have gotten killed. "Not the question I asked."

"But the one you should have."

She had him there, and that truth stung. "I told you to stay put."

A woman from the crowd glanced at them. Shit. They were drawing attention. He steered Anaea around the corner past a thick stone wall and through an open wrought iron gate into the small courtyard of the building kitty-corner to Baltu.

"I said I'd handle it."

Anaea jerked away from him and stormed across the cobblestones along the wall, farther into the yard. She looked glorious, powerful, her cheeks bright with anger. Idly, he noticed her hair seemed to have grown a little bit. It was softer, becoming closer to the pixie cut he'd seen in the dream. He was somewhat surprised he hadn't seen it before, but it didn't really matter. Never had.

"I have no doubt you're able to handle this. But this is my life, too."

He strode to her, but resisted the urge to grab her. "My people are dangerous." Why couldn't she see that? There was evidence enough that a human couldn't survive among drakes without protection.

"I know that." She spun to face him, anger flashing in her eyes.

"Then why?"

"Because." She growled out the word, sending a shiver of excitement through him. "You ordered me."

"I— What—?" The strength and power radiating from her was intoxicating. The desire to be with her was overwhelming.

"I don't take orders anymore."

"It's for your own good."

"Fuck my own good. It's my life. My choice." She shoved him, rocking him back on his new, still-unfamiliar legs and feet.

He snagged her wrist, yanked her to him, and they stumbled against the courtyard wall. Every nerve ending within him ignited. A purr rumbled in his chest, and he brushed his jaw hard against hers. His scent to hers—as if they were actually dragons with scent glands. Mother of All, he'd never encountered someone who awakened all his instincts the way Anaea did. And it just proved how different and incompatible they were.

"Anaea."

She cupped his face, rubbing her thumbs along his jaw. If she didn't stop, he was going to start purring again.

"Anaea, I—"

"Shut up, Hunter."

She planted her lips against his, as if she feared his rejection or her loss of courage. Which was ridiculous on both accounts. Cross-species or not, she was the one he wanted for life. And as for courage, he suspected it flowed, constant and sure, through her veins.

He met her lips with his own hunger. She thrust her tongue into his mouth, licking and teasing, drawing an inferno from deep within him. All thought flew from his mind, consumed by a tremendous need.

He lifted her. She wrapped her legs around his waist, and he turned them, pressing her back to the rough wall. She moaned into his mouth, fueling his frenzy. His blood pounded through him. He had to have her. For real. Right now.

But she deserved more. Certainly more than being taken, without care, in public. She deserved to be wooed properly. Maybe not in a dragon's terms but certainly in human ones.

A chill raced over him. A new, terrible thought popped into his mind. Who was she really kissing? Him or the man whose body he possessed? She hadn't wanted to kiss him earlier, so why now?

He eased away from her lips. It was too soon. She couldn't want this or him. Maybe in the future, maybe once he'd figured out how to keep her safe. But this... this need wasn't for him. It was to ease the tremendous shock she had to be in. It was the only explanation. And the honorable thing to do would be to wait until she was thinking straight.

She dipped her lips to his, but he leaned back. He couldn't take advantage of her like this. He slid her legs from his waist and stepped back.

"Hunter?"

He couldn't look at her, couldn't bear to face how his perceived rejection would make her feel, even if it was the right thing to do.

"We should get back to the hotel."

"What?"

From the corner of his eye he watched her tremble, every line of her body rigid, exuding rage.

"It isn't safe." He was a fool, even if he was a fool for the right reason.

She clenched her fists, opened her mouth and snapped it shut. Then she wilted in on herself.

His heart ached. In the blink of an eye, his warrior dragoness was gone. And it was his fault.

She sniffed. "Fine."

A naea followed Hunter into the hotel suite, her lips still burning from the kiss. She had fantasized of running to Mark, after she realized she'd been a fool and her husband didn't love her. But it hadn't been Mark she kissed in that courtyard, and it wasn't Mark she wanted now.

How could she want Hunter so badly in so short of a time? It didn't make sense, and yet she couldn't deny her yearning to be drowning in his kisses again.

And it was Mark's body.

Her throat tightened. Her life was supposed to be over. Not his. It was too cruel that everyone around her died while she lived.

She threw open the curtains and stared out at the city, unable to focus on anything beyond the glass. God, she wanted Hunter more than she'd wanted anyone before. But he'd lied to her, kept secrets, and bossed her around. Admittedly, it might have been for her own good but she was done with men who wanted to do her thinking for her.

And now he wasn't talking to her. He'd been silent since he'd cut off their kiss, far too early for her liking. She still throbbed with unsatisfied desire. He'd probably realized she was damaged goods, or too independent, or something. There was a lot of her to find fault with. She just wished he'd say something.

Hunter stormed to the window and yanked the curtains closed. He didn't turn to her. The knuckles of his hands, still clenching the curtains, grew white. Anger mixed with something she couldn't recognize rolled off him in red waves more palpable than she'd ever experienced before.

Yep. No love there.

What if it had been a pity kiss? She had been the one to initiate it. Sure, he'd kissed back, but what man wouldn't? Maybe the sensual dreams had put crazy thoughts in her head and made her imagine that the attraction went both ways.

No. That couldn't be true. There were other moments when he'd seemed interested in her. Going to the spa had probably turned him off. She wasn't good and quiet and obedient.

But that had been what John had wanted, not Hunter.

Fine. Whatever.

So she'd screwed up. But he shouldn't have told her to stay put and expected her to do so. Which made it his fault. Okay, that was childish, but she didn't have anything else to hold on to.

"Are we going to talk about what we found or are you going to stand there all night and pout?" she asked.

"No." He didn't turn around.

She clenched her jaw. "You're just going to stand there and ignore me."

"I'm seriously considering it."

Oh, for the love of— "Fine. I'll share first."

Hunter remained focused on the closed curtains clutched between his hands.

"Nero was there."

"I saw that."

Anaea waited for him to continue. He didn't. Swell. "He was having a conversation."

"I saw that, too."

"Let me guess. You speak Italian."

He pursed his lips.

That would be a 'no.' Bully for her. But then, she knew that. It was in his memories, floating through her head. Probably the same way she knew to rub his jaw to turn him on and the reason she wanted to growl her frustration. She no longer knew where he ended and she began, and at the moment she didn't care.

She brushed his shoulder, making him twitch. Frustration bubbled from him, so strong she could feel it.

"What did they say?" he asked, releasing the curtains and leveling his dark gaze on her.

Her lips tingled anew. She didn't care if the attraction was one-sided. She just wanted to kiss him again and again.

She swallowed hard. "I didn't hear much, but Nero seemed to think he couldn't have you asking questions."

"Why?" Hunter leaned close.

If she closed her eyes, she could imagine his breath caressing her face. "He didn't say."

She inched up on her toes and tilted her face to him. Please let him notice the invitation.

"Then I think—" Hunter said.

His lips were close, so close. A fraction more and—

He jerked away. "I think I need to ask some questions."

HUNTER RUSHED INTO THE BEDROOM, SHOULDERING THE DOOR MOSTLY closed. He was honorable. Really. He didn't take advantage of a woman when she was confused. He might flirt a little, but that was different. Honestly. Yep. Sure—

Mother of All, she was driving him crazy, and it was too easy for him to lose focus.

He had to concentrate on who was trying to kill them, then get Regis to accept her as a sorcerer, and then he could court her properly—once she'd had time to heal and figure out what she wanted.

Not sooner.

But damn, he yearned to sweep her off her feet and fulfill the promises he'd made to her in her dreams, the promise of being inamorated. The kiss in the courtyard had been almost too much for him.

He grew hard at the memory.

This was a disaster.

He sucked in a breath. It did little to cool his rising passion. He sat on the bed by the phone and forced himself to pick up the receiver and not think about Anaea, naked on top of the sheets.

A purr threatened to escape.

Shit. Cold showers. Ice baths. Killing things.

He punched in Grey's number and waited.

"Hello?" Anger, barely contained, edged Grey's voice.

"Hello to you, too."

"What? Who is this?"

"You have to ask? Who else calls you?" If Hunter wasn't so wound up about Anaea, he'd find Grey's reaction hilarious.

"Hunter? How the hell am I to know? Where are you, and where's Anaea?"

"Safe. Fine." She was more than fine, but he didn't want to get Grey started. Just the thought of Grey thinking about Anaea's safety made his hackles rise.

"Regis isn't going to like that. And just what the hell happened?"

"Regis doesn't have to know." Although how Hunter was going to keep that from his prince was a problem he didn't want to contemplate right now. "And we're not going to talk about it."

"Fine." Grey didn't sound pleased. Well, neither was Hunter, so they could be miserable together.

"Is Nero still at his estate just outside of Newgate?"

"I've heard that tone before. You can't go collecting his soul without a warrant."

"Not having a warrant is the least of my worries. I'm done running."

The line went quiet for so long, Hunter feared his friend had hung up.

"Okay." Grey sighed. "Let me do some checking around. Where are you?"

"The Royal Park."

"Really?" Mischief crept into Grey's voice. "Decided to wine and dine the pretty lady with a fancy suite."

"It's not like that," Hunter said, but his protest sounded pathetic even to his ears.

"Then you go out for a while, and I'll wine and dine her."

"Goodbye, Grey."

"No, really, I'm sure she's worth a trip to the human realm."

"Goodbye, Grey."

Grey chuckled, but it sounded forced.

Hunter hung up. A knock drew his attention, and Anaea stepped into the doorway, her eyes narrowed and her arms crossed.

"We have unfinished business." She radiated strength and defiance. He could practically see her aura even though his body had yet to connect to the earth's magic.

His mind leapt back to the kiss in the courtyard. Boy, did they have unfinished business. But he didn't think that was what she meant. He'd ordered her around in his attempt to keep her safe. And he'd do it again.

"I—"

She was trembling. He could see it even across the room.

His heart skipped a beat. Something was wrong. She was upset, afraid.

"I—"

He rushed to her, but didn't know what to do once close. If he touched her, would she shy away? Mother of All, he just wanted her to stop quivering. His heart was breaking into thousands of little pieces. "Are you hurt?"

"No." She shook her head. "I'm sorry." All defiance melted away.

She turned to go, but he captured her shoulders.

"You can tell me."

"It doesn't matter."

God, if only shaking sense into someone worked. "It matters to me."

"Oh, really?" Her gaze shot up to meet his.

There was his warrior drake. She stirred heat within him just from a look. "Yeah."

"Yeah?"

He nodded.

"Fine." She jerked out of his grasp and widened her stance. "You don't tell me what to do and you don't kiss me unless you mean it."

"I meant it." Boy, had he meant it. But he didn't know if she knew whether she had meant it or not.

"Gee. Looked that way to me when you left me completely unsatisfied in that courtyard."

"You want satisfaction?" A growl bubbled within him. He was unsatisfied, too. More than unsatisfied.

She stepped close, hands on hips, chin tilted defiantly. Everything about her dared him to kiss her.

Anaea's heart pounded. She'd never been so forthright in her life. And she'd never been so confused and frustrated, either. She wanted to kiss Hunter again but she had no idea if he wanted her. How he felt about her mattered. Beyond any explanation or logic, it mattered.

"You want satisfaction?" he asked.

"Only if you mean it."

He grabbed the back of her head and claimed her mouth with his own. His tongue probed her lips with ferocious licks until she was weak and breathless.

Yes, this was what she wanted. This was who she wanted.

With a gasp, he broke the kiss and pressed his forehead to hers. His chest heaved as he drew in air. "I meant that." He took another deep breath and captured her gaze with his. "And I mean this, too."

He picked her up, carried her to the bed, and eased her back, drawing forth an inferno within her from his gaze alone. His lips trailed down her neck, making her shiver with anticipation.

Oh God, yes. It was her dream made real and taken to the next level. Perfect, delicious. Right.

He tugged her sweater from her jeans and ice swept through her.

But this wasn't the dream. Everything about her was wrong. She was broken, scarred. Incomplete. Less of a woman.

She captured his hands, stopping their upward movement.

"Anaea, let me look at you."

She shook her head, her mouth dry. Her voice had abandoned her.

He kissed her hands. "You're beautiful. Let me see you for real, with my own eyes."

"No, I'm—" She swallowed hard. She didn't know how she could explain how she had willingly and desperately maimed herself.

He nuzzled between her hands, pressing tender kisses to her belly. His breath sizzled over her skin. And yet, she couldn't stop shaking. Why couldn't she be like she'd been in her dream? Like she had been... before.

He circled her bellybutton with his tongue. Wet heat blossomed between her legs. She wanted him, wanted to feel normal. But her trembling wouldn't stop. Her gut churned at the thought that he'd turn away from her the moment he truly saw her.

He glanced at her, his gaze simmering with desire and adoration. She looked away, tears burning her eyes.

"Anaea, look at me."

She couldn't. Her vision wavered and she squeezed her eyes shut.

"Anaea."

She took a shuddering breath and a tear escaped. She was such a fool to think she wanted this.

But she did, more desperately than she'd wanted anything. Even to live.

Hunter slid up beside her on the bed and gathered her in his arms, murmuring against her temple. "You have nothing to fear."

That wasn't true anymore. When she'd first met him she'd already accepted her death. She hadn't feared facing the unknown as much as she feared the look on his face when he finally saw all of her.

"I've done things." More tears seeped from between her lashes.

"We've shared a body. I know." He kissed the tears from her cheeks. "It doesn't matter to me." He ran a finger along the waistband of her pants.

Her trembling continued. "But—"

"Please. Let me look at you." He inched his finger higher.

She bit her lip but didn't stop him.

She could do this.

She had to do this.

Face this fear.

He eased her sweater off and she looked away. He'd provided her with a sports bra with the clothes that he'd ordered, but she hadn't had the heart to put it on without a falsie to fill out her right cup. She couldn't bear to see his expression at her scar.

But he didn't jerk back, shudder, or even pause at the sight of her. Instead, he kissed his way across her belly, up her ribcage, and brushed his lips along the puckered edge of her scar, lovingly, reverently. He nudged her cheek with a gentle finger, drawing her gaze. There was no fear, no disgust in his eyes.

You are amazing.

Her trembling stilled. Hunter's yearning and respect and love seeped through her. She could feel his presence within her mind as if he were back in her body. He didn't see her as broken. He never had. Her scar was a testament to her prowess in the battles of her own life. He saw a warrior, an Amazon.

"Your body reflects your spirit. And what I see is magnificent."

She pressed her lips to his, and his passion radiated through her, magnified by her longing, until they were kissing and licking and sucking in a frenzy of need. All remaining fear of her body burned away with the truth of Hunter's desire. He'd realized early on what she'd done. But he belonged to a race of spirits. Physical form didn't matter nearly as much as the soul.

The honesty of his emotions, permeating every fiber of her being, was a balm for her broken heart. It wasn't a cure and wouldn't eliminate any scars, inside or out, but over time wounds healed and scars faded.

She dragged his T-shirt off and slid her body against his, savoring the feel of warm flesh against flesh. He slid his hands all over her with long, strong strokes. Erotic emotions, his emotions, swept through her, fanning the frenzy within her until she thought she'd explode at even the slightest touch.

He leaned back, panting with her, and stripped out of his clothes. Then, with sensually slow movements, he slipped off her pants and panties. He gazed upon her and this time she writhed in anticipation. He'd make her come just with his gaze, if he continued to look at her with such lust for much longer.

He brushed his fingers low along her abdomen. She jerked, more heat surging through her. His fingers trailed lower. Inch by inch. Just a little lower. Just like the dream. Except this wasn't the dream. It was better.

One more inch and he was caressing her core. She arched and writhed, her orgasm quivering on the verge. Then he plunged his finger in her, taking her over the edge, the fire within her exploding in a dizzying rush of light and sensation.

Breathless, she squirmed on top of the sheets. It was magnificent and she craved more. All of it. She yearned for the feel of him within her. He leaned down to kiss her and she wrapped her legs around his waist. Their gazes met, perfect understanding passing between them. He slid inside her, sending waves of glorious sensation pounding through both of them, completing the bond: soul, mind, and body.

ZENOBIA SHIFTED ON THE STONE BENCH IN THE EMPTY HALL. REGIS was late. It might have had something to do with the Handmaiden's sudden disappearance and Baltu burning down—of which, she was only sort of responsible for one of those problems—but in the eight hundred or so years she'd been watching him, he'd never missed a visit to his private Temple of the Mother. He'd always freshened up in his room first then used this simple, narrow hall to get to the temple for half an hour of meditation just after lunch. If Regis had one good quality, it was his devoutness. However, being devout didn't equal good, or even competent, leadership. But it did make him thankfully predictable.

A manic giggle rippled down the hall, followed by the staccato slap of bare feet rushing along the smooth granite floor.

This was her other reason to wait for Regis. The reminder of what her failure would mean and of what had already been taken from her.

Xanthic skipped around the corner, a childlike joy lighting up his wrinkled and sagging face. Her heart contracted and she shoved the emotion deep within her. That wasn't Xanthic anymore. Her lover was gone and had been since the crazy human's soul had overwhelmed him hundreds of years ago.

The jester cartwheeled to her feet, squatted, and stared up at her. Mother of All, she wanted to believe he was still in there, hidden, protected from the soul sickness. That, however, was impossible and no matter how hard she wished it, it wouldn't change.

A wisp of pale orange flickered over him, a hint of Xanthic's aura. For a moment she could see him, see the dragon she'd fallen in love with all those years ago. The glassiness in his eyes was gone, replaced with the fierce intellect she had loved and admired. But it was just her imagination projecting what she wanted to see. Nothing more.

"Lady, lady." The jester blinked, the unfocused insanity returning to his gaze. His manic giggle grated on her nerves and yet she still ached to touch him. This ruined human was all that remained of her connection to Xanthic and she wanted that connection back. She wanted Xanthic.

"He's still in there, you know," Regis said.

"So you keep telling me." Her heart skipped a beat and she bit her lip. She forced her focus to stay on the jester, refusing to give Regis the satisfaction of knowing she hadn't heard his approach and he'd surprised her. "He's served his sentence many times over. Allow him an unoccupied vessel."

"That was my father's judgment. For me, his sentence isn't finished."

Which meant as much as she wished her lover was still in there and sane, he wasn't. He'd never be permitted an unoccupied vessel because his soul was dead and there was nothing to transfer and

Regis wasn't going to admit it. Xanthic's death was no longer the lie Regis had told dragonkind when Xanthic had been caught body hopping. It was now truth.

"Lady. Lady. Duck!" The jester snorted, clutching Zenobia's calf, and ran his mangled hands up her leg.

She shoved him away, knocking him over. Bile burned her throat.

"Is that any way to treat a lover?"

She glared at Regis. The prince took a step back. His guards, a few paces behind him, shifted and dropped their hands to their sword hilts.

"You know, my lord, I'm saving myself for you." She rose from the bench, glided over, and pressed her body against him. "The jester is a thing, a tool for your entertainment."

Nero strode around the corner, his gaze catching Zenobia's. He paused in place for just a heartbeat but his expression remained unreadable.

Zenobia brushed her lips against Regis's jowly cheek, fighting to keep her lunch down. "He's a prison for a foolish drake I fucked once. I'm moving on to more interesting men."

"And she'll eat you alive, my prince," Nero said, flashing her a hint of teeth. "Are you sure you're a green drake? You're looking a lot like a black widow at the moment."

Zenobia eased away from Regis, trailing a hand down the rolls of Regis's neck. "Don't be jealous, Nero. Not everyone can be king."

"No, not everyone can." Something dark flickered across Nero's gaze and for a heartbeat she feared he knew her plans, knew she was creating a human mage strike force to take the throne during the final feast of the *pahar*. But if that were so, why hadn't Regis arrested her? Why hadn't he imprisoned her as he had Xanthic?

"The temple, my lord." Nero gestured down the hall.

The jester rolled on the floor like a dog with an itchy back. "The temple! The temple!"

Zenobia forced back a sneer. "I'll see you in Council, my lord. 'Til then, my prince."

"Doyen Zenobia." Regis reached for her hand, dropping a sloppy kiss on the back of it, then turned and strutted down the hall, the jester cartwheeling after him.

Nero acknowledged her with a slight nod.

"Still afraid of the humans?" she asked.

"Diligence is not fear." He smirked, but it didn't reach his eyes.

Interesting. Perhaps the rumors were true that he wasn't as much of a Traditionalist as he made himself out to be. She'd push more of his buttons, but that might draw unwanted attention. She'd wait until she was queen. Then she'd do more than push buttons.

She flashed a hint of teeth. If there was anyone on the Council she might be attracted to, it was Nero. He wasn't quite as cunning as she was, but he showed promise. "Until the Council, then, Doyen Nero."

"Zenobia." He turned to follow Regis around the corner.

She watched him go and continued staring down the empty hall at the plain granite walls that curved up to the ceiling in a seamless arch. It wasn't a private hall with restricted access. It connected to too many parts of Court for that. But it wasn't a heavily used thoroughfare, either. She fought the urge to hug herself against the sudden chill of emptiness within her. No, she wasn't empty, no matter what she felt in this moment. Her purpose filled her.

A whisper of air fluttered through her hair, and she turned to see who'd gated into the hall behind her. It was Kijani, his face set in his usual grim expression. Without prompting, he spoke his power word and jerked his hand in his focused gesture, activating his earth magic ability to shield their conversation from magically prying eyes and ears.

"Report."

"We're on schedule, and everyone remains stable... for the moment."

Excellent. With luck, her soldiers' sanity would hold until the coup and she wouldn't have to imprison anyone else. When she had the medallion everything would be fine. Although with the Handmaiden missing and no indication when she'd return, the medallion was useless. Of course, that didn't mean she should give up on the medallion. Eventually, the Handmaiden would be back. It had happened before, and there was nothing to indicate that this situation would be different, regardless of the fact that her men's attack in the rebirth chamber must have pissed the Handmaiden off.

"I still want the medallion."

"I've got a team on it."

"Make sure it's heavy with human mages. We need to keep Hunter guessing for as long as possible."

"Yes, Doyen." Kijani pursed his lips and his gaze dipped to the floor.

"Oh, for goodness sake. What is it?"

"Howel's new body has already connected to the earth's magic and has lightning."

"What a pleasant surprise." That was the best news she'd heard all day. Lightning was powerful, and the more of her strike force wielding it, the better. "His original vessel didn't have earth magic, did it?"

"No, Doyen."

The odds weren't good that Howel would be able to activate another human's earth magic before the coup, and while two soldiers were better than one, it would take the human too much time to learn how to use his magic, particularly while under Laoch's mind spell. "Howel has certainly proven his worth to our cause. He should be rewarded. Kill his current human and give him the empty vessel back."

"Yes, Doyen."

It involved more body-hopping but would ensure her strike force was as powerful and sane as possible. Howel would hop back to his original vessel, Kijani would kill the human mage, and Howel would hop back into the unoccupied vessel, heal it, and have lightning. And really. It was just a human. They were tools to be used as dragons pleased. That was the true order of things, the way it should have been from the beginning. Dragons were predators and humans were cattle.

Hunter brushed a finger along Anaea's temple into her hair. It really was closer to the pixie cut she'd had in the dream and not what he remembered from when he'd first met her. She sighed in her sleep, and he drew his hand back. He didn't want to wake her. She was completely at peace. He could sense it. Her emotions and thoughts weren't nearly as strong within him as when they'd shared a body, or when they'd made love, but she was still there, a sensual, warm presence. And she'd known exactly what she'd wanted. She'd had no reservations.

He shouldn't have feared that her desire to be with him was induced by shock. Of course, their new connection helped to ease any doubts. It was surprising, but then, he'd only body-shared once before and so briefly that he had no idea what the consequences really were. This was a fabulous aftereffect. Unlike what they were facing if Regis found out about her. Especially if she had a bit of real sorcerer in her.

The phone rang. Hunter grabbed it before it could ring again and wake Anaea. He could sense her drifting closer to consciousness and wasn't ready for that, wasn't ready for her to carry the weight of her world so soon.

"Yeah," he said into the cordless receiver as he slipped from the bed and padded into the living room.

"You really need to work on your phone etiquette, you know," Grey said.

"I'll take lessons when this is done."

"No, you won't."

"Maybe I will."

Grey snorted. "A few days in a woman's body and…"

Silence filled the line and Hunter swallowed a groan. Grey was likely jumping to conclusions and was going to be right.

"It's not the body but the woman," Grey said.

"Are you calling just to bother me, or have you actually found something?"

"What do you think I am?"

"You're—"

"Don't answer that. This day has been difficult enough. Word is that Nero stays at his house just outside of Newgate during the *pahar*. But he'll leave after the final feast tonight."

That would make sense. If Nero was planning something, easy access back to Court would be useful, particularly if those working for him didn't have the strength to open a gate outside of the city or even have the ability at all.

"I think Nero and I should have a talk."

"Have fun," Grey said.

"You don't get off that easily." He didn't want to drag Grey out of Court, but he needed someone to keep an eye on Anaea—he'd at least learned something from the last time. Besides, all Grey had to do was stay in the suite until Hunter returned.

"Whatever you want, the answer is no."

"You were willing to come to town for Anaea."

"That's when I thought something horrible had happened to you."

"What?"

"Nothing."

"What do you mean, you thought something horrible had

happened?" What the hell had happened while he was trapped in Anaea's head?

"Nothing, and I'm not going to talk about it. What do you want?"

"Hang out in the hotel with Anaea while I talk with Nero."

"Anaea's a big girl. She can look after herself."

That was what Hunter was worried about. "It'll be good for you to get out and see the twenty-first century."

"It's not an emergency." Grey sounded pained. "You're fine. Anaea's fine. The world is right again."

Hunter hadn't thought Grey's dislike of the human realm had turned into a fear. But considering how bad it had turned out the last time he'd gated over for any duration it didn't surprise Hunter. "I'll set up the movie channel for you. You won't have to leave the suite."

"I've got movie channels aplenty in my lair."

Hunter stared at the painting above the desk. Vast, clear sky. He yearned to be there, even if for a moment, a heartbeat. Dreams weren't enough. Did Grey yearn for the same thing? He hadn't even seen sky since that awful night in 1946.

"I'll make it up to you, I promise." Hunter held his breath, waiting for Grey to say something.

Nothing.

"I need you to keep an eye on Anaea and you know I can't bring her back to Court."

"Hunter, I—"

"You know I wouldn't ask if I didn't have to."

Grey groaned. "I know. I'll be there in ten."

"Thanks."

"Mother of All, both of you seriously owe me."

Hunter ran a hand over his smooth head. "Well, you can't hide at Court for the rest of your life."

"Don't start."

"You're right, I know. I owe you."

ANAEA STRETCHED, SAVORING THE FEEL OF HER BODY'S SLIDE AGAINST the sheets. She felt whole, complete, and amazed. She wasn't broken anymore. Of course, she'd never really been broken. She was truly blessed for finding someone who thought she—all of her—was beautiful. Her final days didn't have to be empty anymore and she was sure as hell going to spend them with Hunter. Yes, he wasn't really human. But for her remaining three months, it didn't really matter.

It was crazy. She'd never believed in love at first sight, and perhaps this wasn't exactly 'first sight.' But she knew, deep within her, they were meant to be together. Hunter's presence simmered within her. Wild, feral, magical. She didn't know how much she believed in destiny, but she did know she was connected to Hunter in a more intimate way than she'd ever been with anyone before.

They still had the problem of someone trying to kill him... and her. Without a doubt he would shut her out, do what he felt he needed to do without her, but she wasn't going to let him. Even with her fleeting sense of what dragons were, she knew the female of the species was just as formidable as the male. That woman, Capri, and certainly Zenobia were both powerful. She and Hunter would work this out together, whether he liked it or not.

She concentrated on Hunter's presence within her. He was in the sitting room thinking about something, but she couldn't tell what. She still couldn't read his thoughts unless he wanted her to. He was likely trying to figure out how to stop whoever was after them without getting her involved. It was actually flattering that he cared so much for her he wanted to fight her battles. She really wanted to talk about their next move, but she could tell by his mood that now wasn't the time. Perhaps after a shower.

Perhaps she could entice him to join her.

Now that was a great idea.

She walked to the bathroom and turned on the taps, focusing on how it would feel to have Hunter run his hands over her skin again.

Something rippled through his presence.

She sat on the edge of the tub and waited. But he didn't come. She pressed her hands to her stomach, imagining they were Hunter's.

His emotions rippled again, this time with recognizable desire.

I'm waiting, she thought at him and inched her hands over her abdomen.

The desire swelled with hot need. Then he clamped down on it and she was left suddenly cold. Her throat constricted. He'd obviously noticed her invitation, but she had no idea why he'd refused her.

A male voice rumbled over the hiss of the water and her heart skipped a beat. Hunter wouldn't talk to himself so he was either on the phone or someone was here.

Another voice, masculine but definitely different from the first, replied.

She took a robe from the hook by the door, slipped it on, and eased the door open.

"Well, I'm here." It sounded like Grey.

The thrumming in her chest eased. Hunter had probably called for help or something. Although he didn't strike her much as a 'call for help' kind of guy.

"You'd think I'd asked you to take Jerusalem."

"Been there. Done that. Rather not do it again."

She glanced at the sitting room door but couldn't see either of the men from that angle so she stepped farther into the bedroom, inching closer to the doorway.

"This'll be easy. Keep Anaea here until I get back," Hunter said.

"Independent, is she?"

She couldn't believe Hunter was going off without telling her again. Yeah, she knew he would, but she'd really hoped he wouldn't.

"It's part of her charm. But in this case, I don't want her to get involved."

For the love of— She could strangle him. And if she wasn't wearing only a robe and Grey wasn't here, she would.

"You mean you don't want Regis to find out you've made a sorcerer."

The heat in her chest, Hunter's presence, chilled.

"She's a mage, not a sorcerer."

"Semantics. Regis won't care."

"He won't find out," Hunter said.

"You're playing a dangerous game."

She moved closer to the door, peering into the living room.

"I don't need you to remind me," Hunter growled. It sounded strange coming from Mark.

Hunter stood in the middle of the room. She could see his fury radiating from him and feel it smoldering in her chest. Grey still stood by the front door, duffle bag slung over his shoulder, as if he hadn't committed to staying. He looked pale, his brows pinched together.

"Hey, Anaea is nice enough to me, but you have to face reality. Magic is magic. There's no way you can keep her hidden from Regis forever. There isn't anywhere in the world where you can hide her from the Asar Nergal. And when they find out, it'll be execution for her and rebirth for you."

"She's not a danger."

"Regis won't see it that way."

"I'll make him." Uncertainty flickered through their connection. Hunter didn't believe what he'd just said.

Grey raised an eyebrow. "Really?"

With a growl, Hunter leapt for Grey, grabbing the front of his coat and jerking him close. "Really."

Grey shoved Hunter back and sunk low into a fighting stance. "You and I both know you killed her the moment you transferred into her body. The only way to prevent being reborn is if she's dead."

Hunter hissed and bared his teeth, but didn't attack. Emotions flashed through her. Regret and fear.

"Say I'm wrong."

Need. Desperation. Yearning.

"Say it."

Resignation.

He knew what Grey said was true.

"You can't say it 'cause you know I'm right."

"I'll find a way," Hunter said, his voice low.

Hunter's emotions quieted. Only a hint of his presence simmered within her.

"If you hide her, he'll find her. If you let her go, he'll find her." Grey inched closer to Hunter, reaching a hand out to his friend. "The only kindness you can offer her is how she dies. Your hand would be the gentlest."

Hunter wrenched away from Grey. "We are not having this conversation."

"Yes, we are. If not now then with certainty later."

"Grey, I can't." Hunter's voice hitched in his throat and Anaea's stomach churned. Grey was right and Hunter knew it.

"Yes, you can."

Hunter shook his head. He couldn't and Grey couldn't see it. She wasn't ready to die again either, but she couldn't bear to know the truth and feel Hunter's grief. She would not be responsible for his death.

LIKE A COWARD, HUNTER HAD GREY GATE HIM TO THE EDGE OF NERO'S estate while Anaea was in the shower. He'd wanted to say goodbye, join her in the shower with long kisses and a whole lot more, and forget about the truth Grey wanted him to acknowledge. But that would lead to another glorious round of lovemaking and delay his departure... by a lot.

That, and if Anaea knew what he planned they'd argue. And rightly so. She had the right to determine her life. To having a life in the first place. He wouldn't be able to live with himself if he didn't fix this. He had to fix this.

He sucked in a steadying breath.

Him getting killed wouldn't help her. He needed to focus for the next forty-five minutes until Grey returned to gate him back to her.

He shifted the *asru* bead in his boot to the toe and continued heading to Nero's mansion. While he didn't anticipate Grey would need to use the mini-anchor enspelled into the bead to find him, nothing about the last couple of days had gone as anticipated. And he wasn't going to take any more risks than necessary. Nero's estate sat in the middle of a hundred acres of forest and farmland northeast of Newgate, containing a sprawling house built by Nero in the mid-eighteen hundreds when it was discovered that the main gate into Court was in the area.

Hunter wasn't sure what he was looking for but rummaging through Nero's office seemed like the place to start. What Anaea had overheard at the spa could have referred to anything, but it was the best he had. If he didn't have her to worry about, he'd probably walk up to the front door and start asking questions, with a liberal dose of violence to encourage looser lips. But he did have Anaea, and if something happened, it would be up to Grey to protect her—regardless of the fact that Grey knew her existence meant trouble. He was sure Grey would keep her safe, but he didn't want to burden either of them with that.

Besides, it always helped to be armed to the teeth when bashing down someone's door and Hunter hadn't had the time, nor the access, to obtain his full supply of weapons. All he had was the long sword and hunting knife Grey had brought him. So with stealth being his only available option, he'd just have to pray something conveniently, and quickly, showed up.

Mother of All, he just wanted to get back to the hotel and wrap himself in Anaea and everything she was. His insides twitched with the effort to concentrate on the task at hand instead of running back to her.

Soon. Soon. He'd figure out how to keep her safe from Regis and... No. They would figure it out. Together. He owed her at least that much.

He inched to the edge of the tree line and scanned the vast, empty lawn leading up a slope to a sprawling patio complete with pool and hot tub and beyond that a massive, three-story manor house. Floor-to-ceiling windows on this side of the building revealed a sunroom with white wicker furniture. So far, he hadn't noticed much of a security system, but with the ground open to wildlife big and small, it was probably a hassle to have much of anything. The mansion, however, was likely a different story. Nero was a smart drake and without a doubt had the best technology could offer.

Which meant even if Hunter bypassed the systems he found, there were probably more lurking in the background. Bashing down the door, even without all of his weapons, was looking more and more appealing by the minute. He couldn't believe he'd rushed off without a plan, or research, or anything. He knew better.

Well, shit. He'd have to consider tonight research. Do a little skulking around, try to determine the layout of the mansion, pinpoint some of the security systems. He didn't really want to have to come back, but he didn't see any other option.

He inched along the tree line to a side of the mansion with fewer windows, and dashed across the lawn. Pressing his body to the rough brick, he held his breath, listening for any indication that someone had seen him.

Everything remained quiet.

Good.

He glanced in the closest window. A boardroom, by the looks of it. In the center sat a large table, surrounded by chairs. A whiteboard hung against one wall and opposite it, stood floor-to-ceiling book-cases crammed with thick, hard-covered books. But a boardroom didn't fit at all with what he knew about Nero. Most of the drake's business was overseas in Rome—established before Columbus and all that—and from everything Hunter had heard, Nero kept his business life and personal life separate.

A chatter of voices rose on the sunroom side of the house, and Hunter peered around the corner of the building. About a dozen people had poured out onto the patio, talking and laughing. Their auras flickered in and out of focus.

Good news at last. His new body was starting to connect to the earth's magic already. Although some of the auras didn't look right. But that could be the tentativeness of his connection.

The young dragon he'd seen with Nero at the feast made her way to the front of the group and led them onto the lawn. Her hair was pulled back in a tight ponytail, the ends brushing her waist. She called two youths forward. Both of them had those strange auras. The first, a girl of about eighteen, raised her hand and a ball of light formed in front of her.

The woman nodded and the ball shot across the lawn. The second youth, a lanky teen, dropped to his knees and pressed both hands to the ground. Clumps of sod rocketed from the lawn, inches from the light as if trying to hit it. The ball danced, and the geysers of dirt blasted faster and faster.

If Hunter didn't know any better, he'd say he was watching earth magic training. But drakes didn't teach other drakes. It could mean loss of power within the coterie and Court if the student surpassed the teacher. And there was something really wrong with the auras of the two students. That and their bodies seemed awfully young. Usually the Handmaiden preferred to rebirth into fully grown humans.

Ponytail Woman's aura, however, was strong, radiating wide and dark, promising powerful earth magic.

Another woman, probably in her mid-thirties, with wild red hair, took the place of the boy, and the ball of light stilled, waiting to resume the exercise. The redhead's aura was like Ponytail Woman's. But most in the group had the strange wavering auras and seemed too young.

Hunter's stomach churned. His aura sight wasn't screwed up. He'd gained a rare gift when he'd taken Mark's body. He could see the aura differences between human mages and drakes, something only one percent of dragons could do. Nero was training mages. Depending on how many he had, he could try to take the throne. All he really needed was to kill Hunter and take the medallion.

Regis needed to be warned.

Hunter inched back from the patio, but a man in the back of the group spun around and stared at him. Damn, he had to have enhanced hearing.

Ponytail Woman yelled something he couldn't quite decipher. The ball of light shot toward him, drawing the gazes of the rest of the group.

Oh, shit.

Anaea fought the urge to squirm in her seat as she sat in one of the stiff wing-backed chairs. She knew what she had to do, knew the only way Hunter would be safe was if she was out of the picture.

It was so cruel. The moment she realized she wanted every minute, every second allowed her, was the moment she had to give it all up. Her presence endangered Hunter. If anyone caught a glimpse of her, anywhere, they'd rebirth him, and from his infusion of memories, she knew without a doubt that the spell would strip him of everything that made him who he was. She would not allow herself to be responsible for that.

Perhaps it was a good thing. They'd had an amazing night—if not a couple of troubled days. If they spent the next few months together, it would be so much harder to say goodbye. And she'd still be forced to say goodbye in the end.

"Movie not doing it for you?" Grey slid a sideways glance in her direction.

"No— I mean—" She didn't care what they watched, although Grey seemed particularly excited about watching anything, so long as it was a movie, and he no longer seemed so uncomfortable. No, she couldn't just sit there anymore. Not when she knew what needed to be done. If she did it now, would Grey stop her?

Probably. Hunter had told him to keep an eye on her, and Grey struck her as a friend so loyal he'd go against his better judgment to keep his word. "I'm just a little hungry."

"Oh, right. Movies need food." He leapt over the back of the couch and grabbed the phone off the desk. "Good call. What do you want?"

She shrugged. "Whatever." She needed to do it now before she lost her nerve, and that meant getting away from Grey long enough to do it. Pills weren't an option. She didn't have any. Neither was jumping out a window. The ones in the suite didn't open.

She eyed Grey's sword, leaning against the side of the couch. Too awkward.

That left her with Hunter's razor in the bathroom.

Grey's expression softened and she felt like she was suddenly on display.

She prayed he wouldn't figure out what she was planning.

"I'll think of something," he said.

She offered a weak smile and turned back to the television, watching Danny Kaye switch from fool to suave lover with the snap of Angela Lansbury's fingers. Now she knew what Hunter had meant when he said Grey called the dragon king's jester Giacomo. The king of jesters and the jester of kings. And like the court in the movie, Hunter's Court was filled with dangers for the unwary. She needed to get up, excuse herself, and do it. But against all desire, she didn't move.

Come on, she could do this. Hunter needed this sacrifice. And really, she'd pretty much already made the choice when she'd stood on the Queen Street Bridge—it had just been delayed.

Grey said something into the receiver, and she dragged her attention from the Technicolor images.

"I told them to send up their two most popular dinners and desserts." Grey flopped back onto the sofa.

"Thanks. Why don't I get some ice." Maybe if she got up for a different reason she could force herself into the bathroom.

Grey hopped back up. "No. You just sit there. I don't want Hunter thinking I didn't treat you right."

She swallowed hard. "Why, thank you, sir," she said in a weak imitation of a Southern belle.

"Anything for a pretty lady." He left with the ice bucket.

She ground her teeth. Come on. Do it. It had to be done. For Hunter.

His presence glowed within her. Everything that he was would be lost if he was reborn. She was on death's door anyway. Life had proven she really was worthy of love and as much as she wanted more, she just wasn't going to get it.

I love you.

His presence pulsed.

She clutched the reaction tight to her heart and shoved out of the chair.

Do it now. Before Grey returned.

She forced one foot in front of the other until she was in the bathroom.

Lock the door.

She locked it and broke Hunter's plastic razor in the sink.

Don't think. Just do it.

She shoved the sleeves of her sweater far up her arms, baring her skin.

Seizing the blade, she yanked it down the length of her forearm, elbow to wrist, so fast she didn't feel anything. Her skin looked perfect and she feared she'd missed. Then fire blossomed over her. The wound spread, revealing a long, deep incision. Blood filled it and spilled over her arm.

Now the other, fast.

Her fingers were numbing already. She ran the blade along the other arm.

Blood seeped down both arms drawing thick, bright lines against the white sink. The pain wasn't nearly as excruciating as she expected. But then in the last couple of days, she'd been shot and stabbed. Maybe she was getting used to it. What a horrible thought. Or maybe the blood loss and acceptance of her situation blunted the sensation.

Black specks flickered through her vision, and she leaned over the sink to brace herself. She'd get dizzy soon. She should have done this in the tub to contain the mess. It didn't matter. All that mattered was that, logical or not, she loved Hunter, he loved her, and she was saving his life.

She concentrated on him, wrapping his presence around her, savoring the memory of making love and the fervor of his emotion. *Thank you, my ferocious love.*

Her vision blurred. The black specks disappeared. Something was wrong. She was supposed to be lightheaded and dizzy. What the hell was going on? She wiped the blood from the first incision, revealing a thick red line and no wound.

Her stomach churned.

She wiped the blood from the other arm. Same thing.

No.

No, no, no. She couldn't have healed. Hunter wasn't in her anymore. How was she going to save him if she couldn't kill herself? She was supposed to die so he could live.

Her throat tightened and she swallowed hard against it. It wasn't fair. Her death could have meant something and now she couldn't even kill herself.

With a growl, she threw the glass from the counter across the room. It hit the tiled shower stall and shattered.

Footsteps pounded through the suite. "Anaea?" Grey called through the bathroom door. "You okay?"

Her eyes burned. No, she wasn't okay. She couldn't even kill herself.

"Anaea." He knocked on the door.

God, she was going to have to face the slow, painful cancer death, and Hunter would be reborn.

The knocking increased, and the handle clicked back and forth against the lock.

Except if she could heal her gash, did that mean she could heal her cancer?

The door crashed inward. Grey stood on the threshold, his gaze locked on the blood in the sink.

She'd been too afraid to ask Hunter, too afraid to have any hope. But cancer or no, her presence still endangered him.

"What are you doing?"

"Trying to save Hunter."

"Mother of All, not like this." He yanked a towel from the rack and grabbed Anaea's wrist.

"Apparently not," she said, revealing the healed wounds.

Grey jerked back. "You—" His mouth opened and closed but no words came out.

"You have to do it," she said.

"I what?"

"You made it clear if I'm alive Hunter will be reborn." She shoved past him, going into the sitting room. This had to be done now, before Hunter returned.

"When did you—?" Grey rushed after her.

She grabbed his sword and held it out to him. "You have to take my head."

"Are you crazy?"

"Please." She wasn't going to be responsible for any more deaths, particularly not Hunter's.

"I'm not going to kill you."

She shoved the sword into his hands. "I can't do it by myself."

Hunter dashed across the lawn for the trees. He had to get to cover. A gale slammed into his back, whistling around his head, tugging at his clothes. He stumbled, caught his balance, and lengthened his stride. He could not get caught.

Sudden grief and desperation washed over him. His knees buckled. Anaea was in trouble. Something was wrong. Every instinct within him knew the emotions were hers. His throat constricted. No. Hers did.

The wind slammed into his side, knocking him down.

He scrambled to his feet and pushed his connection with Anaea aside. He had to get out of here first. Then he could comfort her.

Massive chunks of earth shot from the ground. He twisted out of the way, his sheathed sword banging against his thigh. Just a few feet more and he'd reach cover.

The wind slammed him into the closest tree. Light danced across his vision, and he staggered forward. Whoever controlled the wind was powerful.

The ball of light zinged around his head. Earth shot up beside him, slicing up his calf and thigh. The wind captured him again, bashing him into another tree.

Pain raced through Hunter's chest. He gasped for breath. The wind released him, and he lurched into the cover of the trees. Anaea's despair burned through him. She didn't want him to know something. She loved him. It was for the best. But she needed help.

He rushed deeper into the brush, his chest aching. He had to get back to her. With her state of mind, it felt as though she planned something desperate.

Two men crashed through the underbrush, both dragons by their strong auras. The first, a big man with a buzz cut, dove for Hunter. He sidestepped and rammed his fist into the man's temple, but the other man—also enormous, they could have been twins—was on Hunter fast, punching him in the face.

Pain exploded across Hunter's forehead and his vision went black. Sight popping in and out of focus, he elbowed Twin Number Two in the gut. Twin One stood and Hunter kicked out his legs, toppling him back to the ground. Hunter drew his sword and sliced open Twin Two's neck. It wouldn't kill the drake, just hopefully slow him down long enough for an escape.

Twin One grabbed Hunter's leg but Hunter slashed him across the face and kicked free of his grip. Hunter leapt away. The wind seized him, hurtling him, face first, into a massive tree trunk.

"I'M NOT GOING TO KILL YOU." GREY SQUEEZED THE HILT OF HIS weapon, keeping the blade pointed at the ground. "Hunter will have my head."

Anaea bit back a roar. "No, he won't." If Grey didn't kill her now, she was going to lose her nerve.

"I would beg to differ on that one."

Something flickered through Hunter's presence. Shit. He'd sensed her plan and was coming to stop her. A part of her thrilled at the thought. But she couldn't endanger him any longer. It had to be done.

"They'll rebirth him. I won't be responsible for that."

"There's got to be another way." Grey's knuckles on the hand holding the sword turned white.

Hunter's presence flickered again then jumped with fierce determination.

"Please, Grey. You said yourself it had to be done. And we both know Hunter won't do it."

Hunter had to get back to her. He couldn't get caught.

Which meant he still didn't know the details of her plan.

"Anaea, I—"

The suite's door exploded inward. Grey tossed Anaea behind the couch, shielding her body from the shrapnel.

Ears ringing, she peeked around its side. Five men in black trench coats stormed into the room, each carrying a sword. Their auras were weak, fluttery, and she got the sense they weren't dragons.

"What? Only five?" Grey asked, sauntering toward them and bringing up his blade.

"Where's Hunter?" a brawny blond asked, his coat straining against his broad chest.

Anaea stood. Well, she had needed someone to kill her. "I'm here."

Grey glared at her, but didn't argue. He couldn't without revealing that Hunter had done the forbidden and shared a body with a human. Even if these men had gained their magic in the same way, she didn't doubt their master would use the knowledge to destroy Hunter.

"This has nothing to do with you, silver drake. Although thanks to you and the bug in your cell phone, Hunter was easy to find."

The other men chuckled. Grey bared his teeth.

"Now stand back," Blondie said.

"Not a chance." Grey leapt at the closest man, slicing open his gut and dropping him to the floor.

Hunter's presence boiled with frustration.

Blondie stormed toward her. Grey snagged the back of his collar and jerked him back.

Another man with a black goatee stabbed at Grey. He twisted, and the blade lanced across Grey's side while Blondie swung again.

Anaea leapt around the couch and shoved him. His swing went wild, grazing the sleeve of a shorter assailant.

"Would you get back," Grey growled. He dodged another blow, barely holding his own against so many.

There was no way he could defeat all of them and he certainly wasn't going to let them kill her. Which meant she had to help. What they needed was magic. Anaea pulled at the energy within her, but it didn't flood to her hands as before.

Hunter's frustration within her turned icy. What the hell was happening with him?

Blondie jabbed at her. She stumbled back. The fire was there. She could feel it, just out of reach.

Goatee pinned Grey's arms.

Magical power shimmered behind her but it wasn't of her creation. It belonged to someone else.

Anaea jerked around. Jade stepped through a black vortex and grabbed the back of Anaea's sweater.

Blondie raised his blade.

Anaea twisted in Jade's grasp.

Grey roared and the sword plunged toward him.

The world snapped into darkness, twisting with Jade's gate, while the heat of magic fire tingled, unmanifested, under Anaea's skin.

A naea wrenched against Jade's grip. She had to get back to Grey, had to save him, somehow. He couldn't die. Not another one on her hands. Not Hunter's best friend.

The black vortex of Jade's gate whirled around them then jerked to a halt. Jade shoved Anaea, and she tumbled onto the stone floor of Court's gateroom, scraping the palms of her hands. The gate closed with a whoosh, and Jade grabbed the back of Anaea's neck, keeping her from standing.

An insane giggle filled the corridor, sending shivers racing over Anaea.

"You don't look like Nero. No, no, not at all." The jester, Giacomo, stood a few feet away, dressed in his ridiculous harlequin costume. "But this is a pleasant surprise."

"I have business with the king." Jade grasped Anaea's arm and wrenched her to her feet.

Giacomo giggled. "The king is incapacitated."

"You mean indisposed."

"No." Giacomo's expression flashed to serious. "No, I'm pretty sure I mean incapacitated." He wrapped his ruined hands around his neck, stuck out his tongue, and gurgled as if he were being strangled.

Jade rolled her eyes. "Out of my way."

She shoved Anaea forward, but Giacomo seized the front of Anaea's shirt and pulled her down. Anaea struggled against him, but his grip was unexpectedly strong for a man of his stature.

"I don't have time for games," Jade said, her voice low.

Anaea didn't want any of this, either. Please let Grey be safe. Even Hunter's presence seemed muted within her.

"But this is so interesting." Giacomo wiggled his eyebrows. "And I know you've seen it, oh Green One."

"And it needs to be discussed with Regis." She reached for Anaea, but Giacomo snatched Jade's wrist, yanked her around, and slammed her against the wall. Faster than Anaea thought possible, he smashed Jade's head on the granite with a sickening crack and spray of blood. Glassy-eyed, she sagged to the floor, somehow managing to stay conscious.

"But you wanted to talk with the king." Giacomo straightened and wiped the blood from his face. "Regis is a different story. I don't like Regis."

Anaea scrambled back, but Giacomo grabbed her pant legs and jerked her to him. He grabbed her chin again, crushing her cheeks with his thumb and forefinger. "Not until I get a better look at you." He peered at her, just as he had the first time he'd examined her in the king's chamber.

"The lights are on." He snorted and giggled. "But no dragons are home."

Ice raced through her.

"Perfect." The gleam in his eye darkened.

Jade moaned. "Mother of All, you're a—"

In that heartbeat, Anaea could see it around Giacomo, the wavering, muted orange aura of a drake, barely perceptible unless she concentrated. The jester wasn't just some crazy human misused by a dragon and kept for kicks by the dragon king, but a dragon spirit trapped in a ruined vessel. And a drake looking for a new home.

Anaea squirmed. Giacomo's grip threatened to crush her skull. God, she was not going to be taken. He could not have her body. She wouldn't let him.

But he wrenched her forward, mashing his fleshy lips against hers. His teeth cut her skin. He dug his thumbs into the hollows of her cheeks, forcing her jaw open, and rammed his tongue into her mouth.

Her stomach roiled. This was not happening.

Hot energy lanced into her mouth and burned down her throat. The jester's soul oozed into her, slimy, dark, and manic. He bubbled through her, like burning tar that stuck to, and seared, her soul.

She heaved against him, willed him out and back, but he surrounded her, boxed her in like Hunter had when he'd first taken her body. She shoved against the confines. There had to be a weakness, something, a way to break free. She shied away from him, but her body didn't respond to her commands. She thought harder about moving, focused her intent. Nothing.

Oh, Hunter was a fool to leave this. Jester's voice boomed through her and the prison around her soul contracted.

Get out.

Jester laughed. Her body cackled, and Jade twitched, eyes wide, but not healed enough to do anything.

"You're exactly what I thought you'd be, little human sorcerer. A true one, not like Jade here."

Energy ignited within her, a powerful force she'd never experienced before. It surged through every cell in her body, collecting at her hands until flame leapt across her palms.

Jester placed a finger on Jade's cheek. Fire licked her skin and she screamed. A blackened fingerprint marred her cheek, the flesh around it red and oozing.

"Oh, goodie." Jester giggled, the same manic giggle, except now it sounded like Anaea.

No. Please no. She rammed against her prison. Black thoughts of revenge and torture and pleasure slid through her. They would pay. They would all pay. He would kill them all, slowly, and bathe in their blood.

Fire leapt down her forearms. Jester caressed Jade's face, drawing another scream and another. Flames devoured skin and hair, and still Jade screamed. Her body writhed, and Jester laughed.

If Anaea had a stomach under her control, she'd be sick. God, she wanted to be sick. She couldn't close her eyes, couldn't turn away or stop it. Twisted erotic pleasure made her skin tingle. Heat blossomed between her legs. Giacomo was turned on.

Jade shuddered and collapsed, her head a charred, ruined mess that shattered into ash as it hit the stone.

Come, my dear. Giacomo clapped his hands. *We have a prince to kill.*

BLOOD OOZED FROM THE GASH ABOVE HUNTER'S FOREHEAD AND DOWN his temple. A drop hung from his jaw, trembling, making him itchy. If his hands weren't tied to the back of his chair, he'd wipe it away. As it was, he was forced to either catch the irritation with his shoulder or endure it.

He chose the latter.

Besides, he was pretty sure he had a few broken ribs and didn't want to move too much before he healed. He had a feeling he was going to need everything he had to get out of this, even when Grey showed up to help in five minutes. Nero had the medallion, and Hunter had no doubt that the drake would use it.

Ponytail Woman leaned against the wall on the other side of the office, between an eighteenth century settee and the closed door. Her arms were crossed and her gaze locked on him. The young dragon was going to be a terror when she gained a little more maturity. Her earth magic was already strong enough to hurl him around, but from the look in her eye, she still didn't trust herself to keep him under control.

If all of the people he'd seen in the 'magic class' had half of Ponytail's ability, Nero was definitely a coterie doyen to be wary of. In a few decades, his coterie might be powerful enough for a coup... if he wasn't caught and executed for making human sorcerers first.

But if the mages were still green, why try to eliminate Hunter now?

Why not wait until his army was ready? Unless, of course, Hunter had stumbled too close to Nero's plans—although he had no clue how he had—and only the inexperienced mages had been left at the mansion.

Deep within him, Anaea's emotions billowed, but stayed muted behind the wall he'd put between them. Mother of All, he wanted to know how she was doing. Even shoved to the recesses of his mind he could tell she was upset, but not why. And there wasn't a damn thing he could do about it right now.

He swallowed back a growl as the door opened. Nero strode in dressed in a tuxedo, his bowtie hanging, untied, around his neck. It was, after all, the last night of feasts of the *pahar*. Every dragon who was anyone would be there, dressed to his or her finest.

"I see you've traded up to a more suitable vessel, Hunter."

The blood fell from Hunter's chin and hit his thigh with a plop.

Nero tilted his head and drew close. "Or was the last body too crowded?"

Hunter's heart skipped a beat. As soon as he resolved this mess, he was moving Anaea as far from Newgate as possible. Although with Nero's collection of human mages, perhaps the dragon might be more receptive to Anaea than any other, if he could be trusted.

"You have some powerful human sorcerers under your roof." Hunter slid his gaze to Ponytail, who uncrossed her arms and straightened.

"Mages, not sorcerers," Nero said.

Hunter snorted, feigning disgust. Interesting that Nero should make the distinction. This was not a conversation he thought he'd have with any drake, let alone Nero. "Mages. Sorcerers. Whatever. Still, your humans are powerful."

"But none who can call fire."

Hunter shrugged. "Fire is rare."

"You would know, fire drake." Nero called a hint of wind. It swirled around him, a thin whip-like band that lashed out inches from Hunter's leg.

Hunter ground his teeth. He would not flinch, now or ever.

The chair beside him slid around, and Nero perched on the edge. "Sorcerers are also rare. So are those humans, those mages, who have a naturally awakened connection to the earth's magic."

What a load of shit. No human had naturally developed magic for two thousand years. They had to body-share with a dragon. But Nero looked serious, no hint that he was toying with Hunter. What if a rare percentage of humans did develop magic, significant magic, not just seeing auras or holding séances? Wouldn't other humans know about that? But history was full of humans professing to have —and being accused of having—extraordinary abilities. If the Asar Nergal knew of them, wouldn't they be killed just like those mages created unnaturally through body-sharing?

"How many in your house are natural?" He rolled 'natural' out with a hint of disdain to determine where Nero's loyalties really lay. Ponytail pushed away from the wall and took a step forward. Interesting. She was protective of the humans. Nero held up a hand, and she stopped.

"Funny how so much power can be contained in such a simple object." Nero reached into his breast pocket and pulled out the medallion.

Damn. It looked like that was the end of the small talk and he still had four more minutes to kill.

Hunter twisted his hands, testing the binding. Tight. No getting out that way.

"The power over life and death," Nero said.

Right, well. This wasn't going to be Hunter's death. Not when he'd finally found someone worth living for.

"Tell me, Hunter. Where does your allegiance lie?"

Hunter stilled and raised an eyebrow at that. Did Nero think he could be bought? Hunter supposed he could be. There was no love between him and Regis, nor the king. They were the most powerful coterie only because the Handmaiden had chosen them two thousand years ago and hadn't changed her mind yet. They controlled the last free medallion, and a dragon without a coterie didn't last long.

But the thought of selling out to save his life put a bad taste in his mouth.

"I can't be bought."

"I didn't think you could. And as much as you are the prince's assassin, you've never taken a soul out of spite or for personal reasons. It's all about the job for you."

"You're so sure about that?" It was true, but he couldn't have Nero thinking that made him weak.

"I'm sure other drakes have gotten in the way. Collateral damage and all that. But you've had the medallion for over a thousand years. You could have taken the throne any time you wished."

Hunter bared his teeth. "Note the key word there: wished." Three minutes.

"I have." Nero dangled the medallion by its chain and flicked it with his finger. It twirled around, catching the light. "I respect you, Hunter. You do your duty, you're not hungry for power like other drakes, and I think you disagree with our prince's policy on sorcerers."

"Get to the point."

The rope around Hunter's hands loosened and dropped to the floor.

"My point," Nero said, "is that I can help you."

Hunter rubbed his wrists, trying to look casual while preparing to fight his way free. "Help me?"

"You now have an untrained mage on your hands. Albeit not a natural one. But that doesn't matter."

"She's not your concern."

Just the mention of Anaea made her presence billow within him again. He struggled to concentrate on Nero.

"She is if I can train her so she doesn't... say... burn down another spa." Nero flicked the medallion again, spinning it in the other direction.

"I'm not sure I follow."

"I run a school for those humans who naturally connect to the earth's magic."

Hunter's surprise must have flashed across his face because Nero leaned back in his chair and chuckled.

"How have you managed to hide so many human mages under your roof without drawing the attention of the Asar Nergal?" Particularly if this school had been going on for a while. It implied Nero was more powerful than imagined, either able to avoid detection magically, or able to politically influence whoever led the team assigned to eliminate all human mages.

Nero raised an eyebrow.

"Is it magic? Wards? What?"

Ponytail rolled her eyes but didn't move from the door.

"It's much simpler than that," Nero said. "I am the Asar Nergal."

And everything about Nero now made sense, particularly his rise in status at Court. Regis feared humans would try to finish off dragonkind. All of his laws were based on protecting dragons from discovery. The leader of the Asar Nergal would be Regis's greatest weapon in self-defense.

"But—"

"Why?" Nero flashed a hint of teeth. A threat if Hunter ever saw one. "I grew tired of killing children who knew nothing and were no danger to dragonkind."

When put that way, Hunter couldn't disagree. Survival wasn't supposed to involve murdering children on the chance that they'd threaten drakes someday. But if they couldn't eliminate the potential threat, he had no idea how dragons could prevent another Great Scourge. And while all of this information was fascinating, it was also dangerous. Teaching and not killing human mages, regardless that they were natural, could get Nero reborn. Actually, it would probably get him tortured for centuries first. Rebirth would be a kindness.

Hunter shifted in his chair. There was only one logical direction this conversation could go now. He knew too much about Nero, and Nero held the medallion. He still had two minutes left.

"Why are you trusting me with this?"

"Because you've seen the truth. If I didn't tell you now, you'd go back to Court and figure it out." Nero dropped the medallion in Hunter's lap.

What the hell? Hunter's heart skipped a beat. He yanked the chain over his head before Nero could take the medallion back. "Why not just rebirth me?"

"You don't deserve it." Nero stood and walked to the sidebar in the far corner. "Besides, I'd rather have an ally. Things are changing, or they will very soon. There's talk of a coup, and human mages are being snuck into Court."

Ponytail didn't look surprised at this, which meant she was privy to Nero's plans, revealing an unexpected openness in their relationship. Maybe she really was his new Third.

"Not new information for me." Well, the sneaking of mages into Court was, but he wasn't going to point that out. This still didn't explain why the young drake had tried to challenge Hunter in the feast hall and had looked to Nero for help, but Hunter wasn't going to bring that up at the moment. Better to keep the conversation political and not personal.

"Zenobia is making non-natural mages. She's convinced a small group of young drakes to make a strike force."

"You know this and you haven't done anything?"

Nero poured himself a drink. It looked like vodka straight up. "I've known for a century now, ever since she cut off that cavern on the outskirts of Court. I've been waiting for the moment when the evidence against her is the most damning. That would be tonight when she stages her coup."

"And how do you know that?"

Nero flashed his teeth. "I have an augur under my roof."

"Really? Bet that's helpful, being the leader of the Asar Nergal."

"You could say that."

An augur, either dragon or human, hadn't been seen since Nostradamus and before him the Oracle at Delphi. Why Nero hadn't made a play for the throne with an augur in his pocket was beyond Hunter. "How reliable are his prophecies?"

"*She's* still young, so not a hundred percent." Nero downed his drink in one fast gulp. "My coterie might seem strange, but it is mine. Their safety takes precedence over everything: my life, your life, even the throne."

Well, that they had in common. There wasn't anything Hunter wouldn't do to protect Anaea.

A whoosh of air swept through the room and Grey appeared at Hunter's side, sword drawn and blood dripping from the blade.

Hunter jerked to his feet. "What the hell?"

Ponytail leapt from the wall and hissed a power word but Nero raised a hand. The air around her trembled, pulling at her hair and clothes, but didn't strike Grey. Thank goodness. The drake didn't look like he could handle any more action. He was splattered, head to toe, in blood. It dribbled from a cut in his mouth and a gash on his forehead, and he clutched his gut as if he held himself together.

An attack on Grey meant—

Hunter's heart skipped a beat. "Where is she?"

Grey's gaze darted between Nero and Hunter. It landed on the rope at Hunter's feet and the medallion hanging from the chain around his neck. He relaxed his fighting stance and lowered his sword, digging the point in Nero's carpet to prop himself up. "Apparently my cell phone is tapped." His words wheezed and gurgled. "We've got to find a more secure way to communicate."

"Where is she?" The predator within Hunter flared. If anything had happened to her—

"Jade took her. But I don't think she had anything to do with the others. They were after the medallion."

"Zenobia needs it for her leadership to remain stable after the coup," Nero said.

Hunter glared at the black drake. He didn't care about Zenobia or her coup. All he cared about was Anaea.

Grey started to sit in the chair Hunter had vacated, winced, and remained standing. "Damn it. I hate getting impaled."

"You'll get over it."

"Not nearly as fast as you."

Which was why Hunter had ended up as the prince's assassin and Grey hadn't. "Why did Jade take her?"

Grey raised an eyebrow.

"Shit." Jade must have noticed Anaea still had an earth magic aura but not Hunter's anymore. "Maybe Jade didn't take her to Court."

Grey coughed more blood. "And maybe I don't have a pierced lung."

He had to get to her, make Regis understand how important she was. He was not going to lose her.

"Nero, can you gate me to my suite?"

"I have a coup to stop." At least the black drake looked genuinely upset. "I can gate you to Court but not anywhere near your suite. I don't have the time."

Hunter's pulse rushed in his ears. "Can you spare anyone?"

"No."

"I'll take you." Grey sucked in a wheezing breath.

"Are you sure?" It was going to be tough for Grey to gate as injured as he was, but Hunter was grateful he'd made the offer.

Grey nodded.

Nero cleared his throat. "I have to go." He met Hunter's gaze, his expression filled with knowing and compassion. "Good hunting."

"You, too."

With a whoosh, both Nero and Ponytail gated from the room. Hunter turned back to Grey, slinging an arm around his back and taking some of his weight. "Let's go."

"There's something else you need to know. She can heal like a dragon."

Hunter froze. Only a human with full true sorcerer ability could heal like that.

"I saw it myself."

"Does Jade know?" Regis was certain to kill her if he knew she was a true sorcerer.

"I don't know. But it won't take her long to figure it out."

Shit. He had to get to Court, had to find Anaea. Now.

Panic raced over him, and Anaea screamed in his head, her voice making his ears ring from the inside out.

Where are you?

The terror eased, replaced with an unspoken question.

Where are you? He didn't have time to figure out how or why they could communicate. The best guess was that she really was a true sorcerer and was unknowingly coming into her full power. Which explained a whole lot about how she could call fire and open a gate without power words or gestures.

Court. God, he killed her. Hunter, I— Her words were cut off.

Anaea?

No response.

Anaea?

His stomach churned. "Gate me to Court, now."

34

J ester's sticky cage shrank around Anaea. She shoved against it, but it didn't budge. Hunter had been there, in her head, for just a moment. She had to reach him again, warn him.

Something shivered through her and she jerked her attention back to the jester. He was drawing energy, pulling it into her body. Her skin tingled but she didn't feel the fire licking inside her. Something was wrong, but the jester's pleasure continued to sweep through her. He was doing something else. Calling something else. But she couldn't figure out what.

She squirmed. Tendrils lashed out from the cage, clinging to her. She thrashed harder.

Now, now, Giacomo said. The bands around her tightened, drawing her mental arms and legs out in opposite directions until she couldn't move. *You're giving me a headache.*

Good. She focused all her frustration at him. *Give me my body back, and your problems will be solved.*

Jester grunted. *Hardly.*

Hatred seethed through her. Her body wasn't going to be his prison. Not like that pathetic ruined human had been. Her body would be the means of his revenge. She was more powerful than anyone but he had realized.

A manic laugh bubbled over her lips and she bit it back. No, the jester did. But he wasn't entirely the jester. The sagging sack of a man cowering in the corner was the jester, driven crazy by Xanthic, the dragon, trapped in his body. And his king and Regis were going to pay for that torture.

Over and over again, if he had any say in it.

Which he did.

He let the laugh escape and touched a finger to the ruined human. Fire engulfed him. He whimpered, his ineffectual twitching fanning the flames. Then he sagged against the wall, the inferno extinguished as suddenly as it started.

Good riddance to that.

Anaea wanted to be sick, wanted to scream and fight. But the bonds held her tight, and she didn't even have eyes within her control.

"Quit your whining."

She jerked against her bonds.

Xanthic had been kept trapped in Court for centuries with a body that couldn't even open a gate, with only enough sorcerer ability to recognize another sorcerer's body when he saw it, and the incessant nattering of that human soul. Mother of All, that man had gone crazy within the first day. Constantine had caught Xanthic body-sharing and prevented him from transferring into an unoccupied vessel as punishment. Then the king had become soul sick and because the crazy human's spirit was overwhelming, it muted Xanthic's aura until no one could see it and no one knew he was trapped. Soon everyone had forgotten—or chosen to ignore—that the jester was also a dragon. After the first hundred years, Xanthic couldn't contain the human's soul anymore.

The bonds around Anaea eased, but the cage shrank even more, squeezing her into a mental fetal position.

That jester's body was supposed to have been the one. Perfect. A great power. But he'd misread the signs. And Zenobia had done nothing to save him. She'd let him rot while she flirted with Regis, flaunting her freedom and forcing him to watch. Now the bitch was using his plan to stage her coup. It was his coup!

Energy crackled through her.

The Mother of All had taken pity. Finally. She'd sent him this sweet, powerful body and given him one last perfect moment of control. Crazy or not, Constantine would pay. Regis would pay. The bitch Zenobia would suffer... then pay. They all would. Tit for tat. And when he was done, he'd enjoy his new tits. It had been far too long.

HUNTER STRODE THROUGH THE GATE, SWORD READY, INTO HIS LIVING room. Empty. Thank goodness. Even though the risk had been fairly minimal, stepping into his suite could have been dangerous. Anyone could have potentially been lying in wait, but getting to his cache of weapons was a priority.

Grey stumbled through behind him, hugging his gut and gasping for air. "You owe me."

Yes, he did and he didn't know if he'd ever be able to pay off the debt. "When this body connects to the earth's magic I'll open any gate you want."

Grey sagged onto Hunter's couch. "If that body connects to the earth's magic."

With a shrug, Hunter marched into his bedroom. He'd deal with that later, once Anaea was safe.

He strapped a long sword and matching dagger to his hip. They felt a little mismatched to his new body, but he'd get used to it soon enough. He had to. More knives went into ankle sheaths and wrist sheaths and one at his back. Then he shrugged into a double-gun holster and checked his 9mm semi-automatics. They weren't sanctioned weapons, and they wouldn't kill a dragon, but they could slow one down—a lot if the dragon was a slow healer. And Hunter wasn't going to take any chances if he had to fight his way out. Besides, they would certainly kill a human mage.

He put on his calf-length leather coat, which, indeed, was too broad in the shoulders but the correct length—the Handmaiden had been right—and returned to his living room.

Grey shoved off the couch with a groan. "Ready?"

"I am. You're staying here." The last thing he needed was to worry about Grey. He'd stopped bleeding and the gash on his forehead had sealed up, but the hole in his gut still wept and he looked pale.

"What, and miss all the fun?"

"You'll be more of a hindrance than a help. Besides, Regis is more likely to let me slip Anaea away from Court if there aren't any witnesses."

"That's if he'll let you take her at all."

A growl bubbled within Hunter. "That's not an option I'm willing to entertain."

Grey raised an eyebrow. Hunter could see understanding working across Grey's expression. There weren't many things that would make a dragon so determined but an inamorata was one of them.

Hunter squared his shoulders. He would turn his back on his people, even Grey if necessary, for Anaea. Every cell in his body thrummed for her.

"Hunter." Grey's expression hardened.

The muscles in his neck twitched. There wasn't anything more to discuss. "What?"

"Call me when she's safe."

The knot in his gut eased. "I thought your phone was compromised."

"You know what I mean, you stupid drake. Now get your ass out of here."

With a curt nod to his friend, Hunter slipped into the hall, senses straining for the slightest indication of trouble. The halls of the Dragon Court were empty, which made sense, now that he thought about it. Anyone in Court would be at the final feast of the *pahar*. Still, the quiet made the hairs on the back of his still-unfamiliar neck stand on end. Maybe Zenobia had started her coup and Nero was in the process of stopping her. But it didn't matter. A fight was coming, regardless. Although he supposed it had been a long time in coming. It was surprising he'd been subservient for as long as he had.

Anaea's presence was still muffled within him. He strained to reach her but couldn't and had no idea how she was being contained. Maybe Jade was more of a true sorcerer than she'd let on. Surely, the Handmaiden hadn't gotten involved.

The guards outside Regis's suite were missing. So was the gaggle of sycophants waiting to fawn over him on his way to the feast hall. Hunter could see Regis dismissing the courtiers to deal with Anaea, but not his guards.

Maybe he'd already killed Anaea and gone to the feast.

That thought sent Hunter's heart racing.

No. Regis would want to hold onto Anaea, confront Hunter with the evidence of his guilt, if only to watch Hunter squirm.

But the other possible reasons for absent guards didn't sit any easier with him. It was most likely that Regis was inside, and so was trouble. And Hunter really hated walking into a bad situation blind. He hadn't stayed the prince's assassin for as long as he had through being reckless. Without any other options, however, he had little choice.

He grabbed the door handle. No magic tingled over his skin. The lock wasn't set. He rested a hand on the hilt of his long sword and eased the door open.

Lightning slammed into him, hurling him into the wall at the end of the corridor. Black specks swarmed across his vision, and he gasped against the pressure in his chest.

A figure sauntered toward him.

Anaea.

He blinked, trying to clear his sight. An orange light clung to her, overshadowing a brilliant white aura.

She knelt beside him and tsked.

The pressure in his chest increased, making the specks in his vision whirl faster.

"About time you showed up." She yanked the medallion from his neck with a manic, nails-on-chalkboard giggle.

———

Grey flipped open his phone and dialed Capri's number. Please pick up this time. As much as Hunter had told Grey to hole up in his suite, the shit was going to hit the fan, and Hunter needed help. Getting Anaea out of Court was only one part of the problem. The men in the hotel had magic, at least two with super-human strength and one with extraordinary speed, but they hadn't healed, which meant they had to be human mages. And that meant something big was coming after Hunter and he might not escape Court in time.

He groaned as the pieces of the puzzle the Handmaiden had given him fell together. She had to have seen the future. The spell was difficult and while her visions weren't as accurate as a full augur's, she could do it. Whatever was going to happen, she must have seen it and left him the tools necessary to salvage the situation, trusting he'd figure it out when the time was right.

What he didn't know was why she hadn't stuck around to help or stopped it. But perhaps dragonkind needed to learn a lesson. He wouldn't put that past her.

"Yeah?" Capri said.

"What is it with drakes and phone etiquette?"

"Grey?"

Grey coughed, spiking pain through his chest. "Hunter needs your help."

"You don't sound good."

That sounded like actual concern. If he wasn't in so much pain and so worried about Hunter and Anaea, he'd be thrilled. "Meet me at Gig's and bring a sword." Capri lived somewhere in the human world, and Grey wasn't inclined to find out where. Gig, however, had a suite in Court and Grey knew where that was.

"Done," she said without hesitation.

The line went dead. Grey smashed the phone against the wall and fought past the pain to cast another unanchored gate into the hall outside Gig's suite. His breath burned in his chest, and the hole in his gut still wept blood. Damn, he hated getting impaled. It made concentrating on magic and everything challenging. But at least he was healing.

He snorted. He'd been to the human world twice in as many days and he was still alive. Barely. But barely wasn't dead. Bully for him.

Gig opened the door as Capri rushed down the hall toward them. She had to have gated right after the call and run all the way here from the receiving hall, since she wasn't strong enough to use a gate without an anchor like Grey could.

"Shit, Grey. What happened?" Capri asked.

"Would you believe Hunter has fallen in love?"

"And he beat you up for that?" Gig motioned for Grey to enter the suite, but Grey shook his head.

"He would for his inamorata," Capri said.

She could figure things out so fast. Why couldn't she be interested in him? "Yes to the inamorata." Grey wheezed in another breath. "No to the beating me up. Grab a sword. Hunter needs someone at his back."

Gig rushed inside, but Capri narrowed her eyes.

"I'll explain on the way."

She nodded, her expression still grim. "You're a good friend, Grey."

He squirmed under the truth of that. "I'm an even better lover."

She flashed him a hint of teeth. "So I hear."

35

X anthic drew even more energy. Brilliant light surrounded Anaea and Hunter then vanished. She, Hunter, and Regis stood in the center of chaos. The front of the feast hall writhed with battle. Dragons roared and screamed, swung blades, and shot lightning and stone and ice. Blood and sweat and other things Anaea didn't want to think about slicked the floor. She couldn't tell who was on what side, or who was winning, but there looked to be a good number of the trench-coat wearing assailants in the mix. Hunter staggered to his feet and relief flooded her. Thank God the lightning hadn't killed him.

"What is going on? I demand an explanation," Regis said, his gaze jumping from Hunter to Anaea and back again.

"You demand?" Xanthic snorted. "It's obvious. Someone is stealing my coup! And doing a terrible job at it. But that's what happens when Nero finds out about one's plans." He gated onto the table on the dais and raised his hands. Power surged through her. It raced over her body and poured from Xanthic's palms, exploding in a thunderclap that crashed through the hall. Everyone froze, the sudden silence deafening.

"That's better. Now, where were we? Right, my coup."

"What in the name of the Mother is going on?" Regis screamed, his voice shrill in the quiet.

"The idiot doesn't realize who's in charge now."

"Hunter?" Regis asked.

"I'll take care of this," Hunter growled.

Xanthic snickered and clapped his hands. "The mighty Hunter will take care of this. This should be good."

Energy gathered within Xanthic. Anaea squirmed in her cage.

"Get out," Hunter said to Regis. "I'll explain later."

"No." Regis crossed his arms, looking every bit the petulant child. "You'll explain now."

Hunter's presence within her billowed with frustration for just a heartbeat then was shut off.

"Come on, Hunter. Explain now. In front of everyone." Xanthic hopped off the table onto the front of the dais. "Explain how you body-shared this sweet little human."

Mumbles echoed through the hall and Regis glared at Hunter. "You what?"

Hunter reached into his coat and growled again.

"But you were too stupid to see what you had," Xanthic said in a singsong.

The energy within her continued to grow.

"No, you hopped out as fast as you could. Too dumb to know a true sorcerer even when you're in one."

Xanthic raised a hand and wind whipped through the feast hall. Dragons yelled and rushed for the doors or drew energy to make gates.

"No gating. No leaving." The doors slammed shut, and shimmering cages enveloped the drakes. "You all need to bear witness. There will be a new Royal Coterie." Xanthic glared at the group. "That would be me. But first, a little business to take care of."

He drew more energy, and Anaea's cage wavered for just a moment. A gate whooshed open and Zenobia stood before him, beautiful and perfect, dressed in black with pieces of armor similar to what Anaea had worn during the *wasu tahazu*.

"Not getting your hands dirty, my dear?" Xanthic asked.

Confusion clouded her expression for a heartbeat, and then recognition burned it away. "He said you were dead."

"Actually, he said I was still in there, you just didn't believe him."

"Xanthic, I—"

"What? Planned to save me all along? Thought of me daily?" He stepped close, and a strange sensation slipped through Anaea. It felt like regret.

"If I had known—" Zenobia reached a tentative hand to Anaea's cheek, and Xanthic leaned into the caress. "If only I—"

Fury filled Anaea. "If only," Xanthic sneered. "If only. If only I hadn't whored myself to that whale we call a prince."

Zenobia jerked back, but Xanthic seized her wrist. "This is *my* coup, bitch!"

A new power curled out of Anaea, crawling up her arm and out her hand like a swarm of biting insects. Zenobia screamed. Blood welled on her wrist under Xanthic's grasp but he held tight. His fury burned cold. She needed to suffer like he had suffered. More. Worse. Painful.

He brushed the power across her face. Welts formed, burst, and her cheek collapsed, revealing stringy muscle and pocked bone. She screamed and the bone and muscle reformed, covered with flesh and burst again.

Xanthic giggled and clapped his hands, releasing Zenobia. With a moan, she scrabbled away, blood weeping down her cheek.

"Oh my, I didn't anticipate that you'd heal faster than a disintegrating touch." He giggled, and sexual pleasure billowed over Anaea. This was just too good. She would suffer and suffer, always healing and always disintegrating, until he got around to killing her. Perfect.

He turned his gaze to Regis and Hunter. "I'm king. Any disputers?"

***

REGIS'S CHAMBERS WERE EMPTY, AND THE DOOR HUNG AJAR. CAPRI turned to Grey. He looked marginally better, but sweat still slicked his forehead, and his skin remained pale. He really was a loyal friend. She hoped Hunter knew how good he had it.

"Looks like we missed the fight," Capri said.

Grey nodded. "No bodies. They must be at the feast hall."

"You think he'll risk accusing Hunter in public?" That wasn't good. With the Handmaiden missing since the attack at the rebirth chamber, Hunter's soul could be lost in the medallion. But there weren't a lot of other explanations. Unless those human mages Grey had mentioned had caught up to everyone.

"They have a head start," Gig said.

"Then we'll just have to run." Grey bolted down the hall.

Capri raced after him. Hunter didn't stand a chance if Regis accused him in public. As good as Hunter was, he couldn't survive a fight against every drake who'd be in attendance at the feast. And fight he would if his inamorata's life was on the line.

Grey skidded to a halt in front of half a dozen drakes standing guard before the feast hall doors. They all wore black and all had glazed looks in their eyes. She squinted. Something wasn't right. Four of the six auras flickered, weak and uneven. She'd only seen that once, right before the only human mage she'd ever met called up a cyclone and killed thousands of people. No one else had seen the flickering aura, but she knew she hadn't hallucinated. And now she knew what it meant. Those men weren't dragons, but human mages. Shit.

Grey raised his sword, but he wasn't in any shape to take on all six.

———

ALL THE DRAGONS IN THE FEAST HALL STARED AT ANAEA WITH WIDE eyes, then their gazes shot to the floor.

"Not a defiant one among them," Xanthic said. "Of course, we can't have a new Royal Coterie with the old one still around."

Xanthic jabbed a finger at Regis. Lightning shot toward the prince. Anaea's cage ballooned, slightly, for just a moment. Hunter tackled Regis to the floor and the energy shot past them to the back of the room and burst against the doors, scorching the wood and showering the marble floor with sparks.

More energy surged in Xanthic. The cage expanded again, a little further. Anaea shoved against the gap. Hunter's presence filled her. He was determined, ferocious, and terrified he'd lose her.

I'm still here, she called.

Xanthic shot another bolt. Hunter shoved Regis out of the way and jerked back, but the lightning sliced open Hunter's side.

Xanthic faked a yawn. "This is boring. Do you mind?" He turned to three drakes… no, human mages by the weakness of their auras, but they stared at him, trembling.

"Oh right, take the cage off." He flicked his wrist and the shimmering cage melted around them. "Now kill him and don't make me ask again."

The three mages leapt at Hunter. The first grabbed him and the second slammed his fist into Hunter's face. Hunter's head snapped back.

Anaea bashed against her cage.

Magic fluctuated around the third mage. He was preparing something, but she couldn't tell what.

BOTH DRAKES AND HUMANS GUARDING THE ENTRANCE TO THE FEAST hall raised their blades. A muffled explosion shook the great doors, and they shot nervous glances at each other.

"Gig, a distraction," Capri said, keeping her voice low and not looking back at the young drake. He'd know what to do. He'd sense whatever technology was in the vicinity, hopefully something like a cell phone on one of the assailants, and activate it. She stepped aside and barked her power word, ramming her magic into the minds of the four humans. She couldn't influence the two drakes, but she could take care of the mages. She prayed she was right about the meaning of their flickering auras.

"You're tired," she said. "Go to sleep."

Their weapons sagged in their hands.

The two drakes growled, and Grey rushed at them.

A cell phone rang—Gig working at his finest—and distracted the drakes just long enough for Grey to slice the closest drake's neck.

The humans stumbled back, still blocking the door. Her magic slowed their movements, but not enough. She needed more power.

Grey gasped and brought his sword across the first drake's torso, slicing him open from crotch to sternum. She hoped he was a slow healer. No one wanted to take a dragon's life without a medallion nearby, but she didn't doubt Grey would do it if he had to.

Gig jabbed his short sword at the second dragon, a squat blue drake with a pale aura.

She yearned to help him but all four humans were still a danger. Pain seared Capri's temples. "Go. To. Sleep."

One of the humans dropped to the floor.

"Sleep." She wasn't going to be fast enough, and Grey looked exhausted.

ANAEA COULD ONLY WATCH AS MAGE NUMBER TWO PUNCHED HUNTER in the face again, sending blood and spittle flying into mage number one's face.

With a growl, Hunter jerked a hand free. He pulled a gun from his coat and shot mage number two in the forehead as he came in for another strike. Hunter twisted and killed the man holding him before the first one hit the ground.

His rage swept through Anaea. It fed her, strengthened her. She pounded and pounded at the cage holding her until a crack appeared in her confines.

Hunter shot the third mage between the eyes and rushed up the aisle toward the dais, pulling a second pistol and pointing both at her.

36

Two more humans dropped to the floor under Capri's magic. Her head pounded. The last one started reciting a spell in ancient Egyptian, drawing power.

Gig's strike missed. Grey seized the distraction to slash at the blue drake's legs, but his blade was blocked. Metal clanged against metal. Blue swung at Gig's head. The youngling ducked and Grey tackled Blue, smashing his head against the granite floor.

Capri growled her power word again. Her magic exploded through her skull, and the remaining human mage gasped. His eyes rolled back, and he crumpled to the ground.

Grey rammed Blue's head against the floor again then met Capri's gaze.

She nodded at him and shoved the closest human away from the door. "Open it."

Xanthic jumped from the dais, hands flicking at his shimmering cages, releasing more of Zenobia's mages and screaming, "Kill them! Kill Regis and his assassin!" More than a dozen men, their faces etched with fear, jerked forward and rushed across the hall to Hunter.

Panic filled Anaea. *Do it now, Hunter. Kill him.* The men were going to overtake him, and he wouldn't stand a chance.

Hunter bared his teeth, his guns trained on Xanthic, on her. His index fingers twitched near the triggers but he didn't fire.

The great door swung open. Grey and Gig, doused in blood, and Capri, her aura blindingly radiant, stood in the entrance. They paused for a heartbeat then raced to meet the men.

Anaea dragged her attention back to Hunter. Screams, roars, explosions, and metal screeching against metal filled the chamber. She couldn't look, couldn't bear to see Hunter die. This had to end. Xanthic couldn't be allowed to continue.

Hunter, please. She rammed everything she had at the crack. *Kill him.*

Xanthic sneered and sick satisfaction washed over her.

"What's wrong, Hunter? Can't kill a human?" Xanthic held up the medallion. "Can't kill this human?"

Hunter's hands trembled. He wasn't going to stop her. He couldn't.

"I didn't think so." Magic swept down Xanthic's hands and enveloped the medallion.

Anaea's heart raced. She couldn't lose him.

Someone wailed nearby. Metal caught light, and Grey brought down a mage. Lightning zinged toward him, and Capri tackled him out of the way. No please, not Hunter, not his friends. But she couldn't get control of her body.

The magic within her billowed, and a wind snagged Hunter, dragging him the remaining few feet to Xanthic. She could sense Hunter's flurry of thoughts. He'd failed her, couldn't save her, but had to keep fighting.

The crack in Anaea's cage widened. Just enough. It had to be enough to stop all of this.

Xanthic giggled and shoved the medallion against Hunter's fore-head. Hunter struggled against the wind, but it held him tight, pinning his arms to his sides. Xanthic barked the words to activate the medallion. Blue flame leapt from his hand, surrounding Hunter.

Anaea shoved through the crack, seizing the magic within her, but she couldn't pull it back. It engulfed Hunter, tearing at his soul.

Please, no.

Hunter's gaze met hers. *I love you, inamorata.*

And I won't lose you. She released everything she felt for Hunter: love, respect, awe, determination, into the magic devouring him. She shoved it through the medallion into him.

Hunter dropped to his knees. His red aura blossomed, growing with each beat of his heart. He moaned and glanced up at her.

Her heart stuttered. Something was wrong. He gasped for breath and trembled. Then something cracked and he howled.

"Oh, God. Hunter." She dropped to her knees. Her knees. She had control!

But Xanthic lassoed her essence with a sticky thread. She struggled against it. She needed to stay in control of her body and help Hunter. She shot a mental bolt of light at Xanthic. He absorbed it, and her body released a manic giggle.

Hunter collapsed to his side and hugged his gut. Something writhed under his skin, drawing another scream.

God, she'd killed him.

Xanthic sniggered at the thought.

No, please.

Hunter's face contorted. He heaved onto his hands and knees and the back of his coat split. His gurgled cries turned to growls. His face stretched and turned red. Smoke billowed from his mouth and nose. Flesh peeled away, revealing scales bathed in blood.

His aura surged, surrounding him in a red nimbus, and with a great roar, he spread enormous, leathery wings.

You have something I want, Jester. Hunter's voice rang through her. He spit a blast of fire into the air and peered at her with enormous, slitted eyes.

"You can't have her."

More sticky tendrils wrapped around her. She seized the magic in her, burning at the blackness, but it was too strong. Xanthic's manic desperation made him wild.

A calm sparked within her. She could feel Hunter's fear and love.

And could still feel the ridges of the medallion digging into her clasped hands.

She stared at Hunter. Here, in his true form, he was majestic. His scales shimmered red and gold. Powerful wings curled along his back and the tip of his tail flicked, revealing his rage.

She met his gaze. It was still him. She'd always been able to see his spirit, regardless of what body he was in, and he was filled with absolute love for her. She drew her magic around herself.

Xanthic struggled to rebuild her cage. His sticky tendrils wrapped around her, and his fury swept through her.

But it couldn't touch the love in her heart.

She squeezed the medallion between her palms and activated it with a thought.

Xanthic screamed. His cages around the dragons in the feast hall burst apart and the drakes swarmed Zenobia's men.

Light swept through her, tearing away the darkness, scouring her clean of everything that was Xanthic, sucking his essence into the medallion. Flames danced over her hands, searing her flesh. But it didn't matter. She was a phoenix reborn, rising from the ashes of her empty life into a new one. The life of a true human sorcerer, something that hadn't been seen in over two thousand years. She healed like a dragon, had the lifespan of a dragon, but was so much more than a dragon. She was the reason for all the dragon laws. But they didn't have to fear her, not like the originators of the Great Scourge. Unless, of course, they hurt a member of her coterie.

Hunter spread his wings, roared and spat fire, and all knew he belonged to her.

Then he trembled, his form shrinking, his scales melting away, until he stood once again before her in his human form.

She slid her gaze down his naked body, desire heating her. It was still Mark's body, but it also wasn't. It was the soul inside that counted.

Hunter followed her gaze and coughed, the only indication he was even the slightest bit uncomfortable. "Looks like there are some downfalls to transmutation."

Anaea bit back a grin. "It's only a downfall if we're in public."

"True."

And even though they were still surrounded by the elite of dragon society, she didn't care. All that really mattered was Hunter.

A drake at the back of the room stood and shouted Hunter's name. Others took up the call and it grew into a frenzied chant.

Regis screamed for silence but the crowd kept chanting, over and over again, filling the hall with sound, until Hunter raised his hand and the room went quiet.

"Just because you can transmute doesn't mean you can have the throne," Regis said. He glanced over his shoulder, his expression nervous. Behind him were Nero and Tobias, both covered in blood, holding Zenobia. She crouched between them with Tobias's blade at her neck, rocking and moaning. Anaea didn't want to imagine what Regis would do to her, knowing she'd tried to take his throne and failed. It seemed she'd already received a terrible punishment.

Beyond them, Grey clutched at his gut. Blood trickled down his cheek but his eyes were bright with approval and determination. Capri and Gig stood beside him, also covered in blood, alive and whole. Grey raised his fist in salute and roared Hunter's name, as if daring Hunter to stop him.

A hint of a smile pulled at Hunter's lips, then he turned his attention back to Nero, and his expression darkened. Nero gave a slight nod, and something unspoken passed between them, an understanding of some kind, but Anaea couldn't tell what it was.

"I don't want the throne," Hunter said. "But I do quit."

"You what?"

"I quit. Find yourself another assassin."

Regis huffed and held out his hand. "Then give back the medallion."

Anaea glanced at Hunter. He grinned, his warmth simmering through her. "I don't think so."

"You what—?"

Hunter turned his back on Regis and took Anaea's hands in his. "Let's get the hell out of here."

"Thought you'd never ask."

A gate formed on the dais below them. The world twisted, and then vortex's black nothing engulfed them, sweeping them to safety.

A WEEK AND A HALF LATER, ANAEA STEPPED OUT OF HER BRILLIANT white gate into Hunter's— No, *their* front hall, with a wrapped painting in one hand and an envelope with her medical paperwork in the other. It still felt strange to think of them as a *them*. She really hadn't known him that long, and even after sharing her body with Hunter's spirits, and still, at times, sharing his thoughts with a mental connection they both had yet to gain full control of, a part of her still struggled to believe it.

A hint of heat promising magical flames billowed over her hands, and she leaned the painting against the wall and dropped the envelope on the tiled floor.

Speaking of magic she had yet to control—

The fire now at least gave off a hint of heat before erupting into a full blaze... if she was paying attention. She'd still almost set their bed on fire... and the living room... and the kitchen... and the shower. Their honeymoon phase had just begun and, given Hunter's thoughts that he wasn't even trying to keep private, if they managed to survive her unpredictable sorcerer's power, they'd be in this phase for a long time. At least a couple of centuries if Hunter got his wish. And she wasn't going to argue with that. It didn't matter that only two weeks ago a thought like that would have been crazy. People didn't live that long, magic was a fantasy, and dragons didn't exist. Even if any of that had been true, she still would have had only a few months left to live.

Then she'd met Hunter.

The heat in her hands melted into her skin, pooled around her heart, and turned sensual.

One moment. One kiss. And everything had changed. Her eyes had been opened to a terrifying and beautiful new world, and if giving up the bad meant she'd have to give up Hunter, she wouldn't give up any of it. Whether it was because he'd shared his soul with her or just because this was how being inamorated worked, she craved Hunter with a dragon's ferocity. He wasn't just her lover. He was a partner in everything. It was—in the case of the Dragon Court, literally—them against the world, and together they could face anything. He gave her a balance of spirit she hadn't known she needed, unconditional love—even with her being emotionally and physically scarred—and the challenge to be a better person.

And she had a lifetime, a long, long lifetime, to look forward to.

After all of that, a part of her still couldn't completely believe it. But her cancer was gone, and she now had the test results to prove it.

Three days after they'd escaped Court to this hidden house in Northern Ontario, Hunter had introduced Anaea to Nero, and she'd begun the challenging job of learning to control her magic. She'd never felt so welcome and so out of place at the same time. But she hadn't been able to stop the worry that her cancer still consumed her, so she'd set up an appointment with a new doctor and paid for a rush on every test imaginable to prove, once and for all, how much time she had left.

She'd just returned from her final visit with a clean bill of health. The only evidence she'd ever had cancer was her mastectomy scar.

She'd been so stunned, she'd paid the final bill, took her paperwork, and stumbled out of the office into bright late afternoon sunlight. The sky had been a blazing blue. Clear, warm, everything Hunter had loved before his fall. Everything he loved again now that he had the ability to transmute into his true form. And there, in the shop window beside the doctor's office, had been the painting. A three by two acrylic simply titled Sky One. It expressed the vast warmth and clarity above her in a way that stole her breath, and she knew Hunter had to have it in his new hoard.

"I can't believe the news is bad," Hunter said, stepping into the front hall from the living room looking sexier than hell with his jeans slung low on his hips, his black T-shirt stretched taut against his muscular frame, and two days' worth of stubble on his jaw. His red aura radiated strength and age, and his love for her filled his gaze and her thoughts with a hunger that threatened to set the hall on fire. "I know you went to a doctor's appointment this afternoon instead of going to Nero's."

"I've really got to learn how to control our mental connection." She shrugged out of her light coat and hung it in the closet. Had she really just been standing in the hall lost in thought?

"Yeah, you have." A wicked grin darkened Hunter's eyes, and the fire in body billowed. "But those thoughts earlier about the bedroom and the kitchen counter and the shower… I didn't mind those."

"Oh, you *heard* that, did you?"

He drew closer but didn't touch her, the heat from his body and thoughts sliding across her senses and ratcheting her desire.

She pressed her palm to his chest, unable to just stand there, needing to fulfill the connection and feel the lightning of their attraction snap through her. "Jeez," she said, breathless. "Give the drake his own body, and he's insatiable."

"You should talk." He brushed his lips against hers, drawing more fire through her. "Now tell me the news."

"You already know the news."

"But you need to say it. Make it real. Believe it."

And she did. God help her, she believed all of it, no matter how crazy it seemed. Magic was real. "My cancer is gone." *And I'm in love with a dragon.*

"Imagine how weird it is for me." He brushed his lips across her jaw in a whisper of dragon courtship. "I'm in love with a human."

"But a human who brings shinies." She slipped from his embrace and showed him the painting. "For your hoard."

"For *our* hoard." He wrapped an arm around her and kissed her with a passion that left her breathless and threatened to ignite his clothes with magic flames.

Elation, desire, and certainty flooded into her. She had a spirit as strong as any dragon's, and he had no doubts or regrets. Neither did she.

"Does this mean you're sharing your sky with me?" she asked against his lips.

"Absolutely."

His grip on her tightened, a gate formed under their feet, and in a flash, she was surrounded by twilight sky. They started to plummet, but leathery dragon wings unfurled from his human back, stretched out, and he caught the air current. The first night's stars spun around her and wind caressed her face.

Just like the dream. Their dream. And this time, the only falling they'd do would be into bed and into each other's arms.

Don't miss the next book in the series!

SHATTERED SPIRITS
A Dragon Spirit Novel: Book Two

His love will set her free. Hers will kill him.

For centuries Capri has used her magic to keep dragonkind a secret, living only for her job. A century ago, dragon law forced her to abandon the only man she ever loved, a human, and she swore she'd never love one again. So when a murdered dragon is discovered, Capri jumps to work, only to find the human detective working the case could be her dead lover's twin.

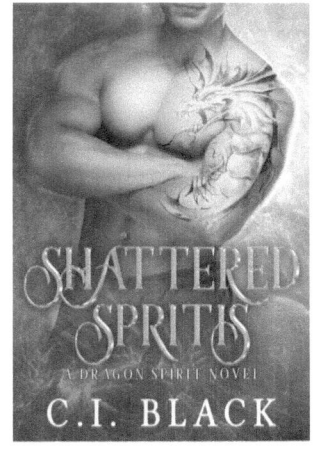

Detective Ryan Miller has always known magic existed. It's the only explanation for the visions of the future that plague his life and jeopardize his career, but when a vision shows FBI agent Capri Jones in danger, he knows he has to stay close and save her. Except the closer he gets the more attraction sizzles between them, the more confusing the case gets, and the more he realizes Capri is keeping secrets. Secrets that once revealed could kill them both.

OTHER BOOKS BY C.I. BLACK

THE DRAGON SPIRIT SERIES

Immortal Coil, Book 1

Shattered Spirits, Book 2

Hoarding Secrets, Book 3

Pursuing Flight, Book 4

THE MEDUSA FILES

Case 1: Written in Stone

Case 2: Heart of Stone

Case 3: Escaped From Stone

Case 4: Carved From Stone

Case 5: Cold as Stone

Case 6: Broken Stone

Case 7: Set in Stone

Case 8: Cut From Stone

Case 9: Shattered Stone

Case 10: Shards of Stone

Case 11: Fallen Stone

Case 12: Trapped in Stone

Case 13: Hard as Stone

ABOUT C.I. BLACK

C.I. Black has always lived in a world of imagination. When she's not daydreaming, she puts her flights of fancy down on paper writing urban fantasy, paranormal romance, and romantic suspense books.

She's the author of The Dragon Spirit series and The Medusa Files series. You can find a complete list of C.I.'s books at www.ciblack.com.